COPY 3

Lodge, David
    Souls and bodies.

160_____   14_____
149_____   22_____
103_____   23_____
  8_____   1_____
150_____   33_____
 12_____   16_____
132_____   35_____
 19_____   38_____

SOULS AND BODIES

Also by David Lodge

NOVELS
The Picturegoers
Ginger, You're Barmy
The British Museum Is Falling Down
Out of the Shelter
Changing Places

CRITICISM
Language of Fiction
The Novelist at the Crossroads
The Modes of Modern Writing

SOULS AND BODIES

David Lodge

William Morrow and Company, Inc.

New York   *1982*

Originally published in Great Britain in 1980 by Martin Secker & Warburg Limited under the title *How Far Can You Go?*

The quotation from "The Lord of the Dance" by S. Carter is reproduced by permission of Stainer & Bell Ltd.

The quotation from "Eleanor Rigby," words and music by Lennon & McCartney, is used by permission of ATV Music. © 1966 Northern Songs Limited for the world.

Library of Congress Cataloging in Publication Data

Lodge, David, 1935–
   Souls and bodies.

   Previously published as: How far can you go?
   I. Title.
PR6062.O36H6   1982   823'.914   81-14026
ISBN 0-688-00933-6   AACR2

Printed in the United States of America

First U.S. Edition

1 2 3 4 5 6 7 8 9 10

To Ian Gregor

What can we know? Why is there anything at all?
Why not nothing?

What ought we to do? Why do what we do? Why and
to whom are we finally responsible?

What may we hope? Why are we here? What is it all
about?

What will give us courage for life and what courage
for death?

Hans Küng, *On being a Christian*

1
How it was

IT IS JUST AFTER eight o'clock in the morning of a dark February day, in this year of grace nineteen hundred and fifty-two. An atmospheric depression has combined with the coal smoke from a million chimneys to cast a pall over London. A cold drizzle is falling on the narrow, nondescript streets north of Soho, south of the Euston Road. Inside the church of Our Lady and St Jude, a greystone, neo-gothic edifice squeezed between a bank and a furniture warehouse, it might still be night. The winter daybreak is too feeble to penetrate the stained-glass windows, doubly and trebly stained by soot and bird droppings, that depict scenes from the life of Our Lady, with St Jude, patron of lost causes, prominent in the foreground of her Coronation in Heaven. In alcoves along the side walls votive candles fitfully illuminate the plaster figures of saints paralysed in attitudes of prayer or exhortation. There are electric lights in here, dangling from the dark roof on immensely long leads, like lamps lowered down a well or pit-shaft; but, for economy's sake, only a few have been switched on, above the altar and over the front central pews where the sparse congregation is gathered. As they murmur their responses (it is a dialogue mass, a recent innovation designed to increase lay participation in the liturgy) their breath condenses on the chill, damp air, as though their prayers were made fleetingly visible before being sucked up into the inscrutable gloom of the raftered vault.

The priest on the altar turns, with a swish of his red vestments (it is a martyr's feast day, St Valentine's) to face the congregation.

"Dominus vobiscum."

There are eight young people present, including one on the altar performing the office of acolyte. They reply, *"Et cum spiritu tuo."*

A creak of hinges and a booming thud at the back of the church indicates the arrival of a latecomer. As the priest turns back to the altar to read the Offertory prayer, and the rest flutter the pages of their missals to find the English translation in its proper place, all hear the hurried tiptap of high-heeled shoes on the tiled surface of the central aisle. A buxom, jolly-looking girl with a damp head-scarf tied over dark curls makes a hasty genuflection and slides into a pew next to another girl whose blonde head is becomingly draped with a black lace mantilla. The wearer of the mantilla turns her head to give a discreet smile of welcome, incidentally presenting her profile to the thickset youth in the dufflecoat just behind her, who seems to admire it. The dark latecomer wrinkles her nose and arches her eyebrows in comical self-reproach. Now there are nine, plus the priest, and a couple of immobile old ladies who are neither sitting nor kneeling, but wedged into their pew in a position halfway between the two postures, wrapped up like awkward parcels in coats and woollies, and looking as though they were left behind by their families after the last Sunday mass and have been there ever since. We are not, however, concerned with the old ladies, whose time on this earth is almost up, but with the young people, whose adult lives are just beginning.

It is apparent from their long striped scarves and their bags and briefcases stuffed with books that they are students at one of the constituent colleges of the University of London, situated not far away. Every Thursday in term, Father Austin Brierley, the young curate of Our Lady and St Jude's, and a kind of unofficial chaplain to the College Catholic Society (for the official chaplain and chaplaincy, embracing the entire University, have appropriately dignified headquarters elsewhere) says mass at 8 a.m. especially for members of his New Testament Study Group, and for any other Catholic students who wish to attend. They do so at considerable cost in personal discomfort. Rising an hour earlier than usual, in cold bed-sitters far out in the suburbs, they travel fasting on crowded buses and trains, dry-mouthed, weak with hunger, and nauseated by cigarette smoke, to be present at this unexciting ritual in a cold, gloomy church at the grey, indifferent heart of London.

Why?

It is not out of a sense of duty, for Catholics are bound to hear mass only on Sundays and holydays of obligation (of which St Valentine's is not one). Attendance at mass on ordinary weekdays is supererogatory (a useful word in theology, meaning more than is necessary for salvation). So, why? Is it hunger and thirst after righteousness? Is it devotion to the Real Presence of Christ in the Blessed Sacrament? Is it habit, or superstition, or the desire for comradeship? Or all these things, or none of them? Why have they come here, and what do they expect to get out of it?

To begin with the simplest case: Dennis, the burly youth in the dufflecoat, its hood thrown back to expose a neck pitted with boil scars, is here because Angela, the fair beauty in the mantilla, is here. And Angela is here because she is a good Catholic girl, the pride of the Merseyside convent where she was Head Girl and the first pupil ever to win a State Scholarship to University, the eldest daughter of awed parents who run a corner-shop open till all hours and scarcely know what a university is for. Naturally Angela joined the Catholic Society in the first week of her first term and naturally she joined its New Testament Study Group when invited to do so, and naturally she goes along to the Thursday morning masses, for she has been conditioned to do what is good without questioning and it scarcely costs her any effort. Not so with Dennis. He is a Catholic, but not a particularly devout one. His mother, who has shouted herself hoarse from the foot of the stairs, at home in Hastings, on many a Sunday morning to get him up in time for church, would be stunned to see him here of his own volition at an early midweek mass. Dennis is fairly stunned himself, yawning and shivering inside his dufflecoat, yearning for his breakfast and the first fag of the day. This is not his idea of fun, but he has no choice, he cannot bear to let Angela out of his sight a moment longer than is absolutely unavoidable, escorting her up to the very threshold of her lecture rooms in the French Department before

3

hurrying off to his own instruction in Chemistry. As soon as ne set eyes on her at the Christmas Hop he knew he must make her his own, she was his dream made flesh in a pink angora jumper and black taffeta skirt. That he was a Catholic gave him an immediate advantage, for Angela trusted him not to be like the other boys she had met at hops who, she complained, held you too close on the dance floor and offered to see you home only in order to be rude. But his faith is a double-edged asset to Dennis, who must act up to the part, not only desisting from rudeness in word and deed, but joining Cath.Soc. and attending its boring study groups and getting up for this early weekday mass in the perishing winter dark for fear that if he does not some other eligible Catholic youth will carry Angela off. Dennis suspects (quite correctly) that Adrian, for instance – the bespectacled youth in the belted gaberdine raincoat, expertly manipulating his thick Roman missal with its four silk markers in liturgical colours, red, green, purple and white – is interested in Angela, and that very probably Michael is too – the boy with the dark slab of greasy hair falling forward across a white snub-nosed face, kneeling some rows behind the others, wearing an extraordinarily shapeless, handed-down tweed overcoat that reaches almost to his ankles when he stands up for the Gospel – but there Dennis is wrong.

Michael is interested not in any particular girl, but in girls generally. He does not want a relationship, he wants sex – though his lust is vague and hypothetical in the extreme. At the Salesian grammar school on the northern outskirts of London which he attended before coming up to the University, a favourite device of the bolder spirits in the sixth form to enliven Religious Instruction was to tease the old priest who took them for this lesson with casuistical questions of sexual morality, especially the question of How Far You Could Go with the opposite sex. *"Please, Father, how far can you go with a girl, Father?"* The answer was always the same, though expressed in different ways: your conscience would tell you, no further than you wouldn't be ashamed to tell your mother, as far as you would let another boy go with your sister. Michael listened to this with lowered eyes and a foolish grin on his face, never having been any distance at all with a real girl. He has not advanced since then. Any reasonably personable female, therefore, will do for his purely mental purposes, as long as she has perceptible breasts. If Angela should happen to take

4

off her coat first in the Lyons cafeteria where they will all have breakfast after mass, he will look at her breasts lasciviously, but if Polly (the latecomer) should be the first he will look at her breasts with equal lasciviousness, though they are of quite a different shape, and the breasts of the women sitting opposite him in the Tube will do just as well, and so will the breasts pictured in the photographic art books displayed in bookshops in the Charing Cross Road – indeed, these will do better because, though not actually present in the flesh, they are uncovered, and thus attest more strikingly to the really amazing, exciting fact of the mere existence of breasts. As for female pudenda, well, Michael isn't (as we say nowadays) into them yet, he doesn't even have a verbal concept for that orifice that he can think with comfortably – cunt being a word that he, and the others present at this St Valentine's mass, have seen only on lavatory walls and wouldn't dream of pronouncing, even silently, to themselves; and though Michael has seen the word vagina in print, he is not sure how to pronounce it, nor is it a word that seems to do justice to what it signifies. He is not at all sure about that, either, never having seen one that was more than three summers old, but anyway breasts are quite enough to keep him in a fever of excitement at the moment. Breasts, and the underclothing that goes with them, are sufficient to be going on with. There is no shortage of reminders of these things, or at least his mind is finely tuned to pick up their vibrations at the slightest opportunity. Give Michael a newspaper double-page spread to scan, with, say, two thousand words on it, and his eye will zoom in on the word *cleavage* or *bra* instantly. American psychologists have since established by experiment that the thoughtstream of the normal healthy male turns to sex every other minute between the ages of sixteen and twenty-six, after which the intervals grow gradually longer (though not all that long), but Michael does not know this; he thinks he is abnormal, that the pollution of his thoughtstream is the work of the Devil, and that he is grievously at fault in not only not resisting temptation, but in positively inviting it. For instance, he walks along the Charing Cross Road at every opportunity, even if it involves a considerable detour; and he reads in the Union Lounge, a frowzy basement room filled with damaged furniture and cigarette smoke, the cheap popular papers that are most likely to include the word *cleavage* and pictures of girls displaying that feature, or rather gap –

that fascinating *vide*, that absence which signifies the presence of the two glands on either side of it more eloquently than they do themselves (or so the structuralist jargon fashionable in another decade would put it, though to Michael in February 1952 cleavage is just second-best to actual bare tits, which newspapers obviously can't show, something to keep you going until it is time for another saunter down the Charing Cross Road). He does these things knowing that they will give him impure thoughts. An impure thought, he has been told by a boy who had been told by a priest in confession, is any thought that gives you an erection, and it doesn't take much to give Michael one of those. It is almost a permanent condition of his waking hours. (Twenty-one years later he learned from a magazine article about the making of pornographic films in Los Angeles that the producers of such films employed special stand-by studs in case the male lead couldn't manage an erection; you didn't have to act, all they ever filmed was your penis, all you had to do was to get it up, and into the female lead; and he thought, ruefully, that would have been the job for me when I was young – ruefully, because he was having trouble himself getting it up then, and not even reading such an article in a magazine, with pictures of naked girls with their legs apart, would do the trick. He was passing blood with his bowel movements at that particular time, and was more apt to think of death than sex every other minute.) But in 1952 he has erections, which is to say impure thoughts, very frequently. These, he thinks, are probably only venial sins, but he masturbates quite often too, and that is surely a mortal sin.

Before we go any further it would probably be a good idea to explain the metaphysic or world-picture these young people had acquired from their Catholic upbringing and education. Up there was Heaven; down there was Hell. The name of the game was Salvation, the object to get to Heaven and avoid Hell. It was like Snakes and Ladders: sin sent you plummeting down towards the Pit; the sacraments, good deeds, acts of self-mortification, enabled you to climb back towards the light. Everything you did or thought was subject to spiritual accounting. It was either good, bad or indifferent. Those who succeeded in the game eliminated the bad and converted as much of the indifferent as possible into the good. For instance, a banal bus journey (indifferent) could be turned to good account by silently reciting the Rosary, unobtrusively fingering the beads in your pocket as you trundled along. To say the Rosary openly and aloud in such a situation was more problematical. If it witnessed to the Faith, even if it excited the derision of non-believers (providing this were borne with patience and forgiveness) it was, of course, Good – indeed heroically virtuous; but if done to impress others, to call attention to your virtue, it was worse than indifferent, it was Bad – spiritual pride, a very slippery snake. Progress towards Heaven was full of such pitfalls. On the whole, a safe rule of thumb was that anything you positively disliked doing was probably Good, and anything you liked doing enormously was probably Bad, or potentially bad – an "occasion of sin".

There were two types of sin, venial and mortal. Venial sins were little sins which only slightly retarded your progress across the board. Mortal sins were huge snakes that sent you slithering back to square one, because if you died in a state of mortal sin, you went to Hell. If, however, you confessed your sins and received absolution through the sacrament of Penance, you shot up the ladder of grace to your original position on the board, though carrying a penalty – a certain amount of punishment awaiting you in the next world. For few Catholics expected that they would have reached the heavenly finishing line by the time they died. Only saints would be in that happy position, and to consider yourself a saint was a sure sign that you weren't one: there was a snake called Presumption that was just as fatal as the one called Despair. (It really was a most ingenious game.) No, the vast majority of Catholics expected to spend a certain amount of time in Purgatory first, working off the punishment accruing to sins, venial and mortal, that they had committed in the course of their lives. They would have been *forgiven* these sins, you understand, through the sacrament of Penance, but there would still be some detention to do in Purgatory. Purgatory was a kind of penitential transit camp on the way to the gates of Heaven. Most of your deceased relatives were probably there, which was why you prayed for them (there would be no point, after all, in praying for a soul that was in Heaven or Hell). Praying for them was like sending food parcels to refugees, and all the more welcome if you could enclose a few indulgences. An indulgence was a kind of spiritual voucher, obtained by performing some devotional exercise, promising the bearer so much off the punishment due to his sins, *e.g.*

forty days' remission for saying a certain prayer, or two hundred and forty days for making a certain pilgrimage. "Days" did not refer to time spent in Purgatory (a misconception common in Protestant polemic) for earthly time did not, of course, apply there, but to the canonical penances of the mediaeval Church, when confessed sinners were required to do public penance such as sitting in sackcloth and ashes at the porch of the parish church for a certain period, instead of the purely nominal penances (recitation of prayers) prescribed in modern times. The remission of temporal punishment by indulgences was measured on the ancient scale.

There was also such a thing as plenary indulgence, which was a kind of jackpot, because it wiped out *all* the punishment accruing to your sins up to the time of obtaining the indulgence. You could get one of these by, for instance, going to mass and Holy Communion on the first Friday of nine successive months. In theory, if you managed to obtain one of these plenary indulgences just before dying you would go straight to Heaven no matter how many sins you had committed previously. But there was a catch: you had to have a "right disposition" for the indulgence to be valid, and a spirit of calculating self-interest was scarcely that. In fact, you could never be quite sure that you had the right disposition, and might spend your entire life collecting invalid indulgences. It was safest, therefore, to dedicate them to the souls in Purgatory, because the generosity of this action would more or less guarantee that you had the right disposition. Of course the indulgences wouldn't then help *you* when you got to Purgatory, but you hoped that others down below might do you the same service, and that the souls you assisted to heaven would intercede there on your behalf. The Church of Christ was divided into three great populations, connected to each other by prayer: the Church Militant (on earth), the Church Suffering (in Purgatory) and the Church Triumphant (in Heaven).

Do the young people gathered together in the church of Our Lady and St Jude on this dark St Valentine's Day believe all this? Well, yes and no. They don't believe it with the same certainty that they believe they will have to sit their Final Examinations within the next three years; and about some of the details in the picture they are becoming a bit doubtful (most of them, for instance, have given up collecting indulgences, as something rather childish and undignified), but in outline, yes, they believe it, or at least they are not sure it is safe not to believe it; and this deeply engrained eschatological consciousness (eschatological, another useful word, meaning pertaining to the four last things – death, judgement, heaven and hell) is probably the chief common factor behind their collective presence here at mass. Only Miles, the tall, sleek figure swaying slightly on his feet during the Credo like a reed in the wind, tilting a handsomely bound old missal to catch the feeble electric light, is positively relishing the service, and he is a convert of fairly recent standing, so it is all delightfully novel to him – the gloomy, grubby ornateness of the church interior, the muttered, secretive liturgy (for only certain parts of the mass are in dialogue, and the Prayer of Consecration to which Father Brierley now turns is his alone), the banks of votive candles flickering amid frozen Niagaras of spent wax, and the sanctuary lamp glowing like an inflamed eye, guaranteeing the presence of God Himself in this place – all deliciously different from the restrained good taste of the chapel at his public school. As to the others, most of them will not be displeased when mass is over and they can hurry off to a day of largely secular concerns and pleasures. They are here not because they positively want to be, but because they believe it is good for their souls to be at mass when they would rather be in bed, and that it will help them in the immortal game of snakes and ladders.

But it is not doing Michael's soul any good at all if, as he thinks, he is in a state of mortal sin. For no matter how many good deeds or acts of devotion you perform, you get no heavenly credit for them if you are not in a state of grace. But is masturbation a mortal sin? There are times when he thinks it can't be. Is it possible that if he should die in the act (an all too vivid picture of himself discovered in bed, frozen by *rigor mortis* like a plaster statue, with his eyes turned up to the ceiling and his swollen member still clasped in his fist) that he would suffer eternal punishment just the same as, say, Hitler? (In fact there is no guarantee that Hitler is in Hell; he might have made an Act of Perfect Contrition a microsecond after squeezing the trigger in his Berlin bunker.) It seems self-evidently absurd. On the other hand, you could argue by the same method that, say, having proper sex with a prostitute isn't a mortal sin, either, and if that isn't, well, what is? Just thinking about it gives him a huge erection under his conveniently baggy coat, at the very moment when Father Brierley elevates the Host at the Consecration, thus heaping iniquity upon iniquity, sacrilege upon impurity. He could, of course ask a priest's advice on the problem – but that is part of the problem, he can't bring himself to confess his sin for shame and embarrassment. (And is that so surprising – would you, gentle reader? Did you, gentle Catholic reader?) This means that he can't go to Communion either, for one may only receive the Eucharist in a state of grace, otherwise it is a sacrilege. Therefore, when the Communion bell rings at these Thursday masses, Michael is the only one left kneeling in his pew. At first, when this was noticed, he used to hint that he had broken his fast – swallowed water when he brushed his teeth; or thoughtlessly nibbled a biscuit; and when this excuse wore thin he ingeniously pretended to have Doubts about the doctrine of Transubstantiation. He kept coming to mass, he confided to the others, in the hope that one day his faith would be restored. Father Brierley tried to convince him that he was being over-scrupulous, upon which Michael rapidly developed Doubts on other major doctrines, such as the Trinity and Papal Infallibility.

The others are rather impressed by Michael's Doubts, and Polly, catching sight of his pale and mournful visage as she herself returns from the altar rail, is apt to recall the words of Gerard Manley Hopkins (she is reading English):

> O the mind, mind has mountains, cliffs of fall
> Frightful, sheer, no-man-fathomed. Hold them cheap
> May who ne'er hung there!

All go out of their way to be nice to Michael and to encourage his failing powers of belief. In fact, of course, he believes the whole bag of tricks more simply and comprehensively perhaps than anyone else present at this mass, and is more honest in examining his conscience than many. Polly, for instance, frequently comforts herself with a moistened forefinger before dropping off to sleep, but wouldn't dream of mentioning this in Confession or letting it prevent her from taking the Sacrament. After all, she only does it when she is half-asleep and no longer, as it were, responsible for her actions. It is almost as though it belongs to someone else, the hand that slips under the waistband of her Baby Doll pyjamas and sliding between her legs rubs, rubs, gently, exquisitely, the little button of flesh the name and nature of which she does not yet know (though years later she will join a women's gynaecological workshop whose members squint through optical instruments at their own and each other's genitals, looking for signs of cystitis, thrush, polypi and other female afflictions, and will know her way around the uterus as familiarly as she now knows the stations on the Inner Circle line between her digs and College). Of course, she does not bring herself to climax – not the panting, writhing kind of climax demonstrated in films such as those Michael will read about twenty-one years later. Rather, she rocks herself to sleep on wavelets of sensation rippling out from the secret grotto at the centre of her body. When she wakes in the morning she has wiped the act from her memory. It helps her to do this that she has no name for it. "Masturbation" is not an item in her vocabulary – or Michael's, for that matter, though he does have his own idiomatic phrase for it, which Polly does not. Neither does Angela, who does not need one anyway, because she doesn't indulge in the practice. She has imbibed more deeply than Polly the code of personal modesty impressed upon convent-educated girls. She keeps her body scrupulously clean, she dresses it carefully and attractively, but she does not examine it or caress it in the process. Her movements at toilet are brisk and business-like. Her complexion gleams with health. She has scarcely ever had an impure thought, whereas Polly has had quite a few. Admittedly, Polly's convent school, a rather posh one in Sussex, for boarders, was a less chaste environment than Angela's in which to grow up. There was inevitably gossiping and giggling and smutty talk between the girls when they were left on their own, whereas Angela went to and fro between school and home every day, with scarcely a moment free, what with studying, games, and helping with housework and the shop, for idle thoughts or words.

As for Ruth, the thickset, bespectacled girl in boots and a school-style navy raincoat, kneeling in the front row, she has put the whole business of sex behind her long ago, *i.e.*, at the age of sixteen. For a while in early adolescence she daily inspected her pimply, pasty complexion, her thick yet flat-chested torso, her lank, colourless hair, wondering if she was merely going through "a phase", whether she would break through this unpromising chrysalis one day and emerge a beautiful butterfly, as she had seen other girls do. But alas, there was no such metamorphosis, she was stuck with her plainness and resigned herself to it, became a great reader and museum visitor and concert-goer, got interested in religion in the sixth form and, much to the surprise of her frivolous and vaguely agnostic parents, announced one day that she had been taking instructions from the local Catholic priest and was intending to be received into the Church.

All the young people present at this mass (and, of course, the celebrant) are virgins. Apart from Michael and Polly, none of them masturbates habitually and several have never masturbated at all. They have no experience of heavy petting. These facts run directly counter to statistical evidence recently tabulated by members of the Kinsey Institute for Sexual Research in Indiana, but these young people are British, and in any case unrepresentative of their age group. They carry a heavy freight of super-ego. To get to the University they have had to work hard, pass exams and win scholarships, sublimating the erotic energy of adolescence into academic achievement; and if ever a sultry evening or a bold glance took them off-guard and set them yearning for nameless sensual satisfactions, the precepts of their religion taught them to suppress these promptings, these "irregular motions of the flesh" as the Catechism called them. They are therefore sexually innocent to a degree that they will scarcely be able to credit when looking back on their youth in years to come. They know about the mechanics of basic copulation, but none of them could give an accurate account of the processes of fertilization, gestation and birth, and three of the young men do not even know how babies are born, vaguely supposing that they appear by some natural form of Caesarian section, like ripe chestnuts splitting their husks. As to the refinements and variations of the act of love – fellatio, cunnilingus, buggery, and the many different postures in which copulation may be contrived – they know them not (with the exception of Miles, who attended a public school) and would scarcely credit them were they to be told by Father Austin Brierley himself, who knows all about them in a theoretical way from his moral theology course at the seminary, for it is necessary that a priest should know of every sin that he might have to absolve. Not, he thanks God, that he has ever had to deal in the confessional with any of the more appalling perversions described in the textbooks, veiled in the relative decency of Latin – unspeakable acts between men and women, men and men, men and animals, which seem to someone who has voluntarily renounced ordinary heterosexual love not so much depraved as simply unintelligible.

He is not thinking of such matters now, of course, he is thinking of the mass he is celebrating, the sacred privilege he enjoys of changing the bread and wine into the Body and Blood of Jesus Christ, Redeemer. It is very hard to generate an appropriate sense of awe towards something done so often – once a day every day and three times on Sundays. Concentration is so difficult, distraction so easy. When he turned to face the congregation earlier at the Offertory, for instance, he couldn't help checking who was present and feeling a little twinge of disappointment that Polly's dark curls and rosy cheeks were missing; and then, as he turned back and heard the unmistakable tiptap of her high heels, he had to suppress a smile which might have been caught by his server, Edward. Edward is a first-year medical student with a humorous, rubbery countenance, hung between a pair of oversized ears, that stands him in good stead in comic opera and rugby-club concerts, but for liturgical purposes he twists it into an expression of such impressive solemnity that Austin Brierley almost feels nervous when celebrating mass under his scrutiny.

When Father Brierley pauses sometimes like this in the middle of the celebration, he is not, as Edward and the others suppose, rapt in private prayer, but struggling to eliminate from his mind such extraneous thoughts as Polly's late arrival, and to concentrate on the Holy Sacrifice. This is hard precisely because of the rapport he feels with the students. The congregation on an ordinary Sunday, mostly made up of poor Irish and Italians employed in the catering and hotel trades, is just a dense, anonymous mass, coughing and shuffling and shushing their babies behind his back, so that it is easy for him to shut them out from his mind; but these students are different – they are intelligent, well-mannered, articulate, and not very much younger than himself. They have no idea how much he depends upon them for human contact, how the New Testament study circle and the Thursday masses, which for most of them are quasi-penitential exercises, are for him the sweetest hours of the week.

Now the moment of his communion has come. He holds the consecrated host in his left hand while beating his breast with his right fist, as he recites the *"Domine, non sum dignus."* Lord, I am not worthy that Thou shouldst enter under my roof. . . . Behind him, summoned

13

by Edward's bell, the little congregation has gathered at the altar rail, and they join in the prayer: *"sed tantum dic verbo et sanabitur anima mea."* Say but the word and my soul shall be healed. Having reverently received the host and drunk from the chalice, the priest pauses for a moment in silent thanksgiving before turning to face his little flock. He holds up a host before them. *"Ecce Agnus Dei; ecce qui tolit peccata mundi."* Behold the Lamb of God; behold Him who taketh away the sins of the world.

Looking, as it were, over his shoulder, at the congregation, you can remind yourselves who they are. Ten characters is a lot to take in all at once, and soon there will be more, because we are going to follow their fortunes, in a manner of speaking, up to the present, and obviously they are not going to pair off with each other, that would be too neat, too implausible, so there will be other characters not yet invented, husbands and wives and lovers, not to mention parents and children, so it is important to get these ten straight now. Each character, for instance, has already been associated with some selected detail of dress or appearance which should help you to distinguish one from another. Such details also carry connotations which symbolize certain qualities or attributes of the character. Thus Angela's very name connotes angel, as in Heaven and cake (she looks good enough to eat in her pink angora sweater) and her blonde hair archetypecasts her as the fair virtuous woman, spouse-sister-mother figure, whereas Polly is a Dark Lady, sexy seductress, though not really sinister because of her healthy cheeks and jolly curls. Miles, you recall, is the ex-public schoolboy, a convert; his handsomely bound old missal bespeaks wealth and taste, his graceful, wandlike figure a certain effeminacy. There is Dennis, Angela's slave, burly in his dufflecoat, the scar tissue on his neck perhaps proleptic of suffering, and Adrian, bespectacled (=limited vision), in belted gaberdine raincoat (=instinctual repression, authoritarian determination), not to be confused with Ruth's glasses and frumpish schoolgirl's raincoat, signifying unawakened sexuality and indifference to self-display. On the altar is Edward, his rubbery clown's face locked into an expression of exaggerated piety, the first to receive the wafer from Father Brierley's fingers, shooting out a disconcertingly long tongue like a carnival whistle. Back in the pews there is Michael, haggard in his baggy wanker's overcoat and his simulated Doubts, his head weighed down with guilt or the hank of dark hair falling across his eyes, his features slightly flattened as though pressed too often against glass enclosing forbidden goodies; and a girl you have not yet been introduced to, who now comes forward from the shadows of the side aisle, where she has been lurking, to join the others at the altar rail. Let her be called Violet, no, Veronica, no Violet, improbable a name as that is for Catholic girls of Irish extraction, customarily named after saints and figures of Celtic legend, for I like the connotations of Violet – shrinking, penitential, melancholy – a diminutive, dark-haired girl, a pale, pretty face ravaged by eczema, fingernails bitten down to the quick and stained by nicotine, a smartly cut needlecord coat sadly creased and soiled; a girl, you might guess from all this evidence, with problems, guilts, hangups. (She is another regular masturbator, by the way, so make that three, and she is not quite sure whether she is a virgin, having been interfered with at the age of twelve by a tramp whose horny index finger may have ruptured her hymen, or so she confided to Angela, who was shocked, and told Ruth, who was sceptical, having received from Violet an entirely different story of how she had been painfully deflowered by a holy candle wielded by her cousin in the course of an experimental black mass in the attic of his house one day when their parents were out. Really, you didn't know what to believe with Violet, but she was certainly a source of interest.)

Let's just take a roll call. From left to right along the altar rail, then: Polly, Dennis, Angela, Adrian, Ruth, Miles, Violet. Michael kneeling in his pew. Edward and Father Brierley on the altar. And of course the two old ladies, who have somehow levered themselves into the central aisle, and shuffled forward with painful slowness on their swollen feet to stand (for if they should kneel they might never be able to get up again) at the altar rail, their heads nodding gently like toys on the parcel shelf of a moving car, their eyes watery and myopic, their facial skin hanging from their skulls like folds of dingy cloth. No one takes much notice of them. Austin Brierley knows them as regular attenders at early weekday mass and as parishioners whom he occasionally has to visit at home, carrying the Blessed Sacrament into their depressing bedrooms when they are too ill to go out. Good women, pious women, but of no interest. Both are widows, fortunate enough to be looked after by their grown-up children. There is nothing he can do for them except give them the sacraments, listening to their mumbled, rambling confessions of trivial peccadilloes (sometimes they dry up after the opening Act of Contrition, unable to remember a single sin, poor old dears, and sensing their panic, he prompts them with a likely venial sin or two, though it is becoming increasingly difficult as they grow older and feebler, almost as incapable of envy and anger and covetousness as they have been for decades of lust, gluttony, sloth) and administering Communion, fighting back his own distaste at their trembling, discoloured tongues and loosely fitting dentures. He does so now, giving them Communion first so that by the time he comes to the end of the row they will be at least started on the slow journey back to their pew. Edward, holding the paten under their quivering jaws, scans them with professional curiosity, diagnosing arthritis, anaemia, noting a large growth, presumably benign, on the throat of one; but to the rest of the students the two old ladies might be part of the church's furniture, the dark stained oak pews and the dusty plaster statues, for all the notice they take of them. Which is surprising, in a way, when you consider that, as explained above, a principal reason why they are all gathered here is that they believe it will stand them in good stead in the next world. For here are two persons manifestly certain to die in the near future. You might think the young people would be interested to observe the disposition in which the old ladies approach the undiscovered country from whose bourne no traveller returns, would be curious to determine whether a lifetime's practice of the Catholic faith and the regular reception of its sacraments has in any way mitigated the terrors of that journey, imparted serenity and confidence to these travellers, made the imminent parting of the spirit and its fleshly garments any less dreaded. But no, it has not occurred to any of them to scrutinize or interrogate the old ladies in this way. The fact is that none of them actually believes he or she is going to die.

They know it, cognitively, yes; but believe it, intuitively, they do not. In that regard they are no different from other young, healthy human beings. They look forward to life, not death. Their plans include marriage, children, jobs, fame, fulfilment, service – not the grave and the afterlife. The afterlife figures in their thoughts rather like retirement: something to insure against, but not to brood on at the very outset of your career. Religion is their insurance – the Catholic Church offering the very best, the most comprehensive cover – and weekday mass is by way of being an extra premium, enhancing the value of the policy.

But it is also more than that. For their Faith teaches them that God does not only control the afterlife; He also controls this one. Not a sparrow falls without His willing it. As far back as they can remember, the cradle Catholics among them have been encouraged to pray for good fortune in this life as well as in the next: fine weather for the School Sports Day, the recovery of a lost brooch, promotion for Daddy, success at the Eleven Plus. There is a convent somewhere in the south of England which advertises in the Catholic press the services of its nuns, praying in shifts twenty-four hours a day for whatever intentions you care to send them in return for donations to their charitable cause (*"Send no money until your prayer is answered – then give generously"*) and which is heavily in demand around the time that GCE results are expected. You might think that the time to pray was before the examinations were taken, otherwise it was asking God to tamper with the marks, but that was not the way these Catholics looked at it. God was omnipotent, and it would cost Him no effort, should He be so minded, to turn back the clock of history and make the tiny adjustment that would allow you to put the right answer instead of the wrong one and get a Pass instead of a Fail and then set the mechanism ticking again without your marker or the rest of the world or indeed you yourself being any the wiser. If such prayers were not always answered this did not show that the system did not work, but merely that God had decided that it wouldn't be in your interest to gratify your wish or that you didn't deserve it. One way or another, it was obviously prudent to keep on the right side of God, as long as you believed in Him at all, since then, even without your asking, He might reward you by ensuring that the right examination question or the right job or indeed Mr Right turned up when you were most in need.

To be fair to the young people in Our Lady and St Jude's, it must be said that they are not here entirely out of self-interest. To a greater or lesser extent they have all grasped the idea that Christianity is about transcendence of self in love of God and one's neighbour, and they struggle to put this belief into practice according to their lights, trying to be kind, generous and grateful for their blessings. Admittedly, Angela is the only neighbour for whom Dennis has any love to spare at the moment, and Michael feels too hopelessly abandoned to sexual depravity to make much of an effort at being good in other ways, but Angela neglects no opportunity to do a good deed, shopping for an old lady or baby-sitting for her landlady: and Ruth is a more systematic philanthropist, helping in the nursery of a Catholic orphanage on one afternoon a week, sometimes taking Polly along with her – and, although Polly can never be relied upon, when she does turn up she entertains the children more successfully than Ruth, so that Ruth has a struggle not to feel jealous; and Adrian is a cadet in the Catholic Evidence Guild, and spends every Sunday afternoon at Speaker's Corner at the foot of the Guild's rostrum, lending moral support and learning the tricks of the trade against the day when he will take on the atheists and bigots of the metropolis in his own right; and Miles is a tertiary of the order of Carmelites and wears under his beautifully laundered white shirts and silk underwear an exceedingly itchy scapular the discomfort of which he offers up for the souls of all his Protestant forebears who may be languishing in the Purgatory in which they did not believe; and Edward plans to practice medicine for at least two years in the mission fields of Africa when he has qualified; and Violet is liable to sudden, alarming fits of self-mortification and good works, such as fasting for a whole week or descending upon bewildered tramps under the arches of the Charing Cross Embankment, offering them rosaries which they accept in the hope of being able to sell them later for the price of a cup of tea, and, if they have sores, little bottles of Lourdes water, which the tramps drink in the expectation of its being gin and then disrespectfully spit out on to the pavement when they discover it isn't.

Violet is the last to receive Communion. Placing the host on her tongue, Father Brierley murmurs, as he has murmured to each of the communicants, *"Corpus Domini Nostri Jesu Christi custodiat animam tuam in vitam aeternam. Amen."* May the Body of Our Lord Jesus Christ preserve thy soul to life everlasting. He turns back to the altar to perform the ablutions – purifying his fingers and the chalice with water which he then swallows to ensure that no crumb of the consecrated host, no drop of the consecrated wine, should remain unconsumed and therefore at risk of irreverent or unseemly treatment. Any entire hosts that remain are locked away in the tabernacle above the altar, its door screened by a little gilt curtain. Meanwhile the communicants have returned to their places, where they kneel in silent thanksgiving, their eyes closed, their heads bowed.

This is a difficult business for nearly all of them. For what is it that has happened, for which they are to give thanks? They have received the Body and Blood of Christ. Not literally, of course, but under the appearances of bread and wine – or rather bread alone, for it is not at this date Catholic practice to administer Communion under both kinds to the laity – and not really bread either, for the host bears very little resemblance to an ordinary loaf. A small, round, papery, almost tasteless wafer has been placed on their tongues, and they have swallowed it (without chewing it, an action deemed irreverent by those who prepared them for their First Communions) and thus received Christ into themselves. But what does *that* mean? The consecrated host, they know, has not changed in outward appearance, and if Dennis, say, were, like sacrilegious scientists in Catholic cautionary tales, to take one back to the laboratory on his tongue and analyse it there, he would discover only molecules of wheat. But it would be sacrilege to do so precisely because the host *has* changed into the Body and Blood, Soul and Divinity, of Jesus Christ, Saviour. In the language of scholastic philosophy, the substance has changed but the accidents (empirically observable properties) have not. The doctrine of transubstantiation, as they have been reminded often enough in RI lessons, is a mystery, a truth above reason. That is all very well, but it means that the mind has little to grip on when it comes to making one's thanksgiving after Communion. In fact, the more intently you think about the mystery, the more irreverent and disedifying your thoughts are apt to become. At what point, Dennis cannot help wondering, does the miracle of transubstantiation reverse itself, since it cannot be that Christ submits himself to the indignities of human digestion and excretion? Is it as the host begins to dissolve on the tongue, as it passes the epiglottis, or as it travels down the oesophagus that Christ jumps from His wheaten vehicle and into your soul? Such speculations are not conducive to pious recollection. There are, of course, set prayers which one can say, but they don't mean a lot either.

"*O Lord Jesus,*" Adrian reads from his missal, "*I have received Thee within myself, and from within the sanctuary of my heart into which Thou hast deigned to descend, do Thou give to Almighty God, in my name, all the glory that is His due.*"

Adrian, who has a good logical mind, might well ask by what right he can describe his heart as a sanctuary, and how Christ, being God, can give glory to God, or putting that aside, why He should be bothered to do so in his, Adrian's name, when he, Adrian, is perfectly capable of giving glory to God himself. But Adrian is conditioned not to ask such awkward questions, and while reading these words with a vague feeling of piety, thinks of something else. In fact, within thirty seconds of kneeling down and bowing their heads, most of them are thinking of something other than the Eucharist – of breakfast, or study, or the weather, or sex or just the ache in their knees.

It is easier for them when Father Brierley, having read the Last Gospel, comes to the foot of the altar and kneels to recite the customary prayers to Our Lady.

"Hail Holy Queen, mother of mercy; hail our life, our sweetness and our hope! To thee do we cry, poor banished children of Eve; to thee do we send up our sighs, mourning and weeping in this vale of tears . . ." Only the converts actually listen to the words and try to make sense of them – to the rest it is just a familiar pious babble; but all can think, as the baroque rhetoric of the prayer lifts them up on its surging cadences, of Our Lady, a sweet-faced woman in blue and white robes, with her arms and hands lifted slightly and extended forward, as she is depicted in a thousand cheap statues in Lady Chapels up and down the land. Praying to her for help is much easier than puzzling over transubstantiation.

Nevertheless, all feel better for having attended the mass, as they assemble outside the church porch, greeting each other, laughing and chattering, donning scarves and gloves against the cold, damp air. All (all except Michael anyway) feel cheerful, hopeful, cleansed, at peace. Perhaps this is indeed the presence of the Lord Jesus in them, and not just the lift of spirits that naturally comes with the termination of mild boredom and the expectation of breakfast.

Father Brierley has unvested with almost unseemly haste in order to race round the back of the church in time to greet his little flock before they move off to the Lyons cafeteria. "Good morning, Angela, good morning, Dennis, good morning, Polly – overslept this morning?" He laughs too heartily, showing teeth stained with nicotine, breaks open a packet of Player's and presses cigarettes upon the boys who smoke. The students stamp their feet and shift the weight of their bags and briefcases from one hand to another, impatient to be off, but unwilling to seem discourteous. Violet takes one of Father Brierley's cigarettes, rather to his consternation, for he does not like to see women smoking in public. Some badinage is exchanged about St Valentine's Day, and Father Brierley, desperately aiming at an effect of good-humoured tolerance of harmless fun, doubles up with forced laughter.

"Did you get my Valentine?" Dennis murmurs to Angela.

She smiles. "Yes. I got two, actually."

Two! Dennis is immediately stricken with jealous fear. "Who sent you the other one?"

"I haven't the foggiest."

Eventually the cigarette ends are stamped into the muddy pavement and the little band begins to shuffle off in the direction of the Tottenham Court Road. "Goodbye, Father!" they call; and Austin Brierley, thrusting his hands deep into the pockets of his cassock, and rocking backwards and forwards on his heels, calls back, "Goodbye, goodbye, see you on Monday, at the study group. First Epistle to the Corinthians."

"Aren't you coming to the St Valentine's Party, Father?" Ruth cries, and then winces as Polly pokes her in the ribs.

"No, no, I think not," the priest replies. "There's a meeting of the Legion of Mary . . ."

"What did you do that for?" Ruth mutters, rubbing her side.

"We don't want him there tonight, he's such a wet blanket," says Polly *sotto voce*, and flashes Father Brierley a brilliant smile over her shoulder.

He blushes, and turns back to the church porch, which the two old ladies have just reached after a laborious arm-in-arm shuffle up the nave, and dutifully pauses to exchange a word with them. Then he makes his way back to the presbytery, where his congealing breakfast awaits him and, behind the *Daily Telegraph* propped on the other side of the table, his parish priest.

"Many there?" enquires the parish priest, without lifting his eyes from the *Daily Telegraph*.

"Nine," says Austin Brierley. "Plus Mrs Moody and Mrs O'Dowd, of course."

The parish priest grunts. Austin Brierley takes the cover off his bacon and egg. It is only eight forty-five and the best of the day is already over.

It begins to drizzle again as the students make their way along the pavements in twos and threes. Rather reluctantly (for the rolling of it is a work of art), Miles unfurls his rapier-thin silk umbrella and gallantly holds it over Violet's head. "Did you know, Miles," she says, "that Our Lady of Fatima left a message about how the world will end which was sealed up and given to the Pope and mustn't be opened till 1960?"

"My dear, how exciting! He must be awfully tempted to have a peep at it."

"They say he has, and it was so terrifying, he fainted."

"You must know," says Dennis to Angela. "You must have some idea."

"Well, I haven't. It wasn't signed, like yours. You're not supposed to sign Valentines, you know," she says, a little tartly, because she is getting irritated by Dennis's persistent questioning. "That's the whole point of them."

"What about the writing on the envelope? Couldn't you recognize that?"

"Oh, for heaven's sake, Dennis, let's drop the subject."

As they draw nearer the Tottenham Court Road, secular London engulfs them with the hiss and roar of traffic, and crowds of jostling, fretting pedestrians hurrying to work. No Lord Jesus in *them*, anyway, by the look of it; their faces are drawn, their eyes anxious or vacant as they cluster on the pavement's edge, waiting for the traffic lights to change. Flags fly at half-mast on some buildings for the recent death of King George VI, and a newspaper placard announces, THE NEW ELIZABETHANS: SPECIAL FEATURE.

"Did you know you were a New Elizabethan, Michael?" Ruth asks.

Michael, who is gazing lustfully at an unclothed and headless mannequin in a shop window, starts. "What? eh?" he says, flicking back his lank forelock.

"We're the New Elizabethans, apparently."

"Gadzooks! Zounds! Marry come up! Buckle your swash!" cries Edward, waving his tattered, broken-winged umbrella in the air. And as the traffic lights change he leads them across the road, crying, "Once more unto the breach dear friends, once more!" Some of the other pedestrians stare, amused or disapproving. Grinning and giggling, the students straggle after Edward, enjoying the feeling of being young and irresponsible. Their gait has a different rhythm to that of the businessmen and typists hurrying to work. They have no lectures before ten o'clock, or if they have, they will cut them in order to have breakfast. And they *are* dear friends, Ruth thinks to herself; she has never had so many friends before, and it is such a relief to know that the friendship does not depend on one's being pretty or wealthy or smart, but simply on having the same beliefs in common; and she feels blessed, walking along the Tottenham Court Road behind Edward and Polly, who are discussing a sketch to be performed at the St Valentine's party.

It is deliciously warm in the basement of the Lyons cafeteria, a steamy, tropical heat emanating from the kitchens and the hot-water urns. They take off their coats and scarves, heap them with bags and briefcases in a corner, and relieve their hunger and thirst with baked beans and bacon, toast and sticky buns, cups and cups of dark, sweet tea. Ruth stirs two heaped teaspoonfuls of sugar into her cup: it will soon be Lent and she will be giving it up. As indulging a sweet tooth is her only weakness of the flesh, this will be no light penance.

"I hope everyone is coming to the party," says Polly, who has sat up half the night cutting out paper hearts for decorations. "Or are you all going to the Union do instead?"

All disown this intention with laughter and mock indignation. Union do's, especially on St Valentine's night, are notoriously dissipated affairs, involving the construction in a corner of the Lounge of a dimly-lit, cushion-lined grotto designed expressly for snogging, if not worse.

"Are you going to the Cath. Soc. party?" Adrian asks, glancing between Angela and Dennis. The "you" could be singular or plural. Dennis thinks it is meant to be interpreted as singular and addressed to Angela, and that Adrian must be the sender of the second Valentine. "No," he says, "I've got an experiment to write up."

"Oh, we must go, we must all go," says Angela. "Polly will be disappointed if we don't."

"I think I may drop in for an hour," says Adrian.

"All right then, if you really want to," says Dennis grimly to Angela.

Momentous things happen at or around the St Valentine's party. Walking Angela to the prefabricated hut in the College precincts where it is to be held, and unable to bear his jealousy any longer, Dennis stops suddenly under a dripping tree in Russell Square and apologizes abjectly for his boorish behaviour of the morning, recklessly declares his love for her, and asks if she will marry him. Angela is moved, overwhelmed, by this sudden gush of emotion; and feeling her heart knocking, the blood coming and going in her face and, as Dennis takes her in his arms underneath her overcoat, unwonted sensations in her vagina, decides that this must indeed be love, and murmurs into his ear that she loves him too, but she cannot promise to marry him till they know each other better and have their degrees, which is nearly three years away. He says he doesn't mind waiting, and at that moment he doesn't. They move on slowly through the square, with their arms round one another and keep them round one another for the rest of the evening, rotating slowly under Polly's crepe paper hearts to the theme tune of *La Ronde*, a saucy French film still attracting queues in the West End.

"Have you seen *La Ronde*, Adrian?" says Polly.

"I certainly have not," he replies in his flat Derbyshire accent.

"You should, it's awfully good."

"It's been banned by the League of Decency in America."

"Pooh, why should we take any notice of them?"

"Personally, I think we could do with an organization like that in this country."

"Oh, Adrian, you are the end! Why don't you ask me to dance?"

"I don't dance, as you very well know, Polly. Anyway, I was just going. I have work to do."

While speaking to Polly, Adrian has been watching Angela and Dennis dancing, and has come to a decision. He will not pursue Angela. To try and win her now would entail too much expense of spirit. To prise her loose from Dennis's possessive embrace, he would have to become as infatuated, as abandoned, as Dennis himself, and Adrian is not prepared to pay that price. No woman is worth it, not even Angela. Looking at her perfectly symmetrical features, slightly flushed and softened by the romantic trance in which she moves about the dance floor, and haloed by the soft waves of her golden hair, he feels a wrenching pang of envy and desire, which he ruthlessly suppresses. Very well, then, if not Angela, then no one – at least until his studies are completed. He tugs tight the belt of his double-breasted gaberdine raincoat and marches out into the cold, dark drizzle. Very well, then, he will work, work and pray. If not Angela, then no one – certainly not Polly, a flighty, frivolous girl who will get herself into trouble one of these days, and not Ruth, either, because too plain, and not Violet, too unstable. He will work hard, he will get a good degree, and he will become a star of the Catholic Evidence Guild. One day Angela will stand beneath his rostrum at Hyde Park Corner, and admire, and regret. Thus Adrian.

Meanwhile Polly, slightly tipsy on the cider cup she prepared, and experimentally tasted rather too often, is dancing with Miles, a quickstep. He dances superbly, beautifully balanced on the pointed toes of his gleaming black shoes, but somehow coldly. There is no warmth in the pressure of his long fingers, splayed out across the small of her back, and when she tries to nestle against him he arches away from her, swings her round in a centrifugal flourish, and breaks into a sequence of rapidly executed fishtails that requires all her concentration to follow. At the conclusion of the record, he spins her like a top at the end of his long arm and bows with mock formality. Polly responds with a theatrical curtsey and nearly overbalances. She is gripped by an almost intolerable desire to be cuddled. Seeing Michael on his own, she goes over to him. Divested of his Artful Dodger's overcoat, wearing a clean white shirt, and having slicked back his quiff with a lavish application of Brylcreem, he looks quite presentable.

Michael watches Polly's approach with alarm. He has been appraising her breasts while she has been dancing with Miles and is afraid that she has noticed. This is not in fact the case, but by coming and speaking to him, she effectively puts a stop to the appraisal. They are in the same Department, English, and talk books for a while. Michael's favourite novel at the moment is *The Heart of the Matter*, and Polly's, *Brideshead Revisited*. "But Greene's awfully sordid, don't you think?" says Polly.

"But Waugh's so snobbish."

"Anyway, it said in the *Observer* that they're the two best English novelists going, so that's one in the eye for the Prods."

After a while the restless Polly moves off to change the records on the gramophone, and leaves Michael free to contemplate her breasts again. He wonders what it is like to live with those twin protuberances, quivering and jouncing in front of you at every moment, like heavy ripe fruit on the bough; what it is like to sponge them at the washbasin every morning, rub them dry with a towel, and fit them carefully into the hollow cups of a brassiere, first the left one, then the right. Extraordinary.

Miles, watching Polly move across the room, recognizes with a certain inner panic that he finds her prominent bust and voluptuous hips repulsive. His spiritual adviser, a Farm Street Jesuit, has assured him that he will come to like girls in due course, given prayer and patience, but so far there are no perceptible signs of it. His erotic fantasies are still of young boys in the showers at school, their high, taut buttocks gleaming under the cascade. Perhaps, he had wondered aloud to the Jesuit, he should renounce sex altogether and try his vocation as a priest; but after a great deal of throat-clearing and tortuously allusive argument he gathered that only guaranteed heterosexuals were eligible for the priesthood. That was manifestly untrue of the Anglican clergy, he had protested. And that's why you get all those scandals in the Sunday papers, was the answer.

Neither Michael nor Miles gives a sexual thought, positive or negative, to Ruth, who is cutting sandwiches in a corner of the room. Yet she is a woman, and particularly conscious of it this evening, for her period has just started and she is bleeding copiously under her limp, dowdy dress of navy blue crepe. Normally Angela would have been helping her, for Angela is that kind of girl, never one to stand idly by when there is work to be done; but tonight Angela is blind to everyone else in the room except Dennis, and, looking up from her sandwiches and holding her throbbing head, Ruth watches Angela dancing, and Polly flirting (with Edward now) and feels gloomily that the Christian fellowship of the morning has after all been dissolved by sex. A bitter remark scrawled on the wall of a loo at school comes back to her: *Blessed are the good-looking, for they shall have fun.* Then, ashamed of these envious thoughts, she bows her head over the sandwiches again. Tomorrow she will put in an extra afternoon at the orphanage, where there is no time – or occasion – for envy. It suddenly comes into Ruth's head that she might herself become a nun. She thrusts this idea away, a little frightened by the plausibility of it, for she doesn't want to give up her freedom, she nourishes dreams of becoming a famous botanist, travelling the world to discover new species, and perhaps marrying another famous botanist who will love her for her mind rather than her looks. And her mother would have kittens. At the thought of her parents' likely reaction to such an idea, Ruth grins to herself, not knowing what a nice smile she has, because no one has ever told her.

Later, there is an entertainment in the form of sketches. In one of these, entitled "The Return of St Valentine", Edward plays the part of the Roman martyr's ghost, dressed in a toga and holding on to his head with both hands in case (as he explains) it should topple off, for he was beheaded, who returns to earth in modern London and is bewildered and scandalized by the cult being celebrated in his name. Orgies of snogging in the Students' Union are represented by the miming of an extravagant display of passion on a sofa immediately behind the figure of St Valentine, as he recites the woeful story of his martyrdom in stumbling rhyming couplets. This sofa, raised on a dais, has its back facing the audience, so that all they can see are arms and legs appearing in surprising and suggestive positions above and to each side of the sofa, and various garments being discarded on to the floor. It is all done, rather cleverly, by Polly alone, using her four limbs and a collection of male and female attire. She tosses shoes to the right and left, she throws a bare arm languorously backwards over the side of the sofa, she draws on one leg of a pair of man's trousers and lofts it hilariously in the air, she points a stockinged leg, daringly exposed to the very suspender button, at the ceiling and wiggles her toes in a droll signal of alarm or ecstacy.

At this point Father Brierley makes an unexpected and unnoticed appearance at the party. He is not amused. He is appalled. When items of underclothing – panties, brassieres, Y-fronts – begin to fly through the air, he cries, "Stop, stop, this is too bad!" and turns on the main lights in the room. Edward, startled, freezes in mid-speech, still holding on to his head. The audience blinks, stirs, looks round. Polly, fully dressed, stands up behind the sofa. Austin Brierley is totally disconcerted: first, to find his favourite student responsible for the spectacle, second, that no real indecency has taken place. But he proceeds to do his duty, which is to reproach them for a lapse of moral standards, not to mention taste. Catholic students should set an example to other young people by their purity of mind and body. The Catechism, he reminds them, explicitly forbade attendance at im-

modest shows and dances as an offence against the sixth command-
ment. All the more deplorable was it, therefore, actually to perform
such degrading entertainments. He was surprised, he was shocked, he
was disappointed. He expected an apology, well not an apology, after
all it was Almighty God who was offended, Confession would be more
appropriate, he would leave it to their consciences, they would talk
about it another time, he did not wish to exaggerate, he was not
opposed to harmless fun, but there were lines that had to be drawn. . . .

He stammers to a halt. There is a long silence. All feel the breath
squeezed out of them by embarrassment, and avoid each other's eyes.
Then Edward, who has by now lowered his arms to his side, mutters,
"Sorry, Father, it was only meant to be a bit of fun," and pulls off his
toga, his big ears bright red. Ruth offers the priest a cup of coffee.
Polly looks very white and angry and says nothing. Father Brierley
declines the coffee and leaves. It is only ten o'clock, but the party is
clearly over.

"Well, Polly did get rather carried away, I'm afraid," says Ruth to
Edward, as they stack the chairs and tear up the paper hearts. "You
couldn't see what was going on behind your back."

"Silly girl," says Edward, "I believe she was a bit under the
influence."

By now, Polly is weeping in a corner, comforted by Violet. "You
were super, Polly, honestly, you should go on the stage," says Violet.
"*I* couldn't have done it to save my life."

This isn't, perhaps, the most tactful of remarks, and Polly weeps
more violently than ever. "I'll never go to his stupid study group
again," she vows, "or his stupid Thursday masses." Then, shocked
herself at what she has just said, she stops crying and, after a while,
cheers up.

The incident has broken the spell of romance for Dennis and
Angela. On the tube train back to her digs they have a slight dis-
agreement about it. Angela opines that Polly was a fool to make such
an exhibition of herself. Dennis, disappointed that Angela did not,
like himself, find the sketch erotically exciting, defends it. When they
kiss goodnight on the porch of her digs he tries to push his tongue
between her lips, but she draws back and says gently but firmly,
"Don't do that, pet."

"Why not?"

"Because."

They wrangle for a while about this, the first of many such arguments, until Dennis has to run back to the station for the last train to his own digs on the other side of London. In those days he seemed to have a permanent stitch in his side from running for last trains and buses.

Austin Brierley went home and tossed and turned all night, tormented by the memory of Polly's stockinged leg waving in the air above the back of the sofa. The next morning, on an impulse, he asked his parish priest for counsel.

"You did well to give them a telling-off," said the PP, when Austin Brierley had told his story. "What are you worried about?"

"I keep having impure thoughts about the girl, Father," Austin confessed with a blush. "I can't seem to get the image of her leg out of my mind."

"Pooh, pooh! Have you tried ejaculations?"

"Pardon?"

" '*My Jesus, mercy, Mary help!*' That's a good one."

"Oh, yes, I've tried prayers."

"Pray especially to Our Lady, she'll help you to forget it. It wasn't your fault, you didn't seek the occasion of sin." The PP sniffed and blew his nose loudly into a handkerchief. "Some of these young hussies need their bottoms smacked," he said indignantly, a careless expression in the circumstances, that didn't do anything at all for Austin Brierley's peace of mind.

2

How they lost their virginities

IN the fifties, everyone was waiting to get married, some longer than others. Dennis lost track of the weddings he and Angela attended in that decade – weddings in churches and chapels of every size and shape, and receptions of all sorts, from a champagne and smoked salmon buffet on a Thames riverboat to a cheap sit-down lunch of rectilinear sliced ham and limp salad, with tinned peaches and ice cream to follow, in a dismal school hall in Watford. But somehow the weddings were all the same – organ music, hats, speeches, hilarity, indigestion; and they always ended in the same way, with Dennis and Angela standing on the edge of a crowd, waving goodbye to some grinning couple off to the scarcely imaginable pleasures of the marriage bed. Once, they went to two weddings on the same Satur-day, one in the morning and one in the afternoon, on opposite sides of London, and the second one was like a nightmare, having to eat cold chicken and sausages on sticks and wedding cake, and drink sweet sparkling wine, all over again, and listen to what sounded like the same speeches and telegrams, and exchange small talk with what looked very much like the same two sets of relatives.

As for themselves, there was Dennis's degree to be got, and Angela's degree to be got and his National Service to be done and her postgraduate certificate of education to be obtained and jobs to be found and money to be saved. Some of these time-consuming operations would overlap, but collectively they would account for at least five years and in fact it turned out to be rather longer before they were married. At a well-wined dinner party in 1974 Dennis was to describe their courtship as the most drawn-out foreplay session in the annals of human sexuality. He was alluding to the infinitely slow extension of licence to touch which Angela granted him over the years, as slow as history itself. By November 1952, when *The Mousetrap* opened in the West End, he was allowed to rest one hand on a breast, outside her blouse. In 1953, Coronation Year, while Hilary and Tenzing were scaling Everest, Dennis was persuading Angela to let him stroke her leg, when she sat on his lap, up to stocking-top height. In 1954 food rationing came to an end, Roger Bannister ran the four-minute mile and Dennis got his hand inside Angela's blouse and on to a brassiere cup. Then there was a setback. One day Angela emerged weeping from the confessional of the parish priest of Our Lady and St Jude's, and for a long time there was no touching of legs or breasts in any circumstances. The Comet was grounded and a link established between smoking and lung cancer.

1954 was the year most of the regular Thursday mass-goers sat their Final examinations. They had stopped going to the New Testament Study Group for lack of time, but to have given up the mass as well would have been inviting bad luck. Adrian, indeed, broke his tight-packed revision schedule to go on Student Cross with Edward (whose medical Finals were some years off) reasoning that the loss of preparation time would be more than compensated for by the spiritual merit earned on the pilgrimage. Student Cross, in case you haven't read about it before, consisted of about fifty young men carrying a large, heavy, wooden cross from London to the shrine of Our Lady at Walsingham in half a dozen stages, reciting prayers and singing hymns from time to time, as an act of penance for the sins of students everywhere (no light undertaking) and for the edification of the general public. The general public stared, looked embarrassed or incredulous, sometimes pretended not to see the pilgrims at all. An old lady on the pavement of Enfield's main shopping street inquired, as they were halted at traffic lights, if they were advertising something. Adrian said, "Yes, madam, the Crucifixion." Edward murmured: "And foot-powder." All suffered from blisters, especially Adrian. An experienced walker, he had the misfortune to lose his boots just before the pilgrimage and was obliged to wear new ones, not properly broken in. Soon his feet were covered in blisters, his boots seemed filled with molten fire. Every step was agony, and to ease the pain he tried to walk on the sides of his feet with his legs unnaturally bowed, which gave him cramp. His face was creased with pain, his eyes were glazed. Edward urged him to drop out, but Adrian refused to acknowledge defeat until he keeled over in the middle of the A10 just south of Cambridge and they had to phone for an ambulance. He was sent home in a wheelchair, sitting in the guard's van amid bales of returned newspapers and crates of disgruntled chickens. He tried to console himself with the thought that he had done his best, but it did not seem a good omen for his Finals.

All worked hard in the weeks preceding their examinations, though, as is the habit of students, when they met they pretended otherwise. Violet, however, really wasn't working, or pretending. She found herself incapable of revising, and more incapable the nearer the time of Finals approached. She would go to the Library each morning, open a book and stare at it for hours, turning the pages out of habit, but not taking in a single word; then she would go home to her digs, open another book and stare at that for hours in the same way. She lived mostly on Lucozade and cigarettes, and her hands shook when she lit the cigarettes and poured the Lucozade. She went regularly to the Thursday masses, but when she remarked in the Lyons cafeteria afterwards that she wasn't doing any work the others thought that it was the usual kind of precaution against hubris and paid no attention. They could see that she didn't look very well, but then none of them did. The girls' hair was lank and greasy from neglect, and the boys looked pale and scurfy from lack of exercise and fresh air.

Violet herself came to the conclusion that she was under some kind of spell or curse, that God was punishing her for her sins. She began to go to Confession compulsively, once a day, then more than once, in different churches all over London, hoping to lift the curse. She did not go at the advertised times: there was usually a bellpush somewhere in a Catholic church by which you could summon a priest to hear your confession at any hour of the day or night. She liked to go into some strange, empty church, in the middle of the morning or afternoon, let the door swing shut behind her, muffling the everyday sounds from the street, and walk with echoing footsteps down the aisle to push the bell button for Confession; then kneel beside the confessional wondering what kind of priest her action would pluck from his hiding-place, and whether he would be the one to break the spell. Always she said she wanted to make a general confession for all the sins of her past life. She confessed the same sins to different priests and compared the penances they gave her. Some were lengthier than others, but none of her confessors seemed particularly shocked by what she told them, so she began, at first subtly, then more and more extravagantly, to embellish her sins and to invent totally fictitious ones: she had corrupted her little sister, she had sold herself as a child to an American soldier for chewing gum, she had masturbated with a statuette of the Sacred Heart. These revelations produced a gratifying reaction from the priests – sighs and stunned silences from the other side of the grille, heavy penances and earnest exhortations, until one day a sceptical Franciscan began to question her sharply about details, and reminded her that it was sacrilege to tell anything other than the strict truth in Confession. This threw Violet into a worse state than before, because she was frightened to admit that she had made all the false confessions. She was less able than ever to do any revision and felt certain that she would fail her examinations. She would have tried to kill herself if that hadn't been a surer way than any of going to Hell. When, one Thursday morning at breakfast in Lyons, someone made a flippant remark about Violet's exaggerations, she suddenly burst into uncontrollable hysterics and began throwing crockery at the wall. Edward took her round to the Outpatients Department of the College Hospital, where she was given a sedative and put in a cubicle to rest until her parents could be contacted to take her home to Swindon. Edward explained to the others that it was a nervous breakdown.

Later, Violet wrote to Edward from the West of Ireland, where she was recuperating on her uncle's farm, to thank him for looking after her, and to say that she would not be taking the exams that summer, but was hoping to return to College in due course to do her final year again. The others were very sorry for Violet, but too preoccupied with their own anxieties about Finals to spare much thought for her. Besides, they did not really understand about nervous breakdowns, they did not quite see how a nervous breakdown fitted into the theological framework of sin and grace, spiritual snakes and ladders. Was it your own fault if you had a nervous breakdown, or was it a cross that God had asked you to bear, like TB? They did not know. For most of them Violet's nervous breakdown was the first they had come into contact with, though it would not be the last.

When the examination results were published, Miles got a First in History, Michael got a very good Upper Second and Polly a Third in English, Dennis an Upper Second in Chemistry and Angela a Lower Second in French, Ruth an Upper Second in Botany and Adrian (to his great disappointment, for he had secretly hoped for a First) a Lower Second in Economics. On the whole these results corresponded to the intelligence and/or industry of each of them respectively, rather than to their virtue.

Miles went to Cambridge (where he would have gone as an undergraduate if he hadn't been undergoing a spiritual crisis at the time of the college entrance examinations) to do a PhD, and Ruth went into a convent as a postulant. You are not going to hear much about these two in this chapter because they did not lose their virginities (unless you count mutual masturbation between schoolboys, in which case Miles had lost his already). Ruth did, however, have a kind of wedding when she took her first vows at the end of her novitiate.

She was led into the convent chapel, clothed in a long white dress and veil and carrying a bouquet of white roses, accompanied by two matrons of honour. Angela, who was one of them, thought poor Ruth looked ridiculous in this get-up, and found the whole ceremony faintly morbid. She couldn't get used, either, to Ruth's being called Sister Mary Joseph of the Precious Blood. Together they moved in procession to the altar where the bishop waited.

"What do you ask?"

"The mercy of God and the holy veil."

"Do you ask it with your whole mind and heart?"

"I do."

Here the two matrons of honour had to remove Ruth's headdress, and with a little pair of gold scissors the bishop cut off one lock of her hair.

"Oh Lord, keep thy handmaid, our sister, always modest, sincere and faithful to thy service."

Then Ruth withdrew into a small room, attended by the Mother Superior and two sisters. The matrons of honour had to wait outside, but they knew what was happening behind the door. So did Ruth's mother, who was sobbing audibly in the congregation. Her father had refused to come.

The two sisters helped Ruth off with her bridal dress, and she put on a plain shift of coarsely woven linen and heavy black shoes and stockings. Then she sat on a stool with a towel round her shoulders, and the Mother Superior ran a pair of electric clippers over her scalp until she was cropped like a convict. Then Ruth put on the black habit, the scapular, the cincture and crown, the coif, the band and the veil, reciting a special prayer with each article of dress. When she returned to the chapel for the rest of the ceremony, she was hardly recognizable as the bride in white – and looked much prettier, Angela thought. All you could see of Ruth now was her face from cheekbone to cheekbone and from forehead to chin, which happened to be by far the most attractive part of her. Everything else was concealed by the graceful folds and starched linen of the habit, which had been modelled on the dress of the *bourgeoises* of Bordeaux in the late seventeenth century, when the Order was founded.

Afterwards there was a kind of wedding breakfast, with an iced cake, but of course no sparkling wine or any other kind of alcoholic beverage, though the sisters seemed to get distinctly tipsy on the cake alone, being unused to such rich ingredients in their food. Later, on the pavement outside the convent gates, Ruth's mother clutched Angela's arm and declared that if she didn't have a stiff drink in the next five minutes she would die.

"Don't you think it's a shame, a terrible waste?" she said, when they were seated in the corner of a saloon bar (Angela felt strange, never having been in a pub without Dennis before) and she had drained her first gin-and-lime.

"Well, she'll still be able to use her qualifications," said Angela loyally. "The Order runs a lot of schools." But she could not rouse much enthusiasm, having herself steadfastly resisted years of propaganda for the nun's life at school. She fingered Dennis's ring on her left hand, and felt particularly glad at that moment that she was engaged to be married. That was nearly three years after they took Finals.

Immediately after the examinations were over, and before the results were known, Polly and her fiancé of the moment (she had had a different one in each academic year) invited Dennis and Angela to join them for a camping holiday in Brittany. Polly and Rex would provide the car, borrowed from Rex's father, and all the gear. Angela was a little surprised by this invitation, for she had never been a really close friend of Polly's, but she and Dennis accepted readily enough, and not until it was too late to withdraw did they realize that they were being asked along as chaperones – Polly's parents having agreed to the trip only on condition that they took with them a reliable Catholic couple. Rex was not a Catholic, and frankly suggested to Dennis, as they lay in their tent on their first night in France, that as soon as possible they should aim to pair off with the girls in the two tents. He was rather put out by Dennis's uncooperative response, and offered to lend him some French letters if that was the problem. (It was not – *that* problem was still in the future for Dennis.) So Polly preserved her virginity on that holiday, but only just.

They finally pitched their tents in the south of Brittany, on the far side of the Loire estuary. It was too hot to lie out on the beach in the afternoons, so they took their siestas in the tents that were shaded by pine trees, and it seemed absurd not to do that as couples. But those sultry afternoons were occasions of sin if anything was, lolling on air mattresses in their swimsuits, for it was too hot to wear anything else, sensually drowsy from the lunchtime wine, and looking, as they all did, amazingly handsome and beautiful from the sunshine and exercise. Every day Dennis and Angela lay side by side, holding hands across the space that separated them, and listening to the scuffles and giggles and sighs emanating from the neighbouring tent. By the end of the second week, Polly and Rex had reached the stage of petting to climax, as Polly intimated to Angela, asking her if she thought it was possible to get pregnant that way. Angela was shocked and unhappy. She wanted to return home, she told Dennis the next afternoon, or at least stop pairing off in the two tents. When he wheedled out of her the reason in full detail, he became uncontrollably excited. He rolled over on to her mattress and whispered breathlessly in her ear, "Let's do it, let us do it."

"What?"

"What they do, what Polly said, oh please let's Ange!"

After a pause, she said: "Why not do it properly, then?"

Dennis sat up and stared at her. Was she serious?

She was. Angela was suddenly fed up with acting as a moral referee over their endearments, blowing the whistle at every petty infringement and quibbling endlessly over the interpretation of the rules. Besides, she felt erotically excited herself by Dennis's strong, brown body, bathed in the orange light of the tent's interior. She lifted her arms slightly and, half closing her eyes, pushed out her lips in the shape of a kiss. He had never seen her look so seductive, but instead of increasing his desire, it frightened him.

"No," he said, "we'd better not."

By the following day he had changed his mind, but so had Angela, and she was not to be wooed into offering herself a second time. He had plenty of leisure in which to brood on his missed opportunity (if that was what it was), his victory over selfishness or his failure of manhood (whichever it was) in the next two years, most of which he spent in a desolate barracks in northern Germany. His Upper Second was not quite good enough to win him a postgraduate scholarship with further deferment of his National Service, and he was called up into the Royal Signals.

Basic training seemed like some sort of punishment for a crime he hadn't committed: shouts, oaths, farts, bruising drill, nauseating food, monotonous obscenity, fucking this fucking that, from shivering morning to red-eyed, boot-polishing night. I have described it in detail elsewhere. So have others. It is always the same. When the Catholic Chaplain came round to talk to the RCs in Dennis's intake, he had an impulse to cry, "*Help us! Get us out of here!*" and listened with dismay as the priest told them they were soldiers of Christ and should try to set an example to the other lads. He tried for a commission and failed his War Office Selection Board (they told him he lacked enthusiasm). Eventually he was trained as a wireless operator and posted to an artillery regiment stationed near Bremen. On his pre-posting leave he and Angela got engaged. Travelling to Germany after that leave, sitting up through the night in a railway carriage foetid with the breath and perspiration of seven other soldiers, remembering Angela's pale, gold-fringed face held up to the train window for a last kiss, feeling the collar of his battledress blouse chafing his neck, and knowing that he would have to wear it for another fourteen months, he tried to comfort himself with the thought that, whatever happened, life couldn't possibly hold greater misery for him than he felt at that moment. (He was wrong, of course.)

Dennis wrote every other day to Angela and she almost as frequently to him. She refused many invitations to go out with other young men, and he kept himself chaste. To fill the intolerable tedium of his days and nights, and in a determined effort to wrest some material advantage from his servitude, he studied furiously electronics and information theory by correspondence course, passed every trade test for which he was eligible, and rose to the rank of corporal.

Polly broke off her engagement to Rex shortly after they all returned from Brittany – a morose, ill-tempered journey in which everybody quarrelled in turn with all the others. She was dashed to find that she had only got a Third and went to see her tutor about it. She had a little cry in his room, then she cheered up. She met Michael nervously combing his hair in the corridor outside the Head of Department's room, waiting for an interview. He had got a scholarship to do postgraduate research, and was thinking of doing his thesis on the novels of Graham Greene. "I don't know how you can bear the thought of another year in this place," said Polly, and made up her mind that instant to go abroad. She went to Italy to be a kind of *au pair* girl with an aristocratic Catholic family in Rome, a connection of one of the nuns at her old school. The head of the family was a count, a handsome, charming man who deflowered Polly quite quickly and skilfully on what was supposed to be her afternoon off. Afterwards she cried a little, but then she cheered up. The count gave her a present of money to buy clothes, telling her not to spend it all at once in case it would be noticed. A couple of months later she had an affair with the young Italian teacher from whom she took language lessons. After she slept with him the first time he said he would have offered to marry her if she had been a virgin, but as she wasn't, he wouldn't. Polly said she didn't want to marry him anyway, upon which he sulked.

She came home to England for Christmas, and at a New Year's party got very drunk and went upstairs with a young man whose name she could not afterwards remember. They found an empty bedroom and thrashed about on the bed by the blue light of streetlamps shining through the windows. When the young man pulled off Polly's knickers she crouched on all fours and presented her broad bottom to him, greatly to his astonishment. Both her Italian lovers had taken her in this position and she had assumed it was the usual one. Either this surprise, or the drink he had taken, unmanned the youth, for he was unable to perform, and Polly went back to Italy with a poor opinion of Englishmen. The trouble with Italians, on the other hand, was that they took no contraceptive precautions, and she had had a bad scare when her period was a week overdue once. However, with the help of a girl-friend who worked in the US Embassy, she got herself fitted with a diaphragm by an American doctor, and was therefore well prepared for her next love affair, this time with a photographer who threatened to kill himself if she didn't yield to his passion. She didn't believe him for a moment, but it was an exciting fiction.

By this time Polly had stopped going to mass except for form's sake. She had come to the conclusion that religion was all form and no content. She had watched the count who had seduced her receive Communion the following Sunday, and even if he had been to Confession in the meantime (which she doubted) he certainly hadn't made a Firm Purpose of Amendment, for he made another pass at her on her very next afternoon off. He was a pillar of the Church, with some important function in the Vatican, yet everyone, even his wife, knew that he had a mistress established in a flat on the other side of the Tiber. At first Polly was shocked by the hypocrisy of Roman life, but gradually she got used to it. The trouble with English Catholics, she decided, was that they took everything so seriously. They tried to keep all the rules really and truly, not just outwardly. Of course that was impossible, it was against human nature, especially where sex was concerned.

Polly explained all this to Michael in a coffee bar near the British Museum after her return to England in the autumn of 1955. Coffee bars, equipped with glittering Italian coffee machines that hissed like locomotives, were all the rage in London at this time. Polly impressed

Michael immediately by asking the waiter for "*uno capuccino*" instead of just a white coffee. She had certainly acquired, he thought, a certain worldly wisdom as a result of her year abroad.

"Italians tolerate adultery and brothels because they're not allowed to divorce," she said. "English Catholics have the worst of both worlds. No wonder they're so repressed."

Michael nodded, causing his Brylcreemed forelock to fall forward across his eyes. "It's the Irish Jansenist tradition," he said.

"What's that?"

"In penal days, Irish priests used to be trained in France, by the Jansenists, so that over-scrupulous, puritanical kind of Catholicism got into their bloodstream – and ours too, because, let's face it, English Catholicism is largely Irish Catholicism."

Michael had long ago overcome his own scruples and resumed the full practice of his religion. A sensible priest, to whom he had unburdened himself, had assured him that his was a common problem, no more than a venial sin, as long as he was sorry for having given way to temptation. Since Michael always felt melancholy after masturbating, this was a satisfactory solution. Anyway, he had shed the habit since falling in love with a student of music called Miriam, whom he met at an NUS farm camp, picking strawberries. She was extremely pretty, with green eyes and copper-coloured hair, though, ironically enough, almost flat-chested. It was in fact because she had no bosom worth looking at that Michael had looked more closely than usual at her face and into her eyes, and discovered there a person whom he very much liked. When Polly rang up out of the blue and proposed a meeting, some instinct had warned him against bringing Miriam along, and he was glad he hadn't when Polly began to hold forth about sex.

"So you've got a girl friend at last, Michael," she said, when he made some allusion to Miriam. "Is she a Catholic?"

"She's taking instructions."

"Goodness, it must be serious."

"We're thinking of getting engaged, actually."

"D'you really want to settle down so soon, Michael? Don't you want to have some fun, first?" Polly's expression made it fairly clear what kind of fun she had in mind.

"How can you, if you're a Catholic, Polly? I mean, either you are or you aren't. I am. I often wish I wasn't – life would be more fun, agreed. But I am, and there it is."

"Oh, Michael! Just like a Graham Greene character."

"Have you read his new one?"

"No, what's it like?"

"It's about the war in Indo-China. Not like the others, really." Michael had been impressed by *The Quiet American*, but slightly disturbed too. It seemed morally and theologically confused – there was not the same stark contrast between the Church and the secular world that you got in the earlier novels. Michael's interest was more than academic: in some oblique way the credibility of the Catholic faith was underwritten for him by the existence of distinguished literary converts like Graham Greene and Evelyn Waugh, so any sign of their having Doubts was unsettling. Polly, however, didn't want to talk about Graham Greene, but about her love affairs.

Michael listened, fascinated and appalled. Here was sin incarnate. If Polly were to walk out of the coffee bar now, and under a bus, there was not much hope for her immortal soul. For dissolute agnostics there might be some mercy, but Polly had been instructed in the True Faith. She knew the rules and the penalties for not keeping them, whatever she might say about the instinctive passion of the Italians.

"It's the sun, you see, Michael. It makes everything seem so different." She drained her transparent Pyrex cup, leaving a large red mouth-shape on the rim. Michael, who was practised in eking out a cup of espresso for an hour and a half, watched her with dismay. "Would you like another?" he asked.

"Please, and perhaps just a tiny piece of that chocolate gâteau."

Polly had grown plumper, Michael thought, she looked almost fat, and under the heavy makeup her complexion was not good. By middle age she would be bloated and raddled. He thought of his own lean, lissome sweetheart with complacency.

"Italian men are an awful nuisance," said Polly, "pinching you and ogling you all the time on the street and on buses. But at least they notice you." She looked around the coffee bar at the unnoticing young men, clerks in pin-stripe suits and students in fisherman's knit sweaters and Harris tweed sports jackets. "God!" she sighed. "England is so boring."

That same autumn, Violet went back to College to begin her final year all over again. She had quite recovered from her nervous breakdown, her eczema had cleared up, and she looked very pretty. The Professor in charge of the Department declared that he would personally undertake tutorial responsibility for her work. He was a short man who looked quite tall sitting behind his desk because of his large, handsome head and luxuriant silver-grey beard. He reminded Violet of pictures of God the Father speaking out of clouds. She felt his interest in her progress was a great honour and was determined to prove worthy of it.

The Professor appointed four o'clock on a Tuesday afternoon for her tutorial, which allowed it to overrun the statutory hour. At five o'clock his secretary would knock discreetly and come into the room with letters to be signed. Then, after she had gone, as the corridors of the Department fell gradually silent, and the winter dusk turned to darkness outside the window, he would draw the curtains, and light a single standard lamp for her, shining down on her notebook, leaving him behind his desk in shadow, and bring out a bottle of sherry and two glasses, and then discourse about the classical world to Violet, about things he never alluded to in his lectures, about pagan fertility rites, phallus worship, Dionysian orgies and sacred prostitutes. "I hope I do not shock you, Violet," he would murmur, stroking his beard as if soothing a pet, and she would shake her head vigorously, though in truth she often thought she would have been shocked if he had not been her professor and it had not been a tutorial.

Then, one day, as he was holding forth in his melodious cadences, she knocked over her sherry glass and, jumping to her feet in reflex response, saw to her horror and amazement that he had his fly open and was playing with himself under the desk. She stared at him for a moment, then dropped to her knees and began scrubbing furiously at the carpet with a handkerchief. He rose from his place and came round the desk to stand over her. "Violet," he said, after several minutes had passed. "Get up."

She rose to her feet. "I've got to go," she said.

"Violet," he said. "Have pity on an old man." He tugged and gnawed at his beard as he spoke.

"You're not old," she said, pointlessly.

"I am fifty-five years old and have been impotent for the last fifteen.

My wife has left me. Sometimes I can coax a little juice to flow. It does no harm to anyone, does it?"

Violet went home in a trance, twice nearly being run over, and tossed and turned in bed, wondering what to do. The Professor's appeal had not fallen on deaf ears. She did indeed pity this great man, the distinguished scholar of whom the entire Department stood in awe, so starved of love that he was reduced to the ignoble expedient in which she had surprised him. Violet had a strong impulse to sacrifice herself, to become a sacred prostitute, to heal his broken sex. It would be a sin, technically; but also, she thought, a corporal work of mercy.

She went back into College with this purpose vaguely in mind, and was dismayed to discover a note in her pigeonhole stating that she had been transferred to another tutor. With some difficulty, she managed to obtain an interview with the Professor. He looked at her with fear in his eyes, tugging and gnawing at his beard.

"You realize," he said, "that if you make a complaint I shall deny everything."

Violet was unable to speak.

"In any case," he said, "my conscience is clear. No genuinely innocent girl would have sat there all these weeks listening to what I told you without a flicker of protest."

Instead of being outraged by this insinuation, Violet was completely convinced of its justice. It revived and confirmed her old feelings of guilt. There must be something about her, she thought, that brought out the worst in people: there was her cousin in the attic, and the tramp in the shelter, and now the Professor. And she had to admit that she had derived a certain thrill from the Professor's stories of pagan filthiness. She went back to her digs and opened a book and stared at it for several hours without taking in a word. Then she got a letter from her new tutor asking why she hadn't been to see him. He was a young man, recently appointed to the Department. She went into College to tell him that she was going to withdraw from the course, this time for good, for she could feel another nervous breakdown coming on.

"What will you do?" asked the tutor, who invited her to call him by his first name, Robin.

"I don't know," said Violet. "I might become a nun."

Robin laughed, but not unkindly. He was intrigued by Violet, and besides, she was pretty.

"What was the problem with the Old Man?" he asked casually. "Made a pass at you, did he?"

It was a bold but happy gambit. To Violet it came as a huge relief that this stranger spontaneously assumed that the Professor and not herself might have been responsible for what had happened. She did not tell Robin what that was, but she agreed to carry on with her studies under his supervision. His tutorials also overran the statutory hour, but they were exclusively academic in content. Violet had a lot of work to make up, and he was determined to prove his prowess as a teacher by getting her through Finals.

One day he proposed taking her to see Donald Wolfit in *Oedipus Rex*, as it would help her with her tragedy paper. Robin found her an agreeable companion, deferential but not sycophantic, and full of quaint opinion and anecdote deriving from her Irish Catholic background. (Her parents had emigrated from the West of Ireland to England when she was only three, but for most of the war years she had been educated at a convent boarding school in Ireland, and she returned to the West frequently for holidays.)

"Which of the six sins against the Holy Ghost do you think is the worst?" she said in the Tube, à propos of nothing in particular.

"I don't even know what they are, Violet."

She rattled them off, parrot-fashion, like a child in school: "Presumption, Despair, Resisting the Known Truth, Envy of Another's Spiritual Good, Obstinacy in Sin, and Final Impenitence."

He considered. "Resisting the Known Truth," he said at length.

"Isn't that just typical of a university lecturer! *I* think the worst is Final Impenitence. Imagine, at the moment of death, when you've everything to gain and nothing to lose by being sorry for your sins . . . Final Impenitence." She gave a faint shudder that was not entirely affected. "I had an uncle in Limerick, they say he died raving against the Holy Ghost. 'Get that damned bird out of here!' he kept shouting, on his deathbed. Of course, he was delirious. But it wasn't very nice for Aunty Maeve. It naturally made her wonder about the state of his soul."

Subsequently Robin took Violet out to other plays and films that had no obvious relevance to her course. When he escorted her home afterwards she did not invite him in because, she said, her landlady would not like it (in fact, because her room was like a pigsty and she was ashamed to let him see it). They said goodbye on the porch and shook hands. On the third such occasion, he leaned forward and kissed her on the cheek, and the time after that on the lips. It seemed to Violet that they must be courting; and though Robin never initiated any discussion of their feelings for each other, he did impress upon her the importance of concealing from the rest of the Department the fact that they were meeting outside tutorials. This threw a romantic aura of the clandestine over their relationship. Violet could hardly believe her good fortune. Robin's slim, dark good looks, his soft, supple clothes of velvet corduroy, suede and cavalry twill, his cool self-assurance and his dry, understated conversation, were to her the quintessence of Englishness, the culture which her family affected to despise but secretly admired.

Violet was very happy that spring, and sailed through her exams in June without stress. After she had sat her last paper, Robin took her to an Italian restaurant in Soho for dinner. Between the chicken *alla cacciatore* and the *zabaglione* he reached across the table and covered her hand with his.

"Violet, darling," he said, and her heart thumped, because he had never called her darling before, "you know I care for you very much, don't you?" She nodded. "And I think you care for me?"

"Oh, Robin," she said. "You know I do."

So this was it. She had often wondered what it would be like to be proposed to, and her imaginings had been surprisingly close to reality: soft lights, a bottle of wine, cosy intimacy. It took her some time to realize that it was not exactly marriage that Robin was proposing, at least not yet. He wanted her to spend a weekend away with him somewhere, "To see how we suit each other physically."

"Oh, no," she said, taking her hand away. "I couldn't do that, Robin. Isn't that what they call a trial marriage? Catholics aren't allowed."

But Robin was a very persuasive young man, and played cannily on Catholic belief in his arguments. Wouldn't it, he asked rhetorically, be madness for two people to contract an indissoluble marriage without knowing whether they were sexually compatible?

"But if they loved each other, wouldn't it be bound to come right in the end?" Violet pleaded.

"Unfortunately there are case histories which prove otherwise."

After a few bouts of this kind of discussion, Violet gave in. Robin borrowed a friend's car and took her to a hotel in the country for a weekend.

"For heaven's sake, drive carefully," she said, chain-smoking in the passenger seat. "I'm in a state of mortal sin, you know."

He laughed and glanced sideways at her. "But you haven't done anything yet."

"No, but I mean to, and that's just as bad. Worse, in a way."

"Worse?"

"I couldn't say I was carried away by the impulse of the moment, could I?"

"No," he said gleefully, "you couldn't say that." Robin never knew how seriously to take Violet's religious scruples, but overcoming them certainly gave the adventure an extra *frisson* of excitement.

"Suppose I get pregnant?" she said after a while.

"You needn't worry about that. I shall take the necessary precautions."

"That's another mortal sin on top," she said gloomily.

After they had checked into the hotel, Violet refused to leave their room because, she claimed, everyone in the lobby had immediately guessed they weren't really married; so Robin had to have dinner sent up at considerable extra cost and trouble. Still, he was willing to indulge her on this occasion. When the waiter had cleared away the dishes, Robin knocked on the door of the bathroom, where Violet was hiding, and said: "Time for bed."

"I'm going to have a bath," she said.

He pushed the door hopefully, but it was locked. When she came from the bathroom half an hour later, Violet was swathed in a dressing-gown from her chin to her feet and insisted on total darkness before she would get into bed. Robin found it difficult to fit his contraceptive sheath in these conditions, particularly as it was not an operation he had performed all that often. Violet also kept his erotic drive in check by her continual chatter.

"You've done this before haven't you Robin how many times I mean how many girls were they not compatible or were you not thinking of marrying them anyway did you just want their bodies for a night?"

"For heaven's sake, Violet, do be quiet."

"I'm sorry, Robin, it's just that I'm so nervous."

"Just try and relax."

In the pitch darkness, impeded by the heavy quilt on the bed, he pushed his index finger in and out of Violet's vagina, hoping that he was stimulating her clitoris. The manual of sexual technique that he had studied rather more frequently than he had actually practised intercourse had laid great stress upon this item of foreplay.

"I'm sorry, darling, but that's hurting," Violet said after a while.

He pulled his finger away as though it had been burned.

"It doesn't mean that we're incompatible, Robin," she said anxiously. "It's just that you were rubbing in the wrong place."

"I'm sorry," he said huffily, "to be so clumsy."

"Shall I show you the right place?" she whispered.

This was better. She took his long index finger, that had so often pointed out to her the syllabic pattern of Latin verse, and gently guided it on to her favourite spot. As he rubbed, he felt her pelvis heave like a swimmer lifted by a wave, and her legs opened wide and his own member stiffened in response.

They made love four times that weekend, and on each occasion Violet had an orgasm under digital stimulation, but not during the act itself, when Robin had his. This worried him somewhat in the light of the textbook, so that when Violet asked him if he thought they were compatible he said he thought they both needed time to think over the experience of the weekend. She looked crestfallen. "Let's sleep on it," he said. "We've already slept on it," she said, "we've done nothing else all weekend." He kissed her and said, "You're lovely and I love you, but there's no need to rush into anything." This was as they were preparing to go home.

"I'm not going away with you for another of these weekends, you know," she said.

"Do you have to say it like that?" he said, pained by her lack of tact.

"Yes, because I'm going to Confession at the very first church we come to and I must have a firm purpose of amendment or it won't be any good."

As soon as they returned to London, Robin was buried in examination scripts – not university exams, but "O" and "A" level papers which he marked to enhance his meagre salary. Violet helped him check the marks and fill in the mark sheets. One day as they were doing this she said, "Robin, I think I'm pregnant."

"What? You can't be."

"Those things don't always work, do they? I'm three weeks overdue, and this morning I felt sick when I got up."

"My God." He stared at her, appalled. It was, he supposed, possible that fumbling with his sheaths in the dark he had nicked one with a fingernail or otherwise mismanaged the business.

"I'm not trying to blackmail you into marrying me," said Violet. "But I thought you ought to know."

"If it's true," he said heavily, "you'll just have to get rid of it."

"You mean, have it adopted?"

"I mean have an operation. It can be arranged, I believe, at a price." He looked miserably at the pile of scripts.

"I couldn't do that, it would be murder," said Violet. "I'll just go away somewhere to a Home for Unmarried Mothers and have it adopted and never trouble you again."

"Don't be absurd, Violet," he said irritably. "It's not that I don't want to marry you, it's just that I don't want to rush into it. And I certainly didn't intend starting a family straight away."

But in the end he did marry Violet, and in a Catholic church. His doubts about the wisdom of this step were mitigated by her being awarded an Upper Second class degree – a rare achievement by girls doing Classics. The Professor sent them a handsome present, and they went to Sicily for their honeymoon and looked at antiquities. In the fourth month of her pregnancy, late in 1956, Violet had a miscarriage, and fell subsequently into a deep depression.

England was less boring in 1956 than it had seemed to Polly in the coffee bar with Michael the year before. At Easter there was the first CND march. *The Outsider* and *Look Back in Anger* made a great stir and the newspapers were full of articles about Britain's Angry Young Men. In the autumn there was the Suez crisis and the Hungarian uprising.

Only the last of these events touched off an unequivocal response in our young Catholics. They were not, on the whole, a politically conscious group. Their childhood had been dominated by the Second World War, which their religious education had imbued with a mythic simplicity, the forces of good contending with the power of evil, Hitler being identified with Satan, and Churchill, more tentatively, with the Archangel Michael. After that apocalyptic struggle, mere party politics seemed an anticlimax, no doubt – anyway, few of them took an informed interest in such things, or bothered to think how they would cast their votes when they were twenty-one. Their politics in adolescence were international Cold War politics. The betrayal of the glorious Allied cause by Soviet Russia, the enslavement of Eastern Europe with its millions of Catholics, the inexorable advance of atheistic communism in the Far East – all showed that Satan was as active in the world as ever. Their hero was Cardinal Mindszenty, who had been imprisoned by the Communists in Hungary, and was released by the new provisional government in October 1956. When the Russian Army moved in to crush the rising with its tanks, the widespread feelings of outrage and impotence in Britain were felt especially keenly by Catholics.

One Sunday, while the Hungarian patriots were fighting for their lives in Budapest, a huge march and rally in Hyde Park was organized by students of London University, at which Dennis and Angela were present with Michael and Miriam. Dennis had recently been released from the Army, and was camping in Michael's bedsitter while he looked for a job. Angela was teaching in a school in South London. Miriam was just starting her final year in Music. Michael had finished his MA thesis on the novels of Graham Greene, and was just beginning a Postgraduate Certificate of Education course: though he would have preferred to try for a university post, schoolteaching was the only way of avoiding National Service.

They stood on the trampled grass in the middle of a large, excited crowd, the two girls hanging on to the arms of their fiancés, and listened to the speeches. The announcement that a group of students were forming a volunteer force to join the freedom fighters of Hungary was received with great enthusiasm. "We want volunteers," declared the speaker, a very young man, pale with sleeplessness and the strain of historic decision, "but only if you know how to use a gun."

Of the four of them, only Dennis knew how to use a gun. For a moment or two he contemplated a heroic gesture, for he was genuinely moved by the plight of the Hungarians and the atmosphere of the meeting was heady. He had a brief glimpse of himself, as though through a rift in cloud, manning a barricade, gripping a rifle, hurling a grenade – converting at one stroke all the tedium and futility of his military training into something positive and transcendent. But then he saw himself falling dead across the bodies of Hungarian partisans, or flattened by a Russian tank like a hedgehog on a bypass, and the rift closed. He did not want to die. Especially he did not want to die without having possessed Angela.

Angela, at that moment, was thinking that if Dennis stepped forward to volunteer, she would ask him to make love to her that night without the slightest hesitation or guilt. She saw herself standing before him in the posture of a statue of Our Lady, her arms slightly lifted, her clothes slipping from her like melting snow.

None of them said anything. When somebody came round with a collecting box, Dennis put in more than he could really afford. Later he read in the paper that the volunteers – there were only about twenty of them – had been turned back at the Austrian border.

If Adrian had been present in Hyde Park, he would certainly have volunteered, but at that time he was still doing his military service, as a Second Lieutenant in the Royal Army Service Corps. He had signed on for three years as a Regular in the hope of getting a commission in the prestigious cavalry regiment into which he had been conscripted as a National Serviceman, but he ended up in the despised RASC, in which he could probably have been commissioned anyway. At the time of the Hungarian uprising, which was also the time of the Suez crisis, he was a transport officer in Cyprus, and his frustration and disgust at the turn of events was extreme. His country, instead of flying to the assistance of the gallant Hungarians and Cardinal Mindszenty, was committing itself to a dubious adventure in wog-bashing – that was how Adrian saw it. The actual invasion was so badly organized, however, that he doubted whether the British Army would have been much help to the Hungarians anyway. On the quayside at Limassol, prior to embarkation, one French truck was grouped with every three British trucks, and as the British vehicles had been sprayed with yellow desert camouflage and the French ones had not, this pattern gave away the presence of the trucks to aerial reconnaisance as clearly as could be. When Adrian pointed this out to his CO, he was brusquely told that there was a political reason for it. In Suez, the convoys lost their way, ran out of water, and their wireless equipment broke down. It was a shambles, and an immoral shambles. When Anthony Eden was forced to resign soon afterwards, broken by ill-health, Adrian felt that some kind of justice had been done in Old Testament style. He determined to vote Socialist at the next election. (He had to wait till October 1959 and the Tories won by a hundred seats.)

After his release from the Army, Adrian took a job in Local Government in his home town, Derby. He lived with his parents because they would have been hurt if he had done otherwise, but it was cramped and inconvenient, for they were a large family with several children still at school. It was time, he decided, that he got married. He took dancing lessons and went to parish socials, but the girls he met were afraid of his severe, intense manner. He joined a tennis club, but the girls there found him stiff and priggish. He was not very good, either, at dancing or tennis. In the end he met Dorothy at a weekend conference on Catechetics. Adrian no longer did public speaking for the Catholic Evidence Guild, but he helped with a Sunday School in his parish for children attending non-Catholic schools. Dorothy was doing teacher-training in Religious Education, but she was quite willing to give up her course to marry Adrian, who had a good job and was suddenly very impatient to have sexual intercourse after so many years of continence in the interests of holiness and self-advancement.

Though he knew much more about sex, in a second-hand way, than when he was a student, from barrack and mess-room conversation, from reading the manual of military law, and from censoring the mail of other ranks in the Suez crisis, Adrian was shy of talking about it to Dorothy during their short engagement. She was a virgin, of course – so much so that when, prior to retiring to bed on their wedding night, he kissed her attired only in a dressing-gown, she inquired what hard object he was concealing in his pocket. Under the bedclothes she snuggled up to him happily enough, but when he tried to enter her she went rigid with fear and then grew hysterical. It transpired that she knew almost nothing about how a marriage was consummated. Adrian turned on the bedside lamp, sat up in bed, and lectured her on the facts of life. He was a good lecturer, having benefited by his training in the Army and the Catholic Evidence Guild, though he spoke rather

51

more loudly than was necessary and after a while somebody banged on the wall of the adjoining room (they were spending their honeymoon in a small hotel in the Lake District). Adrian continued his lecture in a lower tone, making three-dimensional diagrams in the air with his fingers. Dorothy watched him wonderingly, with the bedclothes drawn up to her chin.

"Didn't your mother tell you *anything*?" he said.

"Sex was never mentioned at home, Adie."

"Well, but you must have picked up something from somewhere. How did you suppose babies were conceived?"

Dorothy blushed and shifted uneasily beneath the sheets. "I thought it was enough if the man just touched the woman with his . . . I didn't think he actually had to . . . to. . . ."

Adrian sighed. "Would you like to have another try, now I've explained?"

"If you like, dear."

Adrian lay on top of his bride and butted at her dry crotch while she winced and gasped faintly beneath him. When at last he succeeded in penetrating her, he ejaculated immediately. "That wasn't right," he said. "With practice I'll be able to last longer than that."

"It was long enough for me, dear," said Dorothy, and fell fast asleep.

Adrian lay awake for quite a long while. Undoubtedly it had been a disappointment, the sexual act. But then, so had most things in his life – his degree class, his army career – always falling a little short of his ambition, his ideal. And now marriage. Dorothy was a good, kind-hearted girl, utterly devoted to him, but she didn't scintillate, there was no doubt about that, and though she had nice eyes and pretty hair, she was no beauty, her nose was decidedly half-an-inch too long, and her body rather awkward and angular. Adrian had a sudden recall of Angela, whom he not seen for years. Angela in her pink angora jumper – still, it seemed to him, the prettiest girl he had ever met in his life, and he wondered what she was doing now. Married to that chap, no doubt, what was his name, Dennis. Adrian grew gloomier and gloomier. He went through a dark wedding night of the soul. It seemed to him that God had always mocked his efforts. He had always tried to do his best, to do what was right, but always there was this bitter rebuff to his hopes and ambitions. Meanwhile other people, less good, less dutiful, indeed positively mischievous – fornicators, adulterers, unbelievers – prospered and enjoyed themselves. Of course all would get their just deserts in the next world, but he couldn't help feeling some resentment about the lack of justice in this one. He knew for a fact that men who hadn't worked half as hard as himself had got Upper Seconds in Finals, whereas he himself had only got a Lower Second, and sacrificed the chance of winning Angela to boot.

The disloyalty of this train of thought to the young woman sleeping peacefully beside him shocked Adrian out of his melancholy mood. Lying on his back, he made the Sign of the Cross, and said his usual night prayers, which he had omitted in the excitement of going to bed – an Our Father, a Hail Mary and a Glory Be, an Act of Contrition; then he turned over and settled himself to sleep. Tomorrow he would take Dorothy to Great Gable and teach her a few basic rock-climbing skills.

Because he was doing medicine, Edward was still a student of a kind long after his contemporaries had left the University. His main leisure activities were playing rugby and taking part in the College Gilbert and Sullivan Society's productions until, the season before he qualified, someone trampled on him in a loose scrum and damaged a couple of vertebrae, putting an end to his athletic career and bequeathing to him a lifetime of intermittent backache. For recreation that left him with just Gilbert and Sullivan – and girls, for whom he had not previously had much time. The teaching hospital was of course teeming with pretty nurses looking for doctors to marry, and Edward met one of them, Tessa, at the beginning of his houseman's year, when they were on night duty together. Tessa wasn't a Catholic – her family were vaguely C of E – but she was quite happy about getting married in a Catholic church, and bringing their children up as Catholics. This was established long before Edward formally proposed, for after he had taken her out a few times he said, putting on the expression of exaggerated gravity that used to disconcert Father Brierley, that he thought it was only fair to make clear, before they got seriously attached to each other, what the implications were.

"You'd have to take instructions from a priest," he said. "Of course, it makes everything much simpler if the non-Catholic partner converts, but it's not essential."

"Well, I might, you never can tell," Tessa said brightly, her smooth brown cheeks dimpling, and her dark eyes glancing in all directions. They were in the Brasserie of a Lyons Cornerhouse at the time; Tessa had never been to one before and thought that the gay check table-cloths and the gipsy music and the tangy smells of Continental cooking were heaven. At that moment she would cheerfully have agreed to marry a Hindoo if his name had been Edward.

"And there's another thing," said Edward, looking more solemn than ever. "You know about the Catholic teaching on birth control, don't you?" His big ears glowed red with embarrassment, for in spite of his training in anatomy and gynaecology, and the obscene songs that he sang as lustily as anyone else after rugger matches, Edward was remarkably pure-minded and assumed that girls were even more so.

"Well, I believe in large families, anyway," said Tessa, with a giggle, glancing to right and left.

"It doesn't mean," he hastened to assure her, "that the Church is against family planning as such. It's just a question of the method. It's quite all right to use the Rhythm method."

"Much nicer than the other methods, anyway, I should think," Tessa said, and then wondered if perhaps she had revealed a little too much knowledge. She was still technically a virgin, but had had a fairly passionate heavy petting affair the previous year with a post-graduate dentistry student who had hopefully explained to her on several occasions the various means of contraception.

Tessa decided to become a Catholic as soon as she discovered that, if she didn't, they wouldn't be able to have a nuptial mass. She liked the idea of being the focus of attention for a full hour in her bridal dress, kneeling up on the altar (it was the only time in her life, Edward explained, that a woman was allowed into the sanctuary, except of course for cleaning and polishing and arranging the flowers) with organ music, choir-singing, Latin prayers and glowing vestments swirling around her. Most weddings she had been to seemed to her to be over far too quickly, and the Catholic service for a mixed marriage was almost as short and bleak as a Registry Office ceremony – no candles, flowers or even music being permitted.

"You do understand what you're doing, darling?" Edward said anxiously the day before she was received. "You're quite happy about it?"

54

"Oh yes, darling, quite happy." In truth Tessa found a lot of the doctrine inherently implausible, but she could see that it all fitted together, and if Edward believed it, who was she to quibble?

Shortly afterwards, Edward took her to a weekend conference for Catholic engaged couples. There would be talks by priests, doctors and counsellors on such subjects as The Sacrament of Marriage, Getting On Together, and The Rhythm Method, plus Mass and Benediction each day and times for private recollection. Edward had the idea that this experience would help Tessa to feel fully assimilated into her new faith. It was held at a retreat house and conference centre run by nuns, on the northern outskirts of London.

They arrived on a Friday night, late because Edward had been delayed by an emergency at the hospital. An aged and irritable nun admitted them and said that they were not expected until the following morning. "There'll be extra to pay," she grumbled. "What's your name?"

"O'Brien," said Edward.

The nun peered myopically at a list of names pinned to a notice-board. "Come with me," she said, plucking at Tessa's sleeve like a crone in a fairy-tale.

"Shall I wait here?" Edward said.

"You can if you like," said the nun. "But you'll get nothing to eat. The kitchen's all shut up."

"Goodnight then, darling," said Edward, smiling encouragingly at Tessa, and gave her a peck on the cheek. He could see that she was a bit downcast by this chilly reception. The hall was cold and ill-lit, and smelled faintly of boiled cabbage and carbolic soap. Dark oil paintings depicting martyrdoms and miracles loomed from the walls.

"Goodnight," Tessa replied in a small voice.

Afterwards they both recalled that the nun had looked puzzled by this exchange.

Edward waited while Tessa was shown to her room. It was deathly quiet. After a couple of minutes the nun slowly descended the stairs and shuffled across the lobby as if he weren't there. Just as she was about to disappear through a green baize door, Edward called out: "Excuse me, sister, but where is my room, please?"

The old nun looked balefully at him across the black and white flags of the hall. "Number twenty-nine, up the stairs and turn right," she said.

Edward located the room and walked in to find Tessa in her slip, brushing her hair. She dropped the brush in fright, and clasped her arms across her bosom.

"Oh, heavens, Teddy, you did scare me, this place is so spooky, what do you want? Have you come to kiss me goodnight? What will the nuns think?"

Edward explained about the nun's mistake, but gave her a goodnight kiss anyway, a proper one which went on for some time. There were two beds in the room and they made some jokes about that, which aroused them both. They had a common feeling of being back at school, riskily breaking the rules. Eventually Edward went back downstairs to try and find out about his room. He checked the noticeboard in the lobby. On a list he found: *"Mr and Mrs O'Brien – room 29."* All the names on the list were married couples. The sheet was indeed headed, *Conference for Married Couples*, and the programme included talks on The Holy Family, Beating The Seven-Year Itch, and Problems with Teenage Children.

Tessa had locked her door and Edward had to knock for admittance. When he explained that they had come on the wrong weekend, she collapsed on to one of the beds in hysterical giggles. Like many people who are good at stage comedy, Edward did not like to appear ridiculous unintentionally, but after a while he saw the funny side of his mistake too. It was too late to leave and travel back to Town, and although the house was undoubtedly full of empty bedrooms, he didn't want to go prowling around looking for one in case he made another embarrassing mistake. "You'd better sleep here," said Tessa. "And tomorrow morning we'll creep away early."

"All right, then," said Edward.

They undressed very decorously with the light off, but then they collided with each other in the dark and one thing led to another and before long they were in, or on, the same bed, and Tessa's nightdress was up round her armpits and she was moaning and writhing with pleasure in his arms. It was a long time since the dentist had petted her and she had missed such comforts in Edward's chaste courtship. Edward himself was quite out of his depth. Feeling the pressure of an imminent and unstoppable orgasm, he was filled with shame and panic at the thought of spilling his seed all over Tessa and the bedclothes. In his perturbation it seemed to him that their sin would be less, certainly his own humiliation would be less, if they performed the act properly. Desperately he rolled on top of Tessa and, with a fluke thrust at the right place and angle, entered her in a single movement. Tessa uttered a loud cry that, if it was heard in that house, was probably not recognized; and Edward, groaning into the pillow, pumped rivers of semen into her willing womb.

Afterwards he was aghast at what he had done, but Tessa covered his face with kisses and told him it had been wonderful, and he was moved with grateful pride. Tessa herself was delighted: she felt finally absolved from guilt on account of the freedoms she had allowed the dentist (which she had confessed in the vaguest terms on her reception into the Church) and finally sure of Edward's love. The next day they rose while it was still dark and let themselves stealthily out of the house. Their feet crunched resoundingly on the gravel of the drive, and looking back over her shoulder Tessa thought she saw the old nun watching them from a high, lighted window. Outside the gates they hitched a lift from a lorry taking vegetables to Covent Garden. "Not eloping, are you?" quipped the driver, looking at their overnight bags. They often wondered afterwards what the other, the real Mr and Mrs O'Brien thought when they arrived at the convent later that morning to find their bedroom defiled by unmistakable signs of sexual intercourse.

Having made love once, Edward and Tessa were unable to resist further opportunities that came their way, though each time it happened they solemnly vowed it would not recur. Soon Tessa discovered she was pregnant, and they made arrangements to get married rather sooner than they had planned. Edward was excruciatingly embarrassed by all this, guessing (quite correctly) what everyone would be thinking about the reasons for their haste, but Tessa faced it out serenely and did not for one moment contemplate giving up her white wedding and nuptial mass. She had an Empire-line dress made which artfully concealed the very slight swelling of her tummy. Soon afterwards, Edward's training finished and he was called up into the Army Medical Corps. Tessa went to live with her parents in Norfolk and gave birth to a daughter one night when Edward was sleeping out on Salisbury Plain as part of his officer's training. In due course he was posted to a military hospital in Aldershot and Tessa moved into digs there. They waited impatiently for his service to end, so that Edward could start his career as a GP. He had forgotten all about his intention of working for two years in the mission fields of Africa.

Miriam's conversion took longer than Tessa's. Every now and again she dug her heels in and refused to go any further. She had a quick, sharp mind and she was not, like Tessa, theologically illiterate to start with. Her own religious upbringing had been Low Church Evangelical, and she had already reacted against that form of Christianity, its gloomy Sabbatarianism, its narrow-minded insistence on Faith against Works, its charmless liturgy. Since leaving home to attend the University she had ceased to worship, though still considering herself a kind of Christian. Catholicism, to which Michael introduced her, seemed to be just what she was looking for: it was subtle, it was urbane, it had history, learning, art (especially music) on its side. But there was enough of the Protestant left in Miriam to make a lot of Catholic doctrine difficult to swallow, especially in relation to Mary. She was dismayed to discover that "the Immaculate Conception" did not denote the birth of Christ to a virgin, but the dogma that Mary herself was conceived without the stain of original sin. "It doesn't say so in Scripture, and how else would anyone know?" she said. Michael, who had been well schooled in apologetics at school, quoted the salutation of the archangel Gabriel, "Hail, full of grace, the Lord is with thee." Since Mary hadn't been baptized at that point, she couldn't have been full of grace unless she had been exempted from the stain of original sin inherited from Adam and Eve. Miriam yielded to the logic of this argument (when the Catholic Jerusalem Bible was published ten years later she found that "full of grace" was translated as "highly favoured", but the issue no longer seemed important) and shifted her attention to the doctrine of the Assumption of Our Lady into Heaven, which had been defined as an article of faith as recently as 1950 – though, as Michael was quick to emphasize, it had been an important feast of the Church for centuries. "I still don't see the point of it," she said. "Christianity is hard enough to believe in without adding all these unnecessary extras."

Michael himself was uneasy about the Assumption, for which there didn't seem to be one jot or tittle of Scriptural evidence, and referred Miriam to the College chaplain – no longer Father Brierley, who had been moved to a parish at the end of the Northern Line, but Father Charles Conway, a lively and good-looking young priest with an Oxford degree. He suggested that the doctrine might be looked at as a theological formalization of Mary's special place in the scheme of salvation, and of her presence in heaven as a source of help and encouragement to souls on earth. But Miriam had her reservations about that too. She didn't understand why Catholics prayed so much to Mary to "intercede" for them with God. "Do you mean," she asked, her tulip-cut of glossy copper-coloured hair thrust forward with the urgency of her question, "that if A prays to Jesus via Mary, and B prays direct to Jesus, A has a better chance of being heard than B, other things being equal? And if not, then why bother going through Mary?" Neither Michael nor Father Conway had a satisfactory answer to that one.

When she had got over these doctrinal hurdles, or bypassed them (for they were, after all, peripheral to the main deposit of faith) Miriam got into a panic about making her first confession. To go into that dark, cupboard-like cubicle and whisper your most shameful secrets to a man on the other side of a wire mesh might be tolerable if you were brought up to it from childhood, but for herself it seemed humiliating, a violation, a hideous ordeal. "There's nothing to it, really," Michael reassured her, conveniently suppressing the memory of his own agonizings over masturbation not so very long ago. "The priest won't know who you are. And you can go to one *you* don't know, if you like."

"I certainly shan't go to Father Charles, I'd simply die."

"Anyway, you can't have anything very dreadful to confess," he said fondly.

"How would *you* know?" she shot at him, with such anger that he was chastened into silence.

They were queueing, at the time, for gallery seats at the Globe theatre to see Graham Greene's new play, *The Potting Shed*. Michael had been looking forward eagerly to seeing the play, which, to judge from the reviews, confirmed that the author's faith was intact, but he found that he was unable to concentrate on the story of vows, miracles, lost and found belief. Later in life all he could remember about the production was a dog barking off-stage and the peculiarly bilious green of John Gielgud's cardigan. (Could it possibly have been, he wondered, a sartorial pun on the author's name?) For most of the performance he was brooding jealously on Miriam's hint of grave sin in her past. Though Michael was no longer so helplessly obsessed with sex as in late adolescence, he still thought about it quite a lot. He looked forward to the night of his wedding (provisionally planned for the coming spring) as a feast that would be rendered all the more delicious by the prolonged abstinence that had preceded it. To lie with his beloved in the same bed, free to explore her body at will, above, below, between, to assuage the long ache of unsatisfied desire in total abandonment, without fear or guilt at last – that would surely be a rapture worth waiting for. The thought that Miriam might not, after all, have waited – that she might already have tasted some of the sweets of sex with another boy, or even boys, tormented him. It did not occur to Michael that she might have been referring to masturbation, for he did not know that girls masturbated (his reading in English fiction had not uncovered this fact). But, as it happened, that was not what Miriam was alluding to. Her most shameful secret was that at school she had joined in the persecution of a girl whom nobody liked and who had eventually been driven to attempt suicide. Miriam and her friends had been in great terror as this event was investigated, but the girl in question had nobly declined to tell on them. The worst thing of all was that when the girl returned to school they all hated her more than ever, and after a while her mother took her away.

After *The Potting Shed*, on the Tube ride back to the little flat in Highbury that Miriam shared with another girl, Michael was silent and morose; and instead of going in for a cup of coffee, as was his custom, he kept Miriam talking in the shadow of a plane tree in the street.

"Did you have any boy friends before me?"

"You know I didn't, I told you."

"Nobody at all?"

"Nobody serious."

"You did have some, then?"

Miriam soon got to the source of his mood, and poured scorn on it. "The trouble with you is that all you think about is sex," she said. "You can't imagine people feeling guilty about anything else, can you?"

60

He admitted it, joyfully. "It's the Irish Jansenist tradition," he said.

Soon afterwards, Miriam made her first confession, without telling anybody in advance. She went to Westminster Cathedral, the most anonymous place for the purpose she could think of. Crowds poured in and out of the doors, and sat or kneeled or sauntered about, staring up at the great walls and arches of sooty, unfaced brick. It felt like some huge and holy railway terminus. All along one wall were dozens of confessionals, some offering the facility of a foreign language. Miriam, kneeling in a pew while she got her courage up, considered making her confession in French, a subject in which she had done well at A level, but decided that she would not be able to manage the Act of Contrition. Eventually she plunged into one of the ordinary confessionals at random and gabbled out the formula she had been taught by Father Conway: " Bless me Father for I have sinned this is my first confession." She added: "And I'm terrified." She was lucky with her priest and came out feeling wonderful, spiritually laundered. She never told Michael about the girl at school who had been on her conscience until long after they were married, by which time he was no longer curious.

The wedding night to which he had looked forward for so long got off to a bad start when they were shown into a room at their hotel with twin beds. Michael, inexperienced in such matters, had omitted to specify a double. When the porter had withdrawn, he expressed his regret.

"Ask them to give us another room," Miriam suggested.

Michael imagined himself going downstairs and walking up to the receptionist in a crowded, but silent and attentive lobby, and saying: *"Could I have a room with a double bed in it, please?"* "You ask them," he said to Miriam.

"No *thanks!*"

They giggled and kissed, but the twin beds were decidedly a disappointment. They were narrow and spaced well apart and the headboards were screwed to the wall.

"Oh, well," said Miriam, "never mind." She opened her suitcase and began to unpack. A cascade of confetti fell to the floor as she shook out a dress. "That Gwen!" she said, referring to one of her bridesmaids.

"Hold on a minute," said Michael.

Looking neither to right nor left, he marched out of the room, down the stairs, and up to the reception desk.

"Yes, sir?"

Michael took a deep breath. "Er . . . what time is dinner?" he said.

"Dinner is served from six-thirty, sir."

"Ah." He lingered, squinting at the ceiling as if trying to remember something else.

Michael often recalled that moment of acute embarrassment. He recalled it, for instance, in the summer of 1968, when he was checking into a hotel in Oxford, where he was attending a meeting of GCE examiners, and a young man in a white suit, with blond hair down to his shoulders, came up to the desk and asked the price of a double room. In the background, nonchalantly scanning a newspaper, a girl hovered. "Do you have your luggage with you, sir?" said the clerk, evidently well used to handling such requests from randy under-graduates. The young man didn't have any luggage and was refused the room; but what struck Michael was that he wasn't in the least embarrassed or disconcerted by the refusal, departing with a peace sign and a broad grin, squeezing his girl friend's waist as they left the lobby. "Whereas I," he said one weekend in February 1975, recalling his honeymoon in 1958, "was legally married. All I wanted was a double bed so that we could consummate it in reasonable comfort. And I was tongue-tied. Beads of perspiration literally stood out on my face."

"Is there anything else, sir?" said the receptionist in 1958, as Michael stared at the ceiling. Without looking the man in the eye, he mumbled out a request for a room with a double bed, and was given one without fuss. He ran back to Miriam, grasping the key like mythical treasure wrested from a dragon. He felt hugely heroic, masculine, dominant: a true husband. When they got to the new room, he locked the door and carried Miriam across to the double bed. They lay on it and necked, occasionally sitting up to divest themselves of a garment (shades of Polly's St Valentine's striptease) until they were both undressed down to their underwear. Solemnly Michael un-did the fastener of Miriam's brassiere and drew it from her shoulders. "Do you mind that they're so small?" she whispered. "They're beautiful," he said, kissing the nipples on her delicate little breasts and feeling them grow hard. "Let's make love," he said, scarcely able to draw breath for excitement. "All right," said Miriam.

She got up off the bed and put on her nightie. Michael put on his pyjamas and drew the curtains against the slanting sunlight (it was about six o'clock in the evening). Then they got into bed, under the bedclothes. Neither of them saw anything odd in this behaviour. It was how they had always envisaged married love.

But then there was a hitch. There seemed to be no way that Michael could get his penis to go in and stay in. In all his long hours of musing on the moment of consummation, he had never anticipated this particular difficulty They struggled and heaved and muttered "Sorry" and "It's all right," but after a while the atmosphere became slightly desperate. Had Miriam grasped Michael's penis and guided it to its target, there would have been no problem, but it never occurred to her to do so or to him to suggest it. None of our young brides even touched their husbands' genitals until weeks, months, sometimes years after marriage. All accepted the first nuptial embrace lying on their backs with their arms locked round their spouses' necks like drowning swimmers being rescued; while these spouses, supporting themselves on tensed arms, tried to steer their way blind into a channel the contours of which they had never previously explored by touch or sight. No wonder most of them found the act both difficult and disappointing.

At last Michael admitted defeat, modestly pulled up his pyjama trousers under the blankets, and got out of bed to find a cigarette. Miriam watched him anxiously. "Perhaps there's something wrong with me," she said. "Perhaps I've got a blockage. I'll go and see a doctor." She was only half joking. They dressed and went down for dinner, silent and sad, smiling wanly at each other across the table. Michael contemplated the prospect of a marriage without sex. After so long a wait, did he love Miriam enough to accept that heavy cross? He reached under the table and squeezed her hand, suffused with a Greeneian gloom, "the loyalty we all feel to unhappiness, the sense that this is where we really belong," as a favourite passage in *The Heart of the Matter* put it. When they returned to their room, he proposed one more try.

"I'm awfully sore," said Miriam doubtfully.

"Haven't you got some ointment, or something?"

She did, as it happened, have some Vaseline with her, which she used for the prevention of chapped lips. Applied to her nether lips it produced almost magical results. Afterwards, Michael put his hands behind his head and smiled beatifically at the ceiling.

"From now on," he said, "I'm always going to give Vaseline for wedding presents."

Angela and Dennis were the last of their College set to get married, and had waited the longest. Dennis had wanted to get married as soon as he was offered his first job, with ICI. When he phoned Angela with the news of his successful interview, late in 1956, he said, "Let's get married at Christmas." Angela felt panic choking her and was scarcely able to reply. Dennis thought it was a bad connection and rattled on unconcerned. "Easter, if you like," he said. "Christmas would be short notice for the families."

When they met the next day, Angela, pale from a sleepless night, told him that she didn't think she was ready for marriage. "Ready, what d'you mean, ready?" he demanded, bewildered. "We've waited five years already, how much longer d'you want?"

Angela found it very difficult to explain. She loved Dennis, she appreciated his loyalty and devotion, she wanted to give herself to him. But the prospect of marriage, a lifetime's commitment, frightened her, and the portents in marriages she knew depressed her, especially her own parents' marriage. While she had lived at home she had sentimentalized it, idealized it. The big, warm, happy Catholic family. The house full of noisy bustle and religious zeal. The boys cycling off early in the mornings to serve at mass, priests and nuns dropping in at all hours, family feasts at Christmas and Easter. Now she saw it all differently, aware that her mother's part in all this had been a lifetime of drudgery, her father's a lifetime of worry. The family was like the shop – a tyrant that kept them slaving from morning till night, so that they never had a moment to themselves. Their sexual life was unimaginable, not simply because it embarrassed her to think about it, but because they seemed so exhausted, so drained of tenderness to each other, by the clamorous demands of their offspring. When she went home for weekends now, she threw herself into the domestic front line at her mother's side –

washed, ironed, swept and hoovered – but it seemed to make no difference: the dirty washing accumulated as fast as ever, people tramped through the house leaving mud and dirt everywhere, the fire smoked in the back parlour and the shop bell pinged insistently. Always she was guiltily pleased to be gone, to be back in her snug and neat little bed-sitter in Streatham. She had a teaching job in a girls' grammar school which she found demanding but satisfying, and her career prospects were good. Her eldest brother, Tom, was training to be a priest, and the rest of the children were still at school. She thought it was her duty to work for at least a few years, sending a quarter of her salary home. That was how she put it to Dennis, though the deeper reason was simply that she was frightened of marriage.

"You can go on working after we're married," Dennis said. "You can go on giving part of your earnings to your Mum and Dad."

"For how long? We'll have children, won't we?"

"Not immediately. We'll use the whatdyoucallit, rhythm method."

"Suppose it doesn't work?"

"Why shouldn't it work? It's scientifically sound."

"Oh, *scientifically*. . . ."

She jeered at his trust in science, uttered wounding remarks about his complacency, his self-centredness. She tried to make herself as unpleasant as possible, to provoke him into breaking their engagement; but he simply sat there, absorbing all her venom, and at last wore her out. All right, he sighed, when she had talked herself out, and was sitting red-faced and dumb, wanting to cry but unable to; all right, he would not press her, they could wait until she was ready. He came over to the divan where she was sitting and put his arm round her shoulders. Why me, she thought, why does it have to be me? Why can't he leave me in peace and find another girl, someone who really wants to get married?

Dennis gave up the post he had been offered with ICI, which would have meant moving to Northumberland, and took a job with an electronics firm in London, on the production side, relying on his Army qualifications for the relevant technical knowledge. This job he saw as a temporary expedient, but in fact it turned out rather well for Dennis, for it was a lively firm in what turned out to be a buoyant market in the sixties. At the time, however, it seemed a waste of his chemistry degree. Dennis's parents were quietly reproachful towards Angela when she visited them in Hastings. They thought Angela was a nice girl, "a lovely girl", but they couldn't understand her hesitation to marry their son and they couldn't forgive her for keeping him waiting against his wishes. As for her own parents, they were thoroughly in favour of Dennis, a good Catholic, a steady chap with good prospects; and since Angela made it clear that in no circumstances would she allow them to pay for her wedding, they were quite eager to see it come off. Eventually Angela capitulated to all this gentle pressure, and not unwillingly; she felt she had put up a creditable fight for . . . whatever it was that had made her hesitate: independence, conscience, realism. I have made no promises I cannot keep, she told herself, when at last she named the day (it was being matron of honour to Ruth that tipped the balance in favour of marriage), I haved warned him, I have warned them all. And then, she did love Dennis, wanted to make love to him properly after all these years of the tiresome game of How Far Can You Go. When they lay on the divan bed in her bedsitter now, she did not resist the advances of his exploring hands over her body and under her dress, and she felt the quickening excitement of his breathing and the hardness of his male parts pressed against her thigh. He gave her a book to read, written by a doctor, about the facts of sex, and she learned from it many things she had not known before, her cheeks burning as she read, and felt additional impatience to be wed, for it seemed to her indecent to have such knowledge without the experience.

As they were arranging their own wedding, and their families lived so far apart, North and South, Angela and Dennis decided to have it in London, at the University church. This was not the church of Our Lady and St Jude's, of course, but a much more venerable structure in the City. They did, however, ask Father Brierley to officiate as they did not know the current University Chaplain; and Father Brierley, still a curate in the parish at the end of the Northern Line, was touched by the request, and agreed gladly. This gave Dennis and Angela the idea of inviting all the regular members of the group that used to attend the Thursday masses. There was no rational reason for this, really – for though some, like Michael and Miriam, were close friends whom they would have invited anyway, others were not and had been out of touch for years, except for the occasional Christmas card. However, they both agreed that Father Brierley would appreciate a reunion, and in some obscure, inarticulate way they both felt a kind of sentimental nostalgia for those dark, cold, Thursday mornings of their first love, when they trekked in from the suburbs for early mass. "Imagine," said Angela, "travelling all that distance without a cup of tea first. Not even a glass of water. How did we do it?" For by this date, autumn 1958, the Eucharistic fast had been considerably relaxed, and one was permitted to drink any non-alcoholic beverage up to one hour before receiving Communion – a concession particularly appreciated by brides preparing for their nuptial mass.

Everyone agreed that it was a very nice wedding. It took place on a fine October day. Angela looked beautiful and Dennis looked like the cat who was finally certain of getting the cream. Miriam played the organ expertly, and Michael was an efficient best man. Angela's brother Tom, who was a year away from ordination, assisted Father Brierley as deacon, and read the Epistle in a fine clear voice:

"Brethren: let women be subject to their husbands as to the Lord, for the husband is the head of the wife, as Christ is the head of the Church. He is the saviour of his body. Therefore, as the Church is subject to Christ, so also let the wives be to their husbands in all things. Husbands, love your wives as Christ also loved the Church. . . ."

Father Brierley's sermon was a little on the heavy side, some thought, but it was sincere, and carefully prepared. This couple, he told the assembled congregation (who scarcely needed to be reminded of the fact) had not rushed into holy matrimony, like so many young people these days. They had tested their feelings for each other over a long period, they had prepared themselves prudently for the great responsibilities of the married state, and now they were calling down God's blessing on their union by this nuptial mass. As St Paul's epistle had reminded them all, the relationship between man and wife was analogous to that between Christ and His Church. ("What's analogous?" Angela's mother whispered to her husband, who shook his head.) Both were founded on Faith, Hope and Love. Dennis and Angela, poised on the threshold of a new life together, did not know exactly what the future held for them: great joys and happiness, certainly, but also trials and tribulations, for such was human life.

(Dennis's father stirred restlessly in his pew; it seemed a rather gloomy sermon for a wedding, he thought – more suitable for a funeral.) The Church also at this time stood on the threshold of a new era. A great Pope, Pius XII, had just died, a Pope who had steered the bark of Peter through the stormy seas of the Second World War, who had defended the right of Catholics to practice their faith in the teeth of Communist persecution, a Pope who had never hesitated to stand up for Christian values against the rampant materialism of the modern world. Even as he spoke to them now, the cardinals of all the nations of the world were gathering in Rome to elect a new Pope in secret conclave. No one knew who he would be, or what problems he would have to grapple with. What they did know was that the Holy Spirit would guide the Conclave's choice, that the man who was chosen would be equal to whatever challenge lay before him, because of Christ's promise that he would be with His Church all days, even to the consummation of the world. Likewise, Dennis and Angela knew that Christ would be with them, too, all days, sharing in their joys and supporting them in their sorrows, until death did them part.

Afterwards, at the reception, there were excited reunions between old friends, many of whom had not seen each other for years. Not everyone had been able to come. Sister Mary Joseph of the Precious Blood wrote to Angela to say that the Rule of the Order forbade attendance at weddings, but she wished them both joy and would remember them in her prayers. Adrian wrote excusing himself and Dorothy on the grounds that Dorothy was pregnant and had been ordered to rest. It didn't sound terribly convincing, but Dennis, anyway, was more relieved than sorry at Adrian's absence. All the others, rather to his surprise, turned up. Edward was there, in his Lieutenant's uniform of the RAMC, which made Dennis feel a little queasy, and Tessa, proudly wielding her new baby. Polly came and wept copiously through the wedding service, making the mascara run down her cheeks in black rivulets, so that she had to retire for an interval afterwards to re-do her face. She was twenty-six and was beginning to want very much to be married herself and have babies like Tessa, and like Miriam, who was four months pregnant and looked blooming in a green maternity dress which she scarcely needed yet. Polly now worked for the BBC as a research assistant, and knew lots of young men, but not one of them had asked her to marry him, as she had the reputation of being a bit of a tart. This was hardly fair to Polly, who had had only two affairs in the last two years, but coming back into contact with all these good Catholics, hearing mass for the first time in ages, looking at radiant Angela and proud Dennis, and feeling sure that, incredible as it might seem, they were going to the nuptial bed as genuine virgins, she herself felt distinctly Magdalenish, and began to wonder whether she should start going to mass again, perhaps even to Confession, and try to make a fresh start. But after her second glass of white wine at the reception she cheered up and began to flirt with all the men at the reception, even Father Brierley.

"I don't suppose you remember me, do you, Father? The Salome of Cath. Soc?"

"Of course I do, Polly, yes indeed, how are you after all these years?" said Father Brierley nervously.

"That was a beautiful sermon, Father."

"Thank you, most kind," Father Brierley murmured, blushing with pleasure.

"Isn't it exciting about the Conclave! Who d'you think will win?"

" 'Win' isn't perhaps the most appropriate – "

"Don't you think it would be fun to have a Yank for a change? Good heavens, there's Miles! Excuse me, Father."

Polly turned aside and began to push her way through the crush, leaving a heavy smell of perfume lingering on the air in her wake. Austin Brierley was relieved to see her go, for her presence had stirred embarrassing memories and a still-vivid mental image of her silk-stockinged leg.

Polly greeted Miles with a faint shriek, to which he responded with expressions of surprise and rapture. They embraced with a great deal of physical flourish but little actual contact, since Polly did not want to have to repair her make-up again, and Miles did not want her lipstick all over his face and shirt collar. A little circle of the bride's relations watched this performance respectfully, recognizing a code of manners more sophisticated and complex than their own. Michael, observing from further off, realized for the first time that Miles was homosexual, something that had never occurred to him in his innocent undergraduate days. What, he wondered, did a Catholic homosexual do? Sublimate, he supposed. It seemed rather hard. On other the hand it was difficult, not being a homosexual oneself, to believe that what homosexuals did with each other would be difficult to give up. It was always a mystery, other people's experience of sex. Even Miriam, though she enjoyed making love, could not explain to him what it felt like, and became evasive and finally frigid if he questioned her too closely.

A little later, Michael chatted with Miles and learned that he had finished his PhD thesis, which was likely to be published, and had recently been elected to a Fellowship at one of the Cambridge colleges. Miles spoke eloquently of the pleasures of Cambridge, dropped a few great names, and enquired kindly, but a shade patronizingly, about Michael's career.

"I'm schoolteaching to stay out of the Army," Michael explained. "How did you get out of it?"

"I failed the medical," said Miles.

"Lucky sod," said Michael, unthinkingly. He added hastily, "I'd like to go into university teaching myself, but I can't afford to be called up, now I'm married and with a baby on the way."

"Really? My congratulations."

"Thanks. We didn't really want to start a family right away, but well, you know how it is. . . ."

"Not from experience," Miles smiled suavely.

"I mean for Catholics. Birth control and so on."

"Oh yes, well, I do sympathize, but on the other hand there is something rather fine about the Church's refusal to compromise on that issue, don't you think? Unlike the Anglicans, poor dears."

It's all very well for you, Michael thought; but said nothing.

The reception was nearly over, the telegrams had been read, and speeches made, and the wedding cake cut and consumed. Angela was beginning to think of retiring to change into her going-away clothes when Violet made a very late and somewhat disturbing appearance at the feast. She looked very ill and anxious, very much as she had looked just before her nervous breakdown in her Final year. Her clothes were dark and heavy and distinctly unfestive, and she carried a large paper carrier bag. She went up to Angela and apologized for being late, giving some complicated explanation of how she had lost her way on the Tube. "I've brought you a present," she said, and produced from the bag a rather untidy parcel tied up in crumpled brown paper. As she seemed to want Angela to open it, Angela did so, and was disconcerted to find inside a complete baby's layette.

"It was for the baby I lost," Violet said. "I'm sure you'll have a use for it one day."

The guests, who had gathered round to see the present, turned away in embarrassment.

"But, Violet," said Angela gently, "you mustn't give me this. You may need it yourself another time."

"No, Robin and I are separated. Anyway, he wouldn't have any more children, he didn't mean us to have that one, it was a mistake, he wanted me to have an abortion, but I wouldn't. He's not a Catholic, you know."

"Angela," said Miriam, seeing that Violet had to be stopped from spoiling Angela's day, "if you don't go and get changed immediately, you're going to miss that train. I'll get Violet something to eat." And with a slightly worried frown, Angela went off to get changed.

"Well, well, poor old Violet," said Michael later, when he and Miriam were alone together, walking back to the Tube station arm-in-arm.

"Was she like that as a student?"

"A bit inclined. She had a sort of nervous breakdown in her last year, had to take a year off."

"It's a shame her losing her baby," Miriam said, covertly feeling her own tummy, like someone touching wood.

"Mmm. Her husband's a bit of a cold fish, too. I met him once."

"She said they were separated."

"A typical Violet overstatement. I gather he's gone to the States for a term. Some kind of exchange."

"But he didn't take her with him."

"Expect he wanted to get away from her for a while. Can't say I blame him. Did you see how she got Father Brierley into a corner? He didn't look as if he was enjoying it one bit."

They walked in silence for a while, thinking their own thoughts.

"Well," said Michael, "it all went off very nicely, in spite of Violet. The organ sounded fantastic in that church."

"And you were a super best man. It was a very funny speech." She sqeezed his hand.

"All the same," he said, "I shan't complain if I don't have to go to another wedding for a few years. I've just about had enough."

"From now on," said Miriam, "it's going to be christenings."

Dennis and Angela's honeymoon was, of course, no freer from awkwardness and disappointment than any of the others, though these feelings were mostly on Angela's side. The book Dennis had lent her had not prepared her for the physical messiness of the act of love, and the orgasms she had read about in its pages eluded her. On the honeymoon Dennis was ravenous for her, begged her to make love twice, three times a night, he groaned and swore in his rapture, said over and over again, I love you, I love you, but always he reached his climax as soon as he entered her, and she felt little except the unpleasant aftertrickle between her legs, staining her new nighties and the hotel sheets. When they got home to their little two-roomed flat, she changed the bedlinen so often that their laundry bill became astronomical (there was nowhere to hang out sheets) and caused their first quarrel; after which she spread towels on the bed when the occasion required it. Then, after a couple of months, she missed her period and felt nauseous in the mornings and knew that she must be pregnant. She told her headmistress that she would be resigning at the following Easter.

3

How things began to change

MIRIAM was quite right. For all of them who married in the nineteen-fifties, except poor Violet, the next decade was dominated by babies. Dennis and Angela, Edward and Tessa, Adrian and Dorothy, Michael and Miriam herself, had produced, by the end of 1966, fourteen children between them, in spite of strenuous efforts not to. That is to say, although each of these couples wanted to have children, the latter arrived more quickly and frequently than their parents had wished for or intended. And the reason for this, of course, was that, obedient to their Church's teaching, they relied upon periodic abstinence as a way of planning their families, a system known as Rhythm or the Safe Method, which was in practice neither rhythmical nor safe. I have written about this before, a novel about a penurious young Catholic couple whose attempts to apply the Safe Method have produced three children in as many years, and whose hopes of avoiding a fourth depend precariously on their plotting a day-by-day graph of the wife's body-temperature to determine the time of her ovulation, and confining their enjoyment of conjugal love to the few days between this putative event and the anxiously awaited onset of her period. It was intended to be a comic novel and most Catholic readers seemed to find it funny, especially priests, who were perhaps pleased to learn that the sex life they had renounced for a higher good wasn't so very marvellous after all. Some of these priests have told me that they lent the book to people dying of terminal diseases and how it cheered them up, which is fine by me – I can't think of a better reason for writing novels – but possibly these readers, too, found it easier to bid farewell to the pleasures of the flesh when they were depicted as so hemmed about with anxiety. Healthy agnostics and atheists among my acquaintance, however, found the novel rather sad. All that self-denial and sacrifice of libido depressed them. I think it would depress me, too, now, if I didn't know that my principal characters would have made a sensible decision long ago to avail themselves of contraceptives.

Why this novel should have been translated into Czech and no other foreign language I cannot explain, for I should have thought that Czech Catholics would have more important things to worry about than problems of conscience over birth control, and I cannot imagine that non-Catholic Czechs would take a great interest in the subject. However, it did elicit, from Mr Cestimir Jerhot of Prague, the nicest request for my autograph I have ever received, or am ever likely to receive. *"Dear Sir,"* he wrote, *"I beg your costly pardon for my extraordinary beg and readings-request, with them I turn at you. I am namely a great reader and books-lover. Among my best friends – books – I have also in my library the Czech copy of your lovely book* 'Den zkazy v Britskem museu'. *I have read it several times and ever I have found it an extraordinary smiling book. I thank you very much for the best readings experiences and nice whiles, that has given your lovely work . . ."*

Thank you again, Mr Jerhot, for your lovely letter. This book is not a comic novel, exactly, but I have tried to make it smile as much as possible.

For Dorothy and Adrian, Tessa and Edward, Miriam and Michael, Angela and Dennis, then, in the early sixties, it was babies, babies, all the way. Nappies, bottles, colic, broken nights, smells of faeces and ammonia, clothes and furniture stained with dribble and sick. Well, that was all right. They were prepared to put up with all that, especially Tessa, who doted on babies, and Dennis, who was thrilled with paternity. The others, too, all had moments of great joy and pride in their infant offspring. Nor were the economic consequences of their fertility an overwhelming concern, though of course the wives had to give up work almost as soon as they were married, and at a time of increasing general affluence they had to be content with cramped, poorly furnished accommodation relative to their peer-group, and acquired cars, TVs and household appliances long after their non-Catholic friends. All this would have been tolerable if they had been erotically fulfilled. But just when they began to get the hang of sex – to learn the arts of foreplay, to lose their inhibitions about nakedness, to match each other's orgasmic rhythms – pregnancy or the fear of pregnancy intervened, and their spontaneity was destroyed by the tedious regime of calendar and temperature chart. For they did not always feel amorous on the permitted days, and if they made the mistake of getting amorous outside the permitted days it was back to the old game of How Far Could You Go. Most galling of all, their efforts to control their fertility always failed anyway, sooner or later. There were times when Angela thought it would be preferable simply to trust to luck and Providence, since it seemed to make little difference in the long run, and the frustration of one's intelligent efforts was almost as bad as the actual consequences – at least it seemed to be so for Dennis, who would pore over their graphs and diaries, trying to pinpoint where they had gone wrong, his scientific self-esteem piqued by failure. More than once they quarrelled over some alleged carelessness or inaccuracy on her part in keeping the record.

During a pregnancy, after the initial vexation and morning-sickness had worn off, and providing there were no gynaecological complications, the couples might enjoy a few months of free and easy sex, but after a new baby was born there would be a long hiatus, for it was not possible to plot the incidence of ovulation with any confidence as long as breast-feeding continued. This circumstance was particularly frustrating for Michael, since Miriam grew the most superb breasts, round and firm as apples, while she was nursing, and he wasn't even allowed to touch them, they were so tender and full of milk. All he could do was sit and watch enviously as his infant sucked and gently kneaded his wife's blindingly beautiful tits – which, by the time he and Miriam could make love again, would have disappeared.

Michael was perhaps the most frustrated of the men at this time, for his erotic imagination, always sensitive to stimulus, was being fed with more and more hints from the outside world, especially fiction. He followed the trial of *Lady Chatterley's Lover* with intense interest, and was one of the first to buy a copy of the Penguin edition when it was published, travelling into the next town to ensure that no one from the Catholic College of Education where he was now employed as a lecturer in English Literature would observe him making the purchase. He read the pages staring in disbelief at the forbidden words so boldly printed there and marvelling at the acts described. He had never much cared for Lawrence's writing, and one half of his mind sneered at the book's overblown rhetoric and portentous neo-paganism, while the other half felt a deep, envious attraction to the idea of phallic tenderness. When he had finished the novel, he passed it to Miriam, but she stopped reading it halfway through. She thought it was unconvincing and badly written; therefore the sex seemed crude and unnecessarily explicit. Michael could not defend the novel on literary-critical grounds, but he was disappointed, for the knowledge that Miriam was reading it excited him, and he had been hopeful that the passage about Connie Chatterley kissing Mellors' penis, which was the most amazing thing he had ever read in his whole life, might have given Miriam some ideas, but she did not get that far. After the publication of *Lady Chatterley's Lover*, Michael observed, the amount and variety of sexual intercourse in contemporary fiction increased dramatically. Whether this was because Lawrence's novel had encouraged more people to have it off more often, in more different ways, than before, or because it had merely encouraged novelists to admit what had been going on all the time, Michael was in no position to judge. He just felt that he was missing an awful lot.

The others did not envy the growing permissiveness of secular society so candidly. Adrian, for instance, imagined that his intense interest and excitement at the Profumo affair in the spring of 1963 was because it illustrated the general rottenness of the British political Establishment, which he was apt to compare unfavourably with the style and idealism of the American administration led by President Kennedy, the first Roman Catholic ever to be elected to that office. Adrian did not admit, even to himself, that he was deeply fascinated by the shameless self-possession of the call-girls, Christine Keeler and

Mandy Rice-Davies, when interviewed about their sex-lives on TV and in the press. They spoke as if there was no such thing as sin in the world. At this time Adrian and Dorothy were abstaining totally and indefinitely from sexual intercourse, since Dorothy's womb was in bad shape following two babies and a miscarriage in quick succession. (At about the same time, President Kennedy was confiding to his friend Ben Bradlee, later editor of the *Washington Post*, that if he didn't have a woman every three days or so, he got a bad headache; and by woman the President didn't mean Mrs Kennedy. But Adrian only read about that many years later in a newspaper excerpt from Mr Bradlee's memoirs.)

Of the four couples, Edward and Tessa probably suffered least under the regime of the Safe Period, for several reasons. They were comparatively well-off, they wanted a large family anyway, and they managed to space their first three children at two-year intervals without too much difficulty. Tessa was a strong healthy girl, with a wonderfully regular menstrual cycle (her graphs, Edward used to say, were a thing of beauty). Edward's problems were more in his professional sphere. A GP in the suburbs of an industrial Midlands city, he had an arrangement with his partners by which he looked after the Catholic patients in the practice requiring family planning advice, and he gave up one evening a week to similar service for the Catholic Marriage Advisory Council. Edward attended seminars arranged by the CMAC and kept up conscientiously with the medical literature on the use of the Safe Period. He instructed his clients in the use of the basal temperature method, and spent many hours beyond the call of duty going over the graphs they submitted to him for interpretation. The failure rate was, however, depressingly high. At first he was inclined to attribute this to lack of care and attention on the part of his patients, many of whom were working-class women unskilled in the use of thermometers and graph paper, but after a few years he began to have graver doubts about the reliability of the method itself, and to dread the faintly reproachful look on the faces of those of his family-planning clients who returned unexpectedly to ask for a pregnancy test.

One night he and Tessa were woken by a frantic banging on the front door. Assuming that he was being summoned to an emergency, Edward grabbed his bag and hurried down the stairs. A stranger with dishevelled clothing and staring eyes exploded into the hall and threw Edward to the ground. *"Safe! Safe! Safe!"* he screamed, banging Edward's head on the floor to emphasize the repetition. Recovering from his surprise, Edward wrestled the man into submission, whereupon he went limp and burst into tears. While Tessa quietened the terrified children, who had been woken by the fracas, Edward took the man into the lounge and gave him a mild sedative. It transpired that Edward had advised his wife on birth control, with the usual result, and that evening she had given birth to a child, their sixth, with some kind of physical malformation which the man could not even bring himself to describe. Tessa came into the room in her dressing-gown in time to hear this story, and scolded the man for relieving his feelings on Edward. "I'm very sorry for you and your wife, especially your wife," she said, "but you really can't blame it on my husband. These things can happen to anybody, at any time."

Edward nodded agreement, but inwardly he was not so sure. There had been four babies born in the practice with non-hereditary congenital abnormalities since he had joined it, and three of them had been born to his family-planning clients. Somewhere in the medical journals he had come across the hypothesis that genetic defects were more likely to occur when the ovum was fertilized towards the end of its brief life-span, and this was obviously more likely to occur with couples who were deliberately restricting their intercourse to the post-ovulatory period. The theory had not been tested by controlled experiment, and his own experience had no statistical significance whatsoever, but still, it was . . . unsettling. Edward did not mention these disquieting thoughts to Tessa, and was very glad he hadn't when shortly afterwards she became pregnant for the fourth time, unintentionally. Tessa took it very well, joked about Vatican Roulette and said you couldn't win them all; but Edward watched her swelling belly with barely disguised feelings of anxiety and dread. He terminated his voluntary work for the Catholic Marriage Advisory Council, and recommended the basal temperature method to Catholic patients in the practice with more caution than previously.

You may wonder why they all persevered with this frustrating, undignified, ineffective, anxiety-creating system of family planning.

78

They wondered themselves, years later, when they had all given it up. "It was conditioning," said Adrian, "it was the projection of the celibate clergy's own repressions on to the laity." "It was guilt," said Dorothy, "guilt about sex. Sex was dirty enough without going into birth control, that was the general feeling." "I think it was innocence," said Edward. "The idea of natural birth control, without sheaths or pills or anything, was very appealing to people with no sexual experience; it took some time to discover that unfortunately it didn't work." "It was fear, the fear of Hell," said Michael. Well, yes, that was at the bottom of it, they all admitted. (They were gathered together in 1969 for the AGM of a pressure group called Catholics for an Open Church, to which they all belonged, and were chatting together afterwards in a pub.)

They had been indoctrinated since adolescence with the idea, underlined by several Papal pronouncements, that contraception was a grave sin, and a sin that occupied a unique place in the spiritual game of Snakes and Ladders. For unlike other sins of the flesh, it had to be committed continuously and with premeditation if it was to have any point at all. It was not, therefore, something that could be confessed and absolved again and again in good faith, like losing one's temper, or getting drunk, or, for that matter, fornicating. (A nice question for casuists: was fornication more or less culpable if committed using contraceptives?) It excluded you from the sacraments, therefore; and according to Catholic teaching of the same vintage, if you failed to make your Easter Duty (confession and communion at least once a year, at Easter or thereabouts) you effectively excommunicated yourself. So, either you struggled on as best you could without reliable contraception, or you got out of the Church; these seemed to be the only logical alternatives. Some people, of course, had left precisely because they could no longer believe in the authority of a Church that taught such mischievous nonsense. More often, those who lapsed over this issue retained a residual belief in the rest of Catholic doctrine and thus lived uncomfortably in a state of suppressed guilt and spiritual deprivation. One way or another, Catholics who used contraceptives were likely to be committing a sin against the Holy Ghost – either Resisting the Known Truth or Obstinacy in Sin – and thus putting themselves at risk of final damnation. So Michael was in that sense right – it all came down to fear of Hell.

"Where we went wrong, of course," said Adrian, "was in accepting the theology of mortal sin."

"No," said Miriam, who had been listening quietly to their comments. "Where you went wrong was in supposing that the Church belonged to the Pope or the priests instead of to the People of God."

They nodded agreement. "The People of God" was a phrase the Catholics for an Open Church approved of. It made them sound invincible.

In the early nineteen-sixties, however, their main hope was that the official Church would change its mind on birth control; that they would wake up one morning and read in the papers that the Pope had said it was all right for them to use contraceptives after all. What a rush there would have been to the chemists' and barbers' shops, and the Family Planning Clinics! In hindsight it is clear that this was a fairly preposterous expectation, for such a reversal of traditional teaching would have dealt a blow to the credibility of papal authority so shattering that no Pope, not even Pope John, could reasonably have been expected to perpetrate it. Miriam was right: instead of waiting for the Pope to contradict his predecessors, they should have made up their own minds. This in fact they did, in due course, but it took a lot of misery and stress to screw them up to the point of disobedience. In the early nineteen-sixties they were still hoping for a change of heart at the top, at least in favour of the Pill, to which, some progressive theologians claimed, the traditional natural law arguments against artificial contraception did not apply.

In other respects the Church undoubtedly was changing. Pope John, against all expectations (CARETAKER PONTIFF ELECTED, Angela and Dennis had read on newspaper placards when they returned from their honeymoon) had electrified the Catholic world by the radical style of his pontificate. "We are going," he declared, "to shake off the dust that has collected on the throne of St Peter since the time of Constantine and let in some fresh air." The Second Vatican Council which he convened brought out into the light a thousand unsuspected shoots of innovation and experiment, in theology, liturgy and pastoral practice, that had been buried for decades out of timidity or misplaced loyalty. In 1962, Pope John actually set up a

Pontifical Commission to study problems connected with the Family, Population and Birth Control. This was encouraging news in one sense, since it seemed to admit the possibility of change, but disappointing in that it effectively removed the issue from debate at the Vatican Council, which began its deliberations in the same year. Pope John died in 1963, to be succeeded by Pope Paul VI, who enlarged the Commission and instructed its members specifically to examine the Church's traditional teaching with particular reference to the progesterone pill. Catholics, especially young married ones, waited impatiently for the result of this inquiry.

Meanwhile, other changes proceeded at a dizzying pace. The mass was revised and translated into the vernacular. The priest now faced the congregation across a plain table-style altar, which made the origins of the Mass in the Last Supper more comprehensible, and allowed many of the laity to see for the first time what the celebrant actually did. All masses were now dialogue masses, the whole congregation joining in the responses. The Eucharistic fast was reduced to a negligible one hour, before which any kind of food and drink might be consumed, and the laity were urged to receive communion at every mass – a practice previously deemed appropriate only to people of great personal holiness and entailing frequent confession. Typical devotions of Counter-Reformation Catholicism such as Benediction and the Stations of the Cross dwindled in popularity. Rosaries gathered dust at the backs of drawers. The liturgy of Holy Week, previously of a length and tedium only to be borne by the most devout, was streamlined, reconstructed, vernacularized, and offensive references to the "perfidious Jews" were removed from the prayers on Good Friday. Ecumenism, the active pursuit of Christian Unity through "dialogue" with other Churches, became a recommended activity. The change of posture from the days when the Catholic Church had seen itself as essentially in competition with other, upstart Christian denominations, and set their total submission to its own authority as the price of unity, was astonishingly swift. Adrian, looking through his combative apologetics textbooks from Catholic Evidence Guild days, before sending them off to a parish jumble sale, could hardly believe how swift it had been. And from the Continent, from Latin America, through the religious press, came rumours of still more startling innovations being mooted – married priests, even women priests, Communion in the hand and under both kinds, inter-communion with other denominations, "Liberation Theology", and "Catholic Marxism". A group of young intellectuals of the latter persuasion, based in Cambridge, founded a journal called *Slant* in which they provocatively identified the Kingdom of God heralded in the New Testament with the Revolution, and characterized the service of Benediction as a capitalist-imperialist liturgical perversion which turned the shared bread of the authentic Eucharist into a reified commodity.

These developments were not, of course, universally welcomed. Evelyn Waugh, for instance, did not welcome them, and wrote furious letters to the *Tablet* saying so. Malcolm Muggeridge did not welcome them, and wrote a polemical piece in the *New Statesman* in 1965 urging "Backward, Christian Soldiers!" But it was none of his business, anyway, Michael thought, reading the article in the College library. What people needed from the Catholic Church, according to Muggeridge, was its "powerful pessimism about human life, miraculously preserved through the long false dawn of science." Reading this, Michael recognized a version of Catholicism he had once espoused. He no longer espoused it. Neither, it seemed, did Graham Greene, whose most recent novel, *A Burnt-out Case*, reflected the evolutionary Utopianism of Teilhard de Chardin's *The Phenomenon of Man*, a book published in 1959 to inter-national acclaim, after having been long suppressed by Rome as heretical.

Miles, on the other hand, considered Chardin a wet and muddled thinker, and reading the same article of Malcolm Muggeridge in the Combination Room of his Cambridge college, nodded gleeful agreement. The *Aggiornamento* or Renewal of the Catholic Church instigated by Pope John looked to Miles more and more like a Protestantization of it, and as he said to Michael and Miriam at the christening of their third child (rather to his surprise he had been invited to be its godfather, and rather to their surprise he had accepted), if you liked that sort of thing the Protestants did it much better, and it was not what he, personally, had joined the Catholic Church for. Michael, at the time something of a fellow-traveller with the *Slant* group, was dismayed by this reactionary declaration, but wishing, ignobly, to avoid a row with Miles, his closest personal link with the great academic world, retired to the kitchen to help his mother-in-law prepare tea.

Miriam did not agree with Miles either – as a convert from Evangelical Protestantism she felt quite at home in the new-style Catholic Church – but she was unable to put her point of view with any force because she was tired from lack of sleep and preoccupied with the needs of her three-week old baby and the jealous demands of the two older children and worried about whether there would be enough cups with handles still on them for their guests. So Miles held forth uninterruptedly, which he was used to doing, being a Cambridge don, while Miriam listened with one ear and cocked the other for sounds of crisis in the kitchen and surreptitiously sniffed the baby to ascertain whether she had soiled her nappy and scanned the crowded living-room for other signs of trouble.

"The trouble with Catholics, my dear Miriam," said Miles, "in this country, at least, is that they have absolutely no taste, no aesthetic sense whatsoever, so that as soon as they begin to meddle with the styles of architecture and worship that they inherited from the Counter-Reformation, as soon as they try and go 'modern', God help us, they make the most terrible dog's breakfast of it, a hideous jumble of old and new, incompatible styles and idioms, that positively sets one's teeth on edge. Do you remember that little church, Our Lady and St Jude's – no, of course you wouldn't, you didn't know Michael in those days. . . . Well, anyway, it was a terribly dingy, dilapidated neo-gothic place without a single feature of interest or beauty in it, but at least it had a certain character, a certain consistency, a kind of gloomy *ambiance* which was quite devotional in its way. You know, banks of votive candles simply dripping with congealed wax, hanging down like *stalactites*, and shadows flickering over painted statues. . . . Well, I happened to be in London on Ascension Day, so I dropped in for an evening mass, and, oh dear, what a transformation! No, not a transformation, that was the trouble, it hadn't been transformed, just meddled with. The candles had gone, and most of the statues, and the oil paintings of the Stations of the Cross, which were admittedly fairly hideous but so heavily varnished that you could scarcely see them, had been replaced with ghastly modern bas-reliefs in some kind of aluminium more appropriate to saucepans than to sacred art, and the altar rails had been removed and at the top of the steps there was a plain wooden altar, quite nice in its way but utterly incompatible with the old high altar behind it – all marble and gold inlay, turreted and crenellated in the gothic style . . . and quite honestly the mass itself seemed to me to be the same sort of muddle, bits of the old liturgy and bits of the new flung together, and nobody quite knowing what to do or what to expect."

"These things take time," said Miriam. 'Catholics aren't used to participating in the liturgy. They're used to watching the priest and saying their own prayers privately."

"Well, I must say that some of the things I'm supposed to say publicly nowadays make me cringe with embarrassment. The Responsorial Psalm on Ascension Day, for instance, what was it? *'God goes up with shouts of joy; the Lord goes up with trumpet blast.'* I mean, *really*! It sounds like a rocket lifting off at Cape Canaveral. Or something even more vulgar."

Miles tittered, and glanced covertly at the clock on the mantelpiece, wondering when he could decently make his departure. He had been invited to stay the night, but had no intention of trying to sleep on the Put-U-Up sofa in the living room which, he had established by a discreet survey of the premises, was the only accommodation for guests. The tiny, semi-detached house, overcrowded with people and cheap furniture so that it was scarcely possible to take a step without bumping into something or somebody, depressed him and made him restless to return to the cool, quiet spaces of Cambridge. It had been a mistake to come. Every now and then he succumbed to a feeling that there was something hollow and empty about his privileged existence, and then he would seize any opportunity to plunge into the ordinary world of domesticity, children, simple living and honest toil. But invariably it was disillusioning. He could see nothing to envy in Michael's existence. How could the spirit develop in such an environment? How right the Church was to insist on a celibate clergy!

That, of course, was the obvious way in which he could make his life less selfish; and he often allowed his mind to play over the possibility, weighing the pros and cons of the various orders – not the Dominicans, certainly, far too left-wing and anarchic, and the Carmelites were not quite learned enough, but both the Benedictines and the Jesuits had distinctive attractions, the former having by far the nicer habit. . . . But it would be tricky, taking orders at the present time, compelled to implement liturgical changes with which one had little sympathy, and wrestle with the squalid intricacies of the birth-control controversy. . . . Besides, he would have to give up the elegancies of college life, the good food and wine, the servants and comfortable rooms, and most important, the mildly flirtatious relationships he enjoyed with young men of the same temperament. Not that Miles ever indulged in anything grossly physical, but he moved on the circumference of circles where such things were indulged in, and derived a certain frisson of excitement from the contiguity.

Aggiornamento came very slowly to Father Austin Brierley's parish at the end of the Northern Line, where the Parish Priest regarded Vatican II and the whole movement for Catholic Renewal as an irritating distraction from the serious business of raising money. Fund-raising, mainly to pay off the debt on his church and to meet the Diocesan levy for Catholic education, was Father McGahern's all-consuming passion. Parochial life was one long round of bingo, raffles, whist-drives, dances, football pools, spot-the-ball competitions, sweepstakes, bazaars, jumble sales, outdoor collections, covenant schemes and planned giving. His addresses from the pulpit consisted of one part homily to three parts accountancy. The church porch was papered with graphs and diagrams in several colours, especially red, illustrating the slow progress of the parish towards solvency. The pastoral side of things he left pretty well entirely to Austin Brierley, who could scarcely cope with all the work. There was nothing selfishly materialistic about the PP's single-minded pursuit of lucre – on the contrary, he denied himself (and incidentally his curate) many home comforts in order to swell the parish funds. Heating in the presbytery was turned down to a barely tolerable minimum in the winter, and the electric light bulbs were of a wattage so low that Austin Brierley was sometimes obliged to read his breviary with the aid of a bicycle lamp.

It was a continual source of surprise to Austin Brierley that the parishioners did not seem to object to this constant harping on the theme of money. Indeed, the more active laymen threw themselves into the various fund-raising campaigns with enormous enthusiasm, competing eagerly with each other to bring in the largest amounts, while the apathetic majority paid up regularly and uncomplainingly. Austin Brierley very much feared that they confused this activity with the business of salvation, and measured their spiritual health on the same scale as Father McGahern's graphs, reassured to see that each week they had crept a little nearer to heaven.

Father McGahern had been in charge of the parish for a long time – ever since it had been a raw, unfinished housing estate, with a prefabricated hut for a church – and he rarely left it except to go home to County Cork for his annual holiday. His parish was a little kingdom, which he ruled despotically, and somewhat idiosyncratically. For example, it was his practice occasionally to interrupt the celebration of mass, and step down to the altar rails to deliver himself of some *ex tempore* exhortation or reproach that seemed to him timely. Thus, if there were an especially large number of latecomers he would take a break between the Epistle and Gospel to remind the congregation of the importance of punctuality in God's house; or if it occurred to him that he had not adequately emphasized some point in his sermon, he would interrupt the Eucharistic prayer to add a postscript. Having to say the mass facing the people seemed to make him especially prone to this kind of digression – the expressions he perceived on their faces perhaps put ideas into his head – and it became a special feature of the new liturgy in this parish. Visitors found it strange and indecorous, or engagingly informal, according to their temperaments. The regular congregation, however, grew quite accustomed to it, and did not manifest any surprise or restiveness when these interruptions became increasingly profane in content, reflecting the priest's preoccupation with money, and bearing much the same relation to the mass as commercial breaks to a television broadcast of a Shakespeare play. "You may not realize it, my good people," he would say, putting down the chalice in the middle of the Offertory, and ambling to the altar rail, "but the cost of heating this church is something shocking these days. I have just paid a bill for one quarter to the North Thames Gas Board for one hundred and twenty-seven pounds. One hundred and twenty-seven pounds for one quarter! Now, the reason it's so high, my dear people, is quite simple. During mass the heaters are warming the space inside the church, but as soon as the doors are opened after mass, whoosh, all the hot air flies out and the cold air flies in. So it would be greatly appreciated if you would leave the church as smartly as possible at the end of mass, and not be hanging about talking in the porch, holding everybody up and keeping the doors open longer than necessary." And back he would go to the altar to carry on with the celebration.

When, one Sunday, he took time out twice in one mass, first to draw the congregation's attention to an increase in fire-insurance premiums, and secondly to say that if any more hymn books disappeared he would have to consider charging a deposit on them, Austin Brierley felt he could be silent no longer. After lunch he made his protest, excited and indignant at first, but gradually petering out, like his outburst at the St Valentine's party years ago. The old priest listened without interrupting him and, when Austin Brierley had finished, remained silent for some minutes, as if stunned by the reproaches levelled at him. At last he spoke.

"Tell me, Father," he said abstractedly, "what do you think of Premium Bonds?"

"Premium Bonds?" repeated Austin Brierley blankly.

"Yes. Why shouldn't we keep the money earmarked for the Diocesan Education Fund in Premium Bonds until it's due to be handed over? Then there'd always be the chance of increasing the money with no risk. What d'you say to that?"

A few days later, Father Brierley went to Archbishop's House. He wasn't able to see the Cardinal himself, but he saw a Monsignor who was quite high up in the secretariat. The Monsignor was sympathetic, but not surprised – Father McGahern's eccentricities were well known to his superiors, it seemed. However, as the Monsignor explained, Father McGahern was an old man, and had not a great many years left to serve as parish priest. It would be difficult to persuade him to change his ways now, and harsh treatment to uproot him.

"Well, uproot me, then," said Father Brierley impulsively. "I can't face another week in that madhouse. Counting-house, I should say." He sat hunched in despair before the Monsignor's desk, his knees together and his joined hands thrust down between his thighs. He was conscious of the Monsignor's shrewd eyes appraising him.

"How would you like to go on a course?"

"What kind of course?"

"Whatever you like. Ecumenical studies, pastoral studies, biblical studies, you name it. You know about this new theological college we've just opened? One of the ideas is that it will provide refresher courses for the secular clergy."

It was on the tip of Austin Brierley's tongue to suggest that it was Father McGahern who stood in most urgent need of a refresher course, but he was not foolish enough to waste such an opportunity. "I used to run a New Testament study group, once," he said reminiscently, "for university students. I shouldn't at all mind picking up that sort of thing again."

The Monsignor looked slightly disappointed at his choice. "You don't think something like Pastoral Studies would be more relevant to your work, Father? Or catechetics?"

"No, Biblical Studies would be just the ticket. I'm terribly rusty. I don't suppose I've read a book on the subject since I left the seminary." He suddenly had a vision, flooding his mind like a sunburst, of himself sitting in a quiet room, slowly turning the pages of a thick, heavy book with nothing to do except finish it. "When can I start?" he said eagerly.

Austin Brierley found that things had changed a lot since his seminary days, especially in the field of biblical commentary. When he was a student, the methods of modern demythologizing historical scholarship had been regarded as permissible only in application to the Old Testament. The New Testament was taught as a historically reliable text, directly inspired by God and endorsed as such by the infallible authority of the Church. It came as something of a shock to discover that views mentioned formerly only to be dismissed as the irresponsible speculations of German Protestants and Anglican divines who could hardly be considered seriously as Christians at all, were now accepted as commonplace by many Catholic scholars in the field. The infancy stories about Jesus, for instance, were almost certainly legendary, it seemed, late literary accretions to the earliest and most reliable account of Jesus's life in Mark. The baby in the stable at Bethlehem, the angels and the shepherds, the star in the sky and the three kings, the massacre of the Innocents by Herod, the flight into Egypt – all fiction. Not meaningless, the books and articles and lectures hastened to add, for these fictions symbolized profound truths about the Christian faith; but certainly not factual, like the events one read about in the newspaper, or for that matter in Livy and Tacitus. And the Virgin Birth itself, then – was that a fiction? Well, opinion differed, but there were certainly many authorities who did not see that the literal, physical virginity of Mary (which was nowhere mentioned in Mark, Paul and John) was an essential part of the Gospel message. If this was accepted, then the doctrines of the Immaculate Conception and the Assumption also ceased to signify, they became dead letters, not worth arguing about. What was important was the figure of Jesus, the adult Jesus, himself. But here, too, a startling amount of sceptical sifting appeared to have taken place. The story of his baptism by John the Baptist was probably historical, but hardly the temptation in the desert, a narrative with obvious folktale characteristics deriving from the Jewish Babylonian exile, like the more spectacular miracle stories, the walking on the water and the draught of fishes. And the Resurrection. . . ? Well, here even the most adventurous demythologizers hesitated (it was another kind of How Far Could You Go?) but a few were certainly prepared to say that the Resurrection story was a symbolization of the faith found by the disciples through Jesus's death, that death itself was not to be feared, that death was not the end. *That* was the essential meaning of the Resurrection, not the literal reanimation of Jesus's corpse, an idea that could not possibly be as meaningful to an intelligent Christian of the twentieth century as it was to the inhabitants of a pre-scientific world.

Austin Brierley almost rubbed his eyes in disbelief sometimes. He read the professional theological journals with much the same mixed feelings of shock and liberation as Michael read *Lady Chatterley's Lover* and the sexually explicit fiction that was published in its wake. Of course the theologians and exegetes were generally more discreet than the novelists. They expressed themselves with elaborate caution in learned journals of tiny circulation, or exchanged ideas with like-minded scholars in private. It was understood that one did not flaunt the new ideas before the laity, or for that matter before the ordinary clergy, most of whom were deplorably ill-educated and still virtually fundamentalists when it came to the interpretation of the New Testament. The main thing was to get on quietly with the work of updating Catholic biblical scholarship while Rome was too pre-occupied with pastoral and liturgical experiment to bother checking up on them. Austin Brierley, however was unable to take this view of the matter. It seemed to him that a dangerous gap was opening up between the sophisticated, progressive theologians and exegetes on the one hand, and ordinary parochial Catholics on the other. The latter still went on believing in the nativity story and the miracles of Our Lord and all the rest of it as literally, historically true. If they woke up one day to discover that their own "experts" hadn't believed these things for years, they would feel cheated, and might understandably give up the practice of their religion in disgust. It was therefore, he concluded, the clear duty of priests like himself to try and educate the laity in the new, modern way of reading Scripture.

When his course was over, Father Brierley returned to his parish at the end of the Northern Line fired with this sense of mission. His first sermon was given on Ascension Day. He expounded the Gospel reading as a dramatic way of expressing the idea that Jesus was united with the Father in eternal life after his death on the cross, and thus promised all men of faith the same union and the same eternal life. To the disciples, to the first Christians, to the authors of the New Testament (especially the authors of Luke and the Acts, in which the Ascension was most elaborately described) it was natural to express this idea as a physical movement upwards in space, for they inhabited a flat world in which "Heaven" was identified with the sky above. Today, of course, we knew that the world was round, that space was curved, that there was neither up nor down in the cosmos, that Heaven was not a place that would ever be discovered by a space probe. To understand the Gospel story, we had to interpret it metaphorically.

After a few more sermons like this, the parishioners complained to Father McGahern, and Father McGahern to Archbishop's House, and Austin Brierley was seconded to another diocese in the Midlands that was allegedly short of priests. Before he left, the Monsignor gave him a sympathetic interview, shook his hand and advised him to go easy on the new biblical scholarship in his new job.

It was a small satisfaction to Austin Brierley that one year later Father McGahern had to be hurriedly retired from his parish, when it came out that he had put the entire proceeds of a special collection for the African missions on a horse in the St Leger. Had the horse lost, the

90

matter could have been hushed up, but as it won at 11-2, the priest was unable to resist boasting from the pulpit about his coup, and the popular press got hold of the story.

Sister Mary Joseph of the Precious Blood took her final vows in 1960. The evening before this solemn ritual, there was a ceremony (borrowed from the Benedictines) that in some ways remained even more vivid to her memory. In front of the assembled community, she had to signify her determination to embrace the life of poverty, chastity and obedience. Two tables were set out before her. On one, neatly folded, were the clothes she had worn on the day she entered the convent as a postulant; on the other, the habit of the order and, in a little dish, the silver ring which would be placed on her finger the next morning to confirm her as a Bride of Christ. She had to bow to the Mother Superior, and place her hand irrevocably on one table or another. If she chose the secular clothes, she was free to leave the convent without reproach. It made it easier to turn to the other table that those clothes looked so dowdy and insubstantial.

Soon afterwards she was sent to a girls' grammar school run by the Order in the North of England, to teach biology and botany. Her qualifications were particularly valued by the convent, which was usually obliged to hand over these subjects, so sensitive and potentially dangerous to faith and morals, to lay teachers. Shortly before Sister Mary Joseph's arrival, there had been an unfortunate episode involving a young married teacher who had taken it upon herself to give her fourth-formers a lesson on human reproduction in the General Science course. The policy of the school, as Mother Superior told Sister Mary Joseph at her first interview, was that there should be no class discussion of such matters before the Sixth Form, and then only within carefully defined limits. "What about menstruation?" Sister Mary Joseph enquired. "We assume that the girls' mothers will attend to that," was the reply. "But of course, we are always available to see the girls on an individual basis. You will find that they come to you when they need help."

Sister Mary Joseph found, however, that they very rarely came to her for that kind of help. Help with preparation for exams, or advice on applying to universities, yes. But everything to do with their sexual development they kept discreetly hidden from the nuns, though even from her own cloistered perspective it was obvious that society at large was becoming increasingly permissive and thus creating acute problems for adolescent girls. Every now and then there would be a sexual scandal of some kind, major or minor, in the school – a girl obliged to leave hurriedly because she was pregnant, a fourth-former caught with a copy of *Lady Chatterley's Lover* in her satchel: glimpses, as through chinks in a fence, of appalling temptations in the world outside. With some of her pupils, especially the brighter and more ambitious ones, Sister Mary Joseph enjoyed close friendship – for a time. But always there came a point of withdrawal on the part of the girl – silent, unexplained, unacknowledged, yet as sensible as the sudden disappearance of the sun behind a cloud, signifying (she was morally certain) that the girl in question had discovered Boys, or possibly, a boy. It was not, at first, a physical withdrawal – the girl might come to her just as often for extra coaching, for walks in the lunch hour – but it would not be the same, a deepening reserve separated them, a no-man's-land of unmentionable experience. It pained Sister Mary Joseph that this should be so, that the girls felt they could not share the crucial problems and anxieties of adolescence with her (nor, she was fairly certain, with any of the other nuns) and she came to the conclusion that the habit and rule of life which the Order had adopted as a sign of its dedication had become an impediment.

When, therefore, in 1965, the call went out from the Vatican Council to all religious orders of women to reappraise their statutes, rules and regulations, to consider what changes might be appropriate to make their vocations more effective in the circumstances of modern life, and Mother Superior convened a series of meetings of all the sisters in the community to discuss these momentous questions, Sister Mary Joseph came out strongly for reform. By the power of her intellect and the force of her eloquence, she carried the day. A television set was introduced into the recreation room. *The Times* was subscribed to. Sugar in tea and coffee was no longer restricted to Sundays and feast days. Permission was no longer required from Mother Superior to take a bath, make a telephone call, or go into town on errands, and sisters were allowed to go out alone, not always in pairs. The 6 p.m. curfew was extended to 10 p.m. For sisters with a full teaching load, meditation and recitation of the Office of Our Lady in Chapel at 5 a.m. was made optional, and the day began normally with mass at six.

The mood in the convent in those days was comparable to that of the French National Assembly in '89. The older generation was fearful and sometimes appalled at the rate of change; the younger and more progressive nuns were drunk on liberty, equality and sorority. They had been schooled in the novitiate to believe that the rules and restrictions of the Order were essential to the pursuit of holiness, necessary ways of subduing pride and crucifying the flesh. When word came from Rome that these rules might in many cases be the fossilized remains of obsolete manners and customs, the accumulated frustration of years exploded like a sudden release of compressed air. Mother Superior escaped, by a narrow margin of votes, having her office abolished and replaced by a committee re-elected monthly. A proposal to allow smoking was defeated only on health grounds, and another to allow attendance at theatres and cinemas was approved. But, without doubt, the subject of the greatest contention, and of the most drawn-out debate, was the question of dress.

Even Ruth (as she now thought of herself again, for the Jacobin nuns in the community began to call each other by their baptismal names rather than their names in religion, which they had not chosen for themselves and had never much liked) – even Ruth, progressive as she was, acknowledged the problems and pitfalls in modernizing dress. The disadvantages of the habit were obvious: it was expensive to make and to maintain (two lay sisters were almost constantly employed sewing, laundering, starching and ironing), it was impractical (particularly in the labs), it was excessively warm in summer, and (though this was disputed) it prevented the wearer from having a normal, relaxed relationship with ordinary people. How to modernize this dress was, however, a difficult and delicate question. When the Order had been founded, its habit differed only in detail from what most women wore at the time in provincial France; but that could hardly be a guideline for them now in the mid-nineteen-sixties, the era of the mini-skirt. As one middle-aged sister, otherwise inclined to liberal opinions, remarked: "After all, a nun does take a vow of chastity and I really don't think you should be able to see the tops of her stockings when she sits down "

"Most women wear tights, nowadays, I understand," said Ruth. But she took the point.

In the end it was agreed that a certain number of the sisters should experiment with various kinds of modernized dress, and that after a trial period the matter should be discussed again. As leader of the progressive party, Ruth felt morally obliged to volunteer, though she did so with misgivings. After the meeting, she went to her cell, took off her headdress and habit, and stood in her shift before the mirror on the inside of her cupboard door. It was something she had not done for many years – ever since being taught "custody of the eyes" as a novice (the mirror was supposed to be used only for checking one's appearance when fully dressed). Now it was almost physically painful to scrutinize herself. Her hair was thin and lifeless from years of confinement under the headdress, and a deep red weal ran across her forehead where the headband habitually pressed against the brow. Her bosom had grown fuller with the years, but her brassieres had been silently removed from her laundry shortly after she became a novice, to be replaced by a stiff bodice that flattened and spread the breasts into a kind of unitary mound. Her hips were as broad and clumsy as ever and (she stood on a chair and hitched up the skirt of her shift) her legs of almost uniform thickness from thigh to ankle. Walk through the gates with that lot dressed up in a tee-shirt and mini-skirt, she reflected wryly, and the populace would flee screaming in terror.

Eventually she settled for a navy tailored costume consisting of jacket and mid-calf skirt, worn with a high-necked blouse and a little cap and short veil, like a nursing sister's headdress. She had her hair cut and permed, and every night put it in curlers, obedient to the injunction of the hairdresser's assistant ("You must do it religiously," the girl had said, without apparent irony). When she and the other guinea-pigs first appeared in school in their new get-up, the effect on the girls was, of course, sensational. There were gasps and titters in Assembly, and a crescendo of whispered comment like bees swarming, before Mother Superior was able to restore order and silence. The volunteers were prepared for that, prepared to be the target for curious stares until the novelty wore off. Still, it was rather discouraging to overhear two girls in the cloakroom saying didn't Sister Mary Joseph look a fright in her new clothes, like a cross between a Meter Maid and a Home Help; and it took all Ruth's

94

self-control not to rush back to her cell and put on the habit again. Nor did the new costume have any perceptible effect of breaking down the emotional reserve between Ruth and her pupils. That, she now began to feel, was caused by something much more fundamental than clothing. One of the married teachers, a woman with whom she got on well, put it to her bluntly when they were discussing the catastrophic fall in new vocations to the order: "Frankly, Sister, girls these days aren't very keen on the idea of perpetual virginity."

Sister Mary Joseph sighed, and supposed she was right.

"It's hardly surprising," the teacher went on, "when you see what they're being fed all the time by the mass media. Just look at this."

She took from her bag a popular women's magazine. "I confiscated it from a girl in 5C this morning – she was reading it in a Library session, cheeky devil. Just look at these letters, and the answers."

Ruth glanced at the page folded back for her perusal. It was an agony column of a familiar type, entitled, *Ask Ann Field*. *"Dear Ann Field,"* the first letter began, *"I am seventeen and have been going out with a boy who I love very much for about six months . . ."* And underneath, in bold type, was Ann Field's answer:

> *Many people today believe that if the couple concerned have a loving and stable relationship, sex before marriage is not necessarily wrong and may be a way of putting a future marriage on a firm foundation. Only you and your boy friend can decide whether this, for you, would be an expression of genuine love or merely selfish exploitation. But if you do decide to commit yourself to such a relationship, for heaven's sake get advice about contraception first. There is, incidentally, no reason why you should not have a white wedding when the time comes.*

"If that isn't encouraging young people to jump into bed with each other, what is?" said the teacher. "How are a couple of teenagers supposed to know the difference between selfish pleasure and true love, I'd like to know?"

Ruth sighed again. "It must be a great responsibility to receive such letters," she said. "I suppose this, whatshername, Ann Field, I suppose she tries to help according to her lights."

The teacher looked surprised at this mild response, and reclaimed the magazine with a slightly aggrieved air, as though confiscating it for a second time. "Well, ten years ago, even five, you'd never have found a magazine like this approving sex before marriage," she said. "*I don't know what things are coming to.*"

Polly would have been gratified by Ruth's remark, had she overheard it, for as it happened she was Ann Field at this particular time. She was also married, to a successful television producer, to whom she had borne, precisely two years apart, a handsome son and pretty daughter; and she lived in a converted oast-house near Canterbury, with an *au pair* to help with the children and a milk-white Mini of her own to run about in. She led a busy, enjoyable life, only slightly marred by occasional twinges of anxiety about Jeremy's fidelity and perpetual worry about putting on weight, the two being connected.

They had met in 1960, when she was assigned to work on a programme with him. Jeremy's first marriage, to a well-known actress, was breaking up, and when the unit went on location in Scotland (it was a documentary about the depopulation of the Highlands, a somewhat lugubrious subject rendered all the more so by Jeremy's mood of the moment) they inevitably had an affair. The affair required more mothering than eroticism on Polly's part – long, introspective monologues from Jeremy in the huge, high-ceilinged bedrooms of Scottish three-star hotels, his head pillowed on her lap while she gently massaged his scalp – but the erotic moments were satisfactory too; and before his divorce proceedings were completed, Jeremy had asked Polly to marry him and had been accepted with alacrity.

It was necessarily a Registry Office wedding, a circumstance that caused Polly's parents some pain. Though well aware that she had not practiced her religion for years, they pretended to be ignorant of her way of life. Now her marriage to Jeremy (whom her mother insisted on referring to as *divorcé*, with a French accent, as if the English word were somehow indelicate) made it all public and irrevocable.

"I don't know where we went wrong, I'm sure," her mother said, snuffling into a dainty handkerchief, while Polly nibbled the end of a Biro and tried to draw up a list of the wedding presents she wanted.

"It's nothing to do with you, Mummy," said Polly. "It's the way things are. Most of the girls I was at school with are divorced and remarried or living with people. D'you remember the name of that stainless-steel tableware we saw in Harrods?"

"Well, I think it's shocking. The money your father paid that convent in fees. . . ."

"Why don't you sue them?" said Polly, trying to tease her mother out of her mood. But she was not amused.

"He's left one wife, how can you be sure he won't leave you?"

"He didn't leave her, she left him," Polly snapped back. But the barbed remark stung and was not easily forgotten.

They started a family immediately (Jeremy had had no children by his first wife) and to this end Polly gave up her job at the BBC, without much regret. However, they agreed that it would be socially irresponsible to have more than two children, and once Abigail was out of nappies and Jason had started playschool, Polly began to feel a certain return of surplus energy, the need for a more than merely domestic interest in life. "Something to keep me occupied while you're away filming," she explained to Jeremy, and added, taking care to smile as she did so: "To stop me worrying about what you might be getting up to with those pretty research assistants."

Jeremy pulled a face. "The last one they gave me had such powerful BO, I could hardly bear to go near her. . . . But seriously, darling, I'll keep my eyes open for an opportunity. Something you could do at home."

"You mean, like addressing envelopes?"

"Yes, sewing mailbags, threading beads, that sort of thing."

What Jeremy came up with, through a friend of a friend, the editor of a woman's magazine met at a party and invited down to the oast-house for a weekend, was Ann Field. The regular contributor, who had done the column for years, was retiring, and they wanted to experiment with a new, more up-to-date approach. Polly wrote some dummy replies to sample letters and was given a three month's trial. She had to travel up to Town once a week, but otherwise worked at home with the help of a dictaphone and a secretary who came out from Canterbury two days a week. The change of tone in Ann Field's column under Polly's tenure provoked an enormous postbag of comment, but when they totted up the pros and cons in the office it came out at 72% in Polly's favour, so she kept the job. She found it fascinating, demanding (she replied to all the letters, not just the ones that were published) and rewarding.

"I think of it as a kind of social work," she would say to her friends.

"I know I'm not trained or anything, but most of the women who write know what they want to do anyway. You just have to reassure them. Of course, sometimes they're in absolutely tragic situations, and then there's not much one can do except sympathize and refer them to the social services."

Sometimes she read letters aloud to Jeremy, especially poignant ones from wives with unfaithful husbands, hoping in this way to keep his conscience well-tuned. Some of the most harrowing letters were from Catholic women (and here she had to tread carefully, because the magazine would not allow her to disturb readers' religious beliefs, even in private correspondence) whose problems invariably derived from the lack of effective birth control: frigidity caused by fear of pregnancy, hideous gynaecological complications caused by excessive childbearing, and desertion by husbands unable to tolerate the consequences of their own feckless fucking, the teeming babies and the haggard spouse. "My God, the Church has an awful lot to answer for," she would mutter to herself, trying to find some comforting word for these pathetic women that was not false or hypocritical. Yet, deep down, Polly still believed in God, and, willy nilly, He was the Catholic God.

She and Jeremy had agreed that the children should make their own decision about religion when they were old enough to decide for themselves. But when Jason was ill one night, with an alarmingly high temperature, and Jeremy was away from home (he was in the States making a programme about the latest theory of how President Kennedy was assassinated) she was deeply troubled by the knowledge that the child hadn't been baptized and therefore, according to the Catechism, if he should die wouldn't go to heaven, but to Limbo. She tried to tell herself that it was all nonsense, that no God worth believing in was going to penalize the souls of innocent children, but it was no use, she couldn't sleep for worrying about it; and in the middle of the night she got up and baptized her son while he was asleep, pouring a trickle of tepid water from a plastic beaker on to his flushed forehead and whispering, "I baptize thee in the name of the Father and of the Son and of the Holy Ghost," as every Catholic was allowed to do in an emergency. Then, thinking that she might as well go the whole hog, Polly went along to Abigail's room and did her too. (She never told Jeremy or the children about what she had done, and when many years later Jason was converted to Catholicism while a student at Oxford, he was baptized all over again without knowing.)

"Here's a juicy one," Polly said to Jeremy one evening as they sat in the living-room after dinner around the open (and essentially decorative) fire, Jeremy going through the weeklies and Polly sifting her Ann Field mail. "I wonder if I dare print it. Listen, darling:

"Dear Ann Field,

I am a Catholic, married to a non-Catholic. Throughout our marriage my husband has used condoms as a method of family planning. Although this is against Catholic teaching, various priests have told me that it is alright for me to submit to it under protest. But now my husband wants me to go on the pill because, he says, condoms are primitive and spoil the act for him. Also, I have never had a proper vaginal orgasm and my husband says that it is because of the condoms too. He attaches great importance to my having a vaginal orgasm. Sometimes I think it means more to him than his own orgasms – "

Jeremy guffawed.

"Quite droll, isn't she?" said Polly, turning to the second page.

"I have asked two priests about taking the pill. The first one said I mustn't and recommended the safe method. But my periods are very irregular, and I have been advised not to conceive again (I have had one baby and several miscarriages). The other priest said it would be all right to take the pill for the sake of a higher good (that is, to preserve the marriage). Before I make up my mind, I would like to know if what my husband says is true, namely – "

"It's frightfully long," said Polly, turning over another page. Then, as her eye fell on the signature at the end of the letter, she let her hands fall limply into her lap. "My God," she said, "it's Violet."

"Violet?"

"Violet Casey. Meadowes, she is now. A girl I knew at College. She married her tutor in Classics. They seem to have moved up north."

"She sounds a rather screwed-up sort of person."

"She was."

"What are you going to do with the letter?"

"Answer it, of course."

"In your own name?"

"Certainly not. She wrote to Ann Field. Ann Field will reply."

"You know, you're getting a bit schizoid about this Ann Field business. Like Jekyll and Hyde."

"Which is which?" Without waiting for an answer, Polly went into her study and dictated a letter to Violet. Afterwards she reversed the tape and played it back:

"Dear Violet comma thank you for your letter full stop as to your main question comma two American researchers in this field have recently established by laboratory experiment that there is no such thing as a vaginal orgasm comma i e underline one that is independent of clitoral stimulation parenthesis Masters and Johnson comma Human Sexual Response underline Boston 1966 close parenthesis full stop however I am sure you and your husband would enjoy more relaxed and satisfying lovemaking if you used the pill full stop your second priest sounds like a sensible man stop yours sincerely Ann Field"

Polly pressed another button on her tape recorder and added a postscript:

"Why not experiment with different positions question mark for instance comma sitting astride your husband comma or kneeling so that he enters from behind question mark"

Polly believed fervently in every woman's right to frequent orgasms, and tried out conscientiously most of the things she read about in the sex manuals and magazines that Jeremy brought back with him from his travels. Jeremy, who had been rather repressed in youth, was making up for lost time. The rediscovery of sex, he was fond of saying, was what the sixties were all about. Every now and then, they sent the children out with the *au pair*, drew the curtains, and chased each other naked around the house, having it off in various unorthodox places, on the stairs, or under the dining-room table, even in the kitchen, where Polly would spread jam or chocolate syrup on her nipples and Jeremy would lick them clean. Their private code-word for sex was "research".

When Robin returned from America, not long after Violet's appearance at Angela and Dennis's wedding, they got together again; for

Robin found that although Violet was pretty impossible to live with, he missed her when she wasn't there. Violet, he decided, was an addiction, like smoking: it made you feel terrible most of the time, but you couldn't do without it. To cement their reunion he agreed to start a family, but Violet had several miscarriages (which she regarded as a Divine judgement on them for previously using contraceptives) before she managed, after an anxious pregnancy and painfully difficult labour, to produce a daughter. Robin was pleased with his little girl, whom they called Felicity, but said enough is enough, no more pregnancies, no more miscarriages, and was supported in this resolve by their doctor. Hence Violet's letter to Ann Field some years later, though there was another motive for writing it which Violet had not mentioned. She was afraid that Robin might have an affair with one of his students if he felt sexually dissatisfied at home.

By this time they had moved to a new university in the North of England for the sake of a big jump in salary for Robin. It was a place that was setting out to pioneer new developments in curriculum and teaching methods – Robin was in charge of a special programme teaching the classics in translation to all humanities students in their first year – and it attracted a lively, rather anarchic type of student, whose morals were a source of considerable scandal to the local community. The students lived in mixed, unsupervised accommodation, freely supplied with contraceptives by the Student Health Service. Robin, who rather regretted his move, sometimes described the University as "the only knocking-shop in the country that also gives degrees." This sardonic stance towards campus permissiveness was reassuring to Violet, but she was well aware that if Robin should take a fancy to one of his students it wouldn't require a weekend in the country and the prospect of marriage to coax her into bed.

When Ann Field's reply came back, Violet showed it to Robin and saw immediately from the expression on his face that she had done the wrong thing. He was furiously angry.

"You must be out of your mind, Violet!" he shouted. "Suppose they print it? I'll be the laughing-stock of the campus."

"They won't print it. Anyway, they never give names."

"What in God's name possessed you, an intelligent woman with an upper second, to write to a trashy woman's magazine for advice on such a subject?"

"I just thought it would be interesting to get an outsider's opinion. Have you heard of this book?"

"I think I read about it somewhere," said Robin. (To be precise, his source was *Playboy*, which he read regularly at his barber's while waiting to get his hair cut, but he did not care to acknowledge this.) "They got a lot of people to copulate in a laboratory, all wired up to machines and computers and things."

"Lord, it's a wonder they had any orgasms at all, in the circumstances," said Violet.

In the same year that Masters and Johnson published the results of their sex research, England won the World Cup at football, which millions saw as the bestowal of a special grace on the nation; John Lennon boasted that the Beatles were more popular than Jesus Christ and, to the disappointment of many, was not struck dead by a thunderbolt; Evelyn Waugh died, shortly after attending a Latin mass celebrated in private by an old Jesuit friend; Friday abstinence was officially abolished in the Roman Catholic Church, and the American Sisters of Loretto at the Foot of the Cross became the first order of nuns to abandon the habit completely. The narrator of Graham Greene's new novel observed: "When I was a boy I had faith in the Christian God. Life under his shadow was a very serious affair. . . . Now that I approached the end of life it was only my sense of humour that enabled me sometimes to believe in Him." In the spring of that year, 1966, at Duquesne University, Pennsylvania, and a little later at Notre Dame University, Indiana, small groups of Catholics began to experiment with "Pentecostal" prayer meetings, praying for each other that they might be filled with the gifts of the Holy Ghost as described in the New Testament – the gift of faith, the gift of tongues, the gifts of prophecy, healing, discernment of spirits, interpretation and exorcism. The results were, to the participants, exciting, but passed unremarked by the world at large. Public interest in the Catholic Church was still focused on the cliff-hanging saga of contraception.

In April it was leaked to the press that four conservative theologians on the Pontifical Commission had admitted that they could not show the intrinsic evil of contraception from Natural Law arguments alone. In other words, they still thought it was wrong, but only because the

Church had always said it was, and could not have been teaching error for centuries. However, as a letter in the *Tablet* pointed out, the Church had once taught that owning slaves was permissible and lending money at interest was a grave sin.

Miriam read the letter out to Michael.

"Who's it from?" he asked.

"Someone called Adrian Walsh."

"Good Lord! I was at college with him. Shows how things have changed. He used to be a real hardliner."

The Catholic press, and even the secular press, was full of correspondence and articles about Catholics and birth control. After reading a good deal of this material, Miriam said to Michael one day: "I've had enough. I'm going on the pill. It's obvious that there's going to be change sooner or later. I don't see the point of risking getting pregnant again." Their third child was then a few months old.

Michael was glad to agree, though he probably wouldn't have had the gumption to take the initiative himself. They continued going to Communion, but not to Confession. People went to Confession less and less frequently, anyway, even the idea of making one's Easter Duty seemed to have been quietly dropped, and that made it easier. Their sex life improved dramatically. From time to time Michael checked his conscience for symptoms of guilt. Nothing.

That summer, they shared a holiday cottage in Devon with Angela and Dennis. In the evenings, when the children had been fed, bathed, anointed with sunburn cream, read to, prayed with, put to bed, put *back* to bed, and had finally gone off to sleep, the four adults lolled, exhausted but content, in the little chintzy parlour and chatted. Dennis and Angela, who had found the cottage and were paying rather more than half of the rent, occupied two wing armchairs on either side of the fireplace, while Michael and Miriam sat between them on a small chesterfield. Each husband and wife had come to look more and more like their partners. Dennis and Angela were fair and well-fleshed, red from exposure to sun and wind. Michael and Miriam were both lean and tanned. Michael's hair still fell boyishly down across his forehead, but he wore it dry, now, not steeped in Brylcreem, while Dennis was beginning to lose his. Miriam, who could never bear to be still, however tired, embroidered, while Angela, six months pregnant with her fourth child, dozed with her hands clasped on her belly. Michael and Miriam, who made most of the conversational running, confided the decision they had made about birth control.

"We may do the same after this one," said Dennis, glancing speculatively at Angela. "She's asleep," he observed.

"I really think you should," said Miriam. "I know I couldn't stand the thought of having another one."

"Don't tempt Providence, darling," said Michael, glancing at the ceiling. "Himself might put a dud pill in the packet."

"Shut up," said Miriam, aiming a slap at him.

"Well, we'll have to see," said Dennis, rubbing the back of his neck where sunburned skin was flaking. "It's really up to Ange." As they hadn't had to worry about safe periods for the last few months, the question had lost some of its urgency for him, and, unlike Michael, he had no financial anxiety about the rapid growth of his family. Dennis had just landed a very good new job with an electronics firm in the Midlands.

"There's a proposal to install contraceptive machines in the students' cloakrooms at college," said Michael.

"You never told me!" Miriam exclaimed.

"In a Catholic Training College? I don't believe it," said Dennis.

"It's a very special machine, designed for Catholics," said Michael. "You put contraceptives in and get money out."

Their laughter woke Angela. "What are you talking about?" she yawned. When they told her, she said, "I don't know. I'm afraid I'd feel guilty even if I was rationally convinced there was nothing wrong with it."

"But *why*, Angela?" Miriam thrust her head forward in the way she had when arguing.

"I don't know – upbringing, I suppose. I'd feel I was cheating, some-how. Take my Mam and Dad. All those children, I don't suppose they wanted half that number. Why should we be able to please ourselves, and much better off too?"

"But you've got four, Angela, or soon will have. Four is enough in all conscience."

"Yes," Angela admitted. "Perhaps four will be enough."

"According to the population experts," said Michael, "it's two too many. If Catholics don't stop breeding soon, we'll all be standing shoulder to shoulder eating recycled sewage."

"Anyway," said Angela, "I'm determined to have this one at home, so that Dennis can stay with me right through." She practiced natural childbirth, and had had fair success with it, in spite of uncooperative maternity wards which (to his secret relief) had not allowed Dennis into the delivery room.

"Will the new house be ready in time?" Miriam asked.

"I think we'll just make it," said Dennis. "You must come and see us when we're settled in. You wouldn't like to be godparents again, I suppose?"

"Why don't you ask Edward and Tessa?" Michael suggested. "They don't live far from where you're going."

"That's a thought."

Upstairs, a child began to cry. Angela and Miriam looked at each other, listening.

"One of ours," Miriam said, and rose to attend to it. "I shan't bother to come down again, so I'll say goodnight." She winked covertly at Michael.

"I'll be up soon, darling," he said.

In October of that year, perhaps disturbed by evidence that increasing numbers of Catholics around the world were, like Michael and Miriam, anticipating a change in the Church's attitude to birth control, Pope Paul declared that there would be no pronouncement on the issue in the immediate future, and that meanwhile the traditional teaching must be rigidly adhered to. Monsignor Vallainc, head of the Vatican Press Office, when asked by journalists how the Pope could say that there was no doubt about the traditional teaching when his own commission had been appointed to investigate it, replied that the Church was in a state of certainty, but when the Pope had made his decision, whatever it was, the Church would pass from one state of certainty to another. This pronouncement was, according to Father Charles Davis, a leading theologian much admired by Austin Brierley, the last straw that broke the back of his faith in Catholicism, and shortly after it was made he left the priesthood, and the Church, and married, amid great publicity. His claims in the press that he had not left *in order* to get married were naturally greeted with some scepticism by his co-religionists, especially those of conservative views. Even Father Brierley preferred to believe that Charles Davis might have been unconsciously motivated by the wish to marry, rather than by intellectual doubts about the truth of the Catholic faith.

At about the same time as the Pope's postponement of a decision on birth control, another event occurred which for many people placed a much greater strain on religious belief of any variety.

It was a wet autumn, and the rain fell heavily and unremittingly, especially in the valleys of South Wales. At Aberfan, a small mining village near Merthyr Tydfil, a large coal-tip, a man-made mountain of mining waste, became waterlogged, honeycombed and sodden like a gigantic sponge. Springs and rivulets oozed from its sides and ran down into the valley below. No one took much notice. On Friday, 21 October, at 9.15 in the morning, just after morning prayers at the village Infants and Junior School, the tip became critically unstable, and with a thunderous, terrifying roar, as though the constipated bowels of the Industrial Revolution had suddenly opened, a colossal, obscene, evil-smelling mass of mud and stones avalanched into the valley, sweeping aside everything in its path, and burying the school, with some hundred and fifty children and their teachers.

The school was due to break up at midday that Friday to begin the half-term holiday, and had the landslide occurred a few hours later, and destroyed an empty building, it would have been called a miracle in the popular press; but as it did not, it was called a tragedy, the part, if any, played in it by God being passed over in tactful silence. On the following Sunday, prayers were offered throughout the land for the bereaved, for the rescue-workers and (in Catholic Churches) for the departed souls of the victims, but few ministers of religion took up the theological challenge of the event itself. One of them was Father Brierley, preaching at the 9.30 mass in his new parish, a dull market town in a flat landscape that seemed almost scandalously safe that weekend.

The traditional response of Christians to catastrophes such as Aberfan, he said, was to regard it as some kind of punishment for man's sinfulness, or to accept it unquestioningly as the will of God. Both reactions were unsatisfactory. For if it was mankind's sinfulness that was being punished, it was totally unjust that the punishment

106

should fall on these particular children and their families. And if it was the will of God, why should we not question it? If God, as Christians believed, was everywhere in the Universe, then He must be prepared to take responsibility for everything in it, and accept the anger and bitterness he aroused in the hearts of men at times like this.

The Biblical text that was most relevant was the Book of Job, the story of the virtuous man who was suddenly visited by the most appalling afflictions – his sons and daughters killed, his prosperity taken away, and his own body afflicted with loathesome sores. Why did God allow this to happen? Job himself could not understand it, and was unconvinced by the arguments of the pious who tried to reconcile him to his fate. He felt utter despair and alienation from God, and while never denying God's existence, had the courage to challenge God to justify himself:

> "Yes, I am a man, and he is not; and so no argument,
>   no suit between us is possible.
> There is no arbiter between us,
>   to lay his hand on both,
>   to stay his rod from me
>   or keep away his daunting terrors.
> Nonetheless, I shall speak, not fearing him:
>   I do not see myself like that at all.
> Since I have lost all taste for life,
>   I will give free rein to my complaints.
> I shall let my embittered soul speak out.
> I shall say to God, 'Do not condemn me,
>   but tell me the reason for your assault.
> Is it right for you to injure me,
>   cheapening the work of your own hands?'"

When he had finished reading this passage, Austin Brierley looked up from his notes and surveyed the congregation. He saw the usual blank, bored faces, a few with their eyes closed, some perhaps actually asleep, mothers with babies in arms anxiously watching their fidgeting older offspring, a man going surreptitiously through his pockets for change to be ready for the Offertory collection. He didn't know quite what he had expected. Tears? Shocked expressions? Heads eagerly nodding agreement? Not really, but he felt disappointed that the response was as flat as on any other Sunday. He hurried to his conclusion.

Eventually, God had spoken to Job, and Job submitted to his superior wisdom and power. The words that convinced him would not, perhaps, convince a modern Job. They would certainly not convince the parents of Aberfan. But that was not the point. The point of the story – which was, of course, a myth, a poem – was that God only spoke to Job because Job complained to God, gave free rein to his complaint and let his embittered soul speak out. We should be less than human if we did not, this dark weekend, do the same on behalf of the victims of Aberfan.

At lunch, the Parish Priest asked him casually if he planned to repeat his sermon at the evening mass.

"Yes, why? Did anyone object to it?"

"Well, I did hear one or two comments passed after the nine-thirty. It seems to have upset a few people."

"Good," said Austin Brierley. "Someone was listening, then."

"You're a queer fellow, Father," said the PP, digging into his apple crumble. "What good does it do, making people doubt the goodness of God?"

"What are we, then, his priests or his public relations officers?" said Austin Brierley fiercely, and immediately apologised.

"You're looking overtired, Father," said the PP kindly. "You could probably do with a holiday."

"I had a holiday a couple of months ago."

"A retreat, then. Or perhaps you'd like to go on a course of some kind."

At about the same time that Sunday, Edward and Tessa were driving along the M1 on their way to the baptism of Dennis and Angela's fourth baby, which had arrived safely, if a little early, at the beginning of October. The rain fell heavily, and cars that passed them threw up great fountains of spray which lashed the windscreen and temporarily overwhelmed the wipers. It had stopped raining at Aberfan, their car radio informed them, which was some small blessing for the rescue workers, still shovelling wearily at the millions of tons of mud. (Adrian was not among them, though on hearing the first news of the catastrophe he had thrown tools into the boot of his car and driven nonstop to South Wales, only to be turned back by the police at Abergavenny; there were more than enough volunteer diggers from the local mining communities, better qualified for the job than himself, the police gave him to understand in the kindest possible way, and only vital traffic was being admitted into the disaster area. So the heroic gesture eluded him once again.) So far, the car radio informed Edward and Tessa, one hundred and forty bodies had been recovered.

"Please turn it off, Teddy," said Tessa, "I can't bear to listen. And do slow down."

'I'm only doing fifty," said Edward, turning off the radio.

"I know, but these conditions are so treacherous." Tessa was not normally a nervous passenger, but she felt there was malice in the elements today. Her three children, strapped to the back seat, and the fourth in her womb, seemed terribly vulnerable. She feared for some cruel accident, a skid or collision that would overwhelm them all like Aberfan. "What a day!" she exclaimed, for the sixth time. "I wish I hadn't decided to come. I should have stayed at home with the children and let you go on your own. It will be too much for Angela, so many people."

"Dennis said she was in great form. Apparently the delivery went very smoothly. He was boasting terrifically about having watched the whole thing. Seemed to forget I might have witnessed one or two births myself."

Dennis and Angela's new house was part of a middle-class housing estate still under construction on the outskirts of a small Warwickshire village. The houses, detached and semi-detached, in four basic designs, stuck up rawly from unturfed, rubble-strewn garden lots separated by wire-mesh fences. There were puddles and mud everywhere. It seemed impossible to get away from the physical ambience of Aberfan. And inside the house, in the lounge, a television screen flickered with monochrome pictures of the wall of sludge, the weary, mudstained figures of the workers, the numbed, grief-stricken faces of the watching mothers. Tessa's two oldest children immediately seated themselves in front of the set, which was being watched by Dennis's parents.

"I think it's terrible," said Dennis's mother. "The way they show everything on television these days. It's not right, interrogating people who've just lost their children."

"There've been a lot of complaints about it," observed her husband.

But neither of them seemed to think of turning the television off – as though the transmission of harrowing pictures were a natural force, like the landslide itself, which had to be borne as long as it lasted.

Dennis offered Tessa and Edward a cup of tea before they all set off for the church. "Ange is upstairs, getting the baby ready," he said. "Go up if you like."

"Becky, come and see the new baby," said Tessa, anxious to get her away from the TV and its morbid pictures. Edward, sipping his tea and nibbling a biscuit, took her place, his attention irresistibly drawn to the screen.

"Ghastly, isn't it?" said Dennis. But there was no real horror in his voice: he was still high on the experience of the birth, which he had found extraordinarily moving, and the pride of his own part in it, for which he had been commended by the midwife. The tragedy of Aberfan could not penetrate this private euphoria. He was also childishly delighted with his new house, and couldn't rest until Edward had been shown round it – the modern, fully-fitted kitchen, the separate utility room for washing machine and deepfreeze, the big garage with his workbench and power tools already installed, the downstairs cloakroom and second loo, the upstairs bathroom with shower and four good-sized bedrooms, in the largest of which they found Angela and Tessa sitting on the edge of the divan bed, chatting, with the new baby lolling between them on a clean nappy.

"So this is our godchild," said Edward, stooping over the baby. "How is she?"

"An absolute angel," said Angela. "Never cries. I have to wake her up to give her her feeds."

Edward's hands lightly caressed the child from her cranium to her feet. He took the tiny hands in his and turned them this way and that, tickled the infant's toes and offered her the knuckle of his little finger to suck. Tessa could tell that something was worrying Edward, that he was spinning out the conversation with the fondly smiling Angela while his fingers and eyes probed. When they got back to their car to drive to the church she said, quietly so that the children in the back would not hear, "There's nothing wrong, is there?"

Edward turned on the car radio. Music flooded the car. A familiar voice with the accent of Liverpool sang:

Father McKenzie, writing the words of a sermon that no one will hear,
No one came near . . .

"Ooh! Beatles!" cried Becky, already hooked on pop music at seven. She clapped her hands in delight.

"Downs' Syndrome," said Edward.

"Oh, my God. Are you sure? She doesn't look like a mongol. The eyes – "

"You can't always tell from the eyes. I'm ninety-nine per cent sure. There are more reliable indications – markings on the hands, for instance."

"And they have no idea?"

"Evidently not. The doctor must have spotted it, even if the midwife didn't. Too scared to break it to them, I suppose. Sometimes the parents don't find out for months. Years, even."

"Oh, my God, how awful for Angela." Tessa clutched her own swollen belly. "What causes it?"

"An extra chromosome, it occurs at conception, nobody knows why. Older women are more at risk, but that wouldn't apply to Angela." He took her hand and squeezed it. "Or to you."

She smiled wanly, acknowledging that he had read her thoughts correctly. Edward did not mention the theory that the Safe Method might be responsible for such congenital defects, and was able to conceal his own alarm at this extra piece of confirming evidence. In fact, both of them were queerly and horribly relieved that the affliction had fallen upon Dennis and Angela, for it somehow made it seem more likely that they themselves would escape unscathed. All day, Tessa had felt that there was some malice in the air, still unsated by Aberfan. Now that it had struck, had shown itself, she felt less threatened.

But the baptism was an ordeal, and she could not forbear to weep as she held the infant's head over the font, and the water splashed on to it, and the child gazed back into Tessa's eyes without uttering a single cry. She was named Nicole, after a French pen friend Angela had kept in touch with since childhood. "Wasn't she good?" said the grandmother afterwards. "Not a murmur!"

"Are you going to say anything?" Tessa asked Edward in the car going back to the house.

"I must. I'll suggest a paediatrician should have a look at the child. I'll have a word with Dennis before we leave."

"Dennis will take it harder than Angela," said Tessa.

"You may be right, but I must tell him first."

After the tea and cakes, while Tessa was getting their children ready for the return journey, Edward asked Dennis to show him how the sander attachment worked on his power tool, and Dennis led the way to the garage. Edward followed, feeling like an assassin with a loaded gun in his pocket.

I did say this wasn't a comic novel, exactly.

4

How they lost the fear of Hell

AT some point in the nineteen-sixties, Hell disappeared. No one could say for certain when this happened. First it was there, then it wasn't. Different people became aware of the disappearance of Hell at different times. Some realized that they had been living for years as though Hell did not exist, without having consciously registered its disappearance. Others realized that they had been behaving, out of habit, as though Hell were still there, though in fact they had ceased to believe in its existence long ago. By Hell we mean, of course, the traditional Hell of Roman Catholics, a place where you would burn for all eternity if you were unlucky enough to die in a state of mortal sin.

On the whole, the disappearance of Hell was a great relief, though it brought new problems.

In 1968, the campuses of the world rose in chain-reaction revolt, Russia invaded Czechoslovakia, Robert Kennedy was assassinated, and the civil rights movement started campaigning in Ulster. For Roman Catholics, however, even in Ulster, the event of the year was undoubtedly the publication, on 29 July, of the Pope's long-awaited encyclical letter on birth control, *Humanae Vitae.* Its message was: no change.

The omniscience of novelists has its limits, and we shall not attempt to trace here the process of cogitation, debate, intrigue, fear, anxious prayer and unconscious motivation which finally produced that document. It is as difficult to enter into the mind of a Pope as it must be for a Pope to enter into the mind of, say, a young mother of three, in a double bed, who feels her husband's caressing touch and is divided between the desire to turn to him and the fear of an unwanted pregnancy. It is said that Pope Paul was astonished and dismayed by the storm of criticism and dissent which his encyclical aroused within the Church. It was certainly not the sort of reception Popes had come to expect for their pronouncements. But in the democratic atmosphere recently created by Vatican II, Catholics convinced of the morality of contraception were no longer disposed to swallow meekly a rehash of discredited doctrine just because the Pope was wielding the spoon. Of course, if the Pope had come down on the other side of the argument, there would no doubt have been an equally loud chorus of protest and complaint from the millions of Catholics who had loyally followed the traditional teaching at the cost of having many more children and much less sex than they would have liked, and were now too old, or too worn-out by parenthood, to benefit from a change in the rules – not to mention the priests who had sternly kept them toeing the line by threats of eternal punishment if they didn't. The Pope, in short, was in a no-win situation. With hindsight, it is clear that his best course would have been to procrastinate and equivocate indefinitely so that the ban on contraception was never explicitly disowned, but quietly allowed to lapse, like earlier papal anathemas against co-education, gaslighting and railways. However, by setting up in the glare of modern publicity a commission to investigate and report on the matter, first Pope John and then Pope Paul had manoeuvred the Papacy into a dogmatic cul-de-sac from which there was no escape. The only saving grace in the situation (suggesting that the Holy Spirit might, after all, have been playing some part in the proceedings) was that it was made clear on its publication that the encyclical was not an "infallible" pronouncement. This left open the theoretical possibility, however narrowly defined, of conscientious dissent from its conclusions, and of some future reconsideration of the issue.

Thus it came about that the first important test of the unity of the Catholic Church after Vatican II, of the relative power and influence of conservatives and progressives, laity and clergy, priests and bishops, national Churches and the Holy See, was a great debate about – not, say, the nature of Christ and the meaning of his teaching in the light of modern knowledge – but about the precise conditions under which a man was permitted to introduce his penis and ejaculate his semen into the vagina of his lawfully wedded wife, a question on which Jesus Christ himself had left no recorded opinion.

This was not, however, quite such a daft development as it seems on first consideration, for the issue of contraception was in fact one which drew in its train a host of more profound questions and implications, especially about the pleasure principle and its place in the Christian scheme of salvation. It may seem bizarre that Catholics should have been solemnly debating whether it was right for married couples to use reliable methods of contraception at a time when society at large was calling into question the value of monogamy itself – when schoolgirls still in gym-slips were being put on the Pill by their mothers, when young couples were living together in what used to be called sin as a matter of course, adultery was being institutionalized as a party game, and the arts and mass media were abandoning all restraints in the depiction and celebration of sexuality. But in fact there was a more than merely ironic connection between these developments inside and outside the Church. The availability of effective contraception was the thin end of a wedge of modern hedonism that had already turned Protestantism into a parody of itself and was now challenging the Roman Catholic ethos. Conservatives in the Church who predicted that approval of contraception for married couples would inevitably lead sooner or later to a general relaxation of traditional moral standards and indirectly encourage promiscuity, marital infidelity, sexual experiment and deviation of every kind, were essentially correct, and it was disingenuous of liberal Catholics to deny it. On the other hand, the conservatives had unknowingly conceded defeat long before by approving, however grudgingly, the use of the Rhythm or Safe Method. Let me explain. (Patience, the story will resume shortly.)

It has always been recognized that the sexual act has two aspects or functions: I, procreation and II, the reciprocal giving and receiving of sensual pleasure. In traditional Catholic theology, Sex II was only legitimate as an incentive to, or spin-off from, Sex I – which of course was restricted to married couples; and some of the early Fathers thought that even for married couples, Sex II was probably a venial sin. With the development of a more humane theology of marriage, Sex II was dignified as the expression of mutual love between spouses, but it was still forbidden to separate this from Sex I, until the twentieth century, when, at first cautiously, and then more and more explicitly, the Church began to teach that married couples might deliberately confine their sexual intercourse to the infertile period of the woman's monthly cycle in order to regulate their families. This permission was still hedged about with qualifications – the method was only to be used with "serious reasons" – but the vital principle had been conceded: Sex II was a Good Thing In Itself. Catholic pastoral and theological literature on the subject of marriage took up the topic with enthusiasm; the bad old days of repression, of shame and fear about human sexuality, were denounced – it was all the fault of St Paul, or Augustine, or Plato – anyway, it was all a regrettable mistake; and married couples were joyfully urged to make love with, metaphorically speaking (and literally too if they liked), the lights on.

This was all very well, but certain consequences followed. If Sex II is recognized as a Good Thing In Itself, it is difficult to set limits, other than the general humanistic rule that nobody should be hurt, on how it may be enjoyed. For example, the traditional Christian disapproval of extramarital sex had an obvious social justification as a means of ensuring responsible parenthood and avoiding inbreeding, but with the development of efficient contraception these arguments lost most of their force, as secular society had already discovered by the mid-twentieth century. Why, therefore, should responsible adults have to be married to share with each other something Good In Itself? Or to take a more extreme example, anal intercourse, whether homosexual or heterosexual, had always been condemned in terms of the deepest loathing by traditional Christian moralists, sodomy being listed in the Penny Catechism as one of the Four Sins Crying to Heaven for Vengeance (the others, you may be curious to know, being Wilful Murder, Oppression of the Poor, and Defrauding Labourers of Their

Wages). But if the sharing of sexual pleasure is a Good Thing In Itself, irrespective of the procreative function, it is difficult to see any objections, other than hygienic and aesthetic ones, to anal intercourse between consenting adults, for who is harmed by it? The same applies to masturbation, whether solitary or mutual, and oral-genital sex. As long as non-procreative orgasms are permitted, what does it matter how they are achieved?

Thus it can be seen that the ban on artificial birth control, the insistence that every sexual act must remain, at least theoretically, open to the possibility of conception, was the last fragile barrier holding back the Catholic community from joining the great collective pursuit of erotic fulfilment increasingly obsessing the rest of Western society in the sixth decade of the twentieth century; but the case for the ban had been fatally weakened by the admission that marital sex might be confined to the "safe period" with the deliberate intention of avoiding conception. In practice, the Safe Method was so unreliable that many couples wondered if it hadn't been approved only because it wasn't safe, thus ensuring that Catholics were restrained by the consciousness that they might after all have to pay the traditional price for their pleasure. Clerical and medical apologists for the method, however, never admitted as much; on the contrary, they encouraged the faithful with assurances that Science would soon make the Safe Method as reliable as artificial contraception. (Father Brierley's Parish Priest, in the course of a heated argument, assured him that "the Yanks were working on a little gadget like a wristwatch that would make it as simple as telling the time.") But the greater the efforts made to achieve this goal, the more difficult it became to distinguish between the permitted and forbidden methods. There was nothing, for instance, noticeably "natural" about sticking a thermometer up your rectum every morning compared to slipping a diaphragm into your vagina at night. And if the happy day *did* ever dawn when the Safe Method was pronounced as reliable as the Pill, what possible reason, apart from medical or economic considerations, could there be for choosing one method rather than the other? And in that case, why wait till then to make up your mind?

Following such a train of thought to its logical conclusion, millions of married Catholics had, like Michael and Miriam, come to a decision to use artificial contraception without dropping out of the Church.

Some couples needed the impetus of a special hardship or particular crisis to take this step (Angela went on the Pill immediately after the birth of her mentally handicapped child; and Tessa, though happily her new baby was born sound and healthy, followed suit, with Edward's full support, neither of them being inclined to take any further risks) but once they had done so it seemed such an obviously sensible step to take that they could hardly understand why they had hesitated so long. It helped, of course – indeed, it was absolutely vital – that, as explained above, they had lost the fear of Hell, since the whole system of religious authority and obedience in which they had been brought up, binding the Church together in a pyramid of which the base was the laity and the apex the Pope, depended on the fear of Hell as its ultimate sanction. If a Catholic couple decided, privately and with a clear conscience, to use contraceptives, there was nothing that priest, bishop or Pope could do to stop them (except, in some countries, making the wherewithal difficult to obtain). Thus contraception was the issue on which many lay Catholics first attained moral autonomy, rid themselves of superstition, and ceased to regard their religion as, in the moral sphere, an encyclopaedic rule-book in which a clear answer was to be found to every possible question of conduct. They were not likely to be persuaded to reverse their decision by the tired arguments of *Humanae Vitae*, and some previously loyal souls were actually provoked by it into joining the rebels (Adrian, who had been teetering on the contraceptive brink for years, was so exasperated by the first reports of the encyclical that he rushed out of the house and startled the local chemist's shop by strident demands for "a gross of sheaths prophylactic" – a phrase he dimly remembered from Army invoices, but which smote strangely on the ears of the girl behind the counter). Of course, there were many Catholics who with more or less resignation continued to believe that the Pope's word was law, and many who disobeyed it with a residual sense of guilt that they were never able to lose completely, and yet others who finally left the Church in despair or disgust; but on the whole the most remarkable aspect of the whole affair was the new-found moral independence of the laity which it gradually revealed. Indeed, it could be said that those who suffered most from *Humanae Vitae* were not married layfolk at all, but the liberal and progressive clergy.

118

Conservative bishops and priests had the satisfaction of seeing their beliefs and pastoral practice endorsed by the Pope, but those who had, in the period of uncertainty immediately preceding the publication of *HV*, interpreted the rules flexibly, or actually argued the case for their revision, were now awkwardly placed. What was for the laity a question of conduct which they might settle privately according to their own consciences, was for the clergy a question of doctrine and obedience that was necessarily public. The Holy Father had spoken, and bishops and priests, whatever their own opinions about the matter, were required to promulgate and enforce his message from the pulpit and in the confessional. Some were only too pleased to do so; but many were not, and feared massive disillusionment and disaffection among the laity if the Church simply reverted to the old hard-line teaching. Bishops were in a particularly difficult position, because they could not reject *Humanae Vitae* without the risk of provoking schism. What the more liberal hierarchies did was to make a minimalist interpretation of the encyclical – to say that, while contraception was, as the Pope affirmed, objectively wrong, there might be subjective circumstances which made it so venial a sin as scarcely to be worth worrying about, and certainly not a reason for ceasing to go to mass and Holy Communion. By this casuistry they accepted *HV* in principle while encouraging a tolerant and flexible approach to its enforcement in pastoral practice. Most of the priests who had been dismayed by the encyclical accepted this compromise, but some were unwilling or unable to do so, and if their bishop or religious superior happened to be conservative and authoritarian, the consequences could be serious.

Such priests were apt to become acutely conscious of internal contradictions in their own vocations. For the more deeply they were driven, by the pressure of debate and the threats of ecclesiastical discipline, to analyse the grounds of their dissent from *HV*, the further they were carried towards an endorsement of sexual pleasure as a Good Thing In Itself. And the further they were carried in *that* direction, the more problematical their own vows of celibacy appeared. As long as sexual pleasure had been viewed with suspicion by Christian divines, as something hostile to spirituality, lawful only as part of man's procreative function in God's scheme, the vow of celibacy had obvious point. Unmarried and chaste, the priest was materially free to serve his flock, and spiritually free from the distractions of fleshly indulgence. But when the new theology of marriage began to emerge, in which sexual love was redeemed from the repression and reticence of the past, and celebrated as (in the words of the Catholic Theological Society of America) "self-liberating, other-enriching, honest, faithful, socially responsible, life-giving and joyous," the value of celibacy no longer seemed self-evident, and a progressive priest might find himself in the paradoxical position of defending the right of the laity to enjoy pleasures he himself had renounced long ago, on grounds he no longer believed in. A similar collapse of confidence in the value of vowed virginity affected nuns.

Of course, it could still be argued that, without families of their own to care for, priests and nuns were free to dedicate themselves to the service of others; but this argument, too, only holds good as long as reliable contraception is forbidden. Otherwise, why should not priests and nuns marry each other, and take vows of sterility rather than chastity, forgoing the satisfactions of having offspring in order to serve the community at large, but still enjoying the consolations of that interpersonal genital communion which, the orthodox wisdom of the modern age insists, is essential to mental and physical health? For that matter, why, given new control over their own biology, should not women themselves be priests? For the prejudice against the ordination of women is demonstrably rooted in traditional sexual attitudes rather than in theology or logic.

The crisis in the Church over birth control was not, therefore, the absurd diversion from more important matters that it first appeared to many observers, for it compelled thoughtful Catholics to re-examine and redefine their views on fundamental issues: the relationship between authority and conscience, between the religious and lay vocations, between flesh and spirit. The process of questioning and revision it triggered off continues, although *Humanae Vitae* itself is a dead letter to most of the laity and merely an embarrassing nuisance to most of the clergy. It is clear that the liberal, hedonistic spirit has achieved irresistible momentum within the Church as without, that young Catholics now reaching adulthood have much the same views about the importance of sexual fulfilment and the control of fertility as their non-Catholic peers, and that it is only a matter of time before priests are allowed to marry and women are ordained. There is, however, no cause for progressives to gloat or for conservatives to sulk. Let copulation thrive, by all means; but man cannot live by orgasms alone, and he certainly cannot die by them, except, very occasionally, in the clinical sense. The good news about sexual satisfaction has little to offer those who are crippled, chronically sick, mad, ugly, impotent – or old, which all of us will be in due course, unless we are dead already. Death, after all, is the overwhelming question to which sex provides no answer, only an occasional brief respite from thinking about it. But enough of this philosophizing.

Early in 1969, nearly everyone who used to attend the Thursday morning masses in the old days at Our Lady and St Jude's received long-distance phone calls from Adrian. Most of them had been out of touch with him for many years, but he spoke to them as if it was only yesterday that they had breakfasted at Lyons in the Tottenham Court Road. He had traced Michael's phone number through a Catholic periodical for which Michael occasionally wrote book reviews, and from Michael he got Dennis's number, and so on. Adrian sat at his desk in the Town Hall where he worked and dialled them all on STD, robbing the ratepayers without qualms because it was in a good cause, and the cause was short of funds. He was chairman of a lay pressure group calling itself Catholics for an Open Church, COC for short, which had recently been formed, in Adrian's words, "to fight *HV* and help priests who are in trouble over it". One of these priests was Father Brierley.

"That meek little man who married Angela and Dennis?" said Miriam. "I'd never have thought he had it in him."

"Seems he read out his bishop's pastoral letter about *Humanae Vitae*, which was pretty hard-line, and then told the congregation it was still a matter of conscience."

"Is that all?"

"Well, then a reporter on the local paper interviewed him and he said that personally he thought the Pope was up the creek, or words to that effect, and some mean-minded parishioner sent a cutting to the bishop."

"And what does Adrian Whatsisname want us to do about it?"

121

"He wants us to join this Catholics for an Open Church thing, and sign an open letter to the Cardinal about Father Brierley and the other suspended priests."

"Sounds like a good idea."

"The College Governors won't like it," said Michael, somewhat sheepishly.

"To hell with them," said Miriam.

"You know I'll be up for promotion soon?"

"To hell with that."

"OK," said Michael. "I'll tell Adrian we'll join."

As always, he admired Miriam's moral certitude. Breathing it in as if she had handed him an oxygen mask, he felt suddenly strong and reckless, excited by the possibilities of Catholics for an Open Church. The spirit of protest was abroad, but Michael had not yet been able to find a cause he could plausibly identify with. He was too old for the student movement, too apolitical for the New Left (*Slant* had finally bored him), too moral (or too timid) for the Counter Culture of drugs, rock and casual sex. He was finding himself pushed to the margins of the decade, forced into a posture of conservatism and conventionality which made him feel as if his youth were disappearing at an ever-increasing speed, like the earth beneath an astronaut. The idea of challenging ecclesiastical authority in the cause of sexual fulfilment for married couples and freedom of speech for priests seemed an opportunity to hitch his wagon to the *Zeitgeist* in good faith. Michael did not, of course, analyse his motives as explicitly as this, and did not understand (he accounted for it purely as impulse buying) why, shortly after sending off his subscription to Catholics for an Open Church, he bought a pair of the new-style trousers with flared bottoms and a copy of the Beatles "white" double album, his first non-classical record. He had joined the sixties, in the nick of time.

Michael wore his new trousers to the first annual general meeting of Catholics for an Open Church, held in London that summer, but it proved to be a sadly unfashionable gathering on the whole. Adrian, in the chair, set the sartorial keynote in his business suit, shiny with wear and bulging at the breast pocket with a quiverful of ballpoint pens, flashes of colour against the dark blue serge like the silk markers of his missal in the gloom of Our Lady and St Jude's. He was going bald but did not seem otherwise noticeably different from those days – still stiff, impatient and dogmatic, though he had moved across the ideological spectrum from Right to Left in the meantime. A cursory glance around the hall, hired for the day from the Quakers, told Michael that he had not joined the equivalent of Californian Flower Power or the Paris student communes. Most of the occupants of the rows of bentwood chairs were ordinary, plain-featured, drably dressed, middle-class couples in their late thirties or early forties, with a sprinkling of older people whose concern about *HV* must, he assumed, be entirely academic. Indeed, some of the younger members seemed anxious to claim a similar disinterestedness. "We find that the Safe Method works perfectly well for us," said one man to Michael and Miriam over coffee, his wife, with her mouth full of biscuit, nodding eager agreement, "but we sympathize with others less fortunate." Another man, with a bushy beard and huge, horny-toed feet in sandals, said, "Have you ever tried *coitus reservatus*? It's highly recommended by Eastern mystics. Of course, you have to learn the meditative techniques that go with it." "A bit risky while you're learning, isn't it?" said Michael. Behind him a woman was saying, "I wouldn't care about the population explosion if only it wasn't happening in our house."

Adrian read out some letters of support, mostly anonymous, for the group's aims, which included some poignant case histories and memorable *cris de coeur* ("What is love? What is conjugal love? Why did God make it so nice?" wrote one correspondent with five children and a wife suffering from high blood pressure). Then a somewhat embarrassed-looking Father Brierley was paraded for their edification, rather like an Iron Curtain defector at a press conference. His sports jacket, trousers and roll-neck shirt were ill-co-ordinated in colour and glinted with the sheen of cheap synthetic fabric. He stammered out a speech of thanks for the group's support – financial as well as moral, for he was not receiving any stipend while under suspension. Catholics for an Open Church had received only a curt acknowledgement of its original letter to the Cardinal, and now Adrian read out the draft of a second, follow-up letter for the meeting's approval. The membership quickly split into two factions, one anxious to be respectful and conciliatory, the other determined to be bold and challenging. Amendments and counter-amendments flew backwards and forwards.

The man in sandals made a determined effort to get *coitus reservatus* into the text somehow or other. Tempers rose. It was hard to tell whether the speakers were more hostile to *HV* or to each other. Adrian grew hoarse and irritable, he glared contemptuously at the members like the captain of a mutinous crew, and Dorothy, who was taking the minutes, put down her pen with a theatrical flourish, folded her arms and lifted her eyes to the ceiling. Then Edward – Edward, who had slipped into the back of the hall unnoticed by Michael and Miriam – stood up and took some of the tension out of the atmosphere with a self-deprecating joke and moved that Adrian and Father Brierley should be left to revise the letter in the light of the comments expressed. Michael seconded the motion and it was carried by a large majority. The meeting was closed, and Adrian announced that Father Brierley would say mass for the members before they dispersed. Strictly speaking, he wasn't supposed to do this while under suspension, but as a jovial African supporter said, mixing his proverbs a little, "Hang my lambs, hang my sheep."

At the mass, real wholemeal bread was consecrated and broken, and handed round in baskets, and the congregation also shared the chalice. At the words, "Let us give each other the sign of peace," several couples embraced instead of giving each other the customary handshake. Michael and Miriam spontaneously followed suit and, because of the novelty of the circumstances, Michael experienced a perceptible erection as their lips touched. He was not abashed, as at a similar occurrence at the St Valentine's Day mass long ago; after all, that was what they were all gathered together here for, to assert the compatibility of *eros* and *agape*, to answer positively the questions, what was love, what was conjugal love, why did God make it so nice? Both agreed that the mass was the most meaningful liturgical event they had ever participated in.

Afterwards, they sought out Edward. "Hello, you two," he said. "What do you mean by joining this seditious rabble?"

"What about you, then?"

"I'm an infiltrator, paid by the Vatican in indulgences. And why are you wearing those extraordinary trousers, old man?"

In spite of his quips, Edward looked tired and drawn, and was evidently in some pain from his old back injury. "There is an operation, but I don't fancy it," he said. "I know too much about surgeons.

124

And hospitals. Forty per cent of my patients who have surgery pick up secondary infections in hospital. Take my advice, stay out of hospital if you possibly can."

"I intend to," said Michael.

"I should knock off that stuff, then," said Edward, with a nod at Michael's cigarette.

"I only smoke ten a day," said Michael.

"Fifteen," said Miriam. "Twenty, some days."

"Each one," said Edward, "takes five minutes off your life expectancy."

"You're a cheerful bugger, I must say," said Michael, stubbing out a rather longer dog-end than usual.

They exchanged news about their families and mutual friends. Adrian and Dorothy joined them.

"I thought Angela and Dennis might have come," said Adrian, with a slight tone of grievance. "They did join."

"Angela rang me, she sent her apologies, but she's tied up organizing some bazaar today. And Dennis isn't much interested in the Church these days. Ever since Anne. . . ." Miriam's explanation tailed away.

"Yes," said Edward, shaking his head, and looking at his toecaps, "That was too bad."

Adrian and Dorothy had not followed this and had to have it explained to them, as will you, gentle reader. Two years after Nicole was born, Dennis and Angela's next youngest child, Anne, was knocked down by a van outside their house and died in hospital a few hours later. I have avoided a direct presentation of this incident because frankly I find it too painful to contemplate. Of course, Dennis and Angela and Anne are fictional characters, they cannot bleed or weep, but they stand here for all the real people to whom such disasters happen with no apparent reason or justice. One does not kill off characters lightly, I assure you, even ones like Anne, evoked solely for that purpose.

"Of course, they blame themselves for the accident, one always does," said Miriam. "Though it could happen to anyone."

They were silent for a moment, trying to imagine what it would be like if it happened to them, and failing.

"Well," sighed Adrian, "I'm not surprised they didn't come. They must have enough on their plate." The last vestige of his romantic interest in Angela dissolved with this news. Before the meeting he had been conscious, against his own reason, of a quiver of expectation at the prospect of seeing her again, a foolish wish to shine in her eyes by his conduct of the meeting. Now the thread of sentimental reminiscence that linked them was finally broken, and he recognized her as irrevocably separated from him, robed in her own tragedy, burdened with a grief that he could neither share nor alleviate.

"Have you been in touch with any others of the old crowd?" Edward asked him.

"Eh? Oh, yes. I got on to quite a few. I spoke to Miles, but he didn't sound very keen to get involved. As a matter of fact, he seemed distinctly hostile. Let me see, who else. . . ? Polly I didn't bother to trace, I gather she left the Church years ago. Ruth was sympathetic, but she was just off to America."

"Good Lord, what for?"

"Visiting various convents, I gather, to see what they've been up to over there since Vatican II."

"She's still a nun, then? And Violet?"

Adrian grimaced and Dorothy rolled her eyes heavenwards. "Ever since Adie got in touch with her," said Dorothy, "she's been ringing him up at all hours."

"To discuss her personal problems," said Adrian.

"She's still married to Robin?"

"Just about."

At Edward's suggestion they adjourned to a nearby pub to continue the conversation, which came round inevitably to the great debate about *Humanae Vitae* and the Safe Method and the question of why they had themselves for so many years persevered with that frustrating, inconvenient, ineffective, anxiety-and-tension-creating régime. "It was conditioning," said Edward, who no longer advised patients on the use of the basal temperature method. "It was the repressive power of the clergy, wielded through the confessional," said Adrian, a strong supporter of the new rite of Penance being mooted in advanced liturgical circles, with general absolution and no invasions of privacy. "It was guilt about sex, the way we were brought up not knowing anything," said Dorothy, who had not yet forgiven her mother for the debacle of her wedding night. "It was fear," said Michael. "Let's face it, it was the fear of Hell."

126

Well, yes, they had to agree that had been at the bottom of it: the fear of Hell. And looking at each other, with faintly embarrassed grins as they sipped their drinks, they realized then, if they had not realized before, that Hell, the Hell of their childhood, had disappeared for good.

5

How they broke out, away, down, up, through, etc.

IN America, Ruth travelled from city to city, from convent to convent, like a medieval pilgrim, making notes about the changes that were taking place in the lives of nuns. She had been awarded a six-month's travelling scholarship for this project, but when her time was up she felt that she had only scratched the surface of the subject and wrote home for permission to stay longer. She relied on the religious communities she visited for food and accommodation, repaying their hospitality with whatever work was appropriate. She did substitution teaching in schools, auxiliary nursing in hospitals, helped look after senior citizens and mentally handicapped children. Sometimes she donned her habit and gave talks about the Church in England to parochial groups. Afterwards people would come up to her and shake her hand warmly, sometimes pressing into it a large-denomination dollar bill "to help with your expenses, sister." At first she was embarrassed by these gifts, but after a while she got used to them, and indeed came to rely on such gratuities for her pocket money.

American nuns, she soon discovered, were in a state of upheaval that made England seem quite tranquil by comparison. In Cleveland,

Ohio, she came across a community that had until recently been enclosed, supporting itself precariously by embroidering priests' vestments, and had suddenly decided to train all its members in chiropody and turned itself into a foot clinic. In Detroit, Michigan, a nun in high boots and a mini-skirt ran a free school for juvenile deliquents and led a successful rent-strike against profiteering landlords. In St Louis, Ruth interviewed a sister who was secretary-general of an organization dedicated to opposing male chauvinism in the Church. She wore a trouser suit and scattered words like "crap" and "bullshit" in her conversation. On the wall behind her head a poster depicted Moses telling the Israelites: *"And She's black . . ."* In Texas, Ruth visited a community of nuns who came down to breakfast with their hair in huge plastic curlers. After a hasty grace ("Good food, good meat, good God, let's eat") they tucked into hot cakes and bacon; then, immaculately coiffed, and clad in smart clothes, they swept off in huge shiny convertibles to their jobs as personal secretaries in downtown Houston. In the evenings they had dates with priests, who took them out to restaurants and movie shows.

Ruth herself had adventures. Travelling through the night on a Greyhound bus, dressed, as was her custom now, in ordinary clothes, she realized that the man in the next seat had placed his hand on her knee. She froze, wondering what to do. Scream? Cut and run? Stop the bus? After half an hour she dared a look sideways. The man was asleep, his limbs limp, his mouth open. Slowly, carefully, Ruth lifted his hand from her knee and restored it to his own. Eventually she slept herself and woke to find her head on the man's shoulder. "I didn't like to waken you," he said with a smile, chafing his numbed arm. Ruth blushed crimson and muttered her apologies. "You're welcome," said the man. At the next rest stop he insisted on buying her coffee and doughnuts and telling her the story of his life. He was a shoe salesman, recently retired, going to spend a vacation with his son and daughter-in-law in Denver. "You'd really like them," he assured her. "They made a trip to London a few years back. You'd have a lot in common. Why don't you plan to stay over in Denver a whiles?" When they got back into the bus, Ruth took a seat next to a black woman with a baby on her lap and pretended not to see the hurt and longing looks the shoe salesman sent in her direction across the aisle. At the time, this episode distressed her, but afterwards she was vexed to think how upset she had been, or "uptight" as the feminist nun in St Louis would have put it. When, some time later, an ugly but genial man tried to pick her up at Dallas airport, she didn't panic, but waited patiently for an opportunity to mention that she was a nun. "No *kidding!*" he said, staring. "Hey, I wouldn't have made a pass at you if I'd known. Jesus – sorry – wow! Hey, I went to a parochial school myself, you know? I mean, I was *taught* by sisters." He seemed almost afraid that they would rise up out of the past to punish him. He took out his wallet and tried to press a donation on her. Fending off the proffered dollar bills, Ruth glimpsed a woman on a nearby bench observing them with disapproval. "Put your money away, you're giving scandal," she said, giggling. She dined off the story more than once.

At last she came to the coast of California, which seemed as far as she could go. Her Mother Superior wrote reluctantly agreeing to a three-month extension of her leave. The letter was fretful and discouraged. One nun had just left the community and another was on the brink. There had been only two new postulants admitted to the mother house that year. By the same post Ruth received a copy of *Crux*, the COC newsletter: Adrian had put her on the mailing list even though she hadn't paid a subscription. It contained articles, news items and book reviews, mostly written by Adrian and Dorothy, correspondence with editorial comments by Adrian, and the text of the third Open Letter to the Cardinal.

Michael had been correct in predicting that the governors of his College, who included several members of the clergy he liked to describe as somewhat to the right of Torquemada in the spectrum of ecclesiastical politics, would disapprove of his membership of Catholics for an Open Church. When the second open letter to the Cardinal, bearing his signature, was published in *The Times* and the *Tablet*, the Principal suggested that it would be in Michael's own interest to resign from the group. His professional association offered to take up the case, but Michael was tired of the place anyway, and applied successfully for a more senior post elsewhere. This was another Catholic College of Education, but only recently established, and known to be progressive in its outlook, dedicated to the spirit of Vatican II, with a lay Principal and a largely lay staff. In preparation

130

for the new life they expected to lead there, Michael and Miriam let their hair grow, he to his shoulders and she to her waist. When Miriam thrust her head forward in the excitement of argument now, a shimmering curtain of copper-coloured hair would fall forward over her green eyes, and she would flick it back with an impatient toss of the head. Michael also grew a moustache, hoping it would distract attention from his snouty nose. He gave up smoking, and Miriam started baking her own bread.

They looked forward to seeing more of some old friends in their new location, for the College was situated on the outskirts of the city where Edward had his practice, and was not far, therefore, from Dennis and Angela's dormitory village. To the same city, in due course, came Father Brierley, to study at the Polytechnic. His dispute with the bishop had been resolved, at least temporarily, like other crises in his priestly life, by sending him on a course – this time for a degree in psychology and sociology.

Father Brierley's bishop was not, in fact, the ogre that Adrian liked to make him out to be. He did not wish to lose Father Brierley, whom he recognized as a sincere, hardworking priest, especially as the diocese was chronically under strength; nor did he personally have very strong feelings about the issue of birth control. The bishop had successfully sublimated his own sexual urges thirty years ago, and didn't understand why Catholic couples couldn't do the same after having a few children. As a young man he would have liked to experience copulation once, just to know what it was like, and to live with that curiosity unsatisfied had been a genuine sacrifice at the time. That people should want to go on doing it, again and again, long after the novelty must have worn off, strained his understanding and sympathy. But he acknowledged that there were a lot of sins worse than spilling the seed, and thought it was very regrettable the way this one issue had come to obsess people.

For the bishop, the controversy was purely a management problem. What Father Brierley said to folk in the confessional was between God and his conscience, but if he was allowed to get away with publicly repudiating *HV*, all the young tearaway curates in the diocese would soon be doing the same, and the older ones baying for a heresy hunt, and then the fat would be in the fire. The bishop put this to Father Brierley, frankly and freely, one man to another, sitting opposite him in the episcopal study in an easy chair, and offering Irish whiskey and cigarettes. Austin Brierley apologized for causing him so much trouble, but stood his ground. The bishop sighed, lit a Senior Service, and asked Father Brierley if he had a girl friend. Austin Brierley flushed and denied the suggestion indignantly.

"Hold your horses, Father," said the Bishop, "it was just a shot in the dark. It's only that every priest I've had trouble with in the past few years has turned out to be in love. The poor fools think they've got problems of faith and doctrine but subconsciously they're looking for a way to get out of Holy Orders and into the arms of some woman or other."

"That isn't my situation," said Austin Brierley.

"I'm glad to hear it," said the Bishop. "But what shall we do with you?"

"Let me go to college," said Austin Brierley. "I'd like to take a degree in psychology."

"What in Heaven's name for?"

"I think it would help me to understand people better. They come to me for advice, but what do I know about ordinary people's problems? All I know about are priests' problems."

The Bishop grunted sceptically. "We've managed for nearly two thousand years without degrees in psychology," he said. But the suggestion had an undeniable appeal. Sending Father Brierley to college would get him out of his parish and out of the limelight for a few years, by which time the controversy over *HV* would have died down. And it would appear a magnanimous gesture on his own part, which would be one in the eye for Mr Adrian Walsh and his society of busybodies. "You'd have to resign from that Catholics for an Open Church nonsense," he said. Reluctantly, Austin Brierley agreed to this condition, but he chose his place of study deliberately to be near some of his friends and supporters in COC, and continued to advise them unofficially on matters of theology and ecclesiastical politics.

Michael and Miriam now belonged to a circle of friends, mostly attached to the College in some capacity, who saw themselves as almost a church within the Church. On Sunday mornings they attended mass in the College chapel, where Father Bede Buchanan, a liberal-minded priest who was a lecturer in the Theology Department and chaplain to the student body, tolerated an experimental, avant-garde liturgy that would have lifted the back hairs on the red necks of the local parish priests had they known what was going on in their midst.

Each week the students chose their own readings, bearing on some topical theme, and sometimes these were not taken from Scripture at all, but might be articles from the *Guardian* about racial discrim-ination or poems by the Liverpool poets about teenage promiscuity or some blank-verse effusion of their own composition. The music at mass was similarly eclectic in style, accompanied by guitar and perhaps flute, violin, Indian bells, bongo drums – whatever instruments and instrumentalists happened to be around. They sang negro spirituals and gospel songs, Sidney Carter's modern folk hymns, the calypso setting of the "Our Father", Protestant favourites like "Amazing Grace" and "Onward Christian Soldiers", and sometimes pop classics like Simon and Garfunkel's "Mrs Robinson" (*"Jesus loves you more and more each day, hey, hey, hey!"*) or the Beatles' "All You Need Is Love". At the bidding prayers anyone was free to chip in with a petition, and the congregation might find itself praying for the success of the Viet Cong, or for the recovery of someone's missing tortoise, as well as for more conventional intentions. At the Offertory, the bread and wine were brought up to the altar by two students, usually a courting couple holding hands and exchanging fond looks, and it wasn't only married couples who warmly embraced at the Kiss of Peace. Throughout the mass the young children of the college lecturers scampered uncontrolled about the room, chattering and fighting and pushing their Dinky cars up and down the altar steps. At Communion, most of the congregation received the Host in their hands rather than on the tongue, and also took the cup, which was brought round by a layman – all practices still forbidden in public worship in England. At the end of mass there was a discussion period in which the congregation was encouraged to pick holes in the homily they had heard earlier.

This liturgy had one indisputable spiritual edge over the old: it was virtually impossible to lapse into some private, secular day-dream while it was going on, because you could never be sure from one moment to the next what was going to happen. By suspending their sense of irony, Michael and Miriam derived an agreeable sense of uplift and togetherness from the occasion, while their children positively looked forward to Sunday mornings, and groaned when, during the vacations, the College masses were suspended and they were obliged to attend the parish church, where they were penned in narrow pews and made to sit, stand and kneel, like well-drilled troops, in unison with the rest of the congregation, and obliged to sing the doleful hymns of yesteryear, "Soul of My Saviour" and "Sweet Sacrament Divine". Moving between these two places of worship, and impersonating the two very different styles of deportment that went with them, Michael sometimes felt like a liturgical double agent.

Catholic friends and relatives who came to stay (they now had a large, comfortable old house, with a proper guest room) were taken to the College mass as a kind of treat, or at least novelty. Adrian, who came down with Dorothy one weekend to discuss COC policy (there was a plan afoot to publish a pamphlet demonstrating the fallibility of *Humanae Vitae*) joined enthusiastically in the College mass and offered a bidding prayer inviting the Lord to open the eyes of those clergy who were resisting the spirit of liturgical renewal. This was apparently an allusion to his own parish priest, with whom he was engaged in a long war of attrition. "You don't know how lucky you are," he said afterwards. "Our PP won't even allow women readers."

"Why not?" said Miriam.

"Menstruation," said Dorothy, who liked to advertise the distance she had travelled from her inhibited youth by being very outspoken. "He thinks women are unclean. He probably thinks we bleed all the time."

"But we'll nail him eventually," said Adrian. "Dorothy will read from that pulpit if I have to organize a strike of altar cleaners to do it."

"Sometimes, at the College mass, we have a woman bring round the cup," said Miriam

"Gosh, do you really!" they exclaimed. "How fantastic!"

But the College liturgy did not always please. One Sunday when Michael's parents were with them, a child taking Communion let the chalice slip and spilled the consecrated wine all over the floor. Michael's father, a retired civil servant, was deeply upset by this occurrence, and muttered audibly that it ought to be reported to the Bishop. "It's not right," he said afterwards, over lunch, still agitated and looking quite grey with shock, "letting the children have the chalice. I don't hold with it, in any case, not even for adults, there's always the risk of an accident. But the way they carry on in that chapel, with any Tom, Dick or Harry taking round the chalice, it's no wonder something like that happens. And all that priest did was mop it up with some old cloth!"

"What did you expect him to do, Dad, eat the carpet?" said Michael. The remark sounded excessively rude when he made it, but his father had irritated and embarrassed him by his public fussing over the incident.

"In my day, the carpet would have been taken up and burned."

"Burned?" Michael forced a laugh. "What good would that do?"

"To avoid desecration."

Michael sighed. "You still have a very magical idea of the Eucharist, don't you Dad?"

"Respectful, I'd call it. Reverent."

"Even granted that you still believe in the transubstantiation – "

"Oh, don't you, then?"

"Not in the sense we were taught at school. Substance and accidents and all that."

Michael's father shook his head.

"But even granted that you still believe it, surely you don't think that Christ is *trapped* in the wine, do you? I mean, you admit that the Real Presence could leave the wine the instant it was spilled, before it hit the carpet?"

"Michael, leave your father alone," said Miriam.

"Yes, stop it, you two," said her mother-in-law. "It's not nice, arguing about religion on a Sunday."

Michael's father waved these interventions away impatiently. "Tell me what you do believe, then, son, about Holy Communion, if you don't believe in transubstantiation. What is it, if it isn't the changing of bread and wine into the Body and Blood of Our Lord, Jesus Christ?" He gave a reflex nod of the head at the Holy Name, and his wife followed suit.

"Well . . ." said Michael, more hesitantly, "it's a commemoration."

"Pah!" expostulated his father. "That's what Protestants say."

"*Do this in memory of me*," Michael quoted.

"*This is My Body, this is My Blood*," his father countered.

"That's a metaphor," said Michael.

"It's a plain statement of fact."

"How could it be? A plain statement of fact would be, 'This bread is bread, this wine is wine.'" He took a slice of Hovis in his fingers and waved it in the air illustratively, exhilarated by the argument, his blood up now, a teacher in full cry. "In 'This is My Body,' the verb *is* can only mean '*is like*' or '*is, as it were*' or '*is analogous to*', because any other sense would be a logical contradiction. God can only speak to men in a language that is humanly intelligible."

His father snorted angrily, baffled but not beaten. "Are you trying to tell me that what the Church has taught for centuries is wrong, then?"

"Yes. No. Not exactly. Concepts change as knowledge changes. Once everybody believed the earth was flat. Only cranks believe that now."

"So I'm a crank, am I?"

"I didn't say that, Dad."

His father grunted, but offered no further resistance. The adrenalin seeped away and Michael was left feeling slightly ashamed of his facile victory.

Miles, who stayed with them one weekend on his way to a conference in Wales, was as dismayed as Michael's father. "My dear Michael," he said, emerging from the College chapel with his hand to his brow, like someone with a migraine, "this is madness. This is anarchy. This is Enthusiasm. Ronnie Knox must be spinning in his grave." Miles drew an analogy between what he had witnessed and the development of antinomian sects in the seventeenth century. "It won't be long," he prophesied, "before you're dancing naked in front of the altar and sharing your wives and goods in common."

"Sounds like fun," said Michael, grinning. "But seriously, Miles, everyone's antinomian nowadays. Catholics are just catching up with the rest of the world. I mean, the idea of sin is right out. They don't even teach it in Catholic schools any more." Michael exaggerated somewhat to tease Miles, who awed him less than of old, perhaps because Miles's academic career had not really fulfilled its early promise. His thesis had not, after all, been published, whereas Michael was beginning to publish essays here and there about youth culture, the new liturgy and the mass media, and had hopes of gathering them into a book. When Michael visited Miles at his Cambridge college he was surprised how little envy he felt – his rooms seemed cold and damp and smelled of gas, the furniture was ugly, the conversation at High Table boring and superficial. Apart from the beauty of the external architecture, the ambience reminded him faintly of his father's golf club as it had been in the early fifties. Miles himself, wearing superbly tailored but unfashionably cut three-piece suits, and always carrying his tightly furled umbrella, seemed psychologically arrested in that earlier era.

Miles certainly felt spiritually orphaned by the times. The Catholic Church he had joined was fast disappearing, and he did not like the new one he saw appearing in its place, with its concert-party liturgy, its undiscriminating radicalism, its rather smug air of uxorious sexual liberation. He admitted to himself that there might be an element of envy in his reaction on the last score, for he was himself still hopelessly screwed up over the sexual question. The homosexual subculture of Cambridge was becoming increasingly overt in its behaviour, and beckoning him to join the party, but he held back on the fringe, prim-lipped and buttoned-up. It was at about this time that the word "gay" became widely current in England in the homosexual sense, but to Miles it had a mockingly ironic ring. One summer he arranged to take a holiday in Morocco with a young colleague of apparently similar temperament, and wondered excitedly whether this would be his first affair, whether the exotic and distant setting would allow him to lose his scruples and his virginity at last, but the young man turned out to be paedophile and spent all his time making assignations with young Arab boys in the marketplace of the town where they were staying. One evening Miles himself cruised the narrow streets diffidently in search of a pick-up, but always drew back when accosted, fearful of being robbed, blackmailed or infected. He flew back to England a week early and settled in tourist-ridden Cambridge to make one more assault on the revision of his thesis for publication. By the end of the vacation he had exactly thirteen pages of uncancelled typescript to show for his pains. "You're blocked because you're sexually repressed," said his friend, back from Morocco, bronzed and sated. "How glib can you get?" Miles sneered, but secretly agreed.

At times when his physical frustration became too much to bear, he took from a locked drawer in his bedroom a small collection of homosexual pornography and masturbated. These acts he coldly confessed at the earliest opportunity to his regular confessor, the now ageing Jesuit. "Is it really better to live like this than to have a proper loving relationship with someone?" Miles asked.

"You know very well that if you were doing that I wouldn't be able to give you absolution. Pray to Almighty God to give you strength."

Miles sank into a deep depression. He spent long hours taking hot baths and slept as much as possible, drugging himself with Valium and sleeping pills – anything to reduce the hours of consciousness to a minimum. He cancelled his tutorials frequently because he could not face them, and his students began to complain. Colleagues avoided his company. Cambridge, which he had always thought of as one of the most privileged spots on earth, became hideous to him, a claustrophobic little place, crammed with vain, complacent, ruthless people who were constantly signalling to each other by every word and gesture, *"Envy me, envy me, I'm clever and successful and I'm having it off every night."*

"Perhaps you should see a psychiatrist," said his confessor.

"He'll only tell me to have sex," said Miles. "That's what they all say, isn't it?"

"I know a Catholic one," said the priest. "A very good man."

After several consultations the psychiatrist said, "I can do nothing for you. Speaking as a doctor, my advice would be: find yourself a partner. Speaking as a Catholic, I can only say: carry your cross."

"That's easily said," Miles observed.

The psychiatrist shrugged. "I quite agree. With many clients there comes a point when one has to say, your problem is what you are."

"Like the old joke about the man with an inferiority complex?"

"Precisely. You *are* homosexual."

"I knew that already," said Miles, getting up to go. "But thanks for confirming it."

Violet also went to a psychiatrist – more than one: she sought them out as she had once sought out confessors, moving restlessly and at random from one to another, hoping to find the one with magic powerful enough to break the spell. She told each one her story and

138

compared their diagnoses. Some said depressive, some schizoid, some prescribed drugs, some group counselling. One prescribed therapeutic sex. When Violet told him about the episode with her professor, he propounded the theory that she had imagined the whole thing. It was clearly a displacement of her desire to have sex with her own father. The guilt generated by this repressed incestuous desire had led her to project it on to other father figures as a violation of her own innocence. She would not be cured until she was able to have a happy, guilt-free relationship with an older man. "I am an older man," he pointed out. When Violet broke off the consultation, he said, "If you make a complaint, I shall deny everything, of course."

Ruth wrote home for a further extension. It was refused. Come home, her Mother Superior urged, you are needed. Sixth Form science is suffering. Ruth procrastinated, equivocated. She did not want to go home. She felt that she was in the middle of some spiritual quest that could not be abandoned, though she did not know where or when it would end. As for Sixth Form science suffering, that was all rot. The real reason why Mother Superior wanted her back was because two more nuns had left the convent and morale was low. One of the women concerned had written to Ruth. "*I'll make no bones about it*," she wrote, "*I left to get married, and not to anyone in particular. I woke up one morning and realized that I couldn't face the rest of my life on my own, without a man, without children. I'm going out with a nice fellow now, a widower with two boys, we met through an agency. I'm taking cookery lessons. When I tried to cook a dinner for John and the children he said it was the worst meal he had ever had in his life. I suppose that after a number of years in a convent your taste buds get anaesthetized . . .*"

Ruth herself did not suffer unduly from the pangs of frustrated sexual and maternal longing, but she did feel that there was something missing from her life as a religious, and that she had to find it before she returned home. She wrote back to her Mother Superior: "*I am going through a crisis about my vocation. I must see it through over here.*" Mother Superior wired: "RETURN IMMEDIATELY." Ruth ignored the summons. She did not know whether she had been suspended. She did not greatly care.

It was a time of intense political activity in America, and priests and nuns were throwing themselves into the struggle for civil rights, for peace in Vietnam, for the protection of the environment. Ruth marched and demonstrated on behalf of the Berrigan brothers, Jesuit priests jailed for burning draft cards and alleged conspiracy against the State, and was herself arrested and jailed for a night. She hitch-hiked to Southern California to support the strike of exploited Chicano grape-pickers. Her picket line was broken up by thugs hired by the employers. Ruth was hit in the chest and pushed to the ground, screaming "You cad!" at her attacker. "Those mothers are mean-looking mothers, ain't they?" said the worker who picked her up and dusted her down. After that experience, Ruth wore her habit on demos and enjoyed a certain immunity from assault, though an element of risk remained. Thus attired, she stood among a crowd of two thousand on a college campus at the height of the Cambodian crisis, chanting, "*Pigs out! Pigs out!*" and fled from a charge of police dressed like spacemen, her eyes streaming from tear gas. "Mean-looking mothers, aren't they?" she gasped to a startled fellow-demonstrator. This term of abuse, which she privately interpreted as a contraction of "Mother Superior", had rather caught her fancy, and she continued to use it freely until enlightened as to its true derivation by an amused Franciscan friar during a sit-in at a napalm factory.

From these experiences Ruth emerged proud and self-reliant. Her life before America, dull and orderly, seemed like an album of mono-chrome photographs in her memory. But still she hadn't found what she was looking for. The euphoria, the inspiring sense of solidarity with one's brothers and sisters, that was generated by marches and demonstrations, soon evaporated. Eventually the columns dispersed, the marchers went their separate ways. "This is the darnedest time," said Josephine, a Paulist sister from Iowa, on one such occasion, just after a big peace rally in San Francisco. The two of them were drinking coffee out of paper cups in a bus-station automat in the middle of the night, waiting for their connections. Blue strip lighting bleakly illuminated the Formica tables and the littered floor. "While the rally's going on, you feel just great, right?" Josephine went on. "Like, people are really digging each other, the barriers are down, and when everybody's singing 'We Shall Overcome', or 'They'll Know We Are Christians By Our Love', you feel it's really true. You think to yourself, gee, this is really great, this is the New Jerusalem, this is what it's all about. But it doesn't last. Soon you're in some lousy automat, zonked out, and the party's over."

"I suppose it couldn't last, in the nature of things," said Ruth philosophically. "You couldn't keep up that intense emotional pitch for long."

"It's not just that. The others on the demo, ordinary people, have got homes, real homes to go back to. Husbands, wives, families. Folks waiting to welcome them back, wanting to hear all about it. That must be real nice." Ruth nodded sympathetically, knowing that Josephine's community did not approve of her radical activities and would not want to know anything at all about that weekend's demonstration. "Whereas, for us, it's just an anticlimax, going back. Anticlimax and loneliness. Gee, I get so depressed after one of these rallies. . . . D'you know what I do, Ruth?" Josephine looked around, and although the automat was empty apart from themselves and a black soldier asleep in the far corner, lowered her voice. "I buy myself a little miniature bottle of Southern Comfort and then I fill me a big deep tub, very hot, and I have a long, long soak. I lie there for hours, taking a sip of Southern Comfort every now and then, and topping up the hot water in the tub. I usually wind up giving myself another kind of Southern Comfort, you know what I mean?"

"No," said Ruth, truthfully. Josephine looked at her with a strange expression – quizzical, sceptical, slightly wicked – and suddenly Ruth guessed what she was talking about, and blushed vividly. "Oh," she said.

"D'you think I'm going crazy, Ruth?" said Josephine. "D'you think I should get out before I'm totally screwed up by this life?"

"I don't know," said Ruth. "Don't ask me. I don't even know about myself."

As well as the Sunday masses in the College chapel, Michael and Miriam and their friends held occasional gatherings in their homes on weekday evenings which they called "agapes", after the common meal or love-feast which accompanied the celebration of the Lord's Supper in the primitive Church. These occasions did indeed make Michael and Miriam and their circle feel a little bit like the early Christians, gathered together in fellowship behind the curtained windows of suburban houses, while all around them people went about their secular pursuits, sat slumped in front of televisions, or drank beer in pubs, or walked their dogs under the streetlamps, quite indifferent to and ignorant of the little cell of religious spirit pulsing in their midst. About a dozen people would be invited and, when everyone had arrived, sat round a table spread with homely and slightly archaic fare – home-baked bread, butter, cheese, dates, nuts and raisins, and wine. The host and hostess would choose some readings, usually from the new Jerusalem Bible, which had "Yaweh" instead of "God" in the Old Testament, and then, with some made-up prayer referring to the Last Supper, they would break the bread and pour the wine into a large goblet. These would be passed round the table from person to person, each taking a piece of bread and a swig from the goblet. Then everyone's glass would be filled and the meal would continue with ordinary conversation, serious at first, but getting more lighthearted as the wine flowed.

When Father Brierley came to the city, they naturally invited him to join them at these occasions, and then they would have a Eucharist, but without any vestments or candles, just all sitting round the table as before, with home-made bread and *vin ordinaire*, broken and blessed and handed round, just like at the Last Supper. A certain theological ambiguity hung over these occasions. Was it a real Eucharist, or wasn't it? Outwardly, only the presiding presence of an ordained priest significantly distinguished the event from their improvised agapes. To some, this was a crucial difference, to others it was a relic of the old "magical" view of the sacraments which they had renounced. In the earliest days of the Church, the commemoration of the Lord's Supper was not restricted to a priesthood, and Austin (as they now called Father Brierley) himself declared that the idea of a special caste exclusively empowered to administer the sacraments was rapidly becoming obsolete. He prophesied a time when the whole elaborate structure of bishops and priests and dioceses and parishes would melt away, house-eucharists would replace the huge anonymous crush of the parochial Sunday mass, and mutual counselling and consciousness-raising groups would replace Confession and Confirmation.

So they stood upon the shores of Faith and felt the old dogmas and certainties ebbing away rapidly under their feet and between their toes, sapping the foundations upon which they stood, a sensation both agreeably stimulating and slightly unnerving. For we all like to believe, do we not, if only in stories? People who find religious belief absurd are often upset if a novelist breaks the illusion of reality he has created. Our friends had started life with too many beliefs – the penalty of a Catholic upbringing. They were weighed down with beliefs, useless answers to non-questions. To work their way back to the fundamental ones – what can we know? why is there anything at all? why not nothing? what may we hope? why are we here? what is it all about? – they had to dismantle all that apparatus of superfluous belief and discard it piece by piece. But in matters of belief (as of literary convention) it is a nice question how far you can go in this process without throwing out something vital.

To the agapes came, on occasion, Edward and Tessa and Angela and Dennis. Tessa found the religious part somewhat embarrassing, especially when the bread was passed round in silence and you could hear the sounds of people munching and swallowing; but that was soon over and then it was quite jolly, with plenty of cheap wine, and perhaps after the food was cleared away some music, even dancing if the spirit moved the group that way – free-form spontaneous dancing to recorded music in the folk-rock idiom, with anyone able to join in and no nonsense about partners. It was almost as good as going out to a real party, which Edward was usually reluctant to do, pleading tired-ness and backache. So Tessa always jumped at an invitation to an agape. People dressed informally for these occasions, but since Miriam and her friends favoured long skirts and kaftans to wear about the house anyway, Tessa did not feel overdressed in her long Laura Ashley cotton dresses, which she bought from the original little shop in Shrewsbury. As far as Tessa was concerned, that you didn't have to go to a ball nowadays to wear a long dress, or adjust your dancing style to the limitations of a partner, were the two great social achievements of the nineteen-sixties. (It was by now the nineteen-seventies, but this group of people were having their sixties a little late.)

Though he pretended that Tessa dragged him along to the agapes, Edward went willingly enough. Since joining Catholics for an Open Church he had been cold-shouldered by his Catholic colleagues in the medical profession – an intensely conservative group in whose collective consciousness the pre-war confrontation between Marie

Stopes and Dr Halliday Sutherland still exerted the power of myth. Even if they disagreed privately with *Humanae Vitae*, they saw the pro-contraception lobby as indistinguishable from the pro-abortion and pro-euthanasia lobbies and did not wish to join such undesirable allies in attacking their own religious leaders. Thus Edward found himself pushed, almost involuntarily, into identification with the radical Catholic Underground, though by natural inclination he was far from radical, and at the liturgical gatherings of the Miriam – Michael circle was apt to worry, with a spasm of atavistic superstition, about what happened to the crumbs left over from the bread that Austin had consecrated (or had he?).

And Angela came, as she had come in years gone by to the Thursday masses at Our Lady and St Jude's, because she was invited, because it was obviously a good thing to join with Catholic friends in prayer and fellowship. She had never had much historical sense or any great interest in metaphysical questions; and since the birth of Nicole and the death of Anne she lived more than ever in the present, attending to the tasks immediately to hand. Looking back into the past was too painful, it filled her with a kind of mental nausea. So Angela rarely reflected on the changes that had taken place in the Catholic Church in her lifetime, and was unperturbed by the variety of liturgical practice and doctrinal interpretation that now flourished in it. Whether one prayed in church or in one's living-room seemed unimportant to her, as long as one prayed. It worried her that Dennis no longer seemed to believe in the efficacy of prayer – indeed he seemed to have little faith left at all. She did not discuss the matter with him, partly because they had got out of the habit of discussing serious, abstract questions, and partly because she was afraid of what state of unbelief might be revealed if she pressed him. They had both changed a lot since the birth of Nicole.

When she was told about Nicole's condition, Angela had two quite distinct yet simultaneous reactions, happening, as it were, at different levels of her self. On one level she was shocked and horrified, fought against the truth as long as she could, and, when it could no longer be denied, abandoned herself to grief and self-pity; but on another, deeper level she felt as though she had been waiting all her married life for this, or something like it, to happen. Till now, Dennis had taken all the worries and responsibilities on his shoulders – money, houses, holidays, even the temperature charts – while she had lapsed into a bovine placidity, slowly completing her domestic tasks by day, with a milky-breathed infant invariably in her arms or under her feet, then falling asleep in front of the television in the evenings. It had been a more comfortable and cushioned existence than she had predicted when they were courting, but now Nicole had arrived to confirm her misgivings, and it was almost a relief to know what her cross was to be. When she had cried herself dry, she pulled herself together and resolved to make Nicole the ablest mongol in the land. She read every book on the subject of mental handicap she could lay her hands on, travelled miles to consult specialists, filled the house with educational toys and equipment, joined all the relevant societies, organized play-groups, toy libraries, and fund-raising events.

When, two years after Nicole's birth, four-year old Anne ran into the road in pursuit of a runaway doll's pram and was knocked down by a dry-cleaner's van, Angela was sufficiently hardened and tempered psychologically to cope with the crisis. It was Angela who prevented Anne from being moved from the gutter where she had been thrown, who sent for a blanket to keep her warm, and went with her to the hospital in the ambulance, while all Dennis could do was to crouch over his little daughter's crumpled form, swearing frightfully and literally tearing his hair, great tufts of it which blew away from his fingers like thistledown. When Anne died that night in hospital, without regaining consciousness, it was Angela who was at her bedside, for Dennis was in shock, under sedation at home. It was Angela who made the necessary arrangements for the funeral and held the family steady through that dreadful time. A great shift of gravity had taken place in the marriage, a transfer of power and will from Dennis to Angela. Anne's death showed it, but Nicole's birth had started it.

To Dennis the diagnosis of Nicole's condition had been a stunning and totally surprising blow. He tried to work out why the possibility of such a thing ever happening had never crossed his mind, and came up with several reasons: Angela's pregnancies had always been quite free from complications, and the first three babies had arrived safe, sound and on time; he had never known anyone who had produced abnormal offspring nor had he had personal contact with any mentally handicapped person in his life. But the more fundamental reason was that he had always subconsciously assumed that he was favoured by Providence, or in secular terms, lucky. There had been setbacks and disappointments in his life, but invariably he had found that if he was patient and industrious the obstacle gave way eventually; and after eight years of marriage he was well pleased with himself and his beautiful wife and bonny children, his new four-bedroomed detached house and company car, his well-paid job as deputy production manager of a prospering electronics firm. As far as he knew, he was earning more than any other man among their college contemporaries, except perhaps Edward, and was fairly confident that before long he would have overtaken him, too. The only significant flaw in his general contentment was the business of birth control, with its attendant frustration and worry, but he was prepared to put up with that – it seemed to be a small price to pay for his other blessings. Because of his upbringing, you see, Dennis could not help crediting his good fortune to God, who was rewarding him for working hard and obeying the rules of the Catholic Church.

The birth of Nicole had rudely upset this simple confidence. Instead of being rewarded, it seemed that he had been punished – but for what? Why me? What have I done to deserve this? was his first thought (it is probably everyone's first thought in misfortune, but those with a religious world-view are especially prone) that wet Sunday afternoon in the garage, as Edward, fiddling with the Black and Decker sander, hesitantly described his misgivings about the child (and for ever after the smell of sawdust was associated in Dennis's mind with bad news, so that when two years later his eldest, Jonathan, rushed into the back garden where he was mowing the lawn and screamed at him to come quickly because Anne had been knocked down in the road, he smelled not grass but sawdust, and felt sick). To Dennis, Nicole's condition was not like the other setbacks in his life, something that might pass away or be overcome; it was fixed and irrevocable, as unalterable as chemistry. People they spoke to about mongolism – Downs' Syndrome, as Angela insisted on referring to it – tried to be encouraging: these children were happy, loveable people, they were often good at music, some had even learned to read. But none of this was any comfort to Dennis. His daughter had been defective from the moment of conception, nothing could undo the effect of that extra chromosome at the primal collision of sperm and egg. Nothing except death. In the early days, Dennis wished very much that the child would die, which naturally increased his sense of guilt – indeed, explained to him why he was being punished, since anyone capable of such murderous feelings obviously deserved to be punished.

Outwardly Dennis seemed to share Angela's determination to make the best of things. He cooperated in the training programme for Nicole – played with her, exercised her, talked to the other children about her, read the literature that Angela brought home and attended some of the public meetings, committees and fund-raising events for the mentally handicapped that she was involved in. But it all seemed to him a vain and futile effort to pretend that the tragedy had not happened, that life could resume its former promise. When he came home from work on her first birthday to find her propped up in her high chair, a lopsided paper hat on her head bearing the legend, *"Downs Babies Rule OK"*, obviously the work of her older brothers, it seemed to Dennis like a sick joke, an unconscious expression of resentment, not, as Angela obviously felt, a sign of their acceptance of the child, and he had to struggle to raise a smile.

Nicole's birthdays were always bad days, but after that first one things became a little easier. The little girl began to show that she had a distinctive personality of her own, and she was infatuated with her father, exhibiting signs of excitement and delight as soon as Dennis came in sight. It was impossible to resist such utterly innocent affection. Then Dennis began to realize how many handicapped people there were, most of them much more pathetic cases than Nicole. Through personal contact, anecdote, visits to schools and clinics, watching television programmes he would formerly have avoided, Dennis became aware of a whole world of suffering at the extent of which he had never guessed: children horribly afflicted physically and mentally, by brain damage, spina bifida, hydrocephalus, rubella, epilepsy, muscular dystrophy, cerebral palsy, autism and God knew what else; children suffering from multiple handicap, children doubly incontinent, children so hopelessly paralysed that they would live their whole lives on stretchers, children with cleft palates and deformed bodies and scarcely human faces. Dennis began to feel that perhaps he was lucky after all. He no longer automatically compared Nicole with normal children, but with children more crippled and retarded. His child became for him a lens with which to see more clearly the real vulnerability of human life, and also a talisman against further hurt. He began to feel that he did not need the pity and sympathy of his friends with normal children – it was they that deserved pity, for they had not yet felt the blow of fate that opened a man's eyes to the true nature of things. He had nothing more to fear. He had, as the Americans put it, paid his dues.

Then Anne was run over and killed and Dennis gave up. He could see no sense at all in the pattern of his life. The idea of a personal God with an interest in his, Dennis's, personal fortune, became impossible to maintain, unless he was a God who took a personal interest in torturing people. For while Dennis was able to see that there was some meaning, some positive moral gain, in the experience of having Nicole, he could see no point whatsoever in losing Anne, nothing except sterile anguish and futile self-reproach. Perhaps the bitterest, most heart-rending aspect of the whole ghastly business was the impossibility of explaining to Nicole what had happened to Anne. ("Where Anne?" Nicole would say for years afterwards, turning up at their bedside in the middle of the night, tugging gently at Dennis's pyjama sleeve, "Where Anne?") If one thing was certain it was that Nicole had done nothing to deserve having Anne taken away from her, and would gain nothing from the experience.

Dennis continued going to mass, for the sake of the family, for the sake of a quiet life, but it had no meaning for him. Nothing had, except small, simple pleasures – a glass of beer at the local, a soccer game on TV – handholds by which he kept moving from hour to hour, from day to day. He worked excessively hard at his job to occupy his mind and tire himself out, staying behind at the office long after everyone else had left and often going in on Saturday mornings to the silent, empty factory. Sunday was the worst day of the week because there were so many hours to fill once they had all got back from church.

When Michael and Miriam invited them to an agape, Dennis found an excuse not to go, and Angela went on her own; but intrigued by her account of the proceedings, he accompanied her on subsequent occasions and derived some entertainment, if not spiritual renewal, from these packed, intense gatherings. It amused him to listen to the conversation, to observe the wildly Utopian ideas that blossomed and bloomed recklessly in the hothouse atmosphere, and to interrupt, with a dry question or two, some confident dismissal of, say, industrial capitalism, by a young lecturer in, say, the philosophy of education, who had never put his nose inside a factory, and whose training and salary ultimately derived from wealth generated by industrial capitalism. Dennis posed his questions mildly and without animus, for he had no ideological commitment to industrial capitalism either – he just couldn't see that there was a better alternative available, certainly not the models currently on offer from Russia or China, where most of these innocent Christian radicals would have withered away in labour camps long ago if they had had the misfortune to live there. It was the same with questions of religion: he couldn't understand why they made such a fuss about what they called the authoritarian structure of the Church, why they worked themselves up into furious anger about the conservatism, paternalism, dogmatism of this or that bishop or parish priest. He could see that it would matter to Austin Brierley – after all, it was his job – and with Austin he sympathized; but he couldn't see why the others didn't just leave the Church if they found being in it so irksome.

"But why should *we* leave, Dennis?" they cried. "It's just as much our Church as theirs."

"But just as much theirs as yours," he pointed out. "Why not live and let live? Everybody do their own thing. Latin masses and novenas for the old-fashioned, and this sort of thing – " he gestured at the table, the wholemeal crusts, the empty wine-glasses, the big Jerusalem Bible – "for the avant-garde."

"Oh, Dennis!" they said, laughing and shaking their heads. "You're such a cynic. If the Church doesn't renew itself totally, it'll just fall apart in the next fifty years."

"It seems to be falling apart already, to me," he said.

So Dennis became a kind of court jester, a licensed cynic, to the group. They recognized that his commonsense was a useful check, or at least foil, to their radicalism, and were apt to glance slyly, almost flirtatiously at him when making some particularly extreme remark. It helped him to play this role that he had aged in appearance more than his contemporaries. His hair was thin and grizzled, his face lined and jowly, and he had a paunch. He smoked thirty cigarettes a day, and when people commented on this said, with a shrug, who wants to live for ever?

Angela was still capable of turning heads when, rarely, she took some trouble over her appearance, but her body had thickened, she suffered from varicose veins and her brows were drawn together in a perpetual frown. When Nicole was four she got her into nursery school and herself began to train as a teacher of the educationally sub-normal, not with any serious intention of getting a job, but in order to learn how best to help Nicole's development. The college was some twenty miles away and their domestic life became one of great logistic complexity, involving the use of two cars and the cooperation of sundry baby-sitters, child-minders and cleaning ladies. They drove fast and rather recklessly along the country lanes around their dormitory village, frequently scraping and denting their vehicles. Angela kept up with her voluntary activities and was frequently going out again when Dennis returned late from work. Once or twice a week, perhaps, if they happened to go to bed at the same time, and Angela was not feeling too tired, they would make love.

It is difficult to do justice to ordinary married sex in a novel. There are too many acts for them all to be described, and usually no particular reason to describe one act rather than another; so the novelist falls back on summary, which sounds dismissive. As a contemporary French critic has pointed out in a treatise on narrative, a novelist can (*a*) narrate once what happened once or (*b*) narrate *n* times what happened once or (*c*) narrate *n* times what happened *n* times or (*d*) narrate once what happened *n* times. Seductions, rapes, the taking of new lovers or the breaking of old taboos, are usually narrated according to (*a*), (*b*) or (*c*). Married love in fiction tends to be narrated according to mode (*d*). *Once or twice a week, perhaps, if they happened to go to bed together at the same time, and Angela was not feeling too tired, they would make love.* Which is not to say that this was an unimportant part of their married life. Without its solace the marriage would probably have broken down under the successive crises of Nicole and Anne. But they themselves could hardly distinguish in memory one occasion of lovemaking from another. Over the years they had composed an almost unvarying ritual of arousal and release which both knew by heart. Their foreplay was a condensed version of their courtship: first Dennis kissed Angela, then he pushed his tongue between her teeth, then he stroked her breasts, then he slid his hand up between her thighs. They usually reached a reasonably satisfying climax, and afterwards fell into a deep sleep, which did them both good. By the next morning they retained only a vague memory of the previous night's pleasure.

It was much the same for most of the other couples. Now that they were using birth control, the sexual act had become a more frequent and, inevitably, more routine activity. For they did not take lovers or have casual copulations with strangers met at parties, or in hotels, or in aeroplanes – the kind of thing they read about in novels (even novels by Catholics) and saw in films and on television. Their sex lives were less dramatic, more habitual, and most of them, especially the men, worried about this occasionally. It was true that there was more sex in their lives than there had been – but was it as much as it ought to be? They had lost the fear of Hell, and staked their claim to erotic fulfilment, but had they left it too late? All of them were nearing the age of forty, they had spent more years on earth after leaving University than before going up, they were approaching – perhaps they had already reached – that hump in man's lifespan after which it is downhill all the way. Death beckoned, however distantly. Their bodies began to exhibit small but unmistakable signs of decay and disrepair: spreading gut, veined legs, failing sight, falling hair, receding gums, missing teeth. The men were aware that their sexual vigour was in decline – indeed it seemed, according to some of the many articles on the subject that began to flood the public prints in the early seventies, that their sexual vigour had begun to decline long before they had ever exercised it, the male's maximum potency occurring in the years from sixteen to twenty-three. Premature ejaculation, which had afflicted most of them in early married life, was no longer a problem; indeed, it could be a matter of some anxiety whether, after a few drinks or several nights' lovemaking on the trot, one could ejaculate at all. As for the women, well, according to the same sources of information, their capacity for sexual pleasure was reaching its peak, but they were all well aware that the capacity of their bodies for arousing desire was rapidly diminishing. Making love with the light on was a calculated risk, unless it was very carefully shaded. Meanwhile, their older children were passing into puberty and adolescence and, stripped for the beach, reminded their parents more forcibly with each passing year of the physical lustre they had themselves lost (or perhaps never had).

The permutations of sex are as finite as those of narrative. You can (*a*) do one thing with one partner or (*b*) do *n* things with one partner or (*c*) do one thing with *n* partners or (*d*) do *n* things with *n* partners. For practising Catholics faithful to the marriage bond, there was only the possibility of progressing from (*a*) to (*b*) in search of a richer sex life.

Michael became an addict of sex instruction films, of which there was a spate in the early seventies, mostly produced in Germany and Scandinavia, ostensibly because he was going to write an article about them, in fact because he enjoyed watching even the most clumsily simulated sexual intercourse, and was prepared to sit patiently through long, tedious conversations between white-coated doctors and bashful clients, and voice-over lectures illustrated by coloured diagrams reminiscent of evening class instruction in motor maintenance, for the sake of a few minutes' practical demonstration by a reasonably handsome nude couple in full colour. Michael, with his literary education, was the least willing of all our male characters to admit that sex might become just a comfortable habit. He wanted every act to burn with a lyric intensity, and it was as if he thought that by studying it on the screen he might learn the knack of being simultaneously inside and outside his own orgasms, enjoying and appraising, oblivious and remembering. There was also the opportunity to master through these films the repertoire of postural variation by which married love might, the white coats assured him, be given a new zest, if one's partner were willing to cooperate, which Miriam was not, alas; until one evening when he coaxed her into accompanying him to one of the seedy downtown cinemas that specialized in such films, and she said, afterwards, thoughtfully, as they walked to the bus stop, "I wouldn't mind trying one or two of those things," and he leaped ecstatically into the road, shouting "Taxi! Taxi!" Well, that had been a memorable night, to be sure, and for the next few weeks it was like a second honeymoon between them, and much more satisfying than the first. He went about his work in an erotic trance, hollow-eyed with sexual excess, his mind wandering in seminars and committees as he planned what variations they would experiment with at night. But it was not long before they had to settle between them the old question of how far you could go. In due course their erotic life became as habitual as before, if more subtly textured. It seemed to Michael that he was no nearer grasping the fundamental mystery of sex, of knowing for certain that he had experienced its ultimate ecstasy, than he had been twenty years before, staring at the nudes in the Charing Cross Road bookshops. Then he began to shit blood and quickly lost interest in sex altogether.

Adrian sent away for an illustrated book on sexual intercourse, delivered under plain cover, which showed forty-seven positions in which coitus could be contrived. He tried to run through them all in one night, but Dorothy fell asleep on number thirteen. When he woke her up to ask which position she had found the most satisfying, she yawned and said, "I think the first one, Adie."

"You mean the missionary position?" he said, disappointedly. "But that's what we always do."

"Well, I don't really mind. Which do you like best, Adie?"

"Oh, I like the missionary position best, too," said Adrian. "It just seems rather unenterprising to do the same thing night after night."

"Why do they call it that?"

The explanation tickled Dorothy, and afterwards, when Adrian heaved himself on top of her, she would sometimes chuckle and say, "What are you doing, you dirty old missionary, you?"

Edward and Tessa experimented with positions not so much for the sake of erotic variety as to ease the strain on Edward's back. They found that the most satisfactory arrangement was for Edward to lie supine and for Tessa to squat on top of him, jigging up and down until she brought them both to climax. At first Edward found this very exciting, but the passivity of his own role in the proceedings worried him, and he frightened himself sometimes with the thought that one day he might be incapable of even this style of copulation.

Tessa herself was in a constant fever of vague sexual longing to which she dared not give definition. Her body sent messages which her mind refused to accept. Her body said: you are bored with this clumsy form of intercourse, you want to lie back and close your eyes and be possessed by a strong male force for a change, your body is a garden of unawakened pleasures and time is running out. Her mind said: nonsense, you are a happily married woman with four fine, healthy children and a good, kind, faithful husband. Count your blessings and find something to occupy yourself now that the children are growing up. So Tessa joined keep-fit classes and a tennis club. But the physical wellbeing that accrued only fuelled the fires of her libido. She exulted in the power and grace of her movements across the court or in the gym. In the changing-rooms afterwards she followed the example of the younger women who walked unconcernedly naked from their lockers to the communal shower heads, while the older and less shapely ones waited timidly for the curtained cubicles to become free. The full-length mirrors on the walls reassured her that her body could stand such exposure. From this exercise she returned home, glowing euphorically, to a jaded and weary spouse. Her body said: it would be nice to fuck. Her mind, deaf to the indelicacy, said: he's tired, he was called out last night, his back is paining him.

Tessa, in short, was classically ripe for having an affair, and in another milieu, or novel, might well have had one. Instead, she bought lots of clothes and changed more times a day than was strictly necessary, collected cookbooks and experimented with complicated recipes, read novels from the library about mature, sensitive women having affairs, and enrolled in the Open University.

In spite of his sardonic remarks about campus permissiveness, Robin was fully conversant with the new polymorphous sexuality from his barbershop reading in *Playboy* and *Penthouse*, and anxious to try a few things himself. In this regard he found Violet suprisingly compliant, though unenthusiastic. In her perverse way she had decided that since she was in a state of mortal sin anyway by taking the Pill, it mattered little what else she did in the sexual line – that her best course of action was to let Robin burn out his lust and then repent everything at one go. Robin, for his part, found the listless, whorish impassivity with which she accommodated herself to his whims disconcerting, and it was as difficult as ever to bring her to a climax by penetration, whatever attitude they assumed. He quickly tired of sexual acrobatics. If he was honest, what he enjoyed most was a slow hand-job performed by Violet while he lay back with his eyes closed and listened to Baroque music on a headset. Violet herself was most readily satisfied by lingual stimulation, and gradually this arrangement became customary, each taking turns to service the other. "If we're just going to do this," Robin pointed out one night, "there's no need for you to take the Pill." "If I wasn't on the Pill, I wouldn't be doing it," she replied. "You're crazy," he said. "Tell me something new," she said.

When Felicity started school, Violet tried to get herself a teaching job, but without success. She lacked a postgraduate certificate, and there was no great demand for women classics teachers. So to occupy herself, she signed on at the local art college to study sculpture. This increased their circle of friends, though Robin did not care for the art college crowd (or their art). Almost every weekend there was a party invitation deriving either from the University or the College. For Violet was socially in demand. She fascinated people, as she had fascinated Robin, by her behavioural volatility. Party hosts invited her because she brought a whiff of dangerous irresponsibility into their rooms, without which no party was truly successful, not the parties of that time and place anyway. Violet rarely disappointed them. Being more or less permanently on Librium or Valium, she was not supposed to drink alcohol, but when she arrived at the house, wherever it was, thrumming from cellar to attic with the bass notes of heavy rock and thronged with people chatting and eyeing each other in dimly lit rooms, she felt herself shaking with excitement and social terror and was unable to resist the offer of a glass of wine. Before long she would get intoxicated, and make a set at this or that man, dragging him on to the dance floor, where she would either attempt to shake herself to pieces in frenzied jiving or, draped amorously round his neck, twitch negligently to the beat of some languorous soul ballad. Occasionally she would disappear with her partner into the dark recesses of the house or garden and allow him to grope her while they kissed with open mouths – sometimes, if she was feeling very abandoned, groping him back, but never allowing proper sex. The men she led on in this way sometimes turned nasty, but she usually had some ready lie to get herself out of the tightest corner: it was her period, she was pregnant and fearful of a miscarriage, she had cystitis, she had forgotten to take her pill. . . . Then the man, with good or ill grace, would desist, and having adjusted their dress, they would return to the party as nonchalantly as they could manage, and studiously ignore each other for the rest of the evening, commencing new flirtations in due course. At about two o'clock in the morning Violet would nearly, or actually, pass out from drink or exhaustion, and Robin would take her home, stumbling over other supine bodies in the hall and perhaps the front garden, and put her to bed. The next day she would drag herself off to mass with Felicity, speechless with hangover and guilt; but the next time they got an invitation to such a party, and Robin tried to refuse it, she would accuse him of being snobbish and of trying to deprive her of a normal social life. He did not know what to do. Sometimes he even thought of writing to Ann Field.

Polly wasn't Ann Field any more. Now she wrote a weekly column under her own name on the women's page of a quality newspaper, a column in which radical and progressive ideas were put forward in a subtly ironic style that undermined them even as it expressed them, an effect which perfectly suited the paper's readership, mostly middle-class professionals and their wives, with leftish views and bad consciences about their affluent life-styles.

Polly herself, who had been an early apostle of the sexual revolution, was beginning to wonder whether things hadn't gone too far. She had of course been happily doing n things with Jeremy for years, but when he showed signs of wanting to do them with n partners, she jibbed. They received an invitation to a swinging party at a country house owned by a film producer Jeremy knew; he pressed her to go, and sulked when she refused. Anxiously she strove to show more gusto in their lovemaking, proposing games and variations that she knew he liked, though she herself found them a little tedious, bondage and dressing up in kinky clothes and acting out little scenarios – The Massage Parlour, The Call Girl, and Blue Lagoon. These efforts diverted Jeremy for a while, but eventually he began pressing her again about going to swinging parties.

"Why do you want to go?" she said.

"I'm just curious."

"You want to have another woman."

He shrugged. "All right, perhaps I do. But I don't want to do it behind your back."

"Why do you want to? Don't we have fun in bed?"

"Of course we do, darling. But let's face it, we've been right through the book together, there's nothing new we can do, just the

156

two of us. It's time to introduce another element. You know, sometimes when we're fucking, my mind wanders completely off the subject, I find myself thinking about shooting schedules or audience ratings. That worries me. And you needn't look at me like that. It's nothing personal. It's the nature of the beast."

"Beast is the word." Polly felt a cold dread at her heart. Was it possible that the flame of sex could be kept burning only by the breaking of more taboos? After group sex and orgies, what then? Rubber fetishism? Fladge? Child porn? Snuff movies? "Where does it end?" she said.

"It ends with old age," said Jeremy. "Impotence. Death. But I don't intend to give in until I absolutely have to."

"You don't think there's anything after death?"

"You know I don't."

"I do."

"That's just your Catholic upbringing."

"I don't know what's more frightening, the idea that there's life after death or the idea that there isn't," said Polly. She thought about death a lot these days – had done so ever since her father died the previous winter. It was a sudden death, a heart attack brought on by shovelling snow. She and Jeremy were skiing in Austria at the time and she was delayed getting back to England by blizzards, arriving barely in time for the funeral. So she never saw her father dead, and in consequence was never quite able to believe that he *was* dead; it was as if he had faded away like the Cheshire Cat, leaving the memory of him, his chuckle, the smell of his pipe tobacco, lingering in the mind, and might rematerialize when one least expected it. Polly decided to make death the subject of her next article, and cheered up immediately. That was in the summer of 1973.

6
How they dealt with love and death

MICHAEL read Polly's article about death on the train to London, travelling to an appointment with a consultant specializing in disorders of the intestine. After weeks of mute terror contemplating the daily evidence of the toilet bowl, he had confided in Edward, who claimed to have been at college with the best gut man in the business, and fixed up the consultation for him. Michael did not know that the article was written by someone *he* had been at college with, because Polly used her married name for her by-line, and because the fuzzy, minuscule photo of her that appeared beside it, all tousled bubble-cut and outsize spectacles, did not resemble the Polly he remembered, and because it never crossed his mind that the Polly he remembered could have achieved such fame.

Michael usually looked forward to Polly Elton's column every Wednesday, but her choice of topic was unwelcome this particular morning, already sufficiently replete with reminders of mortality. It had begun with his collecting a specimen of his own stool, which he had been instructed to bring with him for analysis, in a small plastic container supplied by Edward. This container, which looked rather like the kind you bought ice-cream in at the cinema, and even came supplied with a little wooden spatula (the whole exercise had had a distinctly Dadaist quality) now reposed, wrapped in a plastic bag, at the bottom of his briefcase on the seat beside him.

Usually, Michael looked forward to one of his occasional trips to London as a little holiday, a day off the leash, a minor feast of misrule. The best kind of errand was a meeting with one's editor (Michael's volume of essays, *Moving the Times: Religion and Culture in the Global Village*, had received respectful, if sparse, reviews, and the publishers had commissioned him to write a textbook on the mass media for the growing "liberal studies" market) followed by a long expense-account lunch in a Soho restaurant, with plenty of booze before, during and after. Then it was pleasant, stumbling sated and tipsy out of the restaurant in mid-afternoon, and bidding farewell to one's host, to slip into the stream of London pavement life, drift anonymously with the idle, unemployed, sightseeing, windowshopping crowd, eye the goods and the girls, browse in the record shops, buy remaindered books in Charing Cross Road, and then rest one's feet watching the latest sex-instruction film, before catching the early evening train back to the Midlands. But travelling to the metropolis with a lump of your own shit in your briefcase took all the zest out of the excursion; you could hardly look forward to a day of irresponsible self-indulgence while inhaling the reek of your own corruption – for, unless he was very much mistaken, the container was exuding a distinct niff, in spite of its allegedly air-tight lid. What with that, and the prospect of a painful and undignified rectal examination at the hospital, and the constant obsessive fear of being told that he had cancer of the bowel, the last thing he needed that morning was a lay sermon by Polly Elton on the subject of death. *"Is Death The Dirty Little Secret Of The Permissive Society?"* the article was headed. Restively, he let the paper fall to his lap, and observed with some surprise that the seats around him, nearly full when he boarded the train, were now empty. He opened the briefcase experimentally, and hastily closed it again. The dirty little secret of the permissive society was right there.

It was a warm day, and the smell got worse and worse as his journey proceeded. He crossed London feeling like a leper. In the crowded Tube fellow-passengers quickly cleared a *cordon sanitaire* round him. People on the platform where he changed trains began frowningly to inspect the soles of their shoes. Having time to kill before his appointment, he sat for a while in a square in Bloomsbury, with his briefcase on the bench beside him, and it seemed as though the very pigeons strutting on the path veered away from his poisoned ambience. A madman or drunk in a ragged overcoat, hair matted, eyes wild, sat down beside him and thrust under his nose a magazine open on coloured photographs of naked girls with their legs apart. "Disgusting, that's what I say!" he shouted. "Filthy cunts, showing off their cunts like that, there should be a law." He brought his whiskered face confidentially close to Michael's and leered, revealing a few yellow stumps. His breath stank like a lion-house. "You know what I'd like to do to teach those cunts a lesson?" he said. "I'd – " Then the smell from Michael's briefcase hit him, and his head jerked back. He wiped his nose on the back of his sleeve, sniffed incredulously, and shuffled off, muttering to himself.

The man had left the magazine behind, and Michael leafed through it. His professional eye noted the trend towards masturbation poses in the pictures, pseudo-documentary in the stories. He skimmed an article on the pornographic movie industry in California. "*Standby studs are often used for penetration shots,*" he read. Would have been the job for me once, he thought with rueful irony, remembering how he used to walk about London with an almost permanent erection. Now he clung to Miriam in bed more like a child than a lover, nuzzled and caressed her like a baby wanting to crawl back into the womb, his penis limp and discouraged. "What's the matter?" she would say. "D'you want to make love?" "No, I don't feel like it. I'm worried about my guts." "See a doctor then." "Maybe. I'll see. Just let me hold you. It helps me get to sleep." But Miriam had got tired of being treated like a dummy or doll and threatened to move into another room if he didn't get some advice from Edward. Which had brought him to this square in Bloomsbury.

He stood up and tossed the magazine into a litter basket, strongly tempted to do the same with the contents of his briefcase. What would it be like to be told you had a terminal illness, he wondered. Not that he expected to get a definite diagnosis this afternoon, but the impending appointment at the hospital concentrated the mind wonderfully on such questions. Would it make the idea of death any more real? Odd how, though one knew one was going to die eventually, one never *quite* believed it. Impossible to believe, for that matter, that all these people in the square (it was the end of the lunch-hour and the paths were crowded) would all be dead sooner or later. If there were ten million people in London, all of them dying sooner or later, how was it you hardly ever noticed them doing so, how was it they weren't falling dead in the streets, jamming the roads with their funerals, darkening the sky with the smoke of their cremations? Holding the briefcase well away from his side, he set out for the hospital.

The people he asked for directions in the labyrinthine corridors of the vast building did not linger to give them with any great detail, and it was some time before Michael found the Pathology Lab and handed over his noisome package to a beautiful blonde laboratory assistant whose courteous smile collapsed into an expression of uncontrollable dismay as she took it between an exquisitely manicured finger and thumb. Sorry, he wanted to say, sorry my shit smells so awful, sorry you've got to have anything to do with it, but I've come a long way and its been fermenting in my briefcase for hours. As he fled, it crossed his mind that perhaps the whole errand was a practical joke by Edward, that no one in his right mind would try and carry a tub of fresh faeces a hundred and thirty miles across England by Inter-City and London Transport, unless it was hermetically sealed. Perhaps the whole thing was a hoax. Perhaps there wasn't even a consultant.

But there was, though Michael had to wait a long time to see him: a plump, cheerful man, very carefully shaven, who was reassuring, diagnosed colitis, was confident of clearing it up with cortisone and a diet. Michael felt life and hope flowing back into him; he left the hospital in a carefree, happy mood, stood on the pavement outside blinking in the sunshine, rejoining the living.

He was in the vicinity of his old college. The buildings had scarcely changed, but the students going in and out of them looked very different: hairy, denimed and with more experienced-looking faces. A girl passed Michael with a teeshirt bearing the legend "I AM A VIRGO (This is a very old teeshirt)". Like many of the girls, she was not wearing a brassiere, a new fashion still rarely to be seen in the provinces. Earth has hardly anything to show more fair, Michael reflected, than a fine pair of tits oscillating freely under clinging cotton jersey. With delight, he realized that he was interested in sex again, and began to make plans for a celebration with Miriam that night.

On his way to the Tube, he called in at the bookshop which he had patronized as a student, to check whether they had *Moving the Times* in stock. The shop had vastly expanded its floor space, and he had some difficulty in locating the appropriate section, reluctant to ask for help in case he had to buy a copy of his own book or reveal the narcissistic nature of his interest in it. At last he found two copies on a high shelf in Sociology, and as he took one down a familiar voice behind him said: "Michael! As I live and breathe."

With a guilty start, he turned to find Polly smiling at him through outsize spectacles.

"Polly!" he said. "Good Lord, you're Polly Elton!"

"That's right. Do you read me? How nice! Have I caught you gloating over your own book? Actually, I thought it was awfully good, so did Jeremy, that's my husband, you ought to meet him, he's in television."

"Jeremy Elton – yes, I know his work. Very good." (This was not strictly true. Michael did not think Jeremy Elton's programmes were particularly good; but then, neither did Jeremy think much of Michael's book. "Academic claptrap," had been his verdict when Polly passed it to him.)

"It's so good to see you after all these years," said Polly. "Let me pay for these and then let's have a drink or something." She was carrying a large pile of books by Kate Millett, Germaine Greer and other feminist writers. "I decided it was time I really got to grips with the women's movement," she said, plonking the books down on the table in the wine bar where they ended up. "I always used to say that I didn't need Women's Lib because I was liberated already, but now I'm not so sure. Does, er, I've forgotten your wife's name. . . ."

"Miriam? She's interested, but the pro-abortion thing puts her off."

"Ah, yes," said Polly. "You're still practising Catholics, then?"

"I suppose," said Michael. "What about you?"

"Oh, I'm beyond the pale. Jeremy's divorced, for one thing."

"Well, that needn't make any difference these days."

"Really? You mean the Church accepts divorced couples?"

"Well, not officially. But if you don't make an issue of it, the chances are your PP won't either."

"Goodness, things must have changed a lot in the One, Holy, Catholic and Apostolic Church."

"They have."

"I ought to write a piece about it," Polly mused.

They split a bottle of Liebfraumilch between them before they separated, kissing each other on both cheeks and promising to keep in touch. "You and Miriam must come and stay one weekend," said Polly. Michael said that they would love to, if they could find someone to look after the children. "Bring them, bring them!" cried Polly. "We have ponies and things to amuse them." She managed to say this without appearing to show off, but she had obviously made it, Michael reflected, into a world not only of affluence but also of smartness, sophistication, cultural chic. She looked surprisingly good, too: still plump, but shapely, her complexion creamy, her curls lustrous, her clothes smart and new but obviously not "best". Her blouse was open at the throat just one button more than was strictly necessary, one button more than Miriam would have left unfastened.

As the effect of the Liebfraumilch evaporated on the journey home, Michael's spirits drooped. Polly had made him feel threadbare and provincial, awakening in him appetites so long and deeply repressed that he was surprised at the fierceness of the pangs: a longing for fame, success, worldly goods. The life he and Miriam had made for themselves seemed suddenly drab and petty: the earnest discussion groups, the cosy liturgies, the food cooperatives and the sponsored walks for Oxfam and its Catholic equivalent, CAFOD. What did it amount to, after all? What trace did it leave on the public consciousness?

Catching sight of his face reflected in the train window, as the sky darkened in the east, blurred and distorted and looking like a disappointed pig, he cut short this sulky stream of consciousness and delivered a self-reprimand: how fickle you are! This morning all you wanted was a clean bill of health, but no sooner do you get it than you're dissatisfied again. You should be celebrating your reprieve, not bemoaning your lot.

For a joke, and also to excite himself, Michael phoned Miriam from the station and told her to have her knickers off when he got home.

She did not seem amused. Sounds of riotous children chasing each other up and down the stairs dinned in the background. "We've got Angela's children for the night," she explained. "Her father's been taken ill and she's driving up to Liverpool. Dennis is away on business." When Michael got home he found Miriam tired and harassed. Angela's Nicole was disturbed by the sudden disappearance of her mother and clung to Miriam. She wouldn't settle to sleep until they took her into their bedroom, so there was no lovemaking after all that night.

Before he retired, Michael phoned Edward to tell him what the consultant had said.

"Jolly good," said Edward. "And did you remember to take the specimen?"

"Yes," said Michael. "Didn't half make me unpopular on the train, too."

"Why, how much did you take?"

"Well, I more or less filled the container." At the other end of the line Edward spluttered and snorted. "Why, how much should I have taken?"

"Just enough to cover the end of the spatula."

"Bloody hell," said Michael. "Now you tell me."

Angela's father had been admitted to hospital complaining of pains in his back and chest. The doctors made various tests and X-rays and told him it was bronchitis. They told his wife that it was lung cancer, advanced and inoperable. Hence the distraught phone call which had brought Angela rushing up the M6. She found a melancholy family council gathered in the little parlour behind the shop: her mother, two sisters and two brothers, including Tom, now a curate in a parish on the other side of the city. Their Dad would be coming home the next day and they would have to look after him until he was too ill to stay out of hospital. The question was, should he be told?

"How long . . . ?" somebody wondered. The doctor hadn't been specific. A matter of months rather than weeks. One could never be sure. "Who would tell him?" "I couldn't, I just couldn't," said their mother, and wept. "I would," said Angela, "if we agreed that was the right thing to do." "Why tell him?" said the youngest sister. "It

would just be cruel." "But if he asks   ." said another. "Are you
going to lie to your own Dad?"

It seemed to Angela that they weren't getting anywhere. She
glanced interrogatively at Tom, whose calling seemed to establish him
as the natural decision-maker in the circumstances; though you
wouldn't have guessed he was a priest, she thought, sitting there in
his corduroy slacks and a sweater. Like most priests these days, he
seldom wore the dog-collar and black suit, and it was surprising what
a difference it made. He could have been an ordinary man, home from
work, tired, discouraged, uncertain what to do in the crisis. "What do
you think, Tom?" she said.

Tom lit a cigarette and blew smoke from his nostrils. A grey haze
from previous cigarettes hung in the air. All the men in the family
were heavy smokers, perhaps because cigarettes had always been
readily available from the shop. No reference was made by anyone to
this as the likely cause of their father's disease.

"I see no reason to tell Dad yet," Tom said at length. "We should
try to keep him as cheerful as possible."

Their mother looked at Tom gratefully, but fearfully. "But he must
have time to . . . receive the last . . . sacraments and everything," she
faltered.

"Of course, Mam, but there's no need to rush these things. Let's
make him as happy as we can for the rest of his days."

It was their father's habit to walk the dog around the block last
thing at night. Tom offered to perform this task, and Angela said she
would keep him company. Together they trod the worn, familiar
pavements, while ahead of them Spot darted eagerly from lamp-post
to lamp-post, adding his mite to the city's pollution. Every time
Angela came home, the district seemed uglier, grimier, more
dejected.

"Mam was pleased with your advice, Tom," she said. "But I was a
bit surprised. I thought you'd say Dad had a right to know."

"Of course he has – eventually," said Tom. "But there's no
hurry."

"As long as we don't leave it too late," said Angela, "so that he's too
weak and drugged to take it in . . ."

Tom looked at her sharply. "I do believe you positively want to tell
him."

"Of course I don't, I mean I wish there was nothing to tell, I think it's awful, just when he was thinking of retiring, too . . . but, well, we're supposed to be Christians, aren't we?"

"Certainly," he said drily.

"Well, doesn't that mean we shouldn't be afraid of, well, death?"

"That's easily said."

"I know it's not easy at all, but, well, some friends of Miriam's – you remember Miriam and Michael, at our wedding? Some friends of theirs, Catholics, we met them at Miriam's, well, his mother died recently, some kind of cancer, she knew she had it, so did the family, including the grandchildren, they discussed it quite openly, adults and children together. The old lady didn't want to die in hospital so they kept her at home till the end. On the day she died, she said goodbye to them all, she knew she was going. 'I'll be glad to go,' she said, 'I've had a good life, but I'm old and I'm tired. Don't you go getting upset, now.' And after she died, the family went downstairs and got out some bottles of wine and had a sort of party. Don't you think that's absolutely fantastic?" Angela found that tears were streaming down her cheeks.

"No, I'm afraid I don't," said Tom. "I think it's rather affected, if you really want to know." Then, seeing that she was hurt, he added, "I'm sorry, Angela. The news about Dad has upset me."

Angela blew her nose and acknowledged the apology with a sniff. A little further on, Tom stopped under a wall covered with aerosol graffiti to light a cigarette. Without looking at her, he said: "I think I'd better tell you something. I've applied to be laicized."

"What? Why?" Angela was stunned.

"I want to get married."

"Married? Who to?"

"A girl called Rosemary. I was giving her instructions, and we fell in love."

"In love?" she repeated stupidly

"Yes, it does happen, you know. Happened to you, didn't it?"

"A long time ago," said Angela. "When I was very young."

"Yes, well, in those days I was locked up in a seminary, and hadn't the opportunity." His voice had an edge to it.

"Have you told our Mam? Or Dad?"

"No. And now, I can't, do you see? I'll just have to hang on and keep up appearances until. . . ."

Spot padded back towards them and stopped, legs splayed, ears cocked enquiringly. How nice, Angela thought, to be a dumb un-thinking animal. "Tell me," she said, "are you leaving the Church as well as the priesthood?"

"Why should I?"

"You still believe, then?"

"Oh yes, I believe. Not as much as I used to, admittedly. And not as fervently as they do – " With a smile he indicated the graffiti. Angela read half-comprehendingly: "*Jesus saves – and Keegan Scores on the Rebound*" – "*Steve Heighway Walks On Water.*" Tom said: "You know they call football 'the religion' up here. It's more popular than Christianity, that's for sure."

"What about your vows, then?" Angela said.

Tom looked annoyed. "I don't regard them as binding. I was too young and too naive to know what I was doing."

Angela grunted and resumed walking, her hands thrust into the pockets of her raincoat.

"I assure you, Angela, that if I could continue to be a priest and a married man, I would."

"Have you slept with this Rosemary?"

He turned upon her fiercely. "What do you take me for?"

"I take you for a great big booby, since you ask. What makes you think sex is so marvellous?"

He gripped her arm, hard enough to hurt. "I'm not marrying for sex, Angela, difficult as you and everyone else no doubt may find it to believe. I'm marrying for love, for total commitment to another human being. Have you any idea of the intolerable loneliness of a priest's life?"

"Have you any idea of the intolerable things that can happen in married life?"

He relaxed his grip. "I know you've had a lot to bear."

They walked on in silence, past the pub, the fish-and-chip shop. Their home came in sight.

"It will break Mam's heart," said Angela.

"Thanks," said Tom. "You're a great help."

When Angela returned to pick up her children from Michael and Miriam she told them, in confidence, about Tom's plans. "Mam will take it hard," she said. "She'll think it's a disgrace." No, they assured her, it was so common these days, people scarcely raised an eyebrow. "You remember Father Conway, who instructed me?" Miriam said. "He's the latest." "There won't be any priests left, soon," said Angela. She drove off, the frown on her forehead deeper than ever.

"It always seems to happen between the ages of about thirty-five and forty-five," said Michael, as he and Miriam retired to bed that night. "It's as if they suddenly realize that they're approaching the point of no return as far as sex is concerned." He closed the bedroom door and locked it – a coded gesture between them.

Miriam drew off the nightdress she had just put on and got into bed naked. "How old is Austin, I wonder?" she mused.

"Must be getting on for forty-five, wouldn't you say? D'you think he'll go the same way as all the others?"

"I wouldn't be surprised. If the right woman turned up. He must feel terribly isolated."

Michael got between the sheets. He no longer wore pyjamas. Miriam slid into his arms. "Ah!" he sighed. "Nice. You can't blame them, can you, priests wanting to get married? In the old days, at least they believed they'd get to heaven quicker than other people, have less time in purgatory. Give up pleasures in this world and be rewarded in the next. God pinning a medal on your chest. That was the way they used to promote vocations at school. Now that it's all regarded as mythology, priests must wonder what they've given up sex for."

So Austin Brierley's friends watched his vocation like a guttering candle, wondering when it would go out. The bishop had discovered that he was still consorting with Catholics for an Open Church and had suspended his allowance and forbidden him to say mass or perform other priestly duties. He looked less and less like the priest they remembered. To save money (he had qualified for a student grant, but was still hard-up) he wore clothes bought from Army surplus stores, thick, hard khaki trousers and parkas with camouflage markings, and a forage cap vaguely suggestive of German prisoners of war in World War II. He grew a beard, wispy and a surprising ginger in colour, and his hair, balding at the crown, fell down lankly on each side of his face, giving him a faint resemblance to Shakespeare. He carried round with him at all times a rucksack stuffed with books, papers, cuttings, and the materials for rolling his own cigarettes.

The cuttings were mainly about *Humanae Vitae* and its repercussions. Sometimes Austin thought vaguely of writing a book on the subject. "*Humanae Vitae*, By a Repercussion." Meanwhile he collaborated with Adrian on the text of a pamphlet urging Catholics to make their own conscientious decision about birth control, feeling that in this way he was making some amends for all the times he had given contrary advice in the confessional as a young priest. The books in the rucksack were paperbacks on sociology, psychology, philosophy, sexuality, comparative religion. Austin felt that he had a lot of reading to catch up on – too much. His head was a buzzing hive of awakened but directionless ideas. There was Freud who said that we must acknowledge our own repressed desires, and Jung who said that we must recognize our archetypal patterning, and Marx who said we must join the class struggle and Marshall McLuhan who said we must watch more television. There was Sartre who said that man was absurd though free and Skinner who said he was a bundle of conditioned reflexes and Chomsky who said he was a sentence-generating organism and Wilhelm Reich who said he was an orgasm-having organism. Each book that Austin read seemed to him totally persuasive at the time, but they couldn't all be right. And which were most easily reconcilable with faith in God? For that matter, what was God? Kant said he was the essential presupposition of moral action, Bishop Robinson said he was the ground of our being, and Teilhard de Chardin said he was the Omega Point. Wittgenstein said, whereof we cannot speak, thereof we must remain silent – an aphorism in which Austin Brierley found great comfort.

Going to and from Michael and Miriam's house for their liturgical parties, he often saw their eldest son, Martin, a keen amateur astronomer, crouched over his telescope in the dark garden, sometimes actually kneeling on the frosty lawn, immobile, habited like a medieval hermit in balaclava and a long, baggy, cast-off overcoat of his father's. Austin usually stopped to chat with the boy and through these conversations became seriously interested in the Universe. To the rucksack's contents he added popular books on astronomy, from which he learned with astonishment and some dismay that there were about fifty million stars like the Sun in our galaxy, and at least two hundred thousand galaxies in the Universe, each containing a roughly equivalent number of stars, or suns. The whole affair had been going for a very long time, and had spread over a very wide area. Galaxies now being observed for the very first time had started sending, at a speed of 186,000 miles per second, the light that was now being picked up by our telescopes, many thousands of millions of years before the Earth was even formed. If the history of the Universe was conceived of as a single calendar year, the initial Big Bang occurring on 1 January, then the Earth had been formed towards the end of September, and *Homo sapiens* made his appearance at about 10.30 p.m. on 31 December. Christ was born four seconds before midnight.

Austin stored these facts away in his head alongside the theories of Freud, Marx, McLuhan and the rest, and with the opinions of various theologians about God, not finding it any easier to reconcile them all with each other. Indeed, astronomical quantities tended to make all human thought seem both trivial and futile.

"The silence of infinite space terrifies me," he murmured, squinting one night through Martin's telescope at a faint smear of light that the boy assured him was a galaxy several times bigger than the Milky Way.

"Why?"

Austin straightened up and rubbed the small of his back. 'I was quoting Pascal, a famous French philosopher of the seventeenth century."

"Interesting he knew that space was silent," Martin remarked, "that long ago."

"You mean, there's no noise at all up there? All those stars exploding and collapsing without making a sound?"

"You can't have sound without resistance, without an atmosphere."   '

"So the Big Bang wasn't really a bang at all?"

"'Sright."

"Doesn't it frighten you, though, Martin, the sheer size of the Universe?"

"Nope."

Austin stared up at the sky. It was a clear, cold night, ideal for observing. The longer he looked, the more stars he could see, and beyond them were billions more that one could never see with the naked eye. It was statistically certain, according to the books, that some of them must have planetary systems capable of supporting life. It certainly seemed unlikely, when you thought about it, that the only life in the entire universe should be situated on this tiny satellite of an insignificant star in a suburb of the Milky Way. But if there was life out there, there must also be death. Had those creatures, like us, myths of creation, fall and redemption? Had other Christs died on other Calvaries in other galaxies at different times in the last twenty billion years? Under the night sky, the questions that preoccupied philosophers and theologians seemed to reduce down to two very simple ones: how did it all start, and where is it all going? The idea that God, sitting on his throne in a timeless heaven, decided one day to create the Universe, and started the human race going on one little bit of it, and watched with interest to see how each human being behaved himself; that when the last day came and God closed down the Universe, gathering in the stars and galaxies like a croupier raking in chips, He would reward the righteous by letting them live with Him for ever in Heaven – that obviously wouldn't do, as modern theologians admitted, and indeed took some satisfaction in demonstrating. On the other hand, it was much easier to dispose of the old mythology than to come up with anything more convincing. When pushed to say what happened after death, the most ruthless demythologizers tended to become suddenly tentative and to waffle on about Mystery and Spirit and Ultimately Personal Love. There was now something called Process Theology which identified God with the history of the Universe itself, but as far as Austin could understand it, the only immortality it offered was that of being stored in a kind of cosmic memory bank.

"I'm going in," he said to Martin. "I'm getting cold."

The same evening, Michael took him aside. "Austin," he said, "I want your advice. Martin's becoming a bit stroppy about coming to mass on Sundays. What do you think we should do about it?"

"I should leave him alone, if I were you," said Austin.

"You wouldn't like to have a word with him yourself some time? I mean, about religion in general. Even Catholic schools seem to have given up on theology these days. His RE lessons seem to be all about being nice to immigrants and collecting tights for Mother Teresa."

"Tights for Mother Teresa? I wouldn't have thought she wore them."

"It seems her nuns use old nylons to make mattresses for the dying. They're having a big campaign at Martin's school to collect them. Well, a jolly good cause, I'm sure, but the syllabus does seem to be avoiding the larger questions of belief."

Austin did not reply. The reference to tights and nylons had triggered off a faint memory – light years away, it now seemed – of a shapely leg lofted in the air, stockinged to mid-thigh, rising vertically from a lacy foam of petticoats, and he had not attended to the rest of what Michael was saying.

"I thought," said Michael, patiently, "That you might find an opportunity to have a chat with Martin."

"I have already," said Austin, blinking. "I'm learning quite a lot."

Miles decided that he had to get away from Cambridge for a while to think through his problems. In the Easter vacation of 1973 he made a private retreat at a monastery in Nottinghamshire. He slept in an austere cell, rose with the monks at two and six for the singing of Lauds and Prime, ate with them in the refectory while a novice read from Newman's *Apologia*. At other times he read the Bible in the Douai version and, for recreation, Trollope, and took walks in the grounds of the abbey. The setting was less idyllic than he had anticipated. It was mining country and every turn in the paths brought in sight some pithead or sombre slag-heap. The grass and trees were covered with fine black dust, and the morning dew on the grass and shrubs was faintly inky. But this mournful landscape suited his mood. He seriously considered presenting himself as a postulant for admission to the Order. The regularity of the day's routine – office – sleep – wake – office – sleep – wake – office – eat – work – office – work – eat, and so on, around the clock, seemed to take from one's shoulders the terrible responsibility of being happy and successful: it was like some kind of mechanism for keeping in regular motion a body that left to itself would become inert or spastic. He confided this thought to Bernard, a plump, cheerful young monk whom he found a congenial walking companion in the evenings (though the Order observed the Rule of silence, there was a two-hour recreation period after dinner).

"No, sorry, not true at all," said Bernard. "You wouldn't be able to stand the life if you weren't at peace with yourself."

"Then there's no hope for me anywhere," said Miles.

"Cheer up!" Bernard put his arm round Miles's shoulder. "Never say die. You're gay, aren't you Miles?"

Miles looked at him, startled both by the statement and the manner of its expression. "In a miserable, frustrated sort of way, which is why I never use the word, yes, I am."

"Well, it's nothing to be sad about. Nothing to be ashamed of. God made you that way, didn't He?"

"I suppose so."

"So accept it. Be proud of it. You have qualities straight people don't have."

Bernard let his arm drop from Miles's shoulder and put it round his waist, almost hugging him. Miles felt, in quick succession, surprise, panic, then a comforting reassurance. "That's all very well," he mumbled, "but what about . . ."

"What about physical sex? You'll find it easier to do without it once you've accepted yourself for what you are."

"I wish I could believe that "

"Anyway, there are worse sins. As long as there's love. It may be imperfect, but it can't really be evil if there's genuine love."

"Bernard," said Miles, blinking back tears, "you're the first person who's ever given me hope."

Bernard laughed delightedly. "I've always thought that Hope was the most neglected of the Theological Virtues. There must be a thousand books on Faith and Charity for every one on Hope."

They had come within sight of the monastery buildings. Bernard disengaged his arm from Miles' waist. "You'll be all right," he said, twinkling. And patted Miles lightly but unmistakably on the bottom.

Still Ruth lingered on the coast of California. "*I take it you have severed your connection with the Order*," her Mother Superior wrote, "*No, still looking for an answer*," Ruth wrote back. She received no reply.

One day she had a letter from Josephine, the Paulist nun who flashed upon her inward eye every time she saw an advertisement for a certain brand of bourbon. Ruth opened the letter fully expecting that it would announce that the writer had left her Order, probably to get married. To her surprise, Josephine wrote; "After I got back from San Francisco I nosedived into the usual pits. Then I started to go to a prayer group and it changed my life. I've been baptized in the Holy Spirit, and I've never felt so calm, so happy, so sure of my vocation."

This was not the first testimony Ruth had heard to the growing prayer group movement, or Charismatic Renewal as it was sometimes called, but it was the most impressive.

At this time, in the early summer of 1973, Ruth was earning her keep helping in a residential institution for mentally handicapped adults near Los Angeles – or perhaps it was *in* Los Angeles – she never quite knew where the sprawling city began and ended. The institution was lavishly furnished and equipped with the conscience money of the families who had dumped their defective dependents there, but the work was demanding and sometimes distressing. The place was run by a diminutive red-haired nun called Charlotte who generally wore training shoes and a track suit. She was a Judo black belt and some-times she needed to be.

Ruth showed her the letter. "What d'you think about this charis-matic business, Charlotte?"

"Me? I couldn't exist without it."

"You mean you actually go to one of these prayer groups?"

"Sure. Haven't you tried it?

"I'm afraid it wouldn't be my cup of tea. I'd just be embarrassed."

"Everybody's embarrassed at first. You soon get over that. You wanna come along with me one evening?"

"I'll think about it."

Later Charlotte said, "Hey, Ruth, next weekend there's a Day of Renewal over in Anaheim. A big affair, folks from all over coming to it. There's a plenary session in the morning, then small groups in the afternoon. Wind up with mass. Whaddya say?"

Encouraged by the prospect of a large gathering in which she could be an observer rather than a participant, Ruth agreed to go. The following Sunday Charlotte drove them over to Anaheim, a dull satellite of LA chiefly celebrated as the home of Disneyland. Some two or three hundred people were gathered together in the assembly hall of a Catholic junior high school. There were few seats vacant by the time Ruth and Charlotte arrived, and they had to separate. On the stage, which was festooned with banners declaring "JESUS LIVES" and "PRAISE GOD", was a small band of guitar and accordion players dressed in jeans and plaid shirts, and a priest MC at the microphone who led the assembly in hymns and prayers. Ruth was faintly reminded of a concert party at a Girl Guide rally she had attended many years ago: there was the same air of determined joyfulness and good fellowship about the proceedings. When the MC instructed everyone to hold their neighbours' hands as he prayed for the Spirit to descend upon them all, she stiffened in recoil and surrendered her hand reluctantly to the clammy palm of the stout woman sitting next to her. It seemed such an obvious gimmick to create an illusion of togetherness. The MC invited anyone present to pray aloud as if they were in their own homes and to share their thoughts with others. Several people obliged. The accepted mode of prayer was highly informal, personal, intimate, speaking to God as though he were another person present in the room. "We praise you, Lord, simply because you're alive and with us, and that makes all the difference." "Lord, I just have to tell you that I think you're really great." "Lord, you make the sun shine and the flowers grow, you made everything. You're so wonderful, Lord, you lift us up when we're down, you comfort us when we're sick, you rejoice with us when we're happy. We really love you, Lord. We really praise you." Listening to this drivel, Ruth felt herself burning in one big blush.

The MC introduced a speaker evidently well known to the audience, who applauded him vigorously. He was a tall, bony, middle-aged man, with flat hair combed back from a tanned, wrinkled face. He wore a sports jacket and slacks with a collar and tie. He looked as if he might be a salesman for something agricultural. First he relaxed the audience with a few in-jokes. "Did you know that Bishop Fulton Sheen and Cardinal McIntyre were travelling to the Holy Land for a Charismatic Congress and the Cardinal said to the Bishop, 'If you're going to speak in tongues, I'm going to be walking on the water.'" The audience laughed and clapped. Then the speaker asked if there were any Britishers present. Charlotte, seated a few rows ahead of Ruth, looked back at her expectantly, but Ruth kept her hands clasped firmly in her lap. A few hands went up among the audience.

Well, said the speaker, they would know that the British had an airline called British European Airways, BEA for short, and it had struck him when he was on vacation in Europe and flying BEA from Amsterdam to London that those letters could also stand for true Christian faith: "Believe, Expect, Accept. Believe in God. Expect Him to come to you. Accept Him when he comes. . . ." After talking for a while on the power of prayer, and the difference it had made to his own life, he led the congregation in his favourite hymn, *"Oh, the love of my Lord is the essence."* When they had sung the words of the last verse, he continued to hum the melody into the microphone, and the congregation followed suit, modulating into a variety of strange noises, keening and coaxing and crooning sounds, harmonized like a humming top, punctuated with occasional ejaculations – "Amen!" "Hallelujah!" "Praise Jesus!" Ruth glanced around her. Most of her neighbours had their eyes shut and were swaying in their seats. The stout woman had her fists clenched and was muttering over and over again, "Praise Jesus, Praise Jesus, Praise Jesus." Suddenly, from the back of the hall, a voice was raised high in some foreign language, a strange, barbaric-sounding dialect, full of ululating vowels, like a savage chant. So it was true: people really did speak in tongues at these gatherings. How childish it was, just like abracadabra, anyone could pretend to do it. But in spite of herself Ruth felt her skin prickle with the strangeness of it, the high, confident, fluent tone of the utterance. It stopped abruptly. "Thank you, Jesus," said the speaker at the microphone casually. "Thank you, Jesus," the congregation echoed. "Could we pray for an interpretation?" said the speaker. There was silence for a moment, then the stout woman beside Ruth stood up and said, "The Lord says, 'If any man is in Christ, he is a new creation; the old has passed away; behold, the new has come.' The Charismatic Renewal is the new creation. It is everyone's chance to be born anew. We can be like newborn babes in the Spirit." She sat down. "Thank you, Jesus," said the speaker. "Thank you, Jesus," murmured the rest. "Could we pray for a healing?" said somebody. "Could we pray for my sister's little boy who is seriously ill with a suspected brain tumour?" The speaker asked them all to join hands while he prayed with them. At this point Ruth got to her feet and left.

Charlotte hurried out into the lobby behind her. "What's the matter, Ruth?" she asked anxiously. "You OK?"

"I just couldn't take any more," said Ruth. "I felt faint. Something about the atmosphere."

"Yeah, it is kinda stuffy."

"I mean the emotional atmosphere."

"Take a little walk outside, you'll feel better. This afternoon it'll be the small groups. Quieter. You'll maybe feel more at ease."

"I really don't think I can take any more today, Charlotte."

Charlotte eyed her quizzically. "You're sure you're not fighting something, Ruth?"

"Only nausea. Look, I don't want to spoil your day. I'll meet you back here at four, all right?"

"What will you do till then? Why not join a small group this afternoon, huh? Give the Holy Spirit an even break."

Ruth shook her head and left the building. For a while she walked aimlessly along the rectilinear streets of one-storey houses, each with its little plot of coarse grass over which the sprinkler hoses plied monotonously, then through a commercial district of shops, gas stations, motels and funeral parlours. Most of the shops were shut, as it was Sunday. Ruth felt hungry and thirsty, but there seemed nowhere suitable to go, only drive-in hamburger places which she felt self-conscious of approaching on foot, or dimly lit bars advertising topless dancers. Eventually she found herself among crowds converging on Disneyland, and thinking that this would be as good a place as any to kill time, passed through the turnstiles. There was certainly no shortage of refreshment inside – the only problem was deciding in what architectural facsimile you wanted to consume it: a Wild West saloon or a wigwam encampment or a space-ship or a Mississippi paddleboat. It was a world of appearances, of pastiche and parody and pretence. Nothing was real except the people who perambulated its broad avenues, fingering their little books of tickets, patiently lining up for the Casey Jr Circus Train, the Peter Pan Flight, the Jungle Cruise, the Monorail Ride. Music filtered from loudspeakers concealed in the trees and fountains played and the Stars and Stripes hung limply from a hundred flagpoles. Huge grinning plaster figures of Disney characters proffered litter baskets at every intersection of paths. Children ran about with balloons, ice-cream, candy-floss and popcorn under the complacent eyes of their parents.

One such couple, overweight, brightly dressed, festooned with cameras, sat down on Ruth's bench to rest their feet, and the wife volunteered the information that they had come all the way from South Dakota. "Not just to see Disneyland?" said Ruth, with a smile, but they didn't seem to see anything amusing in the idea. "Well, we're seeing a lot of other places as well," said the woman, "but this is the high-spot of the vacation, isn't that right, Al?" Al said it was right. "He's always been crazy to see Disneyland," said the woman fondly, "ever since I started dating him."

It struck Ruth that Disneyland was indeed a place of pilgrimage. The customers had an air about them of believers who had finally made it to Mecca, to the Holy Places. They had come to celebrate their own myths of origin and salvation – the plantation, the frontier, the technological utopia – and to pay homage to their heroes, gods and fairies: Buffalo Bill, Davey Crockett, Mickey Mouse and Donald Duck. The perception at first pleased and then depressed her. She looked at the crowds ambling along in the smog-veiled sunshine, from one fake sideshow to another, chewing, sucking, drinking, licking, and was seized with a strange nausea and terror. For all their superficial amiability and decency they were *benighted*, glutted with unreality. Ruth began to recite to herself the words of Isaiah: "*For the heart of this nation has grown coarse, their ears are dull of hearing, and they have shut their eyes, for fear they should see with their eyes, hear with their ears, understand with their hearts, and be converted and healed by me.*" But she must have spoken the words aloud, for the woman from South Dakota turned to her enquiringly. "I was just thinking," said Ruth "that if Jesus really lives, you wouldn't know it in here." The woman stared. "Well, I don't go much on religion, myself," she said, uneasily. "My husband used to be a Christian Scientist, didn't you, Al?" Al gave a sickly grin and said they ought to be getting along. They left Ruth sitting alone on her bench, staring back at her over their shoulders from a safe distance.

Ruth got to her feet and walked rapidly in the opposite direction, to the Exit turnstiles. She hurried back to the school. In each of the classrooms a small prayer group was in progress. She went from room to room, looking for Charlotte through the little observation windows in the doors. One door had no window, and she opened it. Half a dozen faces turned in her direction. Charlotte's was not one of them. The stout woman who had sat next to her in the assembly hall smiled at her. "Come and join us. Where have you been?"

"I've been to Disneyland," Ruth said, closing the door behind her, and joining the circle of chairs. The others laughed uncertainly.

"And what did you think of it?"

"I thought it was like the world must have been before Christ came."

There was a surprised silence.

"Walt Disney was a good man, a godfearing man," said someone, a shade reproachfully.

The stout woman said, "I don't think Ruth is really telling us about Disneyland. I think she's telling us something about herself. Isn't that right, honey?"

To her astonishment and acute embarrassment, tears began to roll down Ruth's cheeks. She nodded and sniffed, groping in her handbag for a Kleenex. "All my life as a nun there's been one thing missing, the one thing that gives it any point or sense, and that's, well, real faith in God. It sounds ridiculous, but I don't think I ever had it before. I mean, I believed in Him with my head, and I believed with my heart in doing good works, but the two never came together, I never believed in Him with my heart. Do you understand what I mean?"

The stout woman nodded eagerly. "Would you like us to pray over you, honey?"

Ruth knelt, and the other people present clustered round and put their hands on her head. Even before the woman began to speak, Ruth felt a profound sense of bliss descend upon her.

That night she began to pack her bags for the journey home. She wired her Mother Superior: "BY THE WATERS OF DISNEYLAND I SAT DOWN AND WEPT STOP HAVE FOUND WHAT IVE BEEN LOOKING FOR STOP RETURNING IMMEDIATELY"

As part of her Open University course on the Nineteenth-Century Novel, Tessa had to attend a residential summer school, held at one of the new universities in the north of England. "I believe Robin Whatsisname teaches there," said Edward. "You remember, the chap who married Violet, the dotty girl at Angela and Dennis's wedding. You ought to look them up."

"Oh, I'll be much too busy," said Tessa. She was excited at the thought of the week ahead, her first trip away from home on her own since she had been married, and she did not want to waste precious time paying courtesy calls, especially not on the notorious Violet.

The student body at the summer school consisted largely of mature men and women like Tessa, who could scarcely believe their luck at having a cast-iron excuse to abandon spouses and children for six whole days and do nothing except talk, read and enjoy themselves. There were lectures and seminars in the mornings and afternoons, and for the faster set, drinking and a disco every night. Tessa retired dutifully to her room to read immediately after dinner on the first two evenings, but on the third, the rhythmic thud of amplified music and the hum of voices drew her downstairs to the bar. She hesitated at the threshold, peering in. There was a general effect of blue denim stretched tightly over buttock and crotch, of empty beer glasses and overflowing ashtrays, of flirtation and pursuit.

"Extraordinary spectacle, isn't it?" said a voice at her shoulder. It was George, a middle-aged teacher in her seminar group, a dapper, drily amusing man, with a habit of dropping his head and looking over his glasses when he delivered his opinions about *Anna Karenina*, the week's set text. He looked over them now, delivering his opinion on the roaring throng. "They discuss adultery all day and commit it all night."

"How do you know?" Tessa laughed.

"Well, I'm reliably informed that all the Durex machines in the men's loos are empty," he said. "And it's only Tuesday."

Tessa blushed and looked away.

"I'm sorry, I've shocked you. My apologies," said George.

"No, no," said Tessa, feeling foolish, and to re-establish herself as a mature, sophisticated woman, accepted his offer of a drink. "Are you married, George?" she asked conversationally, when they had found a table.

"No," he said with a smile, "I'm a bachelor. But you're quite safe with me. I don't feel that way about girls. Now I've shocked you again."

"Oh, no," said Tessa earnestly, "how terribly interesting." This was certainly living.

"Same again, both of you?"

It was another member of their seminar, Roy. A rather vain young man, Tessa had already decided, very conscious of his blond wavy hair and china-blue eyes. He had perfected a lazy film-star's smile that slowly uncovered a row of strong white teeth, and he gave the general impression of being about to burst out of his jeans and cheesecloth shirt. They discussed the foibles of their seminar leader, and whether it was better to read criticism before or after reading the original text. Tessa offered to lend Roy a book on the language of fiction that she had found particularly useful. She insisted on buying another round, which George fetched from the bar. Then Roy asked her if she would like to dance.

"Would you mind?" Tessa asked George.

"Please! Enjoy yourselves." He waved them away.

When Tessa stood up, she felt the effect of the three vodka-and-tonics she had swallowed. It was a nice effect. She floated through the crowded bar to a darkened annexe where the music throbbed and boomed. Shadowy figures, luridly stained by shifting coloured lights, writhed, ducked and weaved. Occasionally a splash of light illuminated their features and Tessa recognized with surprise some shy fellow-student or awe-inspiring lecturer magically transformed into a creature of mindless sensual abandonment, twitching and shuddering under the invisible lash of the music. She began to twitch and shudder herself. Her limbs, oiled by the vodka, loosened, her head went back, her arms lifted, her torso undulated elastically to the rhythm.

"Hey, you're terrific!" said Roy, as one record faded and another began.

She smiled dreamily. She had forgotten he was there. "I go to keep-fit classes," she said. "We do modern dance sometimes."

After a while the music changed to a slow, languorous tempo, and the figures in the room began to glue themselves together in couples. Tessa felt Roy's hands low on her hips, his belt buckle pressing into her midriff. Or was it his belt buckle?

"I think we ought to go back to George," she said. But when they returned to the bar, George had gone.

"Another drink?" Roy suggested.

"No thanks," said Tessa. "I must be off to bed. Thanks for the dance."

"I'll come with you to pick up that book," said Roy.

Tessa felt panic rising inside her as she led him up staircases and along corridors to her room. Was he going to make a pass at her, or was she being foolish to even think of it, being nearly old enough to be his mother? "I'll just pop in and get the book," she said, unlocking the door of her room.

"Do you have any instant coffee in the kitchens on this floor?" he asked.

"Yes, do you need some?"

"Thanks," he said, "black with sugar."

"Oh," said Tessa, who had not meant that at all. "All right, just a minute."

Stupid of me, she thought, as she went to the kitchen at the end of the corridor. Still, coffee was a sobering drink. And if he tried anything funny, she would tip her cup over him. She returned to her room with a steaming cup in each hand, rehearsing the words of some firm but courteous dismissal to be delivered after the coffee had been consumed. Not being able to turn the door handle, she tapped with her foot for admission. The door opened, and closed behind her as she walked in. She turned. Roy smiled lazily. He was stark naked. Tessa screamed and threw coffee. Roy swore and hopped round the room, clutching himself. Tessa ran out of the room and hid in the Ladies. Half an hour later, she crept back to find the room empty, a coffee-stained bedspread in the middle of the floor the only trace of Roy's visit.

The next evening, she did not dance, but drank with George in the bar. Roy, steering a girl with dyed blonde hair through the crush by her denimed rump, studiously ignored Tessa. She and George discussed *Anna Karenina*, compared Tolstoy's technique with George Eliot's, agreed to differ about the heroine of *Mansfield Park*. It was a warm night, and the dancers emerged from the disco glazed with perspiration. George proposed a walk around the artificial lake. At the furthest and darkest part he put his arms round Tessa and started kissing her neck. "Stop it, George!" she said. "What are you doing? I thought you didn't feel that way about women?"

"You could cure me, Tessa," he said breathlessly. "I have a feeling you could cure me. Come over there by the trees."

Tessa gave him a push and he staggered backwards, putting one foot into the artificial lake. She ran quickly back to the lights of the hall of residence, laughing, crying.

The next evening, Tessa joined a group of married women of her own age in the bar. They drank shandy or bitter lemon and passed round snaps of their husbands and children. They compared, with affected indifference, the grades they were getting in their courses, and complained about the inconsistencies of the marking system. Tessa was reminded of the ladies who waited for the curtained showers after her keep-fit classes. She left them to make her daily call to Edward.

There was always a queue in the evening for the two pay phones, and as she waited Tessa saw George and Roy weaving unsteadily towards her, their arms round each other shoulders. "Hello, Tessa darling," said George. "We're going for a stroll round the lake. Coming?" He leered at her over the tops of his glasses. Roy smiled lazily.

"I'm phoning my husband," said Tessa, making it sound like a threat. They went off giggling uncontrollably.

The man and the woman using the phones ahead of Tessa put down their receivers simultaneously, exchanged sly smiles, and walked off hand in hand. Tessa seized the nearest phone.

"Hello," said Edward. "How are you, darling? Enjoying it?"

"Yes."

"Interesting people?"

"Oh, yes. A real mixture. Housewives, teachers, sex-maniacs . . . "

He chuckled. "I miss you," he said.

"I miss you, too. What are you doing with yourself in the evenings?"

"Nothing much. I've been to the local once or twice. Michael's invited me round tomorrow night. I thought I'd go. Ruth's staying with them."

"Ruth?"

"Oh, you never knew her, did you? She was at college with Michael and me. She became a nun."

"Oh yes. Didn't she go to America?"

"That's right. And she's come back full of this Pentecostal-charismatic caper, apparently. Prayer groups and speaking in tongues and that sort of thing."

"Doesn't sound very Catholic."

"Sounds like a lot of tosh, to me. I'm surprised, Ruth was always a sensible sort of girl. But I haven't seen her for donkey's years. Tomorrow's the Assumption, by the way. Will you be able to get to mass?"

"I don't know. I expect so."

Edward was always scrupulous about mass attendance on Sundays and holydays of obligation, the legacy of being taught as a child that "missing" was a mortal sin. Tessa, conditioned by the much more casual churchgoing of her Anglican childhood, still found the habits of Catholics in this respect a matter for wonder and occasional irritation. At any mass there would always be a score of people with streaming colds who should obviously have been at home in bed instead of coughing their germs over everybody else, and mothers with yowling babies who couldn't possibly be getting anything spiritual out of the occasion. And if they ever went to a Unity service in one of the neighbouring churches or chapels on Sunday, they had to go to mass as well, because the Unity service, even in these supposedly ecumenical days, didn't "count". She was tempted to ignore Edward's reminder, especially as there was no mass on the campus, but the next evening she felt like a change of scene from the bar and disco, so she took the bus into town and heard Mass in an ugly little church crowded with tired and bored office workers. Afterwards, she strolled round the city's medieval cathedral, magnificent, peaceful and empty.

As she walked back towards the bus terminus, a street name caught her eye. It was the address Edward had given her for Violet. She found the house, number 83, at the end of a terrace of Georgian town houses, and rang the bell. A slim, dark man with receding hair brushed back over his ears answered the door.

"Mr Meadowes?"

"Yes."

Tessa went through the rigmarole of introducing herself. He didn't seem very welcoming, and she began to regret her impulse. "Perhaps I've called at an inconvenient time," she said.

"I'm afraid Violet's in hospital."

"Oh, I'm sorry. Nothing serious, I hope?"

"She's in a psychiatric ward."

"Oh dear."

A little girl of about nine appeared at the door. "This is Felicity," he said. "Won't you come in?"

"Oh, no, thank you but – "

"Robin! Coffee!" a youthful female voice called from the back of the house.

"Please, come in and have a cup of coffee." Robin seemed suddenly anxious that Tessa should stay. He led her down a dark hallway and a short flight of stairs into a large basement kitchen, pleasantly decorated and well-equipped, but in a state of squalid disorder. A plump girl of about twenty in a long cotton dress looked up from the stove and pushed a curtain of hair back from her face. She did not seem pleased to see Tessa.

"This is Caroline," said Robin. "She's a student at the University, and she babysits Felicity when I'm out. I've just been out," he said carefully, "to visit Violet."

"Hallo," said Tessa.

Caroline murmured something inaudible and let the curtain of hair fall back.

"It's such a fine evening, why don't we take our coffee into the garden?" said Robin. "I think we still have one or two unbroken deckchairs."

"I really mustn't stay long," said Tessa, more and more convinced that she had made a bad mistake in calling. The garden was an uncultivated rectangle of weeds and long grass with curiously shaped chunks of masonry scattered about here and there. "Violet's sculptures," Robin explained, putting his feet up on one of them. Felicity wandered off to a swing at the bottom of the garden. Caroline had remained in the kitchen. "How well did you know Violet?" he asked.

"Hardly at all. I think I only met her once. It was Edward who knew her really. What is her . . . problem, exactly?"

Robin emitted a harsh, abrupt laugh. "There have been many theories. Personally, I blame her religious upbringing – you're not a Catholic, are you?"

"I am, actually. A convert."

"Ah, well, that's different. It's the conditioning in childhood that does the damage."

"But not all cradle Catholics are . . ."

"Neurotic? No, but it encourages neuroticism. The kind of Catholicism Violet was brought up in, anyway. A convent boarding school in Ireland. Hell-fire sermons, obsession with sin, purity, all that sort of thing."

"It isn't like that now."

"Isn't it? I'm glad to hear it, but the change has come too late for poor Violet." He rocked the sculpture back and forth with his foot. "She hates herself, you see. I mean, most of us are dissatisfied with ourselves from time to time, but she really hates herself, her body, her mind. She thinks she's no good, so she does something awful to prove to herself that she's no good, then she feels guilty. She isn't happy unless she's feeling guilty. But then she's unhappy *because* she's feeling guilty. Because she's terrified of going to hell."

"Telephone!" Caroline called from the kitchen window.

"Excuse me," said Robin. Tessa sipped the dregs of her coffee and wondered how to make her escape. Felicity came up to her, twirling a skipping rope.

"Do you know when my Mummy is coming home?" she said.

"No, I'm sorry, I don't dear," said Tessa compassionately.

"Is she in a loony bin?"

"No, she's in a hospital, with doctors and nurses taking care of her."

"Mummy said it was a loony bin," said Felicity.

"Oh," said Tessa, nonplussed. "Well, I expect that was just for a joke."

With a little smirk, Felicity changed the subject. "Do you know, Caroline has hair between her legs?"

"So do all women," said Tessa briskly. "So will you when you're grown up, Felicity." .

"Do you, then?"

"Of course. Tell me about the school you go to, dear."

Robin came out of the house. Felicity skipped off to the bottom of the garden, humming a little tune under her breath. Tessa got to her feet. "I must be going," she said.

"Oh, really?" said Robin, gazing thoughtfully after his daughter. "I'll run you back to the University."

"Oh, please don't bother "

In the end, she allowed him to drive her back to the bus terminus. "I hope Violet gets better soon," she said in the car.

"Yes, I hope so. I'm afraid the whole business is having a bad effect on Felicity. She's getting to the stage where she's curious about sex and so on, and I really can't handle it. On the other hand, God knows what Violet would tell her."

"I know an awfully good book," said Tessa. "Called *Where Do I Come From Anyway?* or something like that. I'll send you the details, if you like."

"That would be very kind," said Robin. "Well, here we are, there's your bus. If you're coming into town again, give me a call. We could continue that interesting conversation about Catholicism. Listen to a little music on my hi-fi, if you like that sort of thing."

"I'm afraid I'm going home tomorrow," said Tessa, glad to have this cast-iron excuse.

Back at the University, the bar and disco had reached new heights, or depths, of frenzied hedonism on the last night of the course. Oppressed, and slightly haunted, by the visit she had just paid, Tessa plunged into the throng with a kind of relief. Someone pushed a double vodka and tonic into her fist and she quickly became tipsy. Even the housewives' circle had switched from shandy and bitter lemon to gin for the evening and were tipsy too. They sat, bright-eyed and red-faced, near the entrance to the disco, tapping their feet wistfully to the music. "Why aren't you dancing?" said Tessa. "Nobody's asked us," they said. "You don't need partners for this kind of dancing," said Tessa, and chivvied them into the disco room where they flung themselves about with joyous abandon. The bar closed and more people poured into the room. The heavy chords of a record turned up to maximum amplification were greeted with ecstatic cries of "Stones!" and a wild gyration of limbs. Tessa thought she saw George and Roy dancing in a corner with the dyed blonde in jeans, but, ravished by the brutal power of the music, she no longer cared very much. Her body said: this is almost as good as sex, and without complications.

The mood on campus the next day was melancholy, as the students nursed their hangovers, prepared to terminate their brief love affairs, and braced themselves to return to the bosoms of their families. Tessa, looking in the campus bookshop for something to take home to her children, came across the facts-of-life book she had mentioned to Robin and, on impulse, bought it. She asked the taxi taking her to the station that afternoon to stop at Robin's house and wait. She rang the bell without effect. She scribbled a note of explanation on the wrapping paper and tried to push the book through the letter-box, but it was too big. She went down the side alley to the back of the house, but there was no one in the garden. She peered into the kitchen, but that was empty too, the doors and windows shut. A flight of steps led up from the garden to a small verandah with French windows which seemed to be ajar, though the curtains within were drawn. Pulling these aside just enough to insert the copy of *How Did I Get Here Anyway?* Tessa found herself staring at two naked bodies sprawled on floor cushions in a rosy light. She had time to notice before she fled back to the taxi that Caroline was wearing headphones and that Robin's head was clenched between her fat thighs. On her way to the station she stripped the wrapping paper from the book. "Here," she said to the driver, "have you got any children, or d'you know anybody who could use this?"

The man read the title aloud. "A good question," he said, "I've often wondered myself."

Had the whole world gone sex-mad? Tessa silently posed the question to herself, settling back in the corner seat of her train compartment. She had a sense, exhilarated yet relieved, of having escaped unscathed from a region of danger. The week's experiences had quite appeased her body's hunger for sexual adventure, and she felt happy to be returning to her chaste and blameless married life. She resolved, however, to give Edward a carefully edited account of the summer school, in case he tried to stop her going on another one next year.

When she returned home that evening, Edward was incurious about her experiences, and seemed to have preoccupations of his own. He kissed her warmly and murmured, "Bed."

"Goodness, give me a moment to get my breath," Tessa said, laughing, but pleasantly aroused. She visited the children in their various parts of the house and then went back to the kitchen for a snack. Edward perched on a kitchen stool, with his long legs bent like a grasshopper, sipping whisky while she ate. "I went over to Michael and Miriam's last night," he said. "Ruth was there."

"Oh yes. What was it like?"

"Well, it turned into a kind of charismatic meeting," he said. "Ruth insisted on praying over me."

"Good heavens! Whatever for?"

"For my back. They go in for healing, you know."

"And did you let her?"

"Well, I couldn't very well stop her."

"How very embarrassing."

"The funny thing is," said Edward. "I haven't felt a twinge since. And I did two hours in the garden this morning."

Tessa stared. "You're not serious?"

"Well, there's often a psychosomatic dimension to these back troubles you know. I'm keeping my fingers crossed."

"You mean, your back's *cured*?"

"I don't know," said Edward. "But if you'll come to bed, I'll give it a work-out." He grinned lustfully at her, his big ears glowing.

Edward's lovemaking was more passionate than it had been for a long time. "I must go away more often," Tessa purred. She lay back luxuriously and let herself be possessed by his strong male force. But the next day, when Edward woke, his back was paining him again.

"Oh, well," he said. "I thought it was too good to be true."

"Poor darling," said Tessa, nuzzling against him. Guiltily, she realized that she was relieved as well as sorry. The idea that Ruth might have cured Edward's back had offended her commonsense notion of what the world was like. I shall never be a real Catholic, she thought. I don't really believe in the power of prayer.

When Tessa reported to Edward that Violet was in a psychiatric hospital he was sorry but not really surprised. Half the patients he saw nowadays seemed to be suffering from mental or psychosomatic illnesses, and a large proportion of the prescriptions he wrote were for tranquillizers. Michael and Miriam, who had read R.D. Laing and Ivan Illich, sometimes rallied him about this. "I can't prescribe happiness, which is what most of my patients want," he said, "so I prescribe Valium instead."

"How do you think the human race managed before Valium was invented?" Miriam demanded.

"That's a good question," he admitted. "Of course, there was always alcohol, laudanum, and so on. But I sometimes wonder if there hasn't been a quantum leap, lately, in the average human being's expectation of happiness. I mean, in times past, your average chap was content if he could fill his belly once a day and avoid disease. But now everybody expects to be happy as well as healthy. They want to be successful and admired and loved all the time. Naturally they're disappointed, and so they go round the bend."

Edward advanced his theory partly in self-defence. He did not seriously believe that it accounted for poor Violet's psychological condition, which seemed more like a hereditary curse or congenital defect, with no reason or justice behind it. He still felt a vestigial interest in and responsibility for Violet, remembering vividly the day he had taken her to the hospital after she started throwing crockery around in Lyons cafeteria. As they were driving north that Christmas, 1973, to stay with his parents, Edward thought they might break their journey to call on Robin and Violet. Tessa wasn't keen. "There won't be time," she said. "Anyway, how d'you know she isn't still in hospital?" So Edward phoned Robin at his University to enquire.

"Violet's out of hospital," said Robin. "She's been out for some time."

"Oh, good," said Edward. "She's better then?"

"Well, she is in a way," said Robin. "Though as far as I'm concerned she's just exchanged one form of religious mania for another. She's joined the Jehovah's Witnesses."

"Good God! You're not serious?"

"Someone she met in the hospital converted her."

"But it's all nonsense, isn't it?"

"Complete nonsense. But then, so is Catholicism as far as I'm concerned. Shall I give her a message?"

"Well, we may be driving through your neck of the woods soon," said Edward tentatively.

"Well, do drop in, by all means," said Robin. "Violet will be glad to see you both."

But Tessa declined to share the visit. "You go," she said, "while I take the children round the Cathedral. We're too many to descend on someone just out of a mental ward." So Edward made the visit alone.

It was nearly fifteen years since they had seen each other, but Violet had not changed as much as he had expected. She smiled shyly at Edward when she opened the door to him, and led him into a living-room that was comfortably furnished but seemed oddly bleak. Robin was out. Edward met Caroline, a rather sulky young woman whom Violet introduced as their student lodger but who seemed to comport herself more as a member of the family, and Felicity. Edward asked Felicity what Father Christmas was going to bring her and received the disconcerting reply that Father Christmas wasn't Christian. Felicity looked at her mother for approval as she delivered this rebuff, and was rewarded with a smile. Edward suddenly realized why the room seemed so bleak: there were no cards or decorations in evidence.

Caroline took Felicity off and left Edward and Violet alone. They made small talk for a while, but soon Violet turned the conversation to religion. "Do you read the Bible, Edward?"

"Not much," he admitted.

"Oh, you should, it's a great comfort," she said earnestly. "I got better, you know, through reading the Bible. I'll give you one before you go."

"Well, we have got one at home, actually."

"But this one is different. It's got notes."

"Well, mine's got notes as well," said Edward with a smile.

"Ah, yes, but they'd be Catholic notes," said Violet. "And the Catholic Church is the whore of Babylon, you know."

"Violet," said Edward. "You don't really believe that."

"Oh yes," said Violet. "It's all in the Bible. That's why the Catholic Church used to try and stop people reading it. The Catholic religion isn't true Bible religion, you know."

"Isn't it?"

"No. For instance, there's no hell, like they used to tell us at school, only gravedom."

"Gravedom?"

"That's the meaning of the Hebrew word *Sheol*. And there's no such thing as the soul. When you die, you die, you're just dust, nothing. You can't feel anything, so you can't suffer. You can't be punished. Your spirit goes back to God who created it, until the Coming of the Kingdom."

"What will happen then?" said Edward.

"Then God will resurrect the dead and reign for a thousand years."

"And then what?"

"Then there will be a Judgement."

"Ah," said Edward.

"But you won't be judged on what you did in this life," said Violet. "You'll just have to pass the test."

"What test?"

"To witness your loyalty to God," said Violet. "But after a thousand years of the earthly paradise, with no death or sickness or suffering or violence, a thousand years of happiness and peace for the whole world, who *wouldn't* choose God?"

"And when is this thousand years due to start?" said Edward.

"Quite soon," said Violet, getting up to fetch a book from a bookcase. "The Bible says there will be great earthquakes and pestilence and food shortages. Nation will rise against nation and kingdom against kingdom. You only have to read the newspapers. Here."

She put into Edward's hand a small booklet open on a historical chart headed *Events of History, Past and Present*. It began:

> *4026 BC* — *Adam created*

and ended:

> *1975 AD* — *Man completes 6000 years of history on earth*
> — *UN "horns" devastate Babylon*
> — *Christ destroys nations at Har-Magedon*
> — *1000-year reign starts.*

"Looks as if we'd better make the most of 1974, then," said Edward.

Angela's father died in the spring of 1974. He had to go back into hospital at the end, and visiting him there in a ward full of coughing old men, shortly before he died, Dennis was deeply shocked. The papers that day were full of a terrible air-crash – a jumbo jet had fallen out of the sky near Paris, killing hundreds instantaneously – but cancer seemed to Dennis an excellent argument for dying in an air-crash as he walked away from the hospital with Angela. She had been up and down the motorway regularly in the past few months to visit her father, so was prepared for his wasted appearance, his slow, shadowy gestures, his tired voice, the eyes that seemed to have retired to the back of his skull, like the eyes of some small animal cornered in a cave. He seemed to know he was dying, and had gratefully accepted the Last Sacraments, but throughout his illness he had been very insistent that his condition was not lung cancer, making the point to all his visitors. As it seemed to give him some kind of comfort to believe this, they naturally humoured him. Perhaps it was a comfort to themselves, too, for at the funeral most of the mourners seemed to be lighting up compulsively every few minutes and then hastily stubbing out their cigarettes for fear of appearing irreverent. The ashtray in one of the cars became jammed with dog-ends and began to smoulder so that the vehicle drew up at the cemetery filled with a nicotine fog, the occupants coughing and weeping and clutching their throats as they fell out on to the gravel drive. Dennis had the odd feeling that he was the only person who saw anything grimly funny about this. The note of disregarded black farce persisted. At the reception after the funeral, held at the house of one of Angela's married sisters, there was a rat-tat on the open front door and a penetrating middle-class female voice trilled, "Cancer here!" but the murmur of conversation in the living-room scarcely missed a beat. Dennis went to the door and pushed coins into the woman's collection box. "Thank you *so* much," she said. "Having a party, are you? That's nice." Watching her prance back down the garden path, Dennis pushed a cigarette between his lips; then, on second thoughts, replaced it in the packet. In the car on the way home that evening he told Angela that he was going to give up smoking. She grunted sceptically.

"Did you see that girl of Tom's?" she said. "That Rosemary."

The family occasion had brought back a working-class timbre to her voice. It made him think of tight-lipped housewives in head-scarves gossiping on doorsteps. "She seems quite nice," he said. "Infant teacher, isn't she? Does your mother guess?"

"No. I don't know. I don't think so. Tom's been very clever, the way he introduced her. She's become quite a family friend. I suppose he thinks it'll take off some of the shock when he tells them he's going to marry her."

It was late when they got home and Dennis was tired from the drive, but he felt restless and tense. "Feel like making love?" he said to Angela as they were retiring – diffidently, because she had shown little enthusiasm for sex during her father's illness. Rather to his surprise, she agreed. Why? he wondered, as he went through the ritual of foreplay. Was it some obscure jealousy of Tom's girl that she was appeasing? Or was she pursuing this crazy idea that Christians ought to be cheerful and throw parties when their parents died? It certainly seemed to be on principle rather than for pleasure, for she did not appear to have a climax. But Dennis did, and fell gratefully asleep.

The next day was a Saturday, but Dennis went into his office to see if anything important had cropped up on the previous day. He drove through the gates of the factory with a wave to the security man, and parked in the space that had his car number freshly painted on the tarmac (he was Director of Manufacturing now). He let himself into the empty building with his master key. The air inside smelled stale, slightly tainted with chemical odours, and the benches in the work-shops, the shrouded typewriters in the offices, had a dead, abandoned look. But he always liked being alone in the empty factory, soothed by the peace, the silence, the curious sense of freedom.

On his desk, neatly arranged, was Friday's mail, each item clipped to its appropriate file, a record of incoming telephone calls, and a sheaf of freshly typed letters and memoranda which he had dictated on to tape on Thursday evening. Dennis smiled approvingly. Lynn was an excellent secretary, the best he'd ever had. At first he had found her difficult to relate to – a shy, softly-spoken Welsh girl who dropped her head at the slightest discouragement, and screwed up her lips in a sceptical smile when complimented on her work, as if she suspected irony. Dennis certainly never intended it: over the year and a half she had worked for him she had proved efficient, conscientious and fiercely loyal. He lived in perpetual dread that she would tell him one day she was leaving to get married.

As he addressed himself to his papers, Dennis patted his pockets automatically for his cigarettes, then ruefully remembered that he had given up smoking. The need for nicotine stabbed in his veins, but he controlled it and picked up the first of the letters awaiting his signature. One figure needed correction, and he flipped up the top sheet to emend the carbon copy underneath. The carbon was, however, of a different letter. A love letter evidently – or part of one. Dennis detached the sheet, scanned it and turned it over in bewilderment. There was no apostrophe at the beginning or signature at the end. It looked as though Lynn had been doing some private correspondence while he was away and had got it mixed up with the firm's. Amusement at this discovery quickly gave way to disappointment at her lapse and, more surprisingly, jealousy. Then, as Dennis read the letter more carefully, it suddenly struck him that it was addressed to himself. He began to tremble. His hand shook so violently that he had to lay the sheet of paper flat on the desk to read it. He read it over and over again. There was nothing specific in it, no names or other references that would put its meaning beyond doubt, it was all vaguely expressed longing, protestation, self-abasement, like the words of a popular song: but there were hints of problems and difficulties of age and status that fitted the situation of Lynn and himself.

The need for a smoke had become intolerable. Dennis broke into the firm's hospitality room with his master key and found a couple of stale Rothman's in a cabinet drawer. Lighting up with a spill touched to the electric fire in his office, he inhaled hungrily and considered what to do. The most important thing, obviously, was to find out whether the letter really was addressed to himself. That would have to wait till Monday. In the meantime he decided not to tell Angela, in case he was mistaken. And if he wasn't mistaken . . . ? Well, he would cross that bridge when he came to it. He folded the letter into his wallet and took it home.

Several times in the course of the weekend Dennis surreptitiously examined the letter. Its ambiguity remained unresolved until five past nine on Monday morning. Then, he had only to glance at Lynn's face as she came into his office with the morning's mail to know. She blushed a deeper red than he had ever seen anybody blush before. Then she went very pale. Then she ran out of the room. Neither of them had spoken. She came back a few minutes later, wearing her outdoor clothes.

"Where are you going, Lynn?" he said.

"To hand in my notice," she said. "Save you the trouble."

"What would you want to do a silly thing like that for? You know I can't manage without you."

Lynn hung her head and said nothing.

"Take your coat off and come back and take some letters," he said. "Oh, and by the way, this one you did on Friday doesn't seem to have a carbon. Be a good girl and see if you can find it, will you?"

Neither of them made any further reference to the love letter. Office life went on much as before – almost. Sometimes Dennis surprised Lynn gazing soulfully at him, sometimes she might have caught his eyes resting on her longer than was strictly necessary. She was not a strikingly beautiful girl, but she was pretty in a quiet way, with delicate features, a small waist and fine brown hair falling straight to her shoulders. It astonished and moved Dennis that this fair young thing should have fixed her affections upon his broken spirit and gone-to-seed body, and he could no more bring himself to rebuff her than he could have stamped on a fledgling that had fallen out of a tree and lay helpless and palpitating at his feet. He had not asked her to fall in love with him, he had not wished or intended that she should do so, but since she evidently had, Dennis bowed his head in resignation, he accepted the gift of her devotion almost as if it were another blow of fate, like the birth of Nicole or the death of Anne. Of course, it was much nicer – indeed it in some ways healed the wounds of those events. The secret knowledge that he was loved restored Dennis's will to live. He whistled in the morning while shaving. The economic recession that had plunged his managerial colleagues into deep gloom merely stimulated him to greater efforts at cutting costs. He succeeded in giving up smoking, and took up golf to keep his waistline under control. As the friends who introduced him to the game played on Sunday mornings, Dennis stopped going to mass. Since his eldest, Jonathan, had mutinied against mass attendance anyway, Dennis no longer felt obliged to set an example, and Angela acquiesced with only a token protest. She for her part would sometimes make the long drive to Michael's college for the student mass because Nicole liked the guitars and folk hymns.

At the College (where Michael was now Head of the English Department) sexual morality was in a fascinating state of flux. Many

196

of the students who had come up as good, obedient Catholics had, in the course of their studies, either lost their religious faith altogether or espoused a radical and highly permissive version of it; and it was well-known to the students and some staff that many couples among the student body were having fully consummated relationships under the very roof of the College. The residential accommodation was segregated only by floor, and supervision was not strict. Little ingenuity was needed to smuggle a girl or boy friend into one's room for the night. The teaching staff found the idea of this nocturnal traffic almost as exciting as did the students who were actually conducting it. They debated anxiously with each other their ethical responsibility in the matter. To put a stop to it seemed impossible without invoking the full weight of authority, informing the Principal and the Governors; and once the clergy, especially the Bishop, got any wind of it there was no knowing what would happen – the whole place might be closed down, or a highly puritanical regime imposed which would frighten away all the liveliest and cleverest students. Besides, these members of staff were not at all sure in their own minds whether premarital intercourse was necessarily wrong any more. "I mean," said Fiona Farrell, a colleague of Michael's, a good-humoured spinster of fifty who had a flat in college and a pastoral responsibility for the girls on her floor, "with Bede teaching situation ethics in the Theology Department, it's hardly surprising the young people should decide it's all right to sleep with each other – always providing, of course, that it's a serious interpersonal relationship based on genuine trust and a non-exploitative giving of oneself to another. Isn't that the jargon? I daresay I'd do the same in their place. My God, when I think of my own student days! The nuns at College wouldn't even let us lie out on the lawns in summer."

"You mean with your boy friends?"

"Are you joking? Boys weren't allowed within miles of the place. No, I mean if you took a book into the grounds in summer you had to sit bolt upright on the grass to read it. It was considered immodest to lie on the grass. I don't know whether they were afraid we'd be pollinated by the bees or something. . . ."

Fiona, who had come to terms with her own history of sexual repression by making a running joke of it, was holding forth at a dinner party given by Michael and Miriam for a few friends, including Dennis and Angela. Fiona had got them on to the ever-interesting topic with a spicy anecdote about a cleaner at the college who had that very morning found a contraceptive sheath in the girls' loo on Fiona's floor, and had been restrained with some difficulty from reporting it to the Principal. "Just think," she sighed, "I didn't even know what those things were for until I was thirty-five. I used to think people had been playing about with balloons in the parks."

"Actually, you know," said Michael, "it isn't all cant about serious interpersonal relationships and so on. I reckon most of the students who sleep together while they're here get married eventually."

"Michael finds it rather amazing," said Miriam sarcastically, "that anyone should want to marry a girl *after* he's managed to have sex with her."

"All right, I admit it. That was our generation, wasn't it? You weren't allowed to have sex outside marriage, so naturally having sex came to seem the main point of getting married." He opened a third bottle of Sainsbury's Catalonian Red. "And don't pretend it was a one-sided attitude. Girls hung on to their virginities on the same principle in those days."

"I hung on to mine too long," Fiona moaned. "Now I'd gladly give it away. Or auction it for CAFOD."

"Those long engagements," said Michael. "What were they but institutionalized postponements of consummation? Extended fore-play sessions. What d'you think, Dennis?"

"I think our courtship must have been the longest drawn-out foreplay session in the history of sexuality," said Dennis.

"You could have slept with me if you'd wanted to," said Angela, piqued, and a little intoxicated.

"Oh yes, a likely story!" he retorted.

"You could have – once." Angela challenged and held his gaze, until a long-suppressed memory surfaced, of orange light inside a tent, Angela lying back in a two-piece swim suit, inviting him with her arms, her lips.

"Oh, that," he muttered, blushing. "That was just once."

"Oh! Oh! Tell us, tell us!" they chorused. But Dennis changed the subject, and asked about the Paschal Festival which Catholics for an Open Church were planning for the following Easter. It was to be held at Michael's college and was expected to attract members and fellow-travellers from all over the country.

"Adrian feels the movement needs a bit of a boost," said Michael. "Now that *HV*'s no longer such an issue, we need to open up a wider range of areas for Catholic renewal. It should be quite an occasion. We've invited Dan Figuera, you know, the South American liberation theology man. Ruth is going to do her charismatic bit. And Miles has agreed to be on a panel on sexuality. Did you know he's come out, by the way?"

"Come out?" said Angela blankly.

"Admitted he's gay. He lives with an ex-monk called Bernard now."

"I didn't think Catholics could be practising homosexuals," said Angela.

"Well, officially they can't, of course," said Michael. "But I suppose they can just decide to follow their own consciences, like us with birth control. Or the students who sleep with each other before they get married."

In the car on the way home, Dennis said musingly, "I wonder what would have happened if we *had* made love that day in Brittany."

"With our luck, I'd probably have got pregnant," said Angela. "Then we'd have had to get married, with you in the Army, on National Serviceman's pay. A proper mess." She yawned. "I hate going out mid-week," she said. "I feel so shattered the next day." Angela had a part-time job now, teaching in the ESN school that Nicole attended. They hardly needed the money, but the work gave her satisfaction, and she was able to keep a close eye on Nicole's development.

"No, but supposing you hadn't got pregnant . . . I wonder if we'd have got married at all."

"You mean, once you'd got me into bed, you would have lost interest in marriage – like Michael was saying?"

"No, I was wondering if *you'd* have married *me*. You never really liked it, did you, for a long time, sex?"

"We weren't very good at it for a long time," said Angela.

"That's what I mean. If we'd made love that afternoon, it might have put you off for good."

"Oh, what's the point of speculating," she said. "So many things might have been different. We might never have met at all. I nearly went to Liverpool University instead of London – Dad didn't want me leaving home, God rest him." She sighed and yawned again.

Dennis drove slowly and deliberately, still feeling a little sluggish from the wine at dinner. He debated inwardly whether to propose sex when they got home, and then reflected how unthinkable it would have been to the young man in the orange tent in Brittany that one day he would be free to possess Angela and would be wondering whether to bother. To lift the oppression of this thought, he urged her to make love when they were getting ready for bed. "If you like," she said. But when he came from the bathroom she had fallen asleep with the light on and a towel ready to hand on the bedside cabinet. He could not deceive himself that he was unduly disappointed.

While they were clearing up after the dinner party, Michael and Miriam had a row. She accused him of provoking an embarrassing scene between Angela and Dennis. Nonsense, he said, it was all in fun. We were all a bit merry, except you. That's another thing, said Miriam, you pour out far too much wine, you only think a party's going well if everybody's half-seas over, it's not necessary. I hate dinner parties, anyway, she said, scraping plates angrily into the garbage can, you always tell me to cook too much, and then look at the waste. Yes, said Michael sarcastically, you could feed a whole street in Calcutta for a week on our leftovers. Well, it's true, said Miriam, and while we're on the subject, I want to covenant a tenth of our income to CAFOD. You're insane, said Michael, that's over five hundred pounds a year. If the developed countries are going to help the Third World, said Miriam, they've got to accept a drop in their standard of living. We could do without the car, for instance. I'll give up my car if everyone else will give up theirs, said Michael, but I'm damned if I will otherwise. Is that what you call Christian leadership? said Miriam. It's what I call common sense, said Michael, what use is my five hundred pounds to the Third World, most of it would disappear into the pockets of bureaucrats and middlemen anyway. All right, pay me a proper wage for keeping house, and I'll make my own arrangements, said Miriam. Don't be ridiculous, said Michael. It's not ridiculous, said Miriam, white with anger now. Anyway, I'm fed up with housekeeping, I'll get a job of my own. There aren't any

200

music teaching jobs, said Michael, they've all been cut back in the freeze. I don't want to teach music anyway, said Miriam, I want to be a social worker. A social worker! Michael exclaimed, but you're not trained. I'll train, then, said Miriam, there's a course at the Poly. You're going to train as a social worker, said Michael, at great public expense, and ours too, because you won't get a grant, in order to give half your salary away to the Third World? That's right, said Miriam, any objections? What about the kids, he demanded, you always used to say that you didn't want them to be latch-key children. They're old enough to cope, said Miriam, and if you're so worried about them you can arrange your teaching so that you get home when they do.

Michael snatched up the garbage pail and took it outside to the back garden, where he relieved his feelings by banging the dustbin lids. When he returned to the kitchen with a fully worked out account of why he couldn't reorganize his teaching schedule, Miriam had gone to bed, leaving him the rest of the washing-up. Moodily he made himself a cup of instant coffee. The mild lechery which he had been fuelling throughout the evening with wine and sexy talk had evaporated, and he knew exactly what an unfriendly posture Miriam would have adopted in bed upstairs – her face turned towards the wall, her shoulders hunched, her nightdress pulled down and locked between her ankles. These rows, which had become more frequent of late, frightened him, not so much because of the aggression they released in Miriam but because they made him wonder whether they should ever have married each other. Miriam was a puritan, an ascetic, self-denial was no hardship for her, it was the only way she could be happy, whereas more and more he felt himself to be an epicurean. But it was not clear to him whether they had both changed since they had married, or, brainwashed by the cult of matrimony in their youth, had tacitly conspired to conceal and ignore their real identities. There were times when Miriam seemed like an utter stranger, and their married life like a dream from which he was just beginning to waken. But to what?

Dennis couldn't help wondering whether Lynn was sexually experienced or not. He presumed she must be, if even Catholic students were sleeping together these days, but he knew almost nothing about her private life, except that she was twenty-five, came from South

Wales, and had a flat some miles from the factory. She alluded occasionally to attending evening classes for pottery, but otherwise seemed to have no social life. One day he commented on this enigma to a colleague, who said, "Didn't you know? I thought it'd been all round the shop. She's got a kid."

"A kid?"

"What they call a one-parent family, these days, isn't it? In other words, some bloke put her in the family way, and then scarpered."

"Perhaps she didn't want to marry him," said Dennis.

"Perhaps. Silly girl should've got it adopted, then. Nice girl like her could get married easy. But who'd take on some other bloke's little accident?"

The discovery gave Lynn a new interest and a new pathos in Dennis's eyes. At the same time it made her crush on him a more worrying responsibility. Sometimes he wondered if it would not be kinder to get Lynn transferred to another job, even another factory, so that she could shake off her infatuation and perhaps meet some decent fellow who would be glad to marry her and give the child a father. But he hesitated and procrastinated, because he was unwilling to seem cruel in order to be kind, and because, in truth, he couldn't bear the prospect of parting from her. Then, at Christmas, their relationship changed decisively.

On Christmas Eve, work stopped on the shopfloor and in the stores and offices at midday, and a kind of serial party began, made up of lots of little parties, stretching round the factory like a paper-chain, with a great deal of drinking and seasonal fraternization between management and workers. Dennis did his bit in this respect, touring the different departments with a pocketful of cigars and taking a drink with each group of merrymakers. An atmosphere of boozy bonhomie and tawdry licence spread through the buildings. In the corridors Dennis crunched crisps and broken glass underfoot, skirted couples kissing greedily, mouth on mouth, still holding unfinished drinks and smouldering cigarettes in their outstretched hands, and heard behind the doors of the women's toilets the sound of young girls unaccustomed to liquor moaning and being sick. In the corner of one of the stores a woman packer, her face a raddled, grinning mask of powder and lipstick, was doing high kicks on a table, urged on by a rhythmically clapping crowd. It was the same every year at this season, one afternoon on which the accumulated repressions and frustrations of the rest of the year were discharged in a squalid orgy, the memory of its excesses being quickly buried in the stupor of a domestic Christmas. Usually Dennis merely tolerated the custom with a skin-deep show of party spirit, but today he felt genuinely excited. A project was forming in his head and would not be removed: under cover of this feast of misrule he could safely give Lynn a kiss, something, he realized, he had been wanting to do for some time. There would be nothing odd or untoward about such a gesture – on the contrary, bosses were kissing their secretaries all over the factory. Lynn could not imagine that he meant by it anything more than a friendly sign of affection, nor would it give scandal if they were observed. The more he thought about this idea, and the more nips of scotch he took on his tour of the factory, the more excited Dennis became, and as he approached his own department again he was gripped by a hollow, breathless feeling of erotic expectation more intense than anything he had felt in many years.

"Give us a kiss, then, Dennis!"

Doreen Wills, from Personnel, normally the hardbitten career woman incarnate, was ogling him from the door of the hospitality room, a glass in her hand and a paper hat askew on her upswept hairdo. She pointed upwards to a sprig of mistletoe pinned to the door frame. He gave her a perfunctory peck on the cheek, but she twisted her face round to glue her lips to his. "Happy Christmas, Dennis, darling," she said, breathing gin and sweet vermouth into his face. He responded absently, looking over her shoulder into the room where an impromptu disco was in progress. "You know, I could really fancy you, Dennis," said Doreen. "Come and have a dance."

"Sorry, Doreen, I don't go in for that kind of dancing," he said. "Have you seen Lynn anywhere?"

"Ah! Want to get her under the mistletoe, eh?"

"No, just got some work to finish off," he lied, nettled by the shrewdness of her guess.

"For Christ's sake, Dennis, it's Christmas Eve! Anyway, I think she's gone home."

"Home?" Dismayed, Dennis rushed off to Lynn's office. It was empty, and her coat had gone from its hanger behind the door. Angrily Dennis kicked this door shut, cutting off the sounds of carousing, and strode into his own office by the communicating door. Lynn, dressed in her outdoor clothes, looked up from behind his desk.

"Oh," she said. "I was just leaving you a card." She held out a Christmas card to him like an alibi. He approached her and took it across the desk, in a queer reversal of their usual roles. "It's very nice," he said, glancing at it. "Thank you."

"I had a job getting a religious one," she said. Then, leaning forward to peer at him, "You've got lipstick all over your face."

"Doreen Wills caught me under the mistletoe."

"Lucky you," she said drily. Her back was to the fading light of the December afternoon and he could not discern the expression on her face as she spoke.

"Unlucky, you mean." He rubbed furiously at his mouth with the back of his hand.

"Don't do that, you'll just make it worse. Here, have a Kleenex." She rummaged in her handbag.

"Pity we don't have a bit of mistletoe in here," he said, attempting a light-hearted tone that came out as a strangled croak.

She looked up quickly. "I'll remember to get some next year, then," she said, holding out the tissue.

His hand closed over hers and pulled her gently forwards over the desk. "I can't wait that long," he said, "to wish you a happy Christmas." Supporting herself with her free hand, Lynn turned her cheek to receive his kiss. He had forgotten how soft a young girl's skin could be. "That wasn't much of a kiss," he said, keeping hold of her hand. "Come round here."

She shook her head.

"Please."

"You come, if you want to," she whispered.

Without letting go of her hand, as if performing some stately dance, he stepped round the end of the desk and drew her into his arms.

What followed took Dennis completely by surprise. He had had in mind a single, wistful kiss, a tender but decorous embrace that would convey his appreciation of Lynn and his affection for her, but at the same time confirm their mutual awareness of the circumstances that made any deeper relationship impossible. Lynn, however, clung to him as if she would never be prised loose, she flattened herself against him like a climber marooned on a cliff-face, she shuddered in his arms and sighed and moaned and ran her fingers through his hair and thrust her tongue between his teeth as if she wanted to climb inside his mouth and wriggle down his throat. Dennis's feeble lust was soon swamped by this demonstration. He was appalled by the intensity of the passion he had aroused, and daunted by the task of seeming equal to it. At last Lynn peeled her lips from his, sighed and nestled against his shoulder. Dennis, stroking her back as if comforting a child, stared past her head at the dusk gathering over the company car-park. What now, he thought, what now? What does one do next? What does one say? There was nothing he could say, he realized, after trying out a few phrases in his head, that wouldn't sound either coldly dismissive or recklessly committing. It seemed to Dennis that a stark choice already stared him in the face between being a cowardly prig or an unfaithful husband; that, incredible as it seemed, one kiss had tumbled him irretrievably into a maelstrom of tragic passion and insoluble moral dilemmas.

"Shall I take you home?" he said at last. It was the most neutral thing he could think of, but the way Lynn nodded agreement immediately convinced him that, without intending it, he had sealed some sexual contract with her in the code which governed such matters.

In the car, neither of them spoke, except for her to give, and him to acknowledge, directions. Dennis drove like an automaton. He felt deprived of free will, as if the wheels of his car were locked into grooves carrying him inexorably towards adultery. He felt no excitement or lust, only a sense of doom and a fear that he would fail sexually, humiliating both of them.

He stopped the car outside a semi-detached Victorian villa. "Will you come in?" Lynn said. It did not seem to Dennis that she meant it as a real question or that he had a real choice. He followed her into the ground-floor flat. There was a pushchair in the hall. "I suppose you know I've got a little boy?" she said.

"I heard rumours," he said. "I didn't like to pry." The sight of the pushchair had given him hope of a reprieve. "Where is he now?"

"I've got a friend who collects him from the nursery. She keeps him till I call."

The main room in the flat was furnished as a bed-sitting room. Lynn lit the gas fire, took off her coat, and flopped down on the divan bed. "Too much Cyprus sherry," she said, closing her eyes.

Dennis stooped over her, hopeful again. "Are you all right?"

She put her arms round his neck and pulled him down beside her. Dennis stroked her breasts through the woollen dress she was wearing, put his hand under her skirt and slid it up over legs glazed in nylon tights. Now that he could see no way of avoiding the sexual act, he was impatient to get it over. "Why don't you take this off?" he said, plucking at her dress; and sat up himself to take off his jacket, tie, shoes.

This cannot be happening, he thought. Behind him, Lynn said: "Have you got something?"

"What?"

"You know. . . ."

Dennis stopped in the act of undoing his belt, and turned to face her. She was still fully dressed, her skirt up round her thighs. "Aren't you on the Pill, then?"

"No. Why should I be?"

"I don't know . . . I just thought. . . ."

"I haven't got a fella, you know. And I don't go in for one-night stands."

"I'm sorry, Lynn." Red with embarrassment, he began to do up his belt, put on his shoes, his tie, his jacket. When he was dressed, he turned to her. She had not moved. He pulled down the hem of her skirt. "Can we try and forget this ever happened?" he said.

"No," she said.

He made a helpless shrugging gesture. "Can we have a cup of tea, then?"

She laughed, sighed and sat up. Over tea he heard the story of her life, in brief. Brought up in a small town, chapel-going community; trained as a secretary and went to work for a local legal firm. Was seduced by her boss, a married man, and after an extended affair, became pregnant. Refused to have an abortion and left home to avoid disgracing the family. Dennis couldn't help thinking how close they had come to re-enacting the whole sequence. As if reading his thoughts, Lynn said: "I had to stop you just now – I didn't want it to happen again."

"It was just as well," said Dennis. "I think we were both a bit drunk."

"You won't ever do it now, will you," said Lynn, with a wry smile. "I've missed my chance."

"What chance, Lynn? I'm nobody's chance – certainly not yours." Lynn said nothing. "I should never have started it," he said. "It was all my fault, I apologize." Lynn stirred her tea, smiling enigmatically. Dennis looked at his watch. "I'd better be going."

He kissed her again on leaving, trying to make it a chaste and chastened kiss. She clung to him for what seemed like hours, but did not attempt any further show of passion. He let himself out of the house.

When Dennis got home, Angela was in the kitchen, making mince pies. "What's the matter with your face?" she said.

"It must be lipstick," he said. "Doreen Wills trapped me under the mistletoe."

Angela yelled with laughter. "Poor you!" She was in good humour, he noted. She liked Christmas, all the bustle and preparation and wrapping of presents, the orgy of spending.

"Where's Nicole?"

"In the lounge. There's a Blue Peter Special I said she could watch, in a few minutes."

Nicole was sitting cross-legged on a cushion in front of the television. She was addicted to TV and her watching had to be carefully rationed. She scrambled to her feet and came to give Dennis a hug. "My Daddy!" she sighed, as if he had been away for weeks.

"How are you, love?"

"I'm all right." She drew him gently to a chair facing the TV and sat on his knee, returning her gaze to the screen.

Nicole, at eight, was doing very well. She could swim like a fish, read quite advanced Ladybird books and write her name legibly on Christmas cards. She was cheerful and friendly and related well to other people. Dennis loved her dearly, yet he could never set eyes on her without a pang. All mongols looked more like each other than like their parents, but beneath the characteristic heavy, curved jaw, the snub nose and stubby unfinished ears, the short thick neck and barrel-shaped torso, he could discern a likeness to Angela when he had first met her – as though an X-ray portrait of Nicole would reveal the ghostly image of the beautiful, gifted girl she might have been but for the rogue chromosome. Nicole! How many times had he regretted the choice of that exotic name, suggestive of French chic and feminine allure!

Some old black-and-white film, a romantic melodrama by the look of it, was coming to an end. Hero and heroine were exchanging husky endearments against an obviously painted backdrop of lake and mountains. Violin music swelled in the background. "Waiting for Blue Peter?" said Dennis conversationally.

Nicole nodded, then pointed at the TV. "First they kiss," she explained, "then it's finished." She had seen the endings of a lot of old films.

Perhaps, thought Dennis, it would be all right after all. When Lynn sobered up, she would see the afternoon's events as a moment of madness which they could bury, like her letter, and carry on as before. No harm, thankfully, had been done. Perhaps it would even be easier between them, now that the pressure had been relieved. Pressure, safety valves – with these hydraulic images Dennis sought to reassure himself that all was well, that the episode was closed. But the next morning, while most of the family were still in their dressing-gowns after a late breakfast and the opening of presents, there was a ring on the doorbell and Lynn appeared on the step, a small package wrapped in gift paper in her hand. Her face was white and anxious.

"I bought this for your little girl, Nicole," she said. "I forgot to give it to you yesterday."

"Come in, Lynn," said Dennis, with a sinking heart. "Come in."

In Rome that Christmas, Pope Paul, assisted by the Cardinal Penitentiary, chipped with an ornamental tool at the bricked-up Holy Door in the façade of St Peter's and thus inaugurated the Holy Year of 1975. A Holy Year, in case you are wondering, is a year in which the Pope grants a special plenary indulgence to all those who visit Rome and fulfil the usual conditions. The custom dates back to medieval times. In the corridors of the Vatican there was hope that the Holy Year of 1975 would knit the fraying fabric of the Church together by a worldwide demonstration of homage to the Holy See. This expectation, however, was disappointed. The Holy Year was not a success, not even for the Italian tourist trade. Catholics didn't seem to be as interested as they used to be in obtaining plenary indulgences.

Throughout the world, the Church continued to boil with conflict and controversy. Since the Council, this had been chiefly provoked by the ecclesiastical Left, who wanted to identify the Church with socialism, abolish priestly celibacy, ordain women, demythologize the Scriptures, repeal *Humanae Vitae*, and so on. But now a new threat to unity was emerging on the Right, in the person of a French archbishop called Lefebvre, who was right wing enough to think that Pope Paul was a crypto-communist and that the Vatican Council had betrayed the Catholic faith to modernism. This point of view he cleverly associated with a campaign to bring back the old Latin mass – a cause which aroused ready support in the breasts of older Catholics nostalgic for the spiritual certainties of their youth and dismayed by the rapidity of recent change. Tridentine masses, celebrated in defiance of ecclesiastical authority by priests sympathetic to Lefebvre, attracted large congregations and great publicity. The threat of schism loomed. Frantically, Rome tried to steady the rocking boat: Lefebvre was admonished, but so was the modernizing theologian Hans Küng, for questioning the doctrine of papal infallibility.

The Catholics for an Open Church Paschal Festival was going to be a sort of counter-demonstration to Archbishop Lefebvre's movement, and a showcase for the pluralist, progressive, postconciliar Church, as Michael explained to Polly and Jeremy over aperitifs one weekend in February, when his and Miriam's long-mooted visit to the converted oast-house had finally materialized. The Festival programme was settled in outline: the participants would assemble on Holy Saturday morning and throughout the day there would be a continuous programme of lectures, workshops and panels on theology, liturgy, ethics and pastoral practice, leading up to the Easter Vigil and Midnight Mass celebrated by Father Bede, the College chaplain (since Austin was still under suspension), followed by an agape and all-night party, and culminating in a special Easter Dawn Service which had yet to be devised, but would probably involve sacred dancing by nuns.

"Far out," said Jeremy. "I want to film it. The whole thing."

"Really?" said Michael.

"It's perfect for an Elton special. We'll call it 'The New

Catholics'." Jeremy now worked for a commercial television company and had his own networked documentary every fortnight, called the Elton Special.

"Adrian will be tickled pink," said Michael.

"So will you, admit it," said Miriam, squashing Michael since politeness restrained her from squashing Jeremy. She was suspicious of Jeremy, a small but shapely man, with a handsome head and a mischievous, slightly vulpine smile, like a fox in a fable. She couldn't decide whether she positively disliked him, but she certainly didn't trust him – or, for that matter, Polly, who was a charming and efficient hostess, but slightly abstracted in manner, as if she were all the time wondering what use she could put you to in her next column. The affluence of the Elton ménage also made Miriam feel defensive. If their own style of furnishing was Habitat and Handed-down, this was Heals and Harrods: a kitchen straight out of the colour supplements, an Italian dining suite of solid oak and tubular steel, Scandinavian real-hide module furniture in the living room, Japanese hi-fi and video equipment banked up against one wall like a showroom display, hand-woven curtaining fabrics, wall-to-wall Wilton everywhere, a mosaic-topped coffee table covered with the latest weekly and monthly magazines, and a new hardback novel in its pale lemon jacket that had been widely reviewed in the last few days. Miriam could see Michael covertly fingering everything and examining the brand names in barely controlled paroxysms of envy. The Eltons had two Connemara ponies in their stable, and a swimming-pool and a sauna and a sheepdog and a trail-bike and a rowing machine and a table-tennis table and a Victorian rocking horse and a stunning Swedish *au pair* who made Martin's ears glow bright red just by looking at him. Martin and the other two children were as enchanted by this palace of pleasure as Michael. When it had begun to snow heavily at lunchtime and Miriam anxiously wondered aloud whether they would be able to get away on the following day, her youngest, Elizabeth, had burst out, "Oh, Mummy, I do hope not!" to the great amusement of the Elton children. These, Miriam had to admit, were less spoiled than one might have expected, though infinitely more precocious and sophisticated than her own offspring. Abigail, at thirteen, was already dressing with flair, and had a way of patting her hair with both hands, and of curling up in an armchair, that showed an intuitive sense of her own allure, whereas Miriam's Helen, nearly two years older, was still a tomboy; and Jason, at fifteen, looked as tall and mature as the seventeen-year-old Martin. Miriam watched the interaction of these children with painful interest, scarcely able to restrain herself from intervening to coax from Martin and Helen the qualities she knew they possessed. She wondered fleetingly if she had failed them somehow, they seemed so shy and gauche beside the Eltons; but seeing Michael envying, coveting, flattering, affecting a worldliness that wasn't their true style at all, she braced herself to keep the family's conscience, to resist the blandishments of Mammon.

"Don't you think," she said now to Michael, as they sipped their pre-dinner drinks around the log fire, with the curtains cosily drawn against the snow, "that having TV cameras all over the place will inhibit people?"

"No way," Jeremy intervened. "After a few hours, they'll forget we're there, believe me. Sometimes I can hardly credit it myself, the things people will do in front of the cameras. We were making this programme the other day about a wedding, a sort of portrait in depth of a typical suburban wedding. . . ." He laughed reminiscently, and Polly took up the story.

"Yes, you see, Jeremy wanted to get the expression on the girl's face when she woke up in the morning and realized it was her wedding day, and would you believe it, they let him park a cameraman in her bedroom all night."

"Then he overslept, and we had to get the bride to fake it after all," said Jeremy. "But honestly I think, if we'd asked, they'd have let us tag along on the honeymoon and film their first fuck."

"I suppose they were getting paid," said Miriam frostily. Jeremy admitted that there was usually a fee in such cases. "And shall we get paid if you film our Festival?"

"Oh, I don't think COC would worry about that, darling," said Michael.

"Why not? I don't see why the TV people should get us for nothing."

"Miriam's perfectly right, of course," said Jeremy. "There would certainly be some money in it for your organization." He did not seem in the least discomfited by Miriam's insistence, but rather to respect her for it, "I'll write to your chairman – what's his name again?"

"Adrian. Adrian Walsh."

Polly gave a little shriek. "Not that tall bony boy in Cath. Soc. with glasses and the huge missal?"

"Polly – why don't you come to the Festival with Jeremy?" said Michael. "There'll be a lot of old friends besides Adrian there."

"I don't know if I could bear it," said Polly. "It's just the sort of thing to make one feel incredibly ancient. Perhaps I will. But supposing I got converted back to the Catholic Church? I'd have to leave you, darling," she said, with a mock-disconsolate *moue* at Jeremy, "and make you go back to your horrid bitch of a first wife."

"No, no," said Michael. "If you get converted to our kind of Catholicism you don't have to worry about that kind of thing. You can do whatever you think is right."

"Really?" said Jeremy, pricking his ears.

"Well, within reason," said Michael.

After dinner (home-made asparagus soup, a fragrant chicken casserole, chocolate soufflé, Wine Society Beaujolais) they played a tournament of electronic TV tennis with the children; then, when these had retired to bed, or to listen to pop records in Jason's room, or to watch TV in Abigail's, Jeremy distributed whisky and liqueurs and showed some recent Elton Specials on his video cassette equipment. The programmes were all identical in technique. There was no explanatory commentary, just a montage of images and recorded voices. Jeremy explained that his method was to shoot everything in sight, ask people questions, and then make an edited account of the results. The general effect, Miriam felt, was to make the subjects look rather foolish. In the course of this entertainment, Gertrude came into the room to ask if she could take a sauna bath.

"Sure, you know how to turn it on," said Jeremy.

"Isn't that rather extravagant, darling?" Polly murmured, after the girl had gone. It was the first evidence of the weekend that the concept of extravagance was recognized in this household. Perhaps, Miriam thought, the fact that Gertrude was young and pretty had something to do with it. Jeremy brushed aside the objection. Someone else might like a sauna later.

"I've never had a sauna bath," said Michael. "What's it like?"

"There you are!" cried Jeremy. "We'll all have a sauna together. It can seat four."

"Together?" said Miriam doubtfully.

"It's all right, Miriam, relax." Jeremy twinkled. "We always offer guests the choice: with towels or without."

"With, then," said Miriam firmly.

"What d'you have to do?" said Michael, beady-eyed. "Beating yourself with twigs comes into it, doesn't it?"

"Whisking is optional," said Jeremy. "And we don't have the proper birch twigs anyway. Could fix you up with some tomato canes, if that sort of thing turns you on."

"Basically," Polly explained, "it's a wooden cabin, with a stove in the middle, that gets extremely hot, but so dry that it's not uncomfortable. You sit in it for ten minutes or so, and sweat a lot, and then you go and have a cold shower and then you wait a bit and go back into the sauna and then shower again, as many times as you like."

"I've known Gertrude go through the cycle six times," said Jeremy. "She's a real addict."

"What's the point of it?" said Miriam.

"Well, it's like lying in the sun and then diving into a swimming-pool and then lying in the sun again."

"And what's the point of *that*?"

Jeremy laughed. "It's pleasant."

"It sounds like eating salted peanuts to make yourself thirsty to me," said Miriam.

"That's a good idea," said Jeremy. "Let's all have another drink."

"Not if we're going to sauna," said Polly.

"I've had quite enough to drink anyway," said Miriam. "And so have you, Michael," she added as he held out his glass.

"Tell you what," said Jeremy. I'll mull some wine over the fire afterwards." He bared his sharp-edged teeth. "And show you some of my special bedtime videotapes."

"Not *Deep Throat*, for heaven's sake, darling," said Polly.

"*Deep Throat*? Have you got that here?" said Michael eagerly.

"Friend of mine brought back a pirated tape from the States," said Jeremy. "It's hilarious."

"It's quite disgustingly crude," said Polly.

"I'd be jolly interested to see it, I must admit," said Michael.

"What's it about?" said Miriam.

"Oh, you must have read about it, Miriam," said Polly. "It's about this girl, Linda Lovelace, who can only come when she's sucking men off. A typical male chauvinist fantasy."

"But they surely can't show that in a film," said Miriam.

"Oh yes they can," said Polly.

"Well, don't let's argue about it now," said Jeremy, "let's have our sauna."

Michael and Miriam went to their room, as instructed, to undress and put on bathrobes. "You'll find a couple of spare ones in the cupboard," said Polly, and inevitably these garments were posher than their own dressing-gowns. While Miriam was undressing, Michael came up behind her and ran his hands over her body. "What fun, eh?" he murmured, nibbling her ear.

"I'm not going to watch that film," said Miriam.

"Don't be a spoil-sport, Miriam," he wheedled.

"If he puts that film on," she said, "I'm going straight to bed. To sleep."

"That's blackmail," said Michael, taking his hands away. "That's using your body to extort obedience to your will."

"Well, it's either me or Linda Lovelace," said Miriam. "Take your pick."

"Why d'you want to stop me from watching a blue movie? I mean, why do you feel so threatened by it?"

"That's a phrase you've picked up from Jeremy, isn't it, blue movie? It sounds nicer than pornographic film."

"Whatever you call them."

"I think they're sinful," she said, "since you ask."

Michael looked taken aback. Even to her own ear, "sinful" had a slightly archaic ring. "I don't see what harm they can do to adults," he mumbled, "married people." Then, with a sly grin he added, "You might even learn a thing or two."

"Ah ha!" She pounced on the inference. "Look, I know how it's done, I just don't want to do it." She met his eyes and held them, conscious that their talk was wobbling on a perilous edge between badinage and a serious quarrel. Michael opted for badinage.

"It's only a harmless protein," he said. It was an old joke between them, a line from the sex instruction film they had watched together long ago.

"I get quite enough protein, thank you," said Miriam. "No way."

"That's a phrase you've picked up from Jeremy," said Michael.

"Oh, I don't deny that his style is contagious," said Miriam. "I just don't believe he has any principles."

Jeremy and Polly were waiting for them in the hall, draped in matching kimonos and wearing wellington boots. "There's only one snag about the sauna," said Jeremy. "You have to go through the yard to get to it, and there's a fair amount of snow on the ground. So watch your footing. Here are some wellies for you two."

Shrieking and gasping at the shock of the cold night air, and clutching their bathrobes around them, they galumphed across the yard in their rubber boots, leaving deep footprints in the snow. Jeremy threw open the door of one of the outbuildings, and they tumbled inside. Gertrude looked up, startled, from a slatted pine bench where she was lying, swathed in a hooded dressing gown. There were a couple of other benches, a shower cubicle, and in one corner what looked like a rustic garden shed.

"Is it good and hot, Gertrude?" Jeremy asked.

"Perfect," she replied. "One hundred degrees already."

Jeremy distributed big blue towels, which they exchanged for their bathrobes with varying degrees of decorum.

The heat inside the sauna made Miriam gasp. "Oh!" she said. "I shall never be able to stand this. It's burning my nostrils."

"Breathe through your mouth," said Polly. "And sit down low."

There were two stepped benches on each side of the tiny cabin, with the boxed-in stove on the floor between them. The two couples divided and sat facing each other. Miriam, sitting at the lowest level, found herself staring up between Jeremy's thighs at his surprisingly large genitals. She looked hastily away, then examined his face to see if his self-exposure had been deliberate. His grin, however, was no more mischievous than usual. "OK, Miriam?" he said.

"Now I know what a leg of lamb feels like inside a Romertopf," she said.

"It's more comfortable without a towel."

"Thanks, I'll put up with the discomfort."

"Jeremy," said Polly, "leave Miriam alone."

"I want to make a hedonist of her," said Jeremy. "It's a challenge."

"You're banging your head against a brick wall," said Michael. "I've been trying all our married life."

215

"You weren't much of a hedonist yourself, once," said Polly. "Remember how I shocked you when I came back from Italy? You must have changed."

"The world has changed," said Michael, "and I've been trying to catch up. But Miriam won't let me."

"When did the world change?" said Polly.

"The world changed on or about the tenth of June, 1968."

"Don't you mean May?" said Jeremy. "Paris? *Les évènements?*"

"No, on the tenth of June, 1968, I was in Oxford, checking into a hotel. . . ." He recounted the story of the undergraduate in the white suit who had asked the price of a double room. "I realized then that people were no longer ashamed to admit they wanted to fuck. Now on my own honeymoon – that would have made a programme and a half, Jeremy. . . ." Michael told the story of the twin beds. "I was legally married, dammit. All I wanted was a reasonably comfortable bed to consummate the marriage. God knows, we'd waited long enough. And I was tongue-tied with embarrassment. Beads of perspiration literally stood out on my face."

"Talking of perspiration," said Miriam, who had not enjoyed this narrative, "how much longer do we have to stay in here?"

Jeremy glanced at a clock embedded in the wall. "You two could go and have your shower now. Polly and I will stay a bit longer."

Michael and Miriam emerged from the sauna to find that Gertrude had gone. "Let's shower together," said Michael.

"I wish you wouldn't use that word," said Miriam, as they peeled off their towels and donned shower caps.

"What word?"

"You know."

"Everybody uses it nowadays."

Miriam stepped into the shower stall and Michael squeezed in beside her. "I don't," she said.

"You're not suggesting I picked it up from Jeremy, are you? Actually, I picked it up from D.H.Lawrence. Tha's got a loovely coont, lass," he said, putting his hand between her legs.

Miriam pulled the lever behind his head. Michael yelled and she herself gasped as the cold water drenched them. But the sensation was not unpleasant. They wrapped themselves in their towels again, and Michael knocked on the door of the sauna, receiving a muffled

216

acknowledgement from within. He said quickly as he sat down beside her, "Look, do me a favour – just relax and let me enjoy my weekend, eh? Just this once, indulge me. I don't often get the chance to enjoy *la dolce vita*."

"What good does it do you?"

"I just want to know what it's like. I don't want to die a virgin, *ladolcevita*wise."

"You're such a baby," she scoffed. But she allowed herself to be persuaded back into the sauna for a second go. Jeremy filled a ladle with water and sprinkled a few drops on the stove, which hissed and exhaled a puff of steam. As he moved back to his seat, stepping over Polly, his towel slipped from his waist.

"Oops!" he exclaimed. "Oh, to hell with it, I'm sorry, Miriam, but it just isn't a proper sauna with a towel." He sat down naked.

"I'm going to take mine off too," said Michael, suiting the action to the deed.

"Goodness, how shy-making," said Polly. "Hadn't we better do the same, Miriam?"

"No," said Miriam. Polly hesitated, her breasts already half-exposed, but stayed decent. Miriam was angry, but uncertain what to do. To get up and leave would, she felt, be an admission of defeat as well as making an embarrassing scene. But to sit facing Jeremy's blatant nakedness and knowing grin was also an embarrassment, and a kind of defeat. In the circumstances, all she could think of doing was to close her eyes and try to meditate (she had been to evening classes in transcendental meditation.) But what she found herself thinking about was how different Jeremy's penis looked from Michael's – not only bigger, but a different colour and shape, brown and straight like a heavy rope-end, whereas Michael's was pale and curved and slightly pointed, reminding her, when it was flaccid, of a mouse asleep with its head in its paws. It was very hot. She felt perspiration trickling down her breastbone and on to her belly and between her legs. She leaned back and rested her head against Michael's knees. He massaged her head gently with his finger tips, loosening the skin that was tight across the top of her skull. This was an artful move. She was not fooled, of course – she knew that he knew that she liked having her head massaged, and for that matter he knew she knew he knew. But her anger receded. There was certainly something about heat that sapped the will. She wouldn't have greatly cared, now, if her own towel had slipped off, except that she was self-conscious about her almost non-existent breasts; she imagined Jeremy's quick, disappointed appraisal, and Polly's complacent glance. Michael, of course, had always had a thing about big breasts. Well, he was getting an eyeful now, no doubt.

Michael was all enthusiasm for the sauna. He questioned Jeremy about the cost of buying and running the equipment, and talked of installing one himself. "There must be at least twenty-five things we need more urgently than a sauna," said Miriam. "Where would you put it – in the garage? And cool off under the garden hose?"

"Why not?" said Jeremy. "In Finland they rush outside and roll in the snow."

"Well, we could do that ourselves tonight," Polly observed jokingly.

"Great idea!" said Jeremy. "What about it, folks?"

"Anything you say," said Michael.

"It *would* be rather a lark," said Polly.

"You're all mad," said Miriam, opening her eyes and sitting up. "You'll catch your deaths."

Michael begged her with his eyes to join in, and as they were mustering by the door of the outbuilding, murmured, "Come on, darling, be a sport." She shook her head, and pulled her bathrobe more tightly around her. The whole prank, she was now convinced, was being staged-managed by Jeremy to get them all naked together. "I'll watch you make fools of yourselves," she said.

"Right, strip off, children, and away we go," said Jeremy. "Across the yard and into the paddock. Last one to roll in the snow is a cissy." He dropped his towel from his hips and raced barefoot into the night, followed by Michael. Miriam watched Polly's broad buttocks jouncing in the light that streamed out across the snow from the open door as she waddled after them, squealing and shrieking. In the paddock they raced in circles, yelling and laughing, throwing snowballs, tipping each other up in flurries of powdery snow, rubbing handfuls of it into each other's bare skin. More light was shed on the scene from windows in the house, as curtains were drawn and sashes thrown up. Cries of wonder and encouragement came from the children, hilariously delighted at this untoward behaviour in their parents. It was, Miriam had to admit, a surprisingly innocent and appealing spectacle, a cold pastoral. The wagging breasts and penises, the dark smudges of pubic hair, seemed quite unshocking in that crystal setting. Miriam began to regret that she had not, after all, joined in. It seemed possible, suddenly, that she had been quite mistaken in resisting the momentum of the whole evening, that there was nothing after all to be afraid of, that there might be a kind of pagan salvation, a way back to that state of innocence the poets called the Golden Age, in this shared nakedness, without shame, without erotic intent, this pure, childlike play of naked bodies in the snow. Miriam's hand plucked at the belt of her bathrobe. But it was too late. The others were already running back. Then, as she watched, Michael seemed to stumble and fall, and did not get up. Jeremy and Polly stooped over him, and began dragging and carrying him towards the open door. Miriam ran out to meet them.

"You've killed him!" she screamed.

"He's all right, he's breathing," gasped Jeremy.

"*Breathing*! I should hope he is breathing," Miriam shouted. "Otherwise there'll be a few other people not breathing around here."

Michael soon recovered when they got him inside, wrapped him up and chafed his limbs. "Don't say 'I told you so'," were his first words to Miriam.

"I can't understand it," said Jeremy. "The Finns do it all the time."

"Michael doesn't happen to be a Finn," said Miriam.

"I'll phone Doctor Gordon," said Polly. "Just to be on the safe side."

"I'm perfectly all right," said Michael. "Please don't bother."

"Phone him," said Miriam.

The doctor came and examined Michael, probed him with a stethoscope and took his pulse.

"You fainted because of the shock to your body," he said. "The sudden change of temperature."

"But the other two didn't faint," Michael pointed out.

"Well, they've probably got stronger hearts," said the doctor.

"You mean, I've got a weak heart?"

"Only relatively. But I wouldn't go rolling about in the snow without any clothes on again, especially after getting overheated and putting away a fair amount of drink."

After the doctor had gone, Michael allowed himself to be taken off to bed, without any further reference to mulled wine or *Deep Throat*. In bed, he clung to Miriam more like a child than a lover, his penis as small and soft as a mouse. "So I'm not going to die young of cancer, after all," he said. "I'm going to die young of a heart attack."

"Oh, be quiet and go to sleep," said Miriam. She did not confess that she had been on the point of rushing out into the snow herself. "By the way," she said, for it seemed a good moment to make the announcement, "I've applied to the Poly for admission to the social workers' course."

Michael gave out a grunt which she interpreted as resigned acceptance.

In the kitchen, where they were tidying up, Jeremy said to Polly, "Pity about that. I hope he'll be all right."

"What were you up to, anyway?" said Polly. "What was your little game?"

"What do you think?"

"You must be mad," she said, "to think that you had any chance at all with those two."

"Oh, I don't know," said Jeremy. "Michael was hypnotized by your boobs."

"He always was," said Polly.

"And Miriam kept sneaking glances at my prick."

"So I noticed. But they're still just about the last couple in the world. . . . Apart from the fact that *I'm* not interested in that sort of carry-on, as you very well know."

"Well, that was it, you see. It struck me that if I could persuade a couple of square RCs to have a go at group sex, you couldn't very well drop out."

"That was quite clever of you, I must admit," said Polly.

"Then the silly bugger has to spoil it all by passing out," said Jeremy.

"Poor Michael," said Polly. "How awful if he'd died!"

"Not a bad way to go, actually," said Jeremy. He got out a bottle of whisky and held it up to the light "I can think of worse deaths."

"Aren't you coming to bed?" said Polly.

"No, I think I'll do some work," he said. "Have we got any books on the Catholic Church? I really think that there may be a programme in this Festival thing."

"I think I've got a biography of John XXIII somewhere," said Polly. "Will you read in bed?"

"No, I'll go in the study," said Jeremy. "Just tell me where the book is."

Jeremy read for an hour and a half with total concentration. Then he closed his book and turned out the lights on the ground floor. Quietly he climbed the staircase and entered his bedroom. Polly was asleep, breathing deeply, a glass of water and a bottle of Nembutal tablets on her bedside table. Jeremy touched her shoulder lightly, but she did not stir. He left the bedroom and went softly along to one of the three bathrooms in the house. A few minutes later he emerged, in pyjamas and dressing-gown, but instead of returning to his bedroom he turned in the opposite direction and climbed another flight of stairs to Gertrude's room. He entered quietly, without knocking.

The next morning the snow was beginning to thaw, but Miriam insisted on leaving immediately after breakfast in case the roads got worse, and no one attempted to resist her will. The drive home through the slush was slow and nerve-racking and it was dark by the time they arrived. When Miriam opened the door of the house the phone was ringing. It was Angela.

"Is Dennis there?"

"No, why?"

"We've had a row. He's walked out."

"What about?"

"He's been having an affair with his secretary."

"*Dennis*! I don't believe it."

"I found a letter in his wallet. I was looking for money for mass this morning."

"Oh, Angela!"

"She came round on Christmas morning with a present for Nicole. I thought she was just being nice. She's not really all that pretty. Young, of course."

"Listen, I don't understand," said Miriam. "Why did she write him a letter if they see each other every day at work?"

"Apparently that's what she does, she slips love letters into his correspondence. This one was to tell him that she'd been on the Pill for over a month."

"You mean, they haven't actually. . . ."

"According to Dennis, they both got drunk at the Christmas booze-up at the factory and he took her home and he was going to sleep with her because he thought he ought to – "

"Ought to?"

"Because they'd been snogging, he thought it was expected. He thought she'd be hurt if he didn't."

Miriam couldn't help laughing. "He would! Just like Dennis."

"But then he discovered that she wasn't on the Pill, so they didn't."

"This doesn't sound so bad, after all," said Miriam. Michael came into the room and cocked an enquiring eyebrow. She gestured him away.

"Yes, but then we had this terrible row and I think he's gone to her," said Angela.

"Why?"

"Because I told him to."

"Why did you?"

"Because of this terrible row." Angela sounded impatient, as if Miriam were being slow on the uptake. "He said he'd worshipped me with his body and I'd never shown any gratitude. So I told him to try his secretary."

Miriam was silent, not knowing what to say. It was hard to imagine Dennis moved to the pitch of invoking his marriage vows.

"He said I use Nicole as an excuse for ignoring his needs."

"That was unkind," said Miriam loyally. "And untrue."

"It was unkind," said Angela. "I suppose it might be true. I told him I hadn't got anything out of our sex life for years. That was unkind, but true." Her voice sounded surprisingly calm and slightly drowsy.

"Are you all right, Angela?" said Miriam. "Have you taken anything?"

"Just a couple of Valium. Then I had some sherry."

"That's going to knock you out. You'd better go to bed. I'd come

222

over, but we've only just got back from Kent and the roads are terrible."

"I'll be all right."

"I'm sure Dennis will come back tonight." In the background Miriam could hear Michael and the children arguing peevishly about who should bring something in from the car. She felt a deep anger against Dennis, and a deep compassion for Angela; but how strange it was, and slightly shameful, that the news should make her feel fonder of Michael.

"I never really wanted to marry Dennis, you know," Angela was saying. "I tried to get out of it, but he wore me down. Why didn't he leave me alone?" There was a long, choked silence on the line; then Angela began to cry, like a child, gulping for breath between sobs.

"Angela, listen, hang on, I'm coming over," said Miriam.

Dennis did not return home that Sunday. He drove about aimlessly for several hours, then he had a number of drinks in a pub, then he called on Lynn. She opened the door to him in her dressing-gown – it was early in the evening, but she had been taking a bath and washing her hair. Perhaps if she hadn't been wearing so little and smelling so fragrant, they wouldn't have made love. Dennis had come to her with no such intention, indeed with no intention at all: he was all at sea, tossed by violent waves of anger, guilt, self-pity, anxiety; sure only that if he slunk back to Angela without seeing Lynn, after Angela had dared him to go to her, then he would be broken, unmanned for ever after. So he went to Lynn, who read in his face what had happened as soon as she opened the door, and drew him inside, and into her arms, and into her bed. They made love, clumsily and urgently at first, then a second time with more rapture, then once more with desperate effort, Lynn licking him erect, and Dennis groaning as he squeezed a few last drops of seed from his aching balls. He woke the next morning to a grey drizzle, the suspicious scrutiny of Lynn's two-year-old, Gareth, and the consciousness that he was well and truly crucified on the cross of adultery. He drove Lynn to work, dropping her on a street corner half a mile from the factory gates so that they would not be observed arriving together. He went through the day in a trance, making no decisions. In the evening he met Lynn at the same corner and drove her home. There was a bedsitter vacant in the house, and Dennis rented it. He ate his evening meal with Lynn, and slept in her bed at night, but before dawn he would creep upstairs to his dreary little room, for he did not like to be discovered in her bed by Gareth in the mornings. He made no attempt to get in touch with Angela. He made no plans, and Lynn, to his relief, did not press him to declare any. She managed to conduct their affair as if it were an extension of their office relationship. She was calm, efficient, self-effacing. It was as if she could only express passion in her letters – and in bed, where she clung and coiled herself about him with a fierce intensity that filled him with wonderment, delight and dread in equal proportions. Only then did she seem to be staking some desperate claim on his future, but if he praised her afterwards she would smile ironically just as when he used to compliment her on her shorthand and typing.

The breach between Dennis and Angela sent shock waves rippling through their circle of friends. For many, it marked the end of an era, the end of illusions. "We are not immune," Miriam declared solemnly, and when Michael asked her what she was on about, merely repeated, "We are not immune." By "we" she meant their circle, their peer group of enlightened, educated Christians; and by "not immune" she meant that there was no magic protection, in their values and beliefs, against failure in personal relationships. If anything had seemed solid and indestructible in that sphere, it had been the marriage of Dennis and Angela, which had been founded on so long and faithful a betrothal, and had withstood such cruel trials and tribulations; yet it had succumbed at last to the most banal of matrimonial accidents.

Dennis, of course, was chiefly blamed, especially by the women; yet they could not, in their heart of hearts, entirely absolve Angela from all responsibility, for they had all noted, ever since the death of Anne, some fundamental absence of tenderness in her character which, however understandable in itself, might well, they agreed, in the course of the many conversations and phone calls which enveloped the affair in a web of words, have driven Dennis to another woman's arms. They also blamed Lynn for throwing herself at Dennis, though the discovery that she had a child complicated their response, for they prided themselves on their compassion for one-parent families, especially young women who had refused the easy options of abortion or adoption and were struggling to bring up their babies alone. It was natural enough that a girl so situated might persuade herself that she was in love with her boss, when what she was really in love with was her idealized picture of his family life. Clearly the attraction of Dennis for Lynn was as a surrogate father for her child rather than as a lover. Yet his response had a reckless gallantry about it that some secretly admired.

Michael, meeting Dennis by appointment at a pub one evening to hand over a suitcase of clothes, found him shy and defensive, but was himself overwhelmed – not with envy, exactly, for no one could envy Dennis the moral and emotional mess he had got himself into – but with a kind of admiration mingled with self-doubt. The unexpected presence of Lynn, sitting beside Dennis in the pub, brought home to Michael the astonishing reality of Dennis's affair, and made him feel himself less real. In the modern literature to which Michael was devoted, adultery was the sign of authenticity in personal life, and marriage the realm of habit, conformity and compromise. By rights, therefore, it was he, Michael, who ought to have been sitting in the corner of this pub, holding the hand of the pretty pale-faced girl with the nicely shaped breasts, and Dennis, dull, dependable old Dennis, who ought to have been pushing his way through the swing door with a suitcase full of shirts and underwear, a nervous envoy from the world of bourgeois morality. It was he, Michael, who ought to have been defying bourgeois morality, and yet he knew that he never would, he would never have the courage, or the wickedness, or indeed the provocation. For ever since the weekend in Kent, he didn't know whether it was because she thought he had died in the snow, or because he had agreed to her doing the social workers' course, but Miriam had stopped being aggressive, had indeed become positively sweet-tempered. They seemed to have renegotiated their marriage and to be bound to each other by some new, more pragmatic and, from Miriam's point of view, more equitable contract. He had been content with his bargain until he saw Dennis in the corner of the pub holding Lynn's hand, a man who had torn up his contract and tossed the pieces in the face of the world. He tried to explain all this to Dennis after Lynn had left, early, to relieve Gareth's babysitter, and several beers had loosened his tongue. "It's like *Heart of Darkness*," he said. "You're Kurtz and I'm Marlow. See?"

Dennis shook his head uncomprehendingly. "How's Angela?" he said. "How's Nicole?"

"Fine, fine," said Michael vaguely, forgetting for the moment, in his absorption in his own fate, that Dennis had deserted them.

So different people reacted differently to the news as it spread. Adrian was alarmed that the episode would bring Catholics for an Open Church into disrepute, and interfere with preparations for the Paschal Festival. Edward was saddened and Tessa intrigued. Violet sent extensive, incoherent letters to all parties from the long-stay psychiatric hospital where she was now confined. Ruth prayed fervently for a reconciliation. Miles was not very interested. Polly felt selfishly relieved that the plague had passed over her own house. Dennis himself, after a couple of weeks, was profoundly miserable, and longed only to be honourably released from his involvement with Lynn. He was exhausted from nightly sex, depressed by the meanness of his surroundings, acutely embarrassed by the gossip at work, and hag-ridden with guilt on account of Angela and the children, especially Nicole.

In the end it was Austin who rescued him – Austin who was urged by Miriam to mediate in the affair and attempt a reconciliation, Austin who had a long interview with Lynn, and somehow persuaded her to tell Dennis to go back to Angela, and persuaded Angela to accept him back without injuring his pride, and persuaded Dennis to let Lynn leave the factory and find a new job. So, after three weeks in which the earth had moved, life returned to normal again. Dennis and Angela picked up the threads of their lives together, a little wary of each other, a little chastened, but both hugely relieved. Their children, who had begun to exhibit alarming symptoms of delinquency and emotional disturbance under the impact of the crisis, swiftly reverted to normal. Their friends tactfully pretended that nothing had happened. For the first few weeks they contrived to go to bed at different times, and slept stretched along the outer edges of their double bed, but one night, by some intuitive mutual agreement, they rolled into each other's arms and sealed their reconciliation.

Austin's part in all this was, of course, highly acclaimed. It seemed to them all that there was something poetic, something positively providential, about the way he had repaired the marriage that he had himself solemnized so many years ago. It was a bit of a surprise, admittedly, when he turned up at the Paschal Festival with Lynn in tow; and since Angela was there too it put rather a strain on Christian fellowship and bonhomie. And it made them all blink to see Austin and Lynn happily holding hands at the party that followed the Midnight Mass. But then, there were plenty of things to make one blink at the Catholics for an Open Church Paschal Festival.

7
How it is

WHEN Jeremy's programme about the Paschal Festival was transmitted, Michael recorded it on videotape at the College's Audio-Visual Resources Centre. Because of the furore that followed the broadcast, Adrian asked him to write an account of it for reference purposes. Being rather proud of his media know-how, Michael in fact produced quite a polished transcript. It read, he thought, like a kind of coda to everything that had happened to them in matters of belief He was able to identify all but one of the voices over.

TRANSCRIPT OF THE ELTON SPECIAL, "EASTER WITH THE NEW CATHOLICS", AS TRANSMITTED 24/4/75.

Opening shot of the College playing fields, just before dawn, looking eastwards. Silhouetted against the horizon, a large boulder with a figure seated on it, back to camera. Silence.

Cut to

Close up AUSTIN
AUSTIN: We can't be sure that the Resurrection actually happened.

Cut to

Playing fields. Dawn. Looking westwards. Long shot of some two hundred people sitting on the grass. Camera moves in, pans over faces in close-up. Faint dawn light reflected in their tired, expectant faces. Sound: birdsong.

Cut to

Close up ADRIAN
ADRIAN: I think we can be pretty sure that no Pope will ever try to make an infallible pronouncement again.

Cut to

Playing fields. Looking eastwards. Two women in flowing robes of saffron and blue approach the figure on the boulder. Sound: arpeggio on flute. The figure turns and extends arms. The skirts of her pleated white robe are attached to her wrists and open out like wings. The other two fall back as if astonished and fearful.

Cut to

Close up MIRIAM
MIRIAM: I can imagine circumstances in which I would consider having an abortion.

Cut to

Playing fields. The tip of the sun's disc now appears on the eastern horizon. The three women begin a dance-mime illustrating the story of the two Marys and the angel at the empty tomb in Matthew. Sound: flute and percussion.

Cut to

Close up RUTH
RUTH: Well, why shouldn't nuns dance? I don't see anything funny in the idea. (Laughs) Unless it was me dancing. . . .

Cut to

Playing fields. The sun has risen. It shines through the diaphanous robes of the three dancers. The angel mimes the resurrection of Christ, leaping from the ground. Slow motion.
VOICE OVER (*Ruth*): After all, the psalm says, "Let them dance in praise of his name, playing to him on strings and drums."
On the soundtrack the flute and percussion fade out and are replaced by the communal singing of "The Lord of the Dance":

> Dance, then, wherever you may be,
> I am the Lord of the dance, said he, *etc*.

Cut to

College chapel. Night. The end of midnight mass. The packed congregation is singing "The Lord of the Dance" enthusiastically. A few people begin to dance in the aisles, up towards the altar. More join in.

TITLES (superimposed):

EASTER WITH THE NEW CATHOLICS
THE ELTON SPECIAL

Cut to

Main road, morning. Cars and lorries passing noisily. Zoom in on arrowed AA sign, "COC PASCHAL FESTIVAL".

VOICE OVER (*Adrian*): We were rather chuffed to get our own AA sign. It shows we're not just an eccentric fringe group. . . .

Cut to

Main entrance hall of the College, crowded with people greeting each other, kissing, shaking hands, etc. Queue at desk marked "Registration". Banner on wall: "Catholics for an Open Church. Paschal Festival 75. Peace and Love in the Lord." Roar of conversation.

VOICE OVER (*Michael*): Oh, absolutely all sorts of people – teachers, students, civil servants, housewives, priests, nuns . . . no, I don't think we've got any factory workers. I suppose it's essentially a middle-class movement. . . .

Cut to

Lecture room, nearly full. ADRIAN on rostrum with DAN FIGUERA.

ADRIAN: I know Dan Figuera doesn't look like a Professor of Theology, but – (Laughter. Close up of DAN FIGUERA in battledress blouse) But I assure you that he is, and one of the foremost figures in the exciting Latin American school of liberation theologians. It's a great pleasure and privilege. . . .

Cut to

DAN FIGUERA at the lectern.

DAN FIGUERA: Three questions. One: is Christianity a faith or a religion? I say it is a faith. Two: is its true dimension history or eternity? I say, history. Three: is its aim salvation or liberation? I say salvation *is* liberation. . . .

VOICE OVER (*Austin*): What Figuera is saying, basically, is that Christianity took a wrong turning as early as the first century.

According to him, Christ came to start a revolution, but instead became the object of a cult.

DAN FIGUERA: It's obvious from the New Testament that Jesus and his disciples thought the revolution, which they called the Kingdom of God, was imminent. Instead of making it happen, the early Christians turned Jesus into a religion, exactly like a hundred other religions in the Mediterranean world at the time, complete with mysteries, metaphysics, and priests.

Cut to

College refectory. Lunch. Pan shot of people at tables eating and discussing. Sound: babble of conversation, clash of cutlery, crockery, etc. Shot of table with AUSTIN, EDWARD, TESSA.

AUSTIN: What did you think of it then?

TESSA: I'm afraid I can't buy the idea of Christ as a freedom fighter.

EDWARD: He seemed to be saying that the Crucifixion was more important than the Resurrection. I always thought it was the other way round.

AUSTIN: Well, of course, there is some independent evidence about the Crucifixion. We can't be sure that the Resurrection actually happened.

Long shot of ADRIAN on his feet, rapping on the table for silence.

ADRIAN: The forum on "Towards a new theology of sex" will begin at two o'clock, and afterwards we'll split into buzz groups.

Cut to

Lecture room, afternoon. On the rostrum, seated behind a long table, MILES, FIONA FARRELL, BEDE, DOROTHY, and ADRIAN in the chair.

ADRIAN: We've got on our panel a housewife, a priest, a single woman and a . . . bachelor.

Close up on MILES

VOICE OVER (*Miles*): I didn't really want to come here at all. I don't really have a lot in common with Catholics for an Open Church. I mean, liturgically and theologically, I'm a conservative. I mean, I'd bring back the Latin mass if I had half a chance, and deport Dan Figuera as an undesirable alien. . . . But it *is* a public forum, and I think one has a duty to bear witness to one's convictions.

Cut to

MILES on his feet.

MILES: There must be no more distinctions between Jew and Greek, slave and free, male and female . . . (pause) straight and gay

Cut to

Close up FIONA

FIONA: I do so agree with what Dorothy was saying about sex education. The first time I felt sexual desire I thought I must be sickening for flu. . . . (Laughter) And of course I agree that we ought to tell our young people about contraception and so on, and not be shocked out of our wits if they decide to have sex before marriage or turn out to be homosexual, as Miles was saying, but. . . . But. Where does permissiveness stop, I ask myself. Is there anything that's definitely not on? Is there anything we can all agree is wrong in this field? Abortion, I suppose, but that's not exactly . . .

Cut to

A seminar room. A group of about a dozen women.

MIRIAM: I always used to be strongly opposed to abortion, I signed petitions and marched and so on. I still get angry at the messianic attitude of some of the extreme women's groups, as if abortion was the greatest thing since sliced bread. But now I'm not so sure that it's always and absolutely evil. I can imagine circumstances in which I would consider having an abortion. What about you, Angela? I mean, you've got a mentally handicapped . . .

ANGELA: (inaudible)

MIRIAM: I mean, supposing you found you were pregnant again?

ANGELA: I just can't answer hypothetical . . . I suppose I'd have to consider it.

MIRIAM: You see, I'm not sure Bede's right when he said we must completely dissociate the abortion issue from the contraception issue. I mean, if in spite of taking every precaution, I accidentally become pregnant, what am I supposed to think? That God has punished me for using contraceptives? That he's trying to make a fool of me? Obviously I don't believe in such a God. It seems to me that God has given women the freedom to control our own bodies, and we can't avoid the responsibility of using that freedom.

Cut to

The Refectory. Evening. Dinner is nearly over. ADRIAN raps on the table. BEDE stands up.

BEDE: Just to say that there'll be confessions after dinner in the Chapel. Basically, we'll just sit around and talk about our personal failures and hangups, then at the end I'll give general absolution. If anybody here is still into old-style confession, St Peter and Paul's is just around the corner. . . . (Laughter)

RUTH stands up.

RUTH: And if anyone is interested in a prayer group, there'll be one in the Quiet Room starting at eight.

Cut to

The Chapel. Evening. About twenty people are sitting round in a circle, looking self-conscious.

BEDE: Look, it might help to break the ice if I set the ball rolling. My own problem is anger. A well-known vice of celibates. (Subdued laughter)

VOICE OVER (*Michael*): I haven't been to old-style confession for years and years. Neither have my children. It's really quite extraordinary. Twenty years ago, if you went into a Catholic church on a Saturday evening, you'd always find a queue of people waiting to go to Confession. And looking as though they were hating every minute of it.

VOICE OVER (*Austin*): Oh yes, I think there's still a place for the sacrament of penance, definitely. But it should be collective as well as individual. Just think of all the misery and repression and suffering the Church has caused in the past. Persecuting heretics, Jews. Torture. Burning at the stake. Terrifying people with the fear of Hell. I think we should do penance for that daily.

Cut to

The Quiet Room. RUTH and some others sitting in armchairs and on the floor in a loosely formed circle.

RUTH: Let's just start with a period of silence, just making space for the Holy Spirit.

VOICE OVER (*Ruth*): There's no set form for a prayer group. It's however the spirit moves you. Sometimes we recite set prayers, like the Our Father or the Gloria, sometimes we sing hymns, sometimes one of the group will witness, tell the others what the

233

Lord has meant to them. Perhaps someone will ask to be baptized in the spirit.

Cut to

The Quiet Room. A woman is kneeling and the others are standing round her with their hands outstretched, fingertips touching just above her head.

VOICE OVER (*Ruth*): It's like a second baptism. It's a gift from God. Not everyone receives it. Very few receive it the first time they ask for it. Some people actually fight against it, which is not so surprising, really. Because it changes your whole life.

VOICE OVER (*Miles*): The growth of Pentecostalism in the Catholic Church is certainly remarkable, because it's a style of religious behaviour that's utterly alien to the Catholic tradition – intensely Protestant, in fact. There's no doubt in my mind that it's a reaction against the demythologizing and politicizing of the Faith that's been going on since Vatican II. The really emotive side of Catholic devotion has withered away – Benediction, Latin plainchant, the rosary, and so on. The magic has gone, the sense of the supernatural, which is what people want from religion, ultimately. So they turn to prayer groups – healing and speaking in tongues and whatnot.

Cut to

Close up of RUTH, eyes shut, speaking in tongues.

RUTH: (unintelligible)

VOICE OVER (*Austin*): I think you could say that the crisis in the Church today is a crisis of language.

Cut to

The College forecourt. Night. No lights visible. A crowd holding unlighted candles are gathered round a brazier. BEDE, dressed in white vestments, strikes a spark to ignite the charcoal bricks in the brazier.

BEDE: Dear friends in Christ, on this most holy night, when Our Lord Jesus Christ passed from death to life, the Church invites her children throughout the world to come together in vigil and prayer. . . .

VOICE OVER (*Austin*): That metaphor of the Church as mother is highly misleading. Historically, the Church has been much more like a tyrannical father towards its children.

234

The Easter candle is brought to BEDE. He inserts five grains of incense in the form of a cross on the side of the candle and lights the candle from the fire.

VOICE OVER (*Adrian*): Undoubtedly the developments of the last fifteen years or so have shattered the old certainties for ever. I think we can be pretty sure that no Pope will ever try to make an infallible pronouncement again, for instance.

BEDE holds the candle aloft.

BEDE (chants): Christ our light.

ALL (chant): Thanks be to God.

BEDE, carrying the candle, and preceded by an incense-bearer, leads the people in procession into the College, along darkened corridors.

VOICE OVER (*Polly*): Certainly Catholics are much more tolerant, much more liberal than they used to be. I was brought up as one and the nuns gave us to understand that unless you were a good Catholic, your chances of getting to heaven were pretty slim. Most of the people at this affair don't seem to think that they're in any way superior to Protestants or Jews, Hindus or Muslims, or for that matter, atheists and agnostics. Which is very decent and humble of them, but it does raise the question, why be a Catholic at all, rather than something else, or just nothing?

Cut to

The College Chapel. Dark. Empty. Camera on open door. Faint glow of approaching light. Incense bearer appears, followed by BEDE. He stops on the threshold and lifts the candle high.

BEDE (chants): Christ our light.

ALL: (chant) Thanks be to God.

ADRIAN, immediately behind BEDE, lights his small candle from the Easter candle.

VOICE OVER (*Adrian*): I think one has to be fairly tough-minded about this. Christianity *is* the best of the world religions – none of the others can touch it for universality of appeal. And, for all its historical sins, Catholicism is the best form of Christianity.

Cut to

The corridor leading to the chapel. The light is passed along the procession from candle to candle.

VOICE OVER (*Angela*): Oh, I'll always be a Catholic, I couldn't imagine being anything else. I suppose it's only chance, yes, the way I was brought up. If I'd been born a Baptist or something I daresay I'd be a Baptist. I think you need a religion to get you through life at all, and mine happens to be the Catholic one.

Cut to

The Chapel. BEDE goes to the altar and fixes the Easter candle in its holder. The congregation file in and take their seats, extinguishing candles.

VOICE OVER (*Tessa*): I really don't bother too much about theology, to be honest. A lot of things I had to subscribe to when I joined the Catholic Church even Catholics don't believe now. I sometimes wonder if it matters whether it's true, as long as it helps people to cope. And if it doesn't help people to cope, would it be any use being true?

DOROTHY goes to the lectern.

DOROTHY (reads): "In the beginning God created the heavens and the earth. Now the earth was a formless void. . . ."

VOICE OVER (*Austin*): Catholics, like most other Christians, have accepted that Genesis is a poem, a myth, not a factual account of the creation. It's rather more difficult for them to accept that a lot of the New Testament may not be literally true either.

Cut to

EDWARD at lectern.

EDWARD (reads): "And we believe that having died with Christ we shall enter life with him: Christ, as we know, having been raised from the dead will never die again. Death has no power over him any more. . . ."

VOICE OVER (*Miles*): I do think it's a pity the way they keep meddling with the Bible. "Death has no power over him any more." How feeble it sounds, compared to, "And death shall have no dominion over him."

VOICE OVER (*Polly*): I think death is the basis of all religion, don't you? Hearing mass again after all these years, and in English, I was struck by how many references there are to dying and eternal life, almost every other line. I never realized that when I was young. When my father died, a couple of years ago, I found the ritual a great comfort. I shouldn't be surprised if I called for a priest myself if I knew I was dying.

The congregation relighting candles for the renewal of Baptismal Promises.

BEDE: Do you reject Satan?

ALL: I do.

BEDE: And all his works?

ALL: I do . . .

VOICE OVER (*Ruth*): Oh, yes, I believe in the existence of the Devil, evil spirits, certainly. I think anyone who has been baptized in the spirit is sensitive to these things. I know people in the Charismatic Renewal who have had very frightening experiences.

VOICE OVER (*Miriam*): No, not as an actual being. The Devil I think is a sort of personification of the evil in all of us, the potential evil.

Cut to

BEDE, celebrating mass, turns to face the congregation.

BEDE: The peace of the Lord be with you always.

ALL: And also with you.

BEDE: Let us offer each other the sign of peace.

BEDE advances smilingly upon a girl at the end of the front row and embraces her warmly. The rest of the congregation smile, kiss, shake hands, etc., as BEDE moves along the front row, greeting each person.

VOICE OVER (*Dorothy*): Catholics, English Catholics, anyway, and Irish, have always been very frightened of the body, of physical contact. In our parish they think it's terribly daring to even shake hands with your neighbour.

Cut to

BEDE, facing the congregation, the host in his hand, raises it over the patten.

BEDE: This is the Lamb of God, who takes away the sins of the world. Happy are those who are called to His supper. . . .

VOICE OVER (*Angela*): When my little girl, she's mentally handicapped, wanted to go to Communion with the rest of the family, I didn't see why not. She's always been very interested in the mass, very reverent. Some busybody, a woman in the parish said, "But does she really understand what it's about? Could she explain?" I said, "Could you?" That shut her up.

The people in the congregation begin to come up to the altar to receive communion. BEDE administers the host, which most receive in the hand. DOROTHY and ADRIAN each take round a chalice.

VOICE OVER (*Polly*): In my day it would have been sacrilege to touch the host with your hand. And as for drinking the wine! In fact, the mass is hardly recognizable. It's certainly more comprehensible, but rather flat, somehow. Like a room that's too brightly lit. I think you have to have shadows in religion. Bits of mystery and magic.

VOICE OVER (*Michael*): I suppose it all goes back to primitive ritual, like when a tribe would kill their king and eat his flesh and drink his blood to inherit his strength. Then you got a lot of vegetation gods who were identified with the crops and the vine, bread and wine. I don't think it's surprising that Jesus adopted this archetypal symbolism. That's why it's terribly important to have communion under both kinds. Otherwise you completely mess up the symbolism.

VOICE OVER (*Edward*): I suppose I'm very old-fashioned about this. I believe Jesus Christ is really and truly present in the Eucharist. Don't ask me to explain it. Otherwise it would be just a rather empty ritual as far as I'm concerned.

Cut to

BEDE, smiling, arms outspread, faces the congregation.

BEDE: The mass is ended, go in peace.

ALL: Thanks be to God.

An ensemble of guitars, recorders, percussion, etc., strikes up the tune of "The Lord of the Dance", and the congregation sing:

> I danced in the morning
> When the world was begun
> And I danced in the moon
> And the stars and the sun,
> And I came down from heaven and
> I danced on earth,
> At Bethlehem I had my birth.
>
> Dance, then, wherever you may be
> I am the Lord of the Dance said he
> And I'll lead you all
> Wherever you may be
> And I'll lead you all in the dance, said he, *etc*

A few members of the congregation step into the aisles and begin to dance in a free-form, improvised fashion. More join in. They move up towards the altar. BEDE joins in. All around the altar people are dancing.

VOICE OVER (*Who?*): Undoubtedly the Catholic Church has been turned upside down in the last two decades.

Cut to

The Students' Common Room. Night. Party in progress. Disco music. Shots of TESSA dancing with BEDE, MICHAEL with POLLY, and AUSTIN holding hands with LYNN, tapping his feet.

VOICE OVER (*Who?*): Many things have changed – attitudes to authority, sex, worship, other Christians, other religions. But perhaps the most fundamental change is one that the majority of Catholics themselves are scarcely conscious of. It's the fading away of the traditional Catholic metaphysic – that marvellously complex and ingenious synthesis of theology and cosmology and casuistry, which situated individual souls on a kind of spiritual Snakes and Ladders board, motivated them with equal doses of hope and fear, and promised them, if they persevered in the game, an eternal reward. The board was marked out very clearly, decorated with all kinds of picturesque motifs, and governed by intricate rules and provisos. Heaven, hell, purgatory, limbo. Mortal, venial and original sin. Angels, devils, saints, and Our Lady Queen of Heaven. Grace, penance, relics, indulgences and all the rest of it. Millions of Catholics no doubt still believe in all that literally. But belief is gradually fading. That metaphysic is no longer taught in schools and seminaries in the more advanced countries, and Catholic children are growing up knowing little or nothing about it. Within another generation or two it will have disappeared, superseded by something less vivid but more tolerant. Christian unity is now a feasible objective for the first time since the Reformation.

Cut to

The College playing fields. Dawn. The rim of light on the horizon. The tired but expectant faces of the crowd. The nuns begin their dance mime of the Resurrection.

VOICE OVER (*Who?*): But Christian belief will be different from what it used to be, what it used to be for Catholics, anyway. We must not only believe, but know that we believe, live our belief and yet see it from outside, aware that in another time, another place, we would have believed something different (indeed, did ourselves believe differently at different times and places in our lives) without feeling that this invalidates belief. Just as when reading a novel, or writing one for that matter, we maintain a double consciousness of the characters as both, as it were, real and fictitious, free and determined, and know that however absorbing and convincing we may find it, it is not the only story we shall want to read (or, as the case may be, write) but part of an endless sequence of stories by which man has sought and will always seek to make sense of life. And death.

Freeze frame of dancers leaping from the ground, the sun shining through their robes.

ENDS

The *Catholic Herald* liked the programme, but the *Universe* panned it. The *Telegraph* said it showed that the Catholic Church was now in the same state of confusion as all the other Christian churches. The *Guardian*'s TV critic suggested that the dancing nuns should be signed up for a programme to be called "Top of the Popes". There were many resignations from Catholics for an Open Church after the broadcast. Some members resigned because they thought the image it presented of the organization was too radical, others because it was not radical enough. The bishop of the diocese was displeased for a number of reasons, and disciplined Bede for his part in the proceedings. A specially convened meeting of the College Governors deplored the use of College premises for the event, and Michael, as member of staff responsible, was severely reprimanded. His colleagues rallied round him, and wrote a letter to the Governors in his support. When, however, a couple of years later, the Catholic authorities announced plans to close down the College, as part of the nationwide cutback in teacher training, many thought that the Paschal Festival had contributed to this adverse decision, and Michael became less popular with his colleagues. Offered early retirement or alternative employment as a schoolteacher, he chose the former, and intends to move to London to try his luck as a freelance writer. With his pension and Miriam's salary as a social worker, they should be reasonably secure. Their son Martin is reading Physics at Imperial College and Helen, no longer a tomboy, but a rather stunning young woman of Pre-Raphaelite looks, is reading modern languages at Oxford, where she met Polly's Jason again and, to the astonishment of both families, converted him to Catholicism. When she heard about it, Polly commented cynically that she supposed that even in these liberated days a nice Catholic girl wouldn't sleep with non-Catholic boys. In fact the two young people are quite traditionally and chastely engaged.

The Paschal Festival, which Adrian had hoped would inaugurate a new chapter in the annals of Catholics for an Open Church, seemed rather to hasten its demise as a vital force, perhaps by uncovering the irreconcilable variety of aims and assumptions among its members. Adrian survived a vote of no confidence as Chairman, but resigned anyway. The movement continues in a shadowy form, but without his or Dorothy's participation. They are both, these days, heavily involved in the Catholic Marriage Encounter movement, an importation from America which aims to "make good marriages better" by gathering couples together on residential weekends, lecturing to them about married life, and making them write confessional letters to each other. Edward and Tessa, whom they persuaded to go on such a weekend, found it all rather embarrassing, and not only because the conference centre turned out to be, under a different name, the one where they had first had sexual intercourse. A couple of years ago, Edward decided to risk the operation on his spine, and happily it was a success. He has taken up athletic pursuits again, and he and Tessa go jogging together every evening, cheered derisively by their two younger children slouched in front of the television. The two older ones are at University. It is known to Tessa that Becky is sleeping with her boyfriend, but not to Edward, who would not stand for it, and is sufficiently concerned that she does not go to mass any more. Edward has become an enthusiastic student of the Holy Shroud of Turin, after seeing a film about it a couple of years ago. He will explain in detail to anyone prepared to listen that the image of the man on the Shroud is anatomically perfect, that the wounds shown correspond exactly to those inflicted at the Crucifixion as reported in the Gospels and interpreted by modern historical scholarship and forensic medicine, that pollen tests have proved the fabric has been in Palestine at some point in its history, and that nobody has been able to offer a simple, materialistic explanation of how the image got on to it. Suppose it was scorched into the shroud by radiant energy released at the Resurrection? Edward admits that this is only a theory, but is encouraged by the Shroud in his inclination to ignore the theories of modern theologians and stick to his old fashioned belief in the Divinity of Christ.

After due consideration, Adrian and Dorothy did not invite Dennis and Angela to a Marriage Encounter weekend, fearing that it might reopen old wounds. In fact, that marriage is in reasonably good shape. Shortly after the affair with Lynn, Dennis decided that it was time to make a move, to a new job, a new place, and Angela did not resist the idea. He is now managing director of a small firm manufacturing electronic ignition systems, on the south coast. He has bought a small boat, and spends most of his spare time pottering about on it. Angela is much involved in raising funds for a sheltered community in which they hope Nicole will eventually find a home. The two boys are both at college. Angela's brother Tom is married and has two young babies. To see him with them makes Angela want to laugh or cry at the way their lives have got so absurdly out of synchronization. Tom and Rosemary run a residential home for kids in care.

Austin left the priesthood shortly after the Paschal Festival and, much to everybody's astonishment, married Lynn. Their friends were scarcely less astonished when, nine months later to the day, Lynn bore him a son. Austin was lucky enough to get a research fellowship at the Poly to do a PhD in the sociology of religion. The Department is Marxist in orientation, but divided ideologically between empiricists of the old New Left and younger Althusserians intoxicated by Continental theory. There are factions, arguments, confrontations, pamphleteering and political manoeuvring. It is all very exciting and exhausting, and, to Austin, reminiscent of goings-on in the Catholic Church since Vatican II. He still regards himself as a kind of Catholic, but, partly in the interests of his research, goes to a different church or chapel each Sunday – Catholic, Anglican, Orthodox, Free Church, Quaker meeting house, in rotation.

Violet is not a Jehovah's Witness any more, but a Sufist. While she was in the long-stay psychiatric hospital she read a book about

Sufism, and when she was discharged she went to stay with a Sufist community to learn more about it. Sufism seems to suit her better than Christianity because she has not had a nervous breakdown for two years, nor does she take tranquillizers any more. She lost faith in the Jehovah's Witnesses when none of the things that were supposed to happen in 1975 happened, but her imagination is still markedly apocalyptic. She is convinced that a nuclear catastrophe is imminent, and that Sufists will be the only ones able to cope because they know how to tap the full potential of the human being. She and Robin, whom Caroline eventually deserted for a younger and more virile lecturer at the University, now enjoy a surprisingly tranquil companionate marriage. Violet finds that doing without sex completely is a great relief to the spirit, and Robin, who is himself heavily into yoga and macrobiotic diet, is content with this arrangement, appeasing his lower instincts with occasional clandestine visits to a massage parlour in a neighbouring industrial town. When Polly discovered that Jeremy had been unfaithful to her with Gertrude (and, it emerged, with every other *au pair* girl they had ever had, plus scores of research assistants) she divorced him. The oast-house was sold at a vast profit and Polly invested her share in a feminist publishing house of which she is a director. She lives in a flat in London with her daughter and is deeply involved in the women's movement. Jeremy emigrated to California, where he makes highly profitable pornographic films. Miles is still at Cambridge, but has gone back to the Church of England because, he says, there doesn't seem to be much difference between Anglican and Roman beliefs any more and he prefers the liturgy of the former. An unpleasant scene at the Catholic church where he used to worship, following his appearance on Jeremy's programme, also contributed to this decision. Ruth is headmistress of her school in the North of England, a job which has curtailed her charismatic activities, though she still derives great strength and consolation from a weekly prayer-group attended by interested staff and sixth-formers. I teach English literature at a redbrick university and write novels in my spare time, slowly, and hustled by history.

While I was writing this last chapter, Pope Paul VI died and Pope John Paul I was elected. Before I could type it up, Pope John Paul I had died and been succeeded by John Paul II, the first non-Italian pope for four hundred and fifty years: a Pole, a poet, a philosopher, a linguist, an athlete, a man of the people, a man of destiny, dramatically chosen, instantly popular – but theologically conservative. A changing Church acclaims a Pope who evidently thinks that change has gone far enough. What will happen now? All bets are void, the future is uncertain, but it will be interesting to watch. Reader, farewell!